THE
GILDED
CAGE

Judy Alter

Print ISBN: 978-0-9960131-2-3
Digital ISBN: 978-0-9960131-3-0

Alter Ego Publishing
Fort Worth, Texas

Cover by Barbara Whitehead
Book design by Cypress Editing

THE
GILDED
CAGE

Potter Palmer
and Chicago

Chapter One

The smell. He would never forget the smell. It crept into the railroad car and clung to his clothes and the prickly plush seats on which he'd sat and slept for two days. It was almost strong enough that he thought he could reach out and touch it. A whiff of animal odors, a hint of sewage, but mostly a swamp-like mustiness, oppressively heavy.

The train pulled into a siding somewhere in Chicago, and Potter Palmer prepared to get off. But a mocking voice inside his own head urged him to stay on the train until it went back east rather than get off in a place that smelled foul. He hesitated, peering uncertainly out the window to see only an empty, muddy field with small buildings in the distance. In his mind, he saw Lockport, New York, with its neat frame homes with white picket fences, carefully tended shops, lovely old trees. Or New York City—he could take the train back to the city and carve a sophisticated life for himself there. Then, with sudden determination, he picked up his luggage and stepped from the train. He had made up his mind his future was in Chicago, and he'd be a fool, he thought, if he didn't even give it a try. But a part of him admitted it didn't look promising.

Even as a child in the Quaker village of Potters Hollow, New York, Potter Palmer had longed for activity, for complexity, and the comings and goings of people. The gentle souls of Potters

Hollow, including his own family, led quiet, tranquil lives. No one planned to leave the village; indeed, no one ventured beyond its boundaries any more often than necessary. Potter had known discontent almost since he was old enough to think, but he kept it to himself. A hard worker, he was offered a partnership in the local mercantile store before he was twenty, but it could not hold him. Within a few years, he opened his own store in nearby Lockport, then enjoying a modest boom of sorts. But Lockport was an old and settled town, and his discontent grew, even before the town's boom fizzled. Potter Palmer was a careful man, though, and he studied his choices and in effect made a life plan. New York and Philadelphia were ruled out—too old, too established, not the places to offer opportunity to newcomers. Cleveland? Pittsburgh? Mere specks on the map. Too dull.

He studied whatever he could find in newspapers about Chicago and, finally, like a man playing pin the tail on the donkey with his career, determined that was where he would make his new start. No, a bad smell wasn't going to stop him.

It was 1852, he was twenty-six years old, and he was going to make a fortune. By then, Chicago had the telegraph, gaslights, the Michigan and Illinois Canal that brought oceangoing ships from Montreal, and it was a growing railroad center. A man could make his fortune there.

In Iroquois, the name "Chicago" means "Place of the Bad Smell" or "Place of the Wild Onion." Wild onions grew in abundance in the swampy marshlands where the Chicago River met Lake Michigan. In the late 1830s, Chicago had a population of slightly over four thousand. Potter half regretted that he hadn't arrived ten years earlier, completely overlooking the fact that he had been a young teenager at the time.

By 1850, a series of canals connected Chicago to several shipping ports and it was becoming a trade center, land values were still rising, and a boom was on in Chicago. It was indeed the place for a man like Potter Palmer.

* * *

When Palmer stepped from the train, several local men leaned against an empty freight car on an adjoining track. Their clothes were ragged, their hair unkempt, and their faces sullen, the expression in their eyes flat and dead. Palmer presumed they were waiting for work, loading the car. *If I fail,* he thought, *pray God I save enough money to go back east before I end like those men.* And then, *I won't! By God, I will not fail!*

Palmer knew the men were watching, and he turned to look at them. They never acknowledged his stare nor flinched under it. He decided against trusting his luggage to any of them. He looked for a depot but saw only an open field, an apparently empty shack, and, some distance away, a muddy road where a few draymen waited with their wagons. He turned back to the conductor.

"Is there a stationmaster?"

"Nope."

"Can you help me arrange to get my trunk to the Sherman Hotel?"

The conductor nodded. "See that wagon over there? The one pulled by the dark brown draft horse? Driver is Ed Johnson. You tell him Jake Barney told him to come get your trunk and take good care of it." The conductor liked the way this man looked at a person when he spoke, with a direct clear gaze.

"Thanks." Potter reached into his pocket for a tip, but the conductor waved him away with a cheery, "You'll be needin' that in this town."

There was a wooden walkway of sorts, but by the time Palmer reached the roadway, which was almost as deep in mud as the side of the train track, his pants were wet to his knees and clung uncomfortably to his legs. He hailed Johnson and made the arrangements, paying the drayman in advance. But when Johnson motioned for him to climb up on the seat, Palmer shook his head. "I'll walk. I want to see the city. Which way to the business district?" He plopped his leather grip into the wagon.

Johnson smothered a grin at the idea of a business district and nodded his head to the north. Palmer set off at a determined pace, ignoring the mud as best he could. He followed a plank sidewalk, but passage there was almost as treacherous as in the mud. Loose boards threatened to fly up as he stepped on them, and he was forced to dodge an occasional gaping hole beneath which the mud and muck lurked. A horseman in a hurry came too close to the edge of the sidewalk and threw mud so high it landed on Palmer's coat. There was a distinct wet chill in the air, and Palmer shivered as the cold dampness penetrated his clothes. Garbage flowed in a trough along the edge of the street, and at one point he saw pigs running loose, feasting on the sewage. The smell was still with him. *What have I gotten myself into?*

He walked by buildings that seemed to squat on the ground. There was no space between them and the spongy ground on which they sat. Palmer realized that they had no foundations, no cellars, no sewers. Horses and carts made mud-like hash of the street, and horse dung was mixed in with the mud. But the ground itself, that spongy, mucky wetland, dominated. It gave off the smell of the swamp—or the wild onion.

It was not a long walk to the center of the city, though the chill air and his damp clothes made it seem endless. At Courthouse Square, near Madison and State streets, the courthouse dominated the landscape, an imposing brick building with a tall bell tower. But Palmer looked with more interest at the strange mixture of buildings around it. The marble-fronted Sherman Hotel on one corner, his destination, looked solid and respectable. Opposite the hotel was the First Baptist Church, its tall steeple rivaling the courthouse bell tower in height. But along the far side of the square a vacant prairie stretched, mostly mud with a few wild grasses. At the corner of Randolph and Washington, tumbledown two-story frame houses threatened to sag under their own weight at any moment. In the second-story window of one of these buildings, he saw a sign reading "Carter Harrison, Lawyer."

"Not much of an advertisement for a lawyer," he said to himself.

Noticing a mercantile store to his left, Palmer walked over to it and peered through a dusty window at a jumbled display of goods. Inside, several men in work clothes sat around a coal stove.

"Good day, gentlemen," he greeted them, as he came through the door. In response, they nodded their heads ever so slightly and a couple muttered something that might have been "day." It was not a cordial welcome. Palmer walked around the store, studying the few bolts of cloth, mostly gingham, the ready-made pants piled on a table, the shelves that held a few dusty enamelware dishes and some scant supplies.

At length, a bored-looking man in shirtsleeves and apron came toward him. "Help ya?" he asked without enthusiasm. "Something for the missus?"

Palmer shook his head. "No," he said, "there's no missus." He wondered why he'd felt compelled to confess that. "I'm new in town and just looking around."

The clerk nodded and said, "Anytime," in a distant tone.

Palmer knew that if he came in the next day, the clerk would not remember him.

He was headed toward the hotel when the courthouse bell bonged the hour of five o'clock. It was so loud that Palmer, not normally a nervous man, jumped a little at the sudden sound.

A well-dressed man, passing him, smiled in understanding. "You should hear it when it sounds the alarm for a fire," he said. "Rings the number of the ward so often that the whole city is awake . . . and generally unhappy."

Palmer smiled. This man, whoever he was, was the first to make him feel at all welcome in Chicago. He wondered how the other man had avoided the mud and kept his clothes spotless. Palmer entered the Sherman Hotel, uncomfortably aware of his dirty and disheveled clothes.

To his surprise, the clerk welcomed him warmly. "Mr. Palmer? Of course, we have the reservation you made by wire. And your trunk and grip have arrived. I see you've got a spot or two of our famous mud on you. We can fix that."

Palmer soon found himself settled into a perfectly comfortable room. The walls were wainscoted in a dark wood—stained pine, Palmer suspected. The bed was mahogany and so was the small writing table. A leather easy chair and ottoman offered a place to read, with a gas wall lamp to shine down on the pages. The porter who brought up his bags took his soiled clothes away to be cleaned and advised that the dining room would welcome him until eight o'clock. He could order a brandy with his dinner if he so wished. Potter Palmer definitely so wished. His wariness about Chicago was less now. *This is the Chicago I want for my own. Not that god-forsaken mud hole with men standing around as though they were looking for a handout.* When the porter left, he settled in the easy chair to study the Chicago City Directory he had ordered months before. Its pages were now well thumbed and worn, but Palmer studied it intently.

Dinner in the hotel dining room was ample—a roast of beef with a port wine sauce, potatoes, beets, and a bread pudding for dessert, followed by a good brandy. The room was empty except for two drummers who ate with atrocious manners and one couple who seemed lost in their own conversation and ignored Palmer. He was content with his own thoughts and plans.

Later in his hotel room, he sat at the desk, pulled out the hotel letterhead, and began a letter to his family. "Chicago is all I could have hoped," he wrote, deliberately forgetting to mention the mud, the men lounging by the railroad tracks, the smell.

Shabby men with their hands out and pigs eating garbage tumbled in his dreams that night, and he woke suddenly, sure that a bad smell was stifling him. A few deep breaths calmed him and assured him that the air in his room was clean. He then slept soundly until dawn.

* * *

The Palmer Dry Goods Store opened within a month on LaSalle Street. It was in a fairly new building, not one of those two-story wooden ones that looked close to collapse. Red brick walls on the interior and deeply polished wooden shelves to hold dry goods gave warmth to the store. Palmer had found display cases in an abandoned store and painted them a bright white. The shining clean window boasted "Palmer Dry Goods" in gold lettering, and beneath it passersby could see bolts of material with long pieces pulled out and artfully draped so that the material showed off to advantage. He had ordered the material before he left New York—silk, fine challis, buttery soft wool. But no gingham. Potter Palmer aimed for the carriage trade.

Palmer greeted his first customer himself, standing by the front door. "Good morning," he said. "I'm Potter Palmer. Welcome to my new store."

The woman looked a little startled. "I'm Mrs. Cyrus McCormick," she said. "I . . . I was curious, because your window display is so attractive."

"Thank you, madam. I hope you'll find all my goods are as attractive or more so." Potter knew that Cyrus McCormick's reaper works had been one of the first industries in Chicago. "Mrs. McCormick," he went on, "if a fabric doesn't suit you after you get it home . . . or if Mr. McCormick doesn't like it . . . you bring it right back. I'll give you this little slip guaranteeing that you can exchange what you don't like."

Palmer was an attractive young man, with dark hair, the high forehead that was said to indicate intellect, and intense blue eyes, which he always directed straight at the customer he was then charming.

"Mr. Palmer, I . . . I've never heard of anyone doing business like that."

With a slight bow, he replied smoothly, "Mrs. McCormick, the most important thing to me is to please my customers. You let me know if I can help you with anything else. Some new gloves today?"

Mrs. McCormick went home with a dress length of silk and three new pairs of gloves, and she raved to her husband about the new dry goods store and its unusual owner. No other storekeeper in the city was so generous nor so courteous, and Mrs. McCormick and her friends were soon prompted to buy much more than they intended, simply because there was the possibility of returning items, which they seldom did.

* * *

"Return?" Henry Honoré was incredulous. "How can someone let you return? Does he pay you cash for what you return?" He was a man in his early forties, giving in to middle age portliness and balding, with the habit of rubbing the top of his head when puzzled. He was rubbing it now.

"No, but I get credit so that I can buy more." His wife looked smug as she said that and then whirled away from him.

Honoré sensed a smart businessman. As a developer and investor, he hadn't spent much time in dry-goods stores. He envisioned them as dusty, dim, and crowded. But he knew business. The very next day he made it a point to visit Palmer Dry Goods.

Potter Palmer greeted him by calling him by name. "Mr. Honoré, I'm flattered that you've chosen to visit my store."

As the two men shook hands, Honoré said, "How did you know who I was? We've never met."

"I make it my business to know the important men in Chicago," Palmer replied. Then he grinned, "Don't mean to sound like I'm buttering you up. It's the simple truth. I intend to be one of those important men one day."

"I'm sure you shall," Honoré said. "From what my wife tells me, you're a success as a salesman. She spends far too much money in here."

Both men laughed, and a friendship was born that would last for years and also make the two men business partners in real estate and other ventures.

Henry Honoré was a French Protestant who'd come to the United States as a child. His family settled in Louisville, Kentucky, where they had a hardware and cutlery business and did well enough to afford the traditional two-story white frame house with graceful pillars and three servants to run it. The servants were freed blacks, for the Honorés did not believe in slavery. Young Henry enjoyed the good life, danced with the ladies, and finally married Eliza Carr, who came of old Louisville stock. They had been married seven years—and had three children—when he announced he wanted to leave Louisville.

Eliza was aghast. "Leave Louisville? Where else would we live? This is home!"

"Chicago," he said bluntly. "I want to be part of something that is growing, not these cities where the past is religion."

"Chicago?" she echoed. "That's in the North!"

"Yes, it is. And we won't be taking any slaves with us." Eliza's dowry had included several slaves to run the household, and Henry had immediately freed them, much to the horror of Mother Carr.

In the late 1840s, Henry Honoré could hear the distant roar of trouble coming to the nation, and he was convinced that the South was not the place to be. Nor was slavery an institution he could tolerate. Unlike Eliza, he had no ancestral ties to the region or the way of life.

"I know this will be hard on you," he said apologetically, "but I think it's the right thing to do."

"Bertha will be devastated without her Granny Carr," she said, as if stalling.

"Granny can come to Chicago to visit," Honoré said almost curtly. Granny Carr had never approved of him. She considered him a newcomer by at least two or three generations.

Eliza looked doubtful, but one of the things Henry loved most about her was that she was game for whatever he proposed—well, almost everything. "If you think we should go, Henry, then so do I," she said. "When do we leave?"

So they had come to Chicago, and Henry made his living buying and selling land, land that seemed to increase in value no matter what he did. They lived in the Sherman Hotel for two years until at last Henry had decided on a place to build a house—South Prairie Avenue, near 29th Street. It was on the far edge of the city, with open land enough for children to run and play. He built a two-story, rambling house to accommodate his growing family. Henry Honoré was a content man—and a wealthy one.

* * *

Now, some five years after Potter Palmer's arrival in Chicago, the two men sat on the back veranda of Honoré's house, watching his children play.

"It's time you took a wife, Palmer, if you don't mind my saying so." Henry Honoré lifted his glass in a small toast to the man next to him. "Then you too could be overrun with youngsters!" He chuckled as he said it and looked fondly at his six children.

By then, in the year 1857, Potter Palmer was a highly successful businessman and was considered a civic leader. He was also the city's most eligible bachelor, albeit quite a bit older than most of his competition.

The two men sat in wicker chairs. Prairie Avenue was one of several wooded areas left in the city, and a large lawn stretched between the house and the woods that bordered the Honoré property. On that lawn, the children squealed and laughed over a game of blind man's bluff, led by Bertha, the oldest child.

Twelve-year-old Bertha Honoré was tall, even for her age, and just showing the first slight curves of womanhood. This summer evening, she wore a white muslin dress, caught at the waist with a pink diamond-patterned belt. Her dark hair was long, looped behind her ears and caught with tiny pink bows.

But it was her eyes that captivated Palmer. They were large, dark, and serious. When Palmer arrived, she had looked him directly in the face for just a moment, then cut her eyes to the ground as she extended a hand and said, most properly, "It's very nice to see you again." But in that moment, he'd seen—what? Amusement? Mischief? He wasn't sure, but he knew he'd seen a spark not common to proper young ladies. And he liked it.

"And you," Palmer said, bowing low over the offered hand. Behind him, he heard her brothers giggling, but the girl appeared to maintain her composure, smiled again at him, and turned away, dragging one offending brother behind her by the arm.

If Bertha appeared composed, it was an act. Her thoughts were tumbling. This man, so good-looking but surely almost her father's age, made her feel uncomfortable in a way she couldn't define. While her father and Potter watched, she served as the superintendent of the blindfold and the person who turned the child whose turn it was to be "it," but it was clear that she felt herself too grown up to be part of the game with her sister, Ida, and her brothers—Adrian, Henry, Nathaniel, and Lockwood. Occasionally, she glanced toward her father and his guest, as though making sure they were watching. Then she would turn away with what seemed only the least bit of self-consciousness. When she could, she stole looks at Potter Palmer. He was not at all like her father's other friends.

"As I was saying," Honoré continued, "it's time you took a wife."

"I think I'll wait until that one grows up," Potter Palmer said carefully, nodding his head toward Bertha.

"Pshaw, man," scoffed Honoré, "you'll be an old man by the time Bertha's ready for the altar. I warn you, her mother won't let her marry early. No, sir, that girl's going to have an education and proper training."

Palmer smiled. "I know," he said softly. "That's one of the reasons I'm going to wait for her." He was surprised himself by the sudden resolve he felt. No woman his own age had ever affected him this way, and for a fleeting instant he wondered if it was inappropriate for him to be so interested in a young girl. But Potter Palmer was not given to doubting himself. His decision to stay in Chicago had proved right, and he had no doubt this decision too would prove to be the right one.

Honoré rubbed his head, his characteristic gesture of puzzlement, not sure whether to believe his friend and business associate. He would not, he decided, share this conversation with Mrs. Honoré, at least not yet. Potter Palmer was in his thirties, though

Honoré couldn't pinpoint his exact age. Surely too old for his daughter. Why, when she was forty, the man would be sixty-something. And when she was sixty . . . he would be long dead and gone. No, it was not the kind of union a father wanted for his daughter, especially not one as bright and beautiful as Bertha.

"Well done, Nathaniel," Palmer called, his voice startling Honoré back to the children's game.

"Yes, yes," seconded the children's father. Then, asserting his authority, "Go on now, all of you. Your mother will want you to clean up for dinner." He clapped his hands twice to emphasize his order, and the children scampered for the house, with Bertha following at a more leisurely pace, though she gave every pretense of being unaware of the two men who watched her, each thinking his own thoughts.

"You'll stay for dinner, of course," Honoré said to his guest.

"No, I best not, but thank you for the invitation. I've some business to attend to."

"It's Sunday, man," Honoré protested.

"And tomorrow," Palmer replied, "will be Monday, and there'll be too much to do." Potter Palmer in truth did not want to stay for dinner—an invitation he rarely turned down—because his mind was in a bit of an unaccustomed turmoil over his sudden determination to wait until Bertha Honoré was of marriageable age.

It some ways it would be a marriage of convenience—the Honorés were one of Chicago's leading families, pleasantly wealthy, gently southern yet fiercely loyal to the city in which they now lived. Potter Palmer almost always thought in terms of business, and he knew an alliance with the Honoré daughter would be a smart business move. But there was more. The girl drew him like a magnet—perhaps it was those dark eyes, or the grace of her young body, or the composure that seemed to hide any maidenly confusion. Potter Palmer was neither naive nor virginal—he had known many women, enough to know that attraction could be neither explained nor forced. If it happened, it happened—and it had, indeed, happened for him that afternoon. He would, of course, pray that it happened equally for the young girl, as she grew older. But he was a man of action, and he would augment his prayers with a subtle but determined campaign.

Masking his tumbling thoughts, Palmer followed Honoré into the house, bid his farewell to Mrs. Honoré, and prepared to take his leave.

Just as the two men stood at the door, however, Bertha wandered into the foyer, calling "Henry? Henry, you come here and get your face scrubbed." When she saw her father and his visitor, a slight blush ran across her face, and she said, "Pardon me, I didn't know you were here."

"Of course," Palmer said smoothly. And then, boldly, he began his courtship right then. Taking her hand in his, he said, "You're a good sister, and I think they ought to call you Cissy. It's a lively name, and it suits you. May I call you that?"

The girl looked at him, then glanced at her father. "Yes," she said softly, "you may." Bertha Honoré was not sophisticated enough to realize that she had her first schoolgirl crush, even if it was on a man more than twice her age.

The men walked out on the veranda that wrapped around the house, and Palmer said quietly to his host, "Bertha is an old woman's name. I'll call her Cissy in my mind, if not aloud."

Honoré, at a loss for words, simply shrugged. But he stood on the veranda a long time, watching Palmer's carriage disappear down Prairie Avenue. His hand was on his head again.

* * *

Cissy Palmer—as she soon would be known by friends, even if her parents resisted the name—was filled with nervous anticipation the next time she accompanied her mother to Potter Palmer's store. Had she known the details of the conversation between Mr. Palmer and her father, her confusion would have been almost unbearable. She had thought much about Mr. Palmer since the day he'd given her the name "Cissy." She wondered why he had never married, and then her fantasies began to build about what it would be like to be married to Potter Palmer. With schoolgirl naïveté, she saw herself presiding over a grand household and raising children. She was neither wise enough nor old enough to think about intimacy, either physical or emotional. But she did think about Potter Palmer.

She had tried the name he had given her tentatively on some of her schoolmates at St. Xavier's Academy for Girls. It had received a positive reaction—giggles and swoons. Even though her family still called her Bertha, she began to think of herself as Cissy. And she was pleased when one or two schoolmates addressed her thus, tentatively at first and then more boldly. No matter that the nuns had sternly corrected Eleanor Harrison, saying, "Miss Palmer's name is Bertha. You will not call her Cissy!"

"Bertha?"

"Yes, Mamá?"

"I'm going to Mr. Palmer's store for gloves, but I think you need a new gown for the fall season."

"May I go too, Mamá?" Ida asked. When Ida was uncertain, she tended to develop a nervous tic under one eye. Her eye was twitching now.

Her mother considered a moment and then shook her head. "No, I'll make a separate trip with you, after I've looked over your wardrobe. Today you stay here with the boys."

Eliza Honoré asked George, the yardman, to bring up the landau, and they were soon headed downtown. LaSalle Street was near the river, where Chicago's famous stench was worse than in the residential neighborhoods. Cissy and her mother both carried lace handkerchiefs, scented with French perfume, to put to their faces and cover the odor.

But there was no odor inside Mr. Palmer's store. The owner himself saw them coming and opened the door for them, leaving Cissy wondering if he spent his day looking out the front window for customers. They walked into a brightly lit store, with sunlight pouring through display windows that looked like they were cleaned daily with vinegar water. Scented candles burned on several counters, effectively countering the river smell and any lingering vinegar odor.

"Mrs. Honoré, it is a pleasure." Then he turned to her, and, without batting an eye, he said, "Mademoiselle Cissy, my pleasure."

Looking straight at him, she said simply, "Mr. Palmer." She saw that he looked intently at her, and had she been older and more sophisticated, she would have thought he lingered a moment too long over her hand. But she simply thought it charming. When she saw her mother watching her intently, Cissy reluctantly withdrew her hand. *Does he,* she wondered with a touch of jealousy, *greet my schoolmates this way?* She would never talk to Eleanor Harrison about this, though.

Potter Palmer was very much aware of Cissy's reaction and pleased by it. Later, he would smile to himself at the memory of her expression, the way she fixed her eyes on his. It was, he decided, the second step in what would be a very long and slow courtship.

"I need gloves to match a new gown," Mrs. Honoré said, trying to ignore the exchange between her daughter and this older man. She waved a bit of periwinkle blue silk at him. "They must match this," she said.

"Good, come right this way," and he was off, leading them to the glove counter, waving the shop girl away as he himself searched through the stock for just the right shade. "This pair? No, it is not quite right. Wait! Let me try these." Three or four pairs of gloves later, there was a match, and he announced triumphantly, "Perfect!"

Then, "And for you, Miss Cissy?"

This time, Mrs. Honoré looked long and hard at him, and Potter Palmer wondered briefly if her husband had told her of their garden discussion in the summer or if she was simply an ever-vigilant mother and he had, perhaps, been a little too enthusiastic. He decided it was probably the latter and resolved to tone down his enthusiasm.

"We call her Bertha," Mrs. Honoré said quite formally. "I don't know where this name of Cissy came from."

Cissy blushed and looked at the floor as he said, "Yes, madam, I know her name well. But I must take full responsibility for her new name. I told her when last I was at your home that she was such a good sister, I thought she should be called Cissy."

"Why, Mr. Palmer, how observant of you!" The mother relaxed now and smiled broadly in pride at this recognition of her daughter's virtues. "In truth, Bertha could use a new gown for the fall season. Could you show us some silk?"

"Of course!" And he was off, leading them to a different area of the store, where he pulled out bolt upon bolt of fine China silk, some with paisley prints, others with a moiré design, and some plain colors.

"I don't think Bertha is ready for the prints," Mrs. Honoré decided aloud. "Perhaps a blue?" Raising her voice in a question, she looked at her daughter.

Cissy eyed the prints for a long moment, weighing her options. She decided prints were not worth waging a battle over. "Yes, Mother, I think a Mediterranean blue would be nice." It was a fashionable new color, and it bothered neither mother nor daughter that they had little idea about the Mediterranean and any shades of blue to be found there. Mrs. Honoré compromised, and they chose the blue with the moiré pattern.

A woman in a full hoop squeezed past them, and soon Mrs. Honoré was deep in conversation with Mrs. Joseph Medill, whose husband owned the *Chicago Tribune*. "You just meet everyone you know at Mr. Palmer's store, don't you?" she said with a slight laugh, and Mrs. Medill responded in the affirmative.

"And remember, ladies," Palmer said, "you can exchange anything you find unsatisfactory. I'll issue credit on your account. If those gloves don't match, Mrs. Honoré . . . ." His voice trailed off, implying that she could easily return them. Indeed, his tone suggested he might well come fetch them himself.

The two older women fell into a whispered discussion—Cissy could not tell the subject, but it was plain they wanted neither her nor Mr. Palmer to hear it. Whatever the subject, it was deadly serious, for she could almost hear her mother going, "tsk, tsk." Cissy thought it only polite of her to engage the gentleman who attended them in conversation, though she was somewhat at a loss as to what to say. What could she talk to this man about?

Palmer did not help. He stood quite still, smiling at her, thinking his own private thoughts.

Cissy had heard her father say more than once that men liked to talk about their business. "Why," she asked, "do you allow people to return goods? My father says once something is sold, it is sold."

His eyes twinkled as he answered. He was pleased—more than pleased, delighted—with the astuteness of her question. "It's good business," he replied. "They'll shop here because of that privilege, and they'll buy more than they would any place else."

"So you're a good businessman," Cissy said, and it was not a question.

"Your father thinks so, in spite of his philosophy about returns," he replied, still smiling.

Mrs. Honoré left the store with silk for three dresses, two pair of gloves, a bit of fine lace that Palmer had handled with great care when he showed it to them, and a piece of fine brocade that Cissy's mother thought would make a smoking jacket for her husband.

"If anything proves unsatisfactory . . . ." Palmer said as he escorted them to their carriage, and Cissy raised her eyes, looking at him with a conspiratorial glance. She was beginning to understand Potter Palmer as a businessman. But she had no idea about him as a person, and she was more curious by the minute.

Boldly, Cissy asked, "What were you and Mrs. Medill talking about that made you so serious?"

"Cholera," Eliza said bluntly. "There've been too many cases in the city to ignore."

"What's cholera?"

"A disease that kills," her mother said grimly.

A few years earlier, cholera had killed sixty people in Chicago, and the city was wary. People thought the European immigrants were unclean and brought cholera, and no one understood that filthy water and the fumes of exposed sewage caused it. Privy houses were built too close to wells and polluted the water supply; roadside ditches drained their sewage into the river. It was, Henry Honoré finally told his oldest daughter, a nasty disease that caused vomiting, diarrhea, cramps, and, too often, a miserable death.

After the epidemic, the city put in a new sewer system. But because the city sat at the water level of the lake and river, the brick sewers could not be put underground. They were built down the center of streets, connected by ducts to buildings, and covered with mounds of dirt. By the laws of gravity, they drained into the river. But this construction required raising the grade level of the streets by as much as ten feet in some places.

Owners of buildings were expected to raise their buildings to the new street level. Some refused. A pedestrian could walk along a granite sidewalk, looking into storefront plate-glass windows, and then suddenly find wooden steps that led down to the old level of the street, where there were wooden pavement and shabby buildings.

Some huge buildings were hoisted. George Pullman, who would later gain fame and wealth for his railroad sleeping cars, began his career in Chicago raising buildings. His greatest accomplishment was raising the Tremont Hotel. Workmen dug holes into the foundation of the building and put heavy timbers under it. Then each of several hundred men was put in charge of a jackscrew. At the signal of a whistle, each man turned his jackscrew. The building rose slowly, almost imperceptibly, and was shored up with wood pilings. Masons, waiting nearby, laid new brick footings under it. While the Tremont was being raised, guests continued to come and go. Not a pane of glass was broken nor a plaster wall cracked. Watching building raisings attracted Chicago citizens and tourists alike.

The face of Chicago was beginning to change.

Chapter Two

The railroad and the Civil War brought Harry Collins to Chicago. He was young—over twenty but not much—and good-looking, with thick black hair that he let grow a little long around his ears and clear blue eyes under heavy dark eyebrows. But no woman would have been attracted to him that day as he sat slouched in his railroad seat, a scowl on his face as he stared bitterly at the landscape rolling by and recalled the last scene with his father.

"If you will not fight for your family, you're no son of mine," the old man thundered, his face white with rage. Harry's mother stood silently by, eyes downcast. Scenes between her husband and her youngest son were commonplace. Though she loved the boy dearly, in a way that she had not loved his three older brothers, now gone to war, she was too meek to resist her husband.

Father and son faced each other in front of the marble fireplace in a formal parlor that was more ostentatious than comfortable. A candelabra blazed on one side of the mantel and directly overhead Harry's grandfather, the first Harry Collins, glared down as though in anger at both his son and grandson. Mrs. Collins sat stiffly in a velvet-upholstered chair, her knitting lying untouched in her lap. Her eyes followed her husband, darting occasionally to her son but then riveting back on the older man again.

Harry had said nothing while Henry George Collins, owner of a large and thriving woolen mill in Connecticut, paced back and forth, raving about the black sheep of the family and the constant trouble he'd been ever since he was in knickers and good riddance to bad rubbish. "Your brothers, they're something to be proud of! Went through school with good grades and no trouble, knew their duty when those blasted southerners rebelled. I don't know how you're a part of this family." The old man shook his head, and Ethel Collins gasped softly at her husband's savagery.

Harry had stood still and silent, only a slight twitch at the corner of his left eye revealing his own anger. When his father stopped for breath, he said formally, "Am I dismissed now?" Then he turned on his heel and left the room.

Now, halfway across the country, Harry reflected that his father probably was right. He had always been in trouble, ever since the days he had, not once but three times, put a ball through the neighbor's front window. In prep school he had been caught drinking, and it seemed that whatever the headmaster told him to do was just what Harry did not want to do. *But they shouldn't have forced me into things like prep school. And then the army! Couldn't they see it wasn't fair?*

He straightened in his seat. He'd show them he could amount to something, but when they asked—even begged—he'd never go home again. His face softened when he thought of his mother, and he came close to shedding a tear over the pain he knew he was causing her. But then he stiffened his back . . . and his resolution.

Harry got off the train in Chicago because that was the end of the route. He had not intended necessarily to go to Chicago, but after New York, he'd ridden on through Pittsburgh and Cleveland and other cities more out of indecision than anything else. Aimlessly, he wandered toward the lights of the city, carrying the one small valise he'd packed in haste.

"Cup of coffee," he said, without looking at the waitress in the café he stumbled upon after wandering the city's muddy streets for several hours. It was a small café, with a wooden counter and stools along one wall and only a few wooden tables. None of the chairs matched. The wood walls were sparsely decorated with what appeared to be broadsheets left by various drummers. Harry chose a stool at the counter and propped his chin in his open hands. There were no other customers in the café.

"Right away," said a cheery voice with just a light touch of brogue about it, and then Harry looked up.

She was young, maybe no more than sixteen or seventeen, and she had red hair that flew around her face in wispy curls, in spite of the white kerchief she had tied over her head. She wore a broadcloth dress of tan with a clean white apron over it. Her eyes—Harry looked again and swore they were green! Not only green but also dancing with laughter.

"You're a solemn-looking one," she said as she poured his coffee.

He shrugged, brushing off an instinct to tell her he had every right to be solemn, to spill the whole story of the way his family had treated him to this unknown but friendly young girl. Instead, he said, "I . . . I'm gonna have to get a job and a place to stay. Any idea what's around here?"

"Well, you want to stay out of the patches," she began, laughing.

Dammit, why is she laughing? This isn't funny. Aloud, he echoed, "Patches?"

"You really don't know, do you?" she asked. "I thought everyone knew the patches. That's where the sailors and dockhands and"—she hesitated—"and bad women, people like that, live in tents and boxes."

Harry thought that probably was where he belonged. But his curiosity was up. "What kind of bad people? What do they do?"

Warming to her story, she said, "You really don't know about Conley's Patch and Mother Conley or the Sands, do you? There's saloons and places to gamble, and they have cockfights and dog races and rat killings . . . ."

"Rat killings?" Harry wasn't sure what he imagined.

"They set terrier dogs in little rings with rats and watch the dogs kill the rats."

Harry shuddered. It didn't sound like sport to him. And bad as he might be in his family's eyes, Harry Collins was not much inclined toward the seamy side of life. He had been raised in a genteel atmosphere, much as he resented it at the time.

"They give all us a bad name," she said. "Nobody likes the Irish in this city, and it's because of the patches." Sheila Fitzpatrick had a kind of naïveté about her that assumed everyone understood the problems of the Irish and everyone was basically as cheerful and optimistic as she was. That Harry Collins wasn't optimistic was becoming clear to her, and she found it puzzling. She resolved that she would cheer him up.

Holding his cup out for more coffee, Harry said, "All right, now that I know where I don't want to go, where do I want to go?"

She considered for a minute, and then her eyes lit up as the answer came to her. "There's Mrs. Grady's boardinghouse—I can give you directions, and she's got two or three men there that work for McCormick in his plant. They might get you on."

This time he tried not to let his shudder show. The idea of Harry Collins working in a factory was almost ironic. He was management—or at least his family was—not labor. Then he thought of how his father would gloat with self-righteousness. At least he'd never know. And the hundred dollars he'd left home with was considerably diminished by now, down to forty-five. If he wanted a bed to sleep in and food to eat, he'd have to take whatever job he could find. Then he'd work to better himself.

"Will you tell me how to get there? And may I tell Mrs. Grady you sent me?"

"Oh, yes," she said happily. "Just tell her Sheila Fitzpatrick, down to the City Cafe. She'll know. You just go four blocks down that way"—she pointed out the window—"turn the corner, and it's right there. Big wooden house. She's got a sign in front of it."

"Thanks, Sheila," he said, leaving money for the coffee and a generous bit for her. "I'll be back." He still felt sorry for himself, but his spirits were just a little brightened by his encounter with Sheila.

As he passed a saloon on the way to Mrs. Grady's boardinghouse, a drunk stumbled out, bumping hard into Harry.

"Hey, man!" he complained. "Watch where you're going."

The drunk straightened himself, muttered "Sorry," and then seemed to lose his balance again. Harry instinctively reached a hand to keep him from falling. "Had a bit too much, haven't you? Maybe you should sit down till the world stops spinning." He'd been about to suggest the man sit on the edge of the wooden walkway, until he saw the raw garbage there.

"Be all right," the drunk muttered and staggered away.

Harry Collins didn't realize he'd had his pocket picked until he got to Mrs. Grady's and found his remaining cash gone. He was left with just a few coins in his pocket.

From her name and nationality, Harry expected Mrs. Grady to be large and flamboyant. She was anything but, a sparrow of a woman who spoke in chirping tones without the brogue that lightened Sheila's talk.

"So Sheila sent you. She's a good girl, and if she vouches for you, I've got just the room for you," she said. "Has its own outside door, so you can come and go without going through the house."

That appealed to Harry, though he was somewhat let down when he saw the room. An iron bedstead with a quilt thrown over it and an afghan neatly folded at the foot, a braided rug on the floor, a scarred and scratched chest of drawers, and a wooden rocking chair. It was all neat and clean, though, he noted, taking in the washbowl and pitcher on the oak washstand, the thin towels neatly hung over its bar. "I'll take it," he said, assuring himself he'd move soon. "How much a month?"

"Twenty dollars," she chirped, "in advance."

And that was when he reached in his pocket and found it empty. "I . . . I . . ." he stammered, "I had forty-five dollars when I left the café. I . . . I don't know how I could have lost it."

"Stop and talk to anyone?" Mrs. Grady asked knowingly.

"No, not really. A drunk bumped into me, and I had to sort of steady him."

She nodded. "That's how you lost your money. Oldest trick in town. You have a job?"

"No, I'm new in town. Just stopped at the café on my way from the train."

She eyed him suspiciously. "So Sheila doesn't really know you."

He nodded, and the landlady stared at him a long time, assessing this information. Harry shifted nervously from one foot to the next.

"Well," she said slowly, "you look honest. I'll trust you, and you pay me after you find work. You want on at the reaper plant? One of the men what stays here could take you over there."

Unconsciously, Harry held out his hands as though by way of explanation. "I thought I'd look for something clerical or in a store, first," he said.

She stared at his hands. "Not used to hard work, are you? Well, I wish you luck. Breakfast is at six," she said, turning and leaving the room.

Once he got a paycheck, Harry Collins began to stop in at the City Cafe regularly. He found himself anticipating the end of the day, when he'd have coffee with Sheila before going on to one of the huge suppers that Mrs. Grady served.

"You get hired on?" Sheila asked casually, anticipating what he wanted and pouring his coffee without his asking.

"Not by McCormick," he said. "I'm a clerk and bookkeeper for Abe Goodman." He thought briefly about improving his position in the telling but ended with the truth.

Sheila nodded. Like Mrs. Grady, she looked at the white hands and knew that he'd never done hard work. McCormick's would have been wrong for him. She glanced again at his hands and then looked ruefully at her own, reddened and coarsened already by hot dishwater. "Goodman will never compete with that Mr. Palmer's store," she said wistfully. "I wish I could just go in there to look."

"Well, why can't you?" Harry asked.

"Go on with ye," she said with a laugh, "the likes of me in that fancy store? I guess not." Sheila knew—or thought she knew—that she would receive a cold welcome in a store that catered to the carriage trade. Optimistic she might be, but she was also a realist about herself and her life.

"Well, I'll take you there one day," he blurted out. Raised in privilege, he couldn't imagine that one couldn't go into whatever store one wanted to enter.

"Naw," she said, "Goodman's more my style." After Harry left, Sheila stood dreamily at the counter, picturing herself in Palmer Dry Goods fingering a fine piece of silk, while Harry, beside her, said, "If you want it, it's yours."

* * *

Harry thought Goodman's store was depressing, dark inside, with some goods on high shelves that hadn't had a dusting in years. The place smelled musty, and he wondered if it would ever have any business if it weren't that Goodman let people pay out their bills. Old Mr. Goodman—that was how Harry thought of him—sat at the counter by the front door, in front of a cash register on which he rang up sales and a file in which he kept bills owed and paid. He always had a cigar stub clamped in his teeth, and the ashes usually drifted down onto his black frock coat. He was pleasant enough, Harry thought, but not someone to be too friendly with.

One clerk worked in the store, running errands at Goodman's command and saying over and over, "Yes, Mr. Goodman, yes, Mr. Goodman," until Harry wanted to scream at him. The clerk was young—Sheila's age, Harry suspected—and probably never would be anything in life but a clerk. Harry intended to look for better work soon, but he didn't tell Sheila that. Maybe he'd try that Mr. Palmer's store.

One night, sipping his coffee at the café, Harry Collins met Carter Harrison. "You new in town?" the jovial man asked as he sat down next to Harry.

Unused to such familiarity, Harry replied distantly, "Yes, I am." He saw a large man with a bushy mustache and beard. His clothes were well-made but casually buttoned—his suit coat hung open and a vest beneath was only partially buttoned—and rumpled, as though they were just a bit too small for the frame they covered. But Collins also saw a friendly face, and he was lonely in Chicago.

"Welcome, stranger!" The man's hand reached out for a shake, and his face creased in a real smile. "You'll find this is the best city you ever lived in, bar none. I'll vouch for it. Carter Harrison, that's my name." Then he chuckled. "Lawyer. Office on Randolph Street, by the courthouse. Just let me know if I can help you."

Harry softened a little toward this cheerful man who apparently was offering friendship, not soliciting legal business. "Thanks. I . . . I'm working in Abe Goodman's store, living at Mrs. Grady's."

"Then you're in good hands," Harrison said loudly. "Sheila here send you to Mrs. Grady?" Without stopping, he called out loudly, "Sheila, me sweetheart, come bring me some coffee."

It wasn't lost on Harry that Sheila greeted Harrison as an old and trusted friend. "You been stayin' away from here," she accused mockingly. "Hanging out with the swells, I bet."

"Never, me darlin', not me."

"How's the wife and family?" she asked pointedly. "You got another little one yet?"

"Doc says two more months." Harrison sighed, and for the first time the smile left his face. "She's . . . well, she's feeling poorly, and two months seems like a long time."

"Ah," Sheila said, her hand on his shoulder, "it'll be gone before you know it. And once she has that baby, she'll forget all about feeling poorly. Haven't I watched me mom go through it ten times?"

"Ten times!" Harrison said. "I hope this is our last child. We've already got one of each, and she's lost three that died as babies. Neither of us can take that anymore."

"Go on," she teased, "every child needs a house full of laughing brothers and sisters to grow up in."

Harry Collins thought of his brothers and the solemn home of their childhood and had to bite his tongue to keep back an angry comment.

After that, Harrison often joined Harry in the evenings and sometimes bought him hearty suppers of roast beef, mashed potatoes, and turnips. Once Harry asked if he shouldn't be home with his wife and children, the older man replied, "Wife's asleep by now, and so are the children. Sophie's got a woman to help care for her lately, but I don't much like the meals that nursemaid leaves behind. Besides, I like the company here." He winked at Harry and nodded in Sheila's direction.

Harry was puzzled and suspicious, both jealous and uneasy that Harrison, a married man, was carrying on a flirtation with Sheila. Frequently on these evenings, the talk turned to the war. "I ought to go," Harrison said over and over. "It's every man's duty, but . . . well, I've got children, and, damn it! The city needs me. I swear, a man doesn't know what to do."

Harry said nothing about his own decision to avoid conscription by disappearing into Chicago. If he had remained in his New England home, he would have been drafted, and his father would not have paid for a substitute to be sent in his place. His brothers had volunteered before they were called.

"Another piece of pie?" Sheila asked, and Harry smiled directly at her as he shook his head in the negative.

After Carter Harrison's wife gave birth to a boy, neither Harry nor Sheila saw Harrison for days on end. Harry presumed he was at home with his wife and children, but he was wrong. Harry Collins didn't know his new friend very well. Sensing that the inevitable war between the South and North would have a great impact on Chicago, Harrison was working to put Chicago in the best possible position for that conflict. If he didn't serve his country, he'd save his city.

Chapter Three

Henry Honoré knew that the war would be hard on his family. Like other men, he had sensed for too long that war was coming, ever since the 1858 Lincoln-Douglas debate in Chicago, the first of those long debates between the two presidential candidates. He had gone to listen to the debate, and afterward he told a small group of former Kentuckians gathered at his house that night that Lincoln was the more temperate.

"He'll ruin the South," moaned one of the expatriates. "He has no understanding of our way of life. How could he? He's a farm boy from Illinois."

"And you," Henry Honoré thundered, "are a city boy from Illinois these days. You best remember your loyalties!"

Honoré knew when the Union Army built Camp Douglas, a training post, on Thirty-first and Cottage Grove, not far from his home, that war was imminent. But he did not share his fears with his family. *No sense scaring them,* he told himself. Even when rebels fired on Fort Sumter, he said nothing. His wife did not keep up with the news and, of course, neither did his children. He kept his silence.

But when hostilities became general, he felt he had to speak. On a spring evening, he gathered his family, even his young sons, in the parlor. "We are at war," he announced solemnly.

Eliza knew, in spite of her general dismissal of national news. But Cissy asked, "With who?"

"The southern states," her father said. "It's a war about many things but mostly slavery."

"Slavery is wrong," Cissy said with conviction. She had learned that at her father's knee. With no understanding of the horrors of war, Cissy saw no gray in the issue. Clearly, she thought, it was right to fight to end slavery.

"Yes, but southerners believe that it is their right, and they don't believe that the government can tell them they can't own slaves." He didn't want to go into the more complex issues behind the war—questions of sovereignty and of lifestyle, the old resentments between North and South that had simmered for years.

With a worried frown, Eliza asked, "Will it be a long war?"

"I pray God not," her husband answered. "I think President Lincoln hopes for a rapid victory. The North is much better equipped. But we need to remember that some may see us as southerners."

"We are Chicagoans," Cissy protested. She suddenly stood and began to walk about the parlor.

He sighed. "Yes, but we came from Kentucky, we have family there, and some people might think our loyalty lies there."

Cissy wondered if Potter Palmer would go to war. She knew he came from the North and was loyal and patriotic, but somehow she couldn't imagine him as a soldier. She hoped he would not go.

"Has Kentucky seceded?" Eliza asked.

"No. I've had word that the state government tried hard to work for a compromise between North and South. Now that war comes, it will tear the state apart. But they haven't officially declared for either side."

Eliza's lips quivered as she asked, "What about my family?" She sat on the horsehair sofa, but her posture revealed her anxiety.

Henry Honoré shook his head. "You might write your mother and see if the mail goes through. I know your brothers will either be neutral or loyal to the Union," he said. "They should be safe unless Kentucky does join the Confederacy. We can only pray . . . and try to send what goods we can."

In September 1861, Kentucky officially declared for the Union. The Confederacy established secret recruiting posts, and the Union opened a camp. It was said that in Kentucky, brothers literally fought brothers. President Lincoln supposedly said that although he hoped to have God on his side, he had to have Kentucky. Although the state saw several battles, especially early in the war, Louisville was spared. The Honorés sent food, clothing, and letters of love to the Carr relatives there but received only occasional responses. They lived through the war in constant fear for their relatives, always reading the news, always breathing a sigh of relief when no battle was reported near Louisville.

But even in Chicago, they took precautions. Eliza cautioned her children, "If anyone yells at you or calls you 'rebs,' you come right home and get me."

"What's a reb?" Nathan asked.

"Someone who rebels against his government," Cissy said with great superiority. "Mamá means if anyone accuses us of being southerners."

"We are southerners," Ida said softly. "I've always liked the idea of being from Kentucky."

Her older sister fixed her with a stare. "Well, right now, it's not a good idea, so try to pretend to yourself that you were born in Chicago."

Ida opened her mouth in protest, but their mother raised a hand to silence them.

* * *

Harry Collins tried to ignore the war that raged all around them, though it never came near Chicago. He did scan the casualty lists and was relieved each time when he did not find the name of one of this brothers.

"Do you think you should volunteer?" Sheila asked one night as she poured his coffee.

"Me, volunteer? No, I'm going to build my fortune in this city. Many men here are making a huge profit off the war. I want to do the same."

It was far from the answer Sheila wanted to hear, but she remembered his delicate hands. War would harden them, and she knew that.

Potter Palmer was one of those who grew rich. He amassed a fortune selling cotton to the Union Army. When the South withdrew from the Union, the country lost its supply of cotton. Yet cotton was essential to the war. It was used for wadding to tamp down in muzzle-loading guns before the black-powder projectile was inserted; it was wrapped around premeasured amounts of powder to make cannon cartridges; and it was used as "lint," to wipe, clean, and bind wounds. It could be doubled and soaked with chloroform and pressed over a soldier's nose when anesthesia was needed.

For years, Palmer had been importing fine foreign fabrics. Now he imported cotton from various countries. He traveled frequently, securing the fabric and making contacts with army supply officers to sell it. Other times, he operated his store during the day and conducted his "cotton business" at night. More than once, one of his clerks would enter the store in the morning to find Palmer slumped over his desk, asleep.

"Mr. Palmer?" A gentle, tentative tone.

Palmer would shake himself awake and peer at the clerk. "Oh, Jones, thank you. I guess I dozed off." Then he repaired to the dressing room in the rear of the store, splashed cold water on his face, neatened the goatee that he had recently grown because he thought it made him look older and more sophisticated, and changed his clothes. When the store opened, he was at the door, greeting customers in his usual manner. No woman who entered that store ever guessed that Mr. Palmer was exhausted.

Potter Palmer saw no conflict in the fact that he profited from the war. He was, he thought, too old to serve and, besides, his Quaker background prejudiced him against military service. So did his natural inclination. Someone had to supply the much-needed cotton, and surely the country did not expect him to donate either his time or his goods. Potter Palmer wanted the Union to triumph, but his focus was on the personal fortune he was determined to amass.

Henry Honoré came by Palmer Dry Goods one afternoon. "Palmer," he said, seating himself in a chair next to the owner's desk, "we haven't seen you at the house for months, maybe a year. You're working too hard, man."

Palmer fixed him with a direct stare. "I'm making a lot of money," he said.

Honoré sighed. "That's not what life is about, Palmer."

Palmer looked at him again and considered telling him that he had to make a lot of money so that he could provide luxuriously for the other man's daughter. Instead, he said, "I have plans for the money." Then, changing the subject, he asked, "How is your family?" He wanted to ask, "How is Miss Cissy?" but he forbore.

"They're fine," Honoré answered. "Bewildered by the war. They don't understand why people still see us as southerners."

Palmer looked startled. "I don't think of you as southerners."

"No, and most people don't, but some who don't know better think our Kentucky roots make us Confederate sympathizers. But I didn't come here to talk about us. I came here to tell you I'm concerned about you."

"Thank you," Palmer said, rising from his desk and extending his hand. "I'll be fine."

Honoré was rubbing his head again as he left.

* * *

In 1862, the Union began housing Confederate prisoners of war at Camp Douglas. The first batch of prisoners, captured at the Battle of Fort Donelson in Tennessee, was shipped to Chicago in March 1862. Their arrival occasioned a citywide holiday. The prisoners were unloaded from the cattle cars in which they had been crowded together and paraded through the streets. The route from the train to the prison camp was unnecessarily long and convoluted, so that the men could be seen—and jeered—by as many citizens as possible.

The prisoners carried on their backs and in their arms their only possessions, mostly such cooking utensils as frying pans, skillets, coffeepots, and tin cups and plates. Many were hatless, their clothes tattered and torn, and some were shoeless. As they walked by, citizens damned them as poor and ignorant and damned Jefferson Davis for getting them into a war they could never win.

The Honoré boys had heard the prisoners were coming and clamored to be allowed to go watch their progress.

"It's so close to home," Adrian protested, when his mother forbade him to leave the house.

"You will not go stare at those poor, unfortunate creatures," she decreed.

"Will they have horns and tails?" Lockwood, the youngest, asked.

Eliza was startled for a moment. "Of course not," she said. "Where did you get that idea?"

"Jimmy down the street says rebs have horns and tails."

"That's nonsense," she said briskly. "Don't believe it for a minute. They are men like your uncles in Kentucky."

"Will my uncles be prisoners here?" Nathaniel asked.

She raised her eyes heavenward. "Your uncles are loyal to the Union." Then, changing the subject, "Girls, you come in the dining room and practice your needlework. Boys, you clean your rooms."

The boys groaned and reluctantly started up the stairs. The girls dutifully followed their mother, Ida murmuring, "I wouldn't want to see them anyway." Her eye was twitching again.

* * *

When the Honorés' compatriots from Kentucky met, the men sat in the library, smoking cigars and sipping brandy. Cissy and Ida were expected to join the women who gathered around the dining table knitting socks, hats, and mittens for prisoners at Camp Douglas.

"But, Mamá," Cissy asked one day after the ladies had left, "if we are for the North, why do we help the Confederacy?"

"We're not helping the Confederacy," her mother replied. "We're helping men who need kindness, who are much less fortunate than we are. And we help southern men, because few others around here will."

Henry Honoré was outraged that civilians were allowed to visit the prison camp and stare at the men. When a law was passed prohibiting the visits, an enterprising citizen built an observation tower just outside the prison wall. It was always crowded. Men, women, and children looked over a fifteen-foot wooden wall, topped with a walkway for guards, into a compound of barracks and tents where men wandered in tattered clothes, sometimes barefoot even in winter, and latrines were open. The smell of the camp was worse than Chicago's river smell.

Eliza Honoré sent knit goods and other items she thought the soldiers might need—soap, coffee, stationery, and pens on a regular basis. She campaigned hard to secure winter coats for the prisoners, even soliciting her neighbors, some of whom were among those that thought rebs had horns and tails, even if they weren't visible. Throughout the long war she was able to send slightly over a hundred coats to the camp. "A drop in the bucket," she murmured in discouragement. "I hope they can share."

The war lasted longer than Honoré—and President Lincoln—expected, and there were more prisoners sent to Camp Douglas than it was built to hold. Between 1862 and 1865 over twenty thousand men were interred there, and at least four thousand died of smallpox, cholera, poor medical care, and exposure.

Henry Honoré felt his family was in real danger when the Democrats met in Chicago in the summer of 1864. Rumors flew around the city that the rebels had ten thousand stands of arms hidden in cellars in Chicago and officers stationed in Canada who could reach the city in twenty-four hours.

"You are all to stay in the house," Honoré ordered his family. "The city is filled with riffraff."

"Riffraff?" Cissy questioned, her analytical mind wanting a more precise definition.

"People just looking for trouble," Honoré told his daughter, refusing to stoop so low as to describe the drunks and vagabonds he had seen on the streets. "And," he continued, "the rumors about the Knights of the Golden Circle are really bad."

"Knights of the Golden Circle?" Eliza asked. "The copperheads . . . ."

"They're worse than copperheads. Those are just northerners who sympathize with the South but rarely do anything. The Knights of the Golden Circle are organized to rebel."

"Papá," Cissy protested, "Chicago is our home. We can't let anything bad happen here."

He shook his head. "I'm not sure we can stop it, but it's even more important that nothing bad happen to any of you. You'll stay in this house."

Within days, it was revealed that the Knights of the Golden Circle planned to attack Camp Douglas and free the prisoners. With the help of the freed rebel soldiers, they would seize the polls and allow only those with their sympathies to vote. Then, as a grand finale, they would sack and burn the city.

"Would you have been scared?" Ida asked Cissy, when it was clear that the villains had been caught and the plan thwarted.

"I was scared for Chicago," Cissy replied. In truth, from all she'd heard about the beaten men at Camp Douglas, she doubted they had the strength or nerve to burn a city. On the other hand, her father and his friends all agreed that it wouldn't take much to burn Chicago. It was a wooden city. Most buildings were of pine, which had so much pitch in it that it would burn quickly. Even marble-faced buildings had wooden cornices and signs and many had mansard top stories that were wood covered with felt, tar, and shingles—all combustible. Chicago lived in fear of fire.

The Honorés rejoiced with most of Chicago when word came that General Robert E. Lee had surrendered the Army of the Confederacy to General Ulysses S. Grant at a place with the strange name of Appomattox. Men cheered and shouted in the streets of downtown Chicago, and newspapers printed special editions with banner headlines, such as "We Won!" "Victory over the Confederacy." Eliza Honoré let her sons celebrate on Prairie Avenue in front of their house, but she refused to take any of the children to town, which was where they wanted to be to see what they called "the real celebration."

"Some men might . . . ah . . . get carried away," she said. "You're safer on your own street." She wondered about the men at Camp Douglas—had they gotten the news? Would they be set free? Sent back south by train? Surely they couldn't just turn all those sick and hungry men loose in Chicago.

Joy turned to sorrow just a few days later. On April 15, 1865, a somber Henry Honoré arrived home in the middle of the day, his face white, his eyes almost glazed. "Where's your mother?" he demanded, his voice strained.

"She . . . she took the boys somewhere," Cissy replied. "Ida and I are the only ones at home."

Ida stood timidly behind her sister, her eye twitching.

The words burst out of him, as though with his wife not at home, he had to tell someone. "Lincoln! He was shot last night!"

"Is he dead?" Cissy asked.

Her father shook his head in the affirmative.

"What will happen now?" she asked.

He shook his head again, this time in bewilderment. "God only knows," he said, "God only knows."

Chicago, like the rest of the country, went from deep grief at the news to a burning desire for vengeance. There were stories of men beaten for rejoicing at the president's death, and the *Chicago Tribune* carried a story from the nation's capital about a man who asked a guard at the State Department if the president was really dead. Told that he was, the man said, "I'm damned glad of it." The guard shot him in the head and killed him.

Henry Honoré never got beyond the grief, never thirsted for vengeance, and rebuked his sons when they offered lurid descriptions of what they'd do to John Wilkes Booth, who had been identified as the man who shot the president.

The Lincoln Special, the train carrying Lincoln's coffin, the disinterred coffin of his young son, Willie, and about three hundred mourners, pulled into Chicago at eleven in the morning on May 1. Rather than going into Union Station, it stopped on a trestle near the lake.

Chicago's funeral procession rivaled the huge procession held in New York, going from Michigan Avenue to Lake Street, then Clark Street, and finally to Court House Square. Cissy and Ida were among the girls who ran before the somber procession, strewing flowers in the street.

Lincoln's casket was open for public viewing twenty-four hours, from six o'clock that night until the next evening. Henry Honoré wanted his children to remember this great man, so the family was in the throng that streamed double-file past the bier, the boys solemnly holding their hats over their hearts and the girls dressed in dark colors, looking demurely sad. Both Cissy and Ida had to turn away, and Cissy had to brace Ida, for the president's skin had darkened disturbingly in the days since his death. It was, Cissy thought, a sad last memory to have of a great man, and she tried to banish the image from her mind. She remembered instead the picture of the fallen president that had been plastered over the cowcatcher of the train.

When the Lincoln Special left Chicago, a Pullman car was attached to carry Chicago businessmen who would attend services in Springfield. George Pullman had moved beyond raising buildings and started his career as a manufacturer of specialized railroad passenger cars.

Chapter Four

Chicago changed and grew rapidly after the war, and no one, least of all those getting rich, cared that growth was built on the slaughter of the great buffalo herds to the west and the destruction of forests and prairies closer to home. The city still had pine-plank and wood-block pavement, and it still smelled bad. The new Chicago Stockyards only added to the smell. The enormous facility opened on Christmas Day in 1865 and sometimes held as many as one-hundred and twenty thousand animals. It was four miles southwest of the city, but the smell frequently drifted over residents on the South Side.

Potter Palmer was not the only businessman growing rich in those years. George Pullman began building his elegant railroad parlor cars not too long after the war, and Cyrus McCormick employed over a hundred men at his four-story brick factory and hired many more traveling salesmen and repairmen. Railroads cut across the city in all directions. There were no restrictions on where they could build, and great areas of the city had become freight and storage yards. It wasn't good for residential neighborhoods.

Men came to Chicago looking for work, believing they would one day make a fortune but meanwhile working in its factories and packing plants. Wooden shacks were hastily built to house these men and their families, and the city grew westward faster than anyone could have imagined.

"Decent folks have to move farther south on the shore or north," one of Palmer's competitors complained one day. "Fellow can't look to the west for a place to build a home."

"Yes," Palmer replied, "but the lumberyards are making a lot of money."

"They'll make more again when that tinderbox of a city out there catches fire," replied the other man. "And the patches . . . we've got to do something about those people." He shook his head as though in despair.

* * *

Even after the war was removed from Harry Collins' conscience, he was not pleased with Chicago or with his job. In fact, he'd been fired from Abe Goodman's store, where he'd been a bookkeeper, because he refused to keep regular hours or follow orders. He was now a clerk in a lawyer's office—Carter Harrison had gotten him the job—but he'd already been reprimanded for tardiness.

"Late three times, and not very late at that," he complained to Sheila as he ate pot roast at the restaurant counter. "You'd think they could make a few exceptions."

She nodded cautiously and said nothing. She knew what would happen to her if she were late to the café. She'd be in a sweatshop winding spools of thread! Raised to follow orders and do whatever she had to in order to keep a job, she could not understand Harry's insistence that rules were not for him. But she continued to be fascinated by him, closing her mind to the doubts that occasionally danced through it. Maybe it was his eyes and the way he looked at her, but she saw—or dreamt she saw—in Harry Collins a man who would rescue her from the usual fate of a poor Irish Catholic girl in Chicago.

"I don't know that this is a city where an ambitious man can make his fortune," Harry went on. "I think . . . well, you know, all the swells have it in their palms. McCormick, of course, and that Palmer fellow who made all the money during the war."

"They say he's a very nice man," Sheila said and then was quickly silenced by Harry's stern glance. He had that effect on her, and she lacked the spunk to stand up to him. She didn't want him angry with her. If he were too angry, she feared he would simply stop seeing her.

"Come on," he said, "I'll see you home, if you're ready to go."

She looked at the clock and nodded, beginning to untie her apron. "Right," she said. "Another dollar, another day."

He looked strangely at her but said nothing, and they left together, walking carefully apart.

Harry had been walking her home for a long time by now, but he always refused to come in and "meet the family," as Sheila urged him to do. "Me mother would love to feed you Sunday dinner," she said, looking at him speculatively. "She'd say we needed to fatten you up." She glanced ruefully at her own well-rounded figure, as if to say she'd been eating her mother's cooking too long.

Her family joked about Sheila's reluctant suitor, but her mum had talked seriously to her, urging her to see other men. "This one," Mum had said, "he's too reluctant. It ain't natural to court a lady for so long. He'll never do more than court, and you'll end the old maid."

Sheila refused to see other young men. Her heart was set on Harry Collins, though she could not have explained why.

Now they stood in front of her family's house. It was two story and frame but badly in need of paint and repair. The windows sat a little askew, and the front door hung off its hinges. Bare dirt marked the front of the house, where Harry would have expected to see a picket fence and green grass—well, at least green in summer. Harry sometimes wondered if that explained his reluctance to enter.

"Not tonight," he said, as he always did. But then, boldly, he reached for her hand. Pulling her toward him but without touching more than her hand, Harry Collins gave Sheila Fitzpatrick a sound kiss on the mouth. And he felt her response, gentle and tentative but still a response.

"I've got someplace I've got to be," he said, withdrawing as suddenly as he'd pulled her toward him.

Leaving a dreamy-eyed Sheila behind him, he went to O'Malley's Pub, where he joined a low-stakes poker game and lost every penny of his last paycheck. He wondered if Mrs. Grady would believe he'd been robbed again. Sometimes he saw Harrison at O'Malley's and once the older man even bailed him out of a big loss, but he wasn't there this night.

Lying in his bed that night, angry with himself and the world, Harry Collins thought about Sheila. Maybe if . . . well, if she became more a part of his life, maybe then his luck would change. Then he thought about his father, Henry George the industrialist, and smiled in wry amusement at the picture of the older man welcoming Sheila into the family. Not, Harry thought in quick defense, that she wasn't worth ten of all of them—except of course his mother—but she was not up to what his family thought of as their standing in society. They would be immediately disdainful of her brogue, if nothing else.

He turned over on his lumpy bed and decided that he would spend more time with Sheila, maybe even go in and meet the Fitzpatricks. He wasn't in love; he was just dissatisfied with his life.

"Care to take a walk along the lakeshore Sunday?" he asked.

"Along the lakeshore?" She laughed aloud. "You're still the newcomer, after all this time. It's all swamp and marsh, and we couldn't walk there if we wanted. I wish we could go out to Cottage Grove, where there's trees and big houses to look at and . . . But, no, it's too far to walk."

"We'll go in a hack," he said boldly, thinking that by then he would have his next paycheck.

"Oh, go on," she laughed, "we can't afford that. No, you'll come to supper and meet my family."

"All right," he said reluctantly and then, more brightly, as he remembered his plan, "I'd like that."

His visit to the Fitzpatrick family dinner was neither the disaster Harry feared nor the triumph Sheila had hoped for. The younger Fitzpatrick children behaved fairly well, except for Sean stealing potatoes off Patrick's plate and little Mary Kate screaming without stopping for more corned beef. This good-looking easterner with his fine manners had instantly charmed Sheila's skeptical mother. The slight air of tragedy that hung over him appealed to her Irish sensibilities. Sheila's father had been a little more suspicious, especially when he heard that Harry worked for a lawyer. Daniel Fitzpatrick had the workingman's distrust of the upper class and, particularly, of lawyers.

"Ain't I seen you at O'Malleys?"

Sheila looked startled, and Harry managed to mutter, "Maybe a time or two."

After he had given profuse thanks for dinner, Harry invited Sheila to walk out with him. By no coincidence, they found themselves in front of Mrs. Grady's boardinghouse, where Harry had that room with a private entrance.

"You got to see where I live," he said laughing. "After all, you're the one that sent me here."

"It ain't proper," Sheila protested.

"No one will know," he assured her, "and I'll be a perfect gentlemen."

After that, Harry took Sunday supper with the Fitzpatricks every week, and he and Sheila always walked out afterward, unless the weather was inclement, and then they were both inclined to get testy. Sheila had no doubt any longer about what tied her to Harry Collins.

"We have to get married, Harry," Sheila told him one Sunday night as they lay together in the bed in his room at Mrs. Grady's. "I'm in the family way."

He propped himself up on one elbow and stared at her. "Really? Are you sure?" It wasn't unexpected news, and he was neither angry nor overjoyed.

"Two months late I am now," she said, nodding her head.

Harry had been raised to do the honorable thing, and he would marry Sheila. Besides, maybe his luck would change if he were a married man. He supposed he came as close to loving Sheila as he would anyone, except perhaps a millionaire heiress, and no one with a fortune would look twice at him. At some level, Harry knew he'd ruined his own life. Perhaps Sheila would save it. Deliberately, he banished all thoughts of his mother's reaction.

Leaning over to kiss her, he said, "Of course, we shall marry, right away."

When Sheila's mother wanted to know what the hurry was, Harry smiled and said, "We can't live without each other any longer." Sheila never knew that Harry kept his crossed fingers behind his back when he said that.

Mrs. Fitzpatrick swallowed her own doubts about this easterner who was so slow to court her daughter and then suddenly rushed her into marriage. She knew the probable truth only too well.

They were married in St. Mark's Catholic Church in February 1867. Besides Sheila's large, roaring family, the only guest was Carter Harrison, who had heard about the wedding at the café and who gave the young couple a wedding gift of a hundred dollars.

They moved into a shanty at DeKoven and Clinton streets, furnished it with rough pieces they bought with Harrison's money, and settled down to domestic life. Harry worked in the lawyer's office, and Sheila worked at the café. Their daughter, Juliet, was born six months after the wedding.

* * *

As Henry Honoré had known he would, Potter Palmer changed the face of Chicago's business district. Palmer was convinced that the main business street should run north and south, rather than east and west. He wanted to take his customers away from the river with its smells. State Street, he told Honoré, should be the main business street, and it should be widened considerably.

He built a six-story, marble-façade store at the corner of Washington and State, well back from the street to leave room for the widening that he had proposed to the city council.

"What about the businesses that front on the street at its present width?" Honoré asked. The two men sat in Palmer's private office, after the close of business.

Potter seemed surprised that his friend even had to ask. "Why, they'll have to move them back," he said.

"At their own expense?"

"Of course."

"Many won't do it," Honoré predicted, taking another sip of brandy.

And he was right. State Street soon presented an unusual sight, with some buildings sitting tight against the curb of a newly widened street and others moved back to allow for pedestrian traffic.

Henry Honoré wasn't the only one who visited Palmer in his private office. One day his assistant announced Carter Harrison.

Potter rose from his desk to greet his guest, immediately noticing the rumpled clothes and wild beard on this large man. He would learn that even in well-made clothes of the finest fabric, Carter Harrison always looked rumpled. He always wore a slouch hat and usually had a long cigar clamped between his teeth. Out of deference to Palmer, this day he had dispensed with the cigar.

"Carter Harrison," the guest said, holding out his hand. "I figure we should get acquainted." His speech may have been a little more casual than Palmer's, but the Irish brogue he affected around Sheila and Harry and in O'Malley's Pub had disappeared. Carter Harrison always knew his audience.

It would, however, later surprise Potter Palmer to learn Harrison held a law degree from Yale, spoke fluent French and German, and read incessantly, everything from Greek classics to Charles Dickens works. At the moment, Palmer didn't remember the lawyer's office in a sagging building that he'd noticed the first day he arrived in Chicago. Slightly amused by his guest's forthright manner, Potter urged him to sit and then asked, "And why should we become acquainted?" He did not offer brandy, as he always did to Henry Honoré.

"I live out your way. Built a house on Ashland Avenue, not as far out of the city as yours but still like being in the country. Great place to raise children." He paused a minute. You know, it used to be called Reuben Avenue. Then it became a good joke to call those of us who live there 'rubes.' I changed it to Ashland. Has a nice sound, don't you think?"

"You changed it?" Palmer echoed.

"Well, man, I got the city to do it. Chose the name myself."

Potter wondered if the man were all bluster and brag. He remembered hearing that Harrison kept a large black mare named Kate in a stable near his house and rode up and down the street, as though he were a plantation owner surveying his property. But Potter wasn't sure that living in the same direction, slightly out of central Chicago, gave them that much in common. He waited for the man to continue.

"We both have the same goals for Chicago," Harrison went on, oblivious to his host's silence. "I love this city, and I want to see her thrive. I think Chicagoans want to make money and spend it, and you help them do that. What you did about State Street is one of the best things every happened here. I want to congratulate you."

"Thank you," Potter murmured, puzzled about where the conversation would go next.

"We've got to think into the future," Harrison said.

"Such as?"

"Such as making this city more fireproof. I mean, we can't ever make it fireproof, but we can make it less like a disaster waiting to happen. I ride with a volunteer firefighting company, and I know the kinds of things we've seen."

Like any thinking man in the city, rich or poor, Potter Palmer knew that Chicago was prey to fires and that one day one could be a disaster. "What do you propose?" he asked.

"Changes in building codes," Harrison said, "and increased support for firefighters. We can't do much about the shanties to the west, without making people homeless, but we can see that no more are built of tinder-dry wood, and we can encourage every man jack in the city to join a volunteer company."

Palmer hid a shudder. He would support firefighters with generous contributions, but he could not see himself as a member of a firefighting company any more than he could have earlier imagined himself marching off to war. "Let's make some concrete plans," he said, dipping his pen in the inkwell and pulling up a sheet of paper.

"We might start with zoning laws," Harrison said, and Palmer had the uncomfortable feeling that he was taking dictation. "There's no planning in this city. Shanties sit next to fine homes."

Palmer nodded. He could agree with that.

The two men talked and planned for over an hour. Then Harrison took his leave, shaking his host's hand and saying heartily, "I have a feeling, Palmer, that we're going to work together a lot." He had started out the door when he turned and said, "Oh, by the way, I plan to be mayor of this city one day." And then he was gone before Potter could comment.

When Harrison left, Potter Palmer sat at his desk a long time in thought. He was puzzled. The man was . . . well, not polished, although someone other than Potter might have seen the quality as genuine. Yet Palmer could tell Harrison was sincere in his love of Chicago, and he had good ideas for making it one of the most important cities in the country. One of his goals was to beat out the city's traditional rival, St. Louis. But mayor of the city? Palmer hesitated at that. Knowing that Harrison came from Kentucky, he decided to ask Henry Honoré about him the next time they met.

Honoré proved unhelpful. "Man, Kentucky's a big state. I didn't know everyone there. He's not a part of the Kentucky Regulars—that's what I call those that gather at my house—but I can tell you this, he's a Yale graduate with a law degree. That's pretty impressive." What Honoré didn't tell his friend was that Harrison had as many friends on the wrong side of the law as he did on the right. Harrison was Machiavellian in a way, consorting with corruption to further his long-range goal of fostering Chicago's success.

* * *

The summer of 1867 was momentous for the Honoré family. Henry Honoré moved his family into a home on Chicago's newly fashionable North Side, right on Michigan Avenue. Their house was built of brick, with stone quoins at the corners, though it was wrapped with a wooden veranda and had a wooden roof. Inside, spacious, high-ceilinged rooms had walnut woodwork and oak floors stained dark and covered with Oriental rugs. Mrs. Honoré had decorated with the fashionable cluttered look of upper-class Victorian homes. Chandeliers were elaborate, doorways had decorative corner piers, fabric was draped over tables and picture frames. In the living room, a guitar stood leaning against a corner wall, as though waiting for someone to pick it up and sink onto one of the tasseled floor cushions to strum it.

Upstairs, two bedrooms housed two boys each, while Cissy and Ida each had their own rooms. The boys, who could now roam the marshes of the lakefront, were delighted at the family's move. They caught sand crabs and grasshoppers and all kinds of wildlife that inhabited the marshes, coming home with their treasures in hand, smelling strongly of lake water and marsh. The smell of Chicago followed the Honorés to the North Side.

Ida was dismayed by the move. She would have to leave St. Xavier, where she knew all the girls, and attend a new school. "I don't make friends easily," she wailed to Cissy, "and I liked our old house." She also did not like the way her brothers smelled or the creatures they brought home. "And we're so far from everything!"

"Posh, we're not far. George can take us places in the landau. And the new house," Cissy said with authority, "is ever so much grander. Mamá will be able to entertain large crowds. And it's much more fashionable to live on the North Side now."

Ida didn't care about fashionable.

Cissy wasn't really focusing on the house. She would be leaving for boarding school in the East in late August. St. Xavier's had begun to bore her, and she felt older than all her schoolmates, more sophisticated. At the Convent of Visitation in Georgetown, outside Washington, D.C., no one would know her as Bertha. She could introduce herself as Cissy. Except for moments, the prospect of being away from home didn't bother her, though she knew she'd miss her family. When doubts came to her, Cissy took a deep breath and tried to think about something else. She'd certainly never tell Ida that she had her small fears.

Her mother saw to it that she had the appropriate wardrobe for finishing school. They went to the opening of Potter Palmer's new store, which he was operating with two younger men—Marshall Field and Levi Leiter.

When George pulled the landau up to the front door, a young man in dark blue with rows of brass buttons marching across his chest and white gloves on his hands helped Mrs. Honoré and her daughters from the carriage. Another young man bowed low as he held the door for them, and still another greeted them inside by handing each a fresh red rose. "Fine fabrics are on the first floor," he said. "Gowns on the second, jewelry on the third" and so on, reeling off a directory of the store. The women looked in wonder at white pillars, high open spaces, and draped tables that held swags of beautiful fabrics. Before they could exclaim to one another about the store, Mr. Palmer himself came over to them. Properly, he spoke to the mother first.

"Mrs. Honoré, I am so grateful that you honored our opening and brought your delightful daughters with you." He bowed over each of their hands and said, "Let me show you some of the finest wares." The three admired fabric and beautiful ready-made gowns and fine gold jewelry from Europe for more than an hour, with Mr. Palmer ever at their side.

Finally, Mrs. Honoré said, "Bertha will be leaving in August for school in the East."

Cissy saw him raise an eyebrow and glance at her. "Of course," he said smoothly, "she needs a new wardrobe." She thought he looked tired, although he was as polite and polished as ever.

They chose waists and skirts and everyday dresses of challis and ticking and one wonderful full-skirted silk gown in a small blue-and-gray pattern with floss fringe that waved in the air when Cissy moved her arms. She tried on each dress in a private dressing room, equipped with comfortable chairs in which her mother and sister sat as she pirouetted before them.

"You have no idea," Mrs. Honoré later said to Potter Palmer, "what a relief it is to buy ready-made clothes instead of having seamstresses in the house for weeks on end."

"I am glad to be of service," he said, bowing slightly. "Remember, if anything doesn't satisfy . . ."

She laughed. "I know. We can bring it back. We'll return later to shop for Ida's fall wardrobe."

They were in the store a full four hours. When they left, the carriage was loaded with fabric, ready-made gowns, and shoes, and Eliza Honoré, Cissy, and Ida each carried a small delicate handkerchief edged with Belgian lace, a gift from Mr. Palmer. Eliza's protests that she should buy them fell on deaf ears.

"I insist," he repeated. And then, looking directly at Cissy, "I hope you find school a rewarding experience."

"I'm sure I shall," she said, dropping her eyes. "I'm looking forward to it."

Later, in the carriage, she rhapsodized, "I want to shop there for everything I wear."

"Don't let your father hear you say that. It's an expensive store."

"But it's wonderful, Mamá."

Henry Honoré was waiting for them at home and helped unload the massive quantity of clothing from the carriage. "I suppose you bought out Palmer's store," he said, rolling his eyes heavenward. "I shudder to think of the bill he'll send me."

"Mr. Palmer was very kind to us, Papá. Look, he even gave us these Belgian lace handkerchiefs," Cissy said.

Henry Honoré looked at the glow on his daughter's face, and suddenly he was taken back several years in his mind. He saw Potter Palmer sitting in those wicker chairs on the veranda of the Prairie Avenue house, declaring that he thought he'd wait until Cissy was grown. And now, she was almost grown. As a father, he didn't know what to make of it.

* * *

Instead of being invigorated, as she'd expected, Cissy was bored by her two years at Visitation. She studied manners, French, music, and sewing, with a smattering of geography and history, which she suspected was intended to prepare her for a grand tour of Europe. Nonetheless, she found those subjects the most interesting. She learned to make wax flowers—violets, camellias, and japonicas—a talent she could in no way foresee using in the future.

"I guess I'm expected to marry and make wax japonicas," she moaned one night to her roommate, a girl named Kate from New York City. "It hardly intrigues me—at least the flower part, not the marrying part."

"Women," Kate intoned, "need to be doing significant things, not making wax flowers." She was sitting at her desk, back ramrod straight as she'd evidently been taught, book open before her. "I, for one, will become a suffragette."

"Will you bob your hair and wear bloomers?" Cissy sat at her own desk, her back equally straight.

"If my father will permit," Kate answered, and Cissy turned her head to hide a grin.

* * *

In the summer of 1868, while Cissy was home from school, her mother gave a lawn party for Henry Honoré's business friends. Cissy was carrying a platter of petit fours to a table on the lawn when she almost tripped over Potter Palmer.

"Whoa!" he exclaimed, reaching to steady the tray and brushing his hand across hers in the process. "That was almost a disaster."

She laughed lightly. "But your reactions were so quick, you saved me." She thought her hand burned where he had touched it.

He bowed low, and with just a hint of mockery in his voice, he said, "Always glad to be of service to a beautiful woman. Let's go set that tray down where it belongs."

Cissy handed him the tray and led him to the lawn table, where it was to be placed. She was glad he carried it, for her hands felt shaky now.

"And how is your schooling?" he asked.

She glanced around to see who might be within earshot, and then she answered honestly. "I don't much like it. It's a finishing school, where they teach you manners and the like. But I have only another year to go."

"And then," he asked with amusement, "will you be *finished?* It sounds rather like something that is done to fine furniture." He turned his head and coughed slightly.

Cissy laughed at his cleverness. "It does, doesn't it? Well, I shall be finished when the proper patina is achieved."

"Touché," he said, lifting his glass of champagne in a quick gesture of toast. Potter Palmer admired clever women. "So you are off for yet another year of finishing. Will the patina take?"

"It's my last year. I don't think my parents can find any more Catholic schools to send me to after this."

"But you are not Catholic," he said, with a slight question in his voice.

"No, we're French Protestant. But Mamá says the nuns make ladies out of young girls."

"They've done very well with you," he murmured. And then he had to turn away to cough again.

She knew he had been bold, and she was afraid she blushed. But as she looked at him, she forgot his boldness because she saw again that he looked older than she remembered and more tired. And that cough! She knew, of course, that he'd made himself a very rich man during the war, although that was now several years past. She'd heard the rumors that he'd made seven million dollars and that he always had a beautiful woman with him in his carriage, though he never seemed to settle on one. He summered in Saratoga Springs, New York, and took friends to the stadium he had built for the "White Stockings" baseball team. He was, clearly, the talk of the town. Cissy's mother's Kentucky friends gossiped about him, with a "tsk, tsk" in their voices. "Man like that must be very unhappy," they said.

Cissy never understood why they thought he must be unhappy. In her eyes, he had a wonderful life—plenty of money, more women than she wished he knew, all that travel, and that fine store. She thought just to stand in the store and look around and know you owned it must be a thrill. But, this day, he didn't look like he had a wonderful life. He looked tired.

"You are tired," she said. It was not a question.

He nodded. "The war was hard on me." Then he hastened to add, "Good for business, very good. But I've worked too hard for too long and now the doctors are threatening me."

"With what?" she asked.

He chuckled. "Ill health, unless I rest."

"And are you going to?" She expected he was one of those men for whom relaxation was not possible.

"I'm going to try," he said. "I've leased the store to Field and Leiter. I'm going to Europe. Perhaps we'll both be finished about the same time."

She laughed softly. "Wouldn't that be funny? We'd have to drink a toast to our own . . . our own what? Not finishing, but I don't know what."

"We'll think of something. Until then, I'll hold that as a promise. May I?"

She nodded in agreement and slipped quickly away to hide her uncertainty.

Potter Palmer was sure the decision he made years earlier was the right one. His goal was almost in sight, and he could afford to be patient.

* * *

In June of 1869, Bertha Honoré—the convent would not sanction any name but that on her official papers—was recognized as one of six students receiving highest honors for "uniform excellence of conduct." She took honors in geography, history, and domestic economy, and she was through with finishing school.

"Domestic economy!" her father exploded. "What have I been paying all this money for my daughter to learn?"

"How to run a household," Eliza said quietly. "And she'll be very good at it."

Fleetingly, Henry once again remembered Potter Palmer's words.

In the autumn, when she made her debut in her family's home, Potter Palmer was there.

"You are finished," he said, kissing her hand.

"And you," she replied, lifting her eyes to meet his, "are much improved." She saw that the twinkle was back in his eyes and that he stood straight and moved with assurance. He looked, she thought, considerably younger than he had before he went to Europe.

He laughed. "At least in appearance. I don't know about my inner life." Then he turned serious. "I am better, and I thank you for thinking of it." He was still holding her hand, and she withdrew it with some reluctance, aware of propriety but wanting to keep feeling his touch.

He brought her a glass of sherry and watched while she surveyed the crowd. Now that she had finished with school, she was permitted to sip sherry in public, and she liked it.

A small orchestra was playing the music of Strauss, and he asked if she would care to dance.

"My mother," she said carefully, "would not permit me to waltz." Even as she spoke, Cissy could feel the music sweep over her, and she longed to be on the dance floor. She recognized that what she really longed for was to be in Potter Palmer's arms on the dance floor. But Eliza Honoré was insistent that it was not proper for unmarried women to waltz. Cissy sighed a little inwardly, chafing at the restraints put on her life.

"And have you ever danced the waltz when she was not in attendance?" he asked. It was a bold and impertinent question, and he knew that he was testing his luck.

A smile flickered across her face but was quickly erased. "I have not had that opportunity," she replied carefully, looking deep into the swallow of sherry left in her glass. She knew she would not dance without permission, whether or not her mother was present. The discipline of convent training was strong.

"I would like to offer you the opportunity to dance . . . when the occasion arises, of course, and with proper permission." He felt as though he were in a formal duel, each person sparring, carefully measuring his or her movements against the other.

"Of course. I would like that." And then, as was the pattern of all their brief meetings, she moved quickly away to greet other guests. This time, though, he sensed she did not move away out of confusion, as she had before. It was time, Potter Palmer concluded, to begin his courtship in earnest.

She was not surprised when he suggested he would like to teach her to waltz.

"I would, of course, secure your father's permission," he said most properly. And that he'd done, over Eliza Honoré's objections. They'd waltzed at the next big festivity, given in a private home with a large ballroom.

Potter called at the Honoré home a few days prior to the event, and Cissy, summoned to the parlor by the maid, wondered what he could want of her. And why her heart was beating too fast.

"I understand," he said, positioning himself by the fireplace with his hands clasped behind him, "that you are going to the Fields' party."

She lowered her eyes. "Yes, I am."

"I have asked *both*"—he stressed the word—"your parents for permission to waltz with you at the dance. I understand they will be playing the music of Mr. Strauss."

He had, Cissy realized, gone to a great deal of trouble to find out about the music and to talk to her parents.

"I will look forward to the waltz," she said as calmly as she could.

"So will I, so will I," he said, speaking so low that he was almost talking to himself. Then his tone strengthened. "Since I am to be your dancing partner, I suggest that it is only appropriate that I escort you to the dance."

Cissy had never been escorted anywhere by a gentleman caller. It was fairly well understood that a young woman of Cissy's class and training was escorted to various social functions by her parents, until she was betrothed, at which time, in carefully selected circumstances, she might attend this party or that with the intended. Clearly, Potter Palmer had committed a breach of social manners.

"I don't think my parents would approve that," she said quietly and felt just as she had when she'd first refused to waltz with him—a longing inside of her nearly overrode the obedience she'd been so carefully taught. "I'll attend with them and look forward to seeing you there."

"Of course," he said, eyes twinkling again. "Forgive me for overstepping my place." Taking his leave, he bent low over her hand and then raised his eyes to meet hers.

Cissy returned his look directly, and once again he was not sure what he saw in the depths of her eyes. He thought maybe, just maybe, it was attraction.

* * *

Sheila Collins sat at the rough table in their shanty, cradling Juliet in her arms.

"You baby her," Harry said crossly from across the table. "She's got to learn to take care of herself. She needs to get out with the children around here."

"She's only a little better than two, and the others here are ragamuffins. I'll protect her as long as I can," Sheila said defensively. She recognized that her husband was in one of his moods, and she suspected he'd had one too many pints of beer at O'Malley's before he came home. Harry Collins had proved to be a protective husband and father, and he was more affectionate with Juliet than with Sheila, often telling the child a story after she was in bed at night. Sheila did not know that he was telling himself he was building the family he'd never had as a child. What she did know was that when he'd been to O'Malley's, his old demons seemed to haunt him, as they did this night.

Harry Collins was now working as a stocker in a mercantile store, putting canned goods on shelves. He had been late one too many times to the lawyer's office, and Carter Harrison had been unable to help him. The change had embittered Harry—a facet of his personality Sheila came to recognize too late—and he stopped too often at the pub. Sheila's mother kept Juliet during the day while Sheila worked at the café, and it was her meager pay that kept the family in tough stew meat and potatoes. Some nights it was potatoes without the meat.

"Why can't we have a decent meal?" he'd complain, and Sheila would patiently answer, "Because we cannot afford to buy meat." She worried about Juliet, who was pale and quiet and didn't seem to get enough nourishment, except when she was at her grandparents' house. There was, Sheila thought, much to be said for her father's regular job at the McCormick plant with pay that was better than what Harry earned. But she kept her tongue.

"You seen Mr. Harrison lately?" she asked, hoping to change the subject.

Harry's look was brooding. "A time or two at O'Malley's, same as I've seen your father." There was insinuation in that statement. "But Harrison's got more important friends than us. He visits with the upper crust." Harry had not learned the street vernacular that called people like Potter Palmer "the swells."

"I hear he's working with Potter Palmer," he said, "the one whose store you always wanted to visit. They're planning to improve Chicago." His voice held contempt, as though he did not think there was any hope of improving Chicago.

She gave a light, forced laugh. "Not much hope of that now, is there?"

He looked startled. "Of what?"

She had no idea he had been thinking of the future of her city. "Of me visiting Mr. Palmer's dry goods store," she said.

He stood up and stalked into the sleeping area, muttering over his shoulder, "I'll take you there any time you want."

Sheila Collins knew that she would not go to a store where she could not afford to make a purchase. She would not gawk.

* * *

Cissy Honoré loved to waltz and proved herself graceful and accomplished at it. She and Potter were the talk of the Fields' party—and of society for days afterward.

"A gentle rumor has reached me," Eliza Honoré said to her husband, "that Potter Palmer is . . . ah, unsuitably . . . interested in Bertha. For a man of his age, that is."

"And why is it unsuitable for a man of his age?" he demanded almost gruffly.

His wife thought a moment and then said, "I'd thought she would marry someone . . . more her age."

Henry Honoré sat heavily in a chair in the sitting room. "Potter Palmer has not asked to marry her. He simply wanted to dance with her." Then, watching his wife carefully, he said, "But I expect he will one day want to marry her. What will you do then?"

She was thoughtful a moment. "What will Bertha do?"

"Why, I imagine she'll marry him," answered the father. "I sense that she is attracted to him. I think I've sensed it since the day years ago when he gave her the name Cissy." He paused and watched his wife's face, unable to read her expression. Then he pressed on. "Look at it another way—she's bright and knowledgeable, and most of these young pups I see around the city would bore her to death. Potter would make a good husband, and there'd be no worry about her being taken care of."

Eliza sighed heavily, trying to adjust her dream for her oldest daughter.

After the Fields' party, Potter Palmer was at Cissy's elbow everywhere she went. At parties, he put his name on her dance card as often as he dared. Should she venture out shopping, she inexplicably ran into him, until she once wondered to herself, in amusement, if he were spying on her movements. And, until then only an occasional caller at the Honoré home, he now became a frequent and regular visitor, so much so that on Sundays, when the family gathered for a large and formal dinner, a place was automatically set for him.

"Cissy," Ida asked, "are you really . . . ah, interested in Mr. Palmer? Isn't he awfully old? I mean, all kinds of boys our age are paying attention to you."

Cissy whipped around in her dressing-table chair and stared directly at her sister. "I am, yes, I am interested in Mr. Palmer. Beside him, Sam Medill is a child, always stepping on my toes when we dance. And the Thomas boy drinks too much, even at parties. No doubt he'll be a sot within two years after he convinces some poor girl to marry him. And Bev McGee—he can't put five words together in a sentence." She paused a minute and then went on almost dreamily, "Mr. Palmer talks to me about real things like business and . . . well, mostly business. And he's a divine dancer, moderate drinker . . . I just think he's everything a girl could want."

"In a father," Ida muttered, softly enough that her sister didn't hear her.

When her mother asked her much the same question, Cissy had her answers better organized—or thought she did. "He's clever," she said, "and amusing. He makes me laugh. Bryan Chapman is so deadly serious about everything, from his father's business to my Protestantism, and Keith Thomas and some of the others are never serious about anything. I don't know which is worse. But Potter—"

"Mr. Palmer," her mother interrupted.

"I call him Potter," the daughter said serenely. "We are friends . . . really good friends."

"I think," the mother said slowly, "that he wants to marry you." She did not want to explore the phrase "really good friends" or find out how intimate—only emotionally, of course—her daughter had become with Potter Palmer. Some things, Eliza was convinced, were best left unknown.

But she did ask the question that burned in her mind. "Does it not bother you that he is"—she paused, trying to be delicate in her choice of words and not finding an appropriate way—"so much older than you?"

Cissy answered quickly. "I've thought a lot about that, Mamá. I know when I'm forty, he'll be sixty-three, and when I'm sixty-three . . . well, he'll either be old or dead. But what I finally worked out in my mind is that I shouldn't miss years of being with him because of what might happen in the future." She paused, then added, "That is, of course, if he asks me to marry him."

"I think he will do just that," her mother said.

"Oh, I hope so," Cissy said. "I really do hope so."

Her mother could think of no answer. Cissy had always been independent, but she had also been obedient. Now her mother saw her as headstrong. She knew she could not change the course of coming events.

In time, Potter Palmer formally asked Henry Honoré for his daughter's hand in marriage. The father consulted the mother, and both agreed the decision was up to the daughter. Her response was so instant that all three were surprised.

"Thank heaven," she said. "I've been waiting for him to ask."

"He's old," Ida repeated when told the news, her assessment now definitely tinged with jealousy. Only a year younger than Cissy, she had few beaux.

"And," said Cissy mischievously, "experienced. He knows about women." She left her implication hanging in the air but was completely satisfied with Ida's shocked, "Cissy!"

"And I will," she'd added impishly, "live in a hotel!"

Rejuvenated by his long stay in Europe, Palmer had plunged headlong into business in the city again, and his principal project was the building of the grandest hotel Chicago had yet seen. It would be called the Palmer House, and it would open in 1871. Potter told her that his new hotel was his wedding gift to her, and they would have a private apartment on the top floor. Cissy was enthralled with the idea of living in the midst of the city.

Potter Palmer was forty-five; his bride was twenty-two.

* * *

Carter Harrison handed his mare, Kate, to a doorman outside Palmer Dry Goods in the middle of the business day and burst into the store without waiting for it to be opened for him. "Where's Palmer?" he roared.

"In his office," a clerk said nervously. "Shall I announce you?"

"I'll announce myself," he said, brushing past the clerk and climbing the stairs to Palmer's office on the fifth floor.

He entered without knocking, and a startled Potter Palmer looked up from the blueprints he was studying. In the years since their first meeting, he had come to know Harrison much better and to both appreciate his ambitions for Chicago and despair of some of his behavior. He was not surprised that the man burst into his office this way.

"Harrison," he said calmly, rising.

"Palmer, you old devil," the other man said, holding out his hand. "Let me congratulate you. I hear you're taking yourself a bride. And not just any bride." A grin broke out on his face.

To Potter, this was an intrusion on his personal life. He wondered if Harrison was referring to Cissy's age or her family's wealth. Either way, the man clearly missed the reason he was marrying her. "Miss Honoré has consented to be my bride," he said rather stiffly.

"I heard, I heard. Word's all over town." He didn't tell the groom-to-be that he'd heard the news from Sheila in the City Café, who'd heard it from a customer and had repeated it to him in tones of awe that reflected her astonishment at the way "the swells" lived. "They'll be richer than God," she had said.

"Calls for a celebration, man." Harrison pulled a flask out of his coat pocket.

Palmer was ever the good host. "Put that away, Carter. I've some good bourbon here." He went to the sideboard where a decanter and glasses were set, poured each a finger of bourbon, and handed a glass to Harrison.

"To a long and happy marriage and many children," Carter said, raising his glass to clink it rather roughly against Potter's.

Potter wondered that the glasses hadn't cracked as he took a sip of the bourbon. He would have to remember to add Carter Harrison to the guest list.

"Nice that you and Honoré will have more in common than your real-estate deals," Carter went on. "Mrs. Harrison and I will want to entertain you, of course, after the honeymoon, when it's suitable."

A nicety, Potter thought, *that I wouldn't have thought would enter his mind.* Aloud, he said, "We'll certainly look forward to that," hoping the evening would never come to pass. He was unprepared for Harrison's next comment.

"I married an Indian, you know. Yessir, great-granddaughter of Pocahontas. Makes me proud."

Potter wondered why Harrison's wife's lineage was relevant to a discussion about his own forthcoming marriage.

After Harrison left, Palmer had a disturbing thought. If his forthcoming marriage was the talk of the city, did the gossips think, as he suspected Harrison did, that it was a marriage of convenience? He could never say publicly that it was a marriage of passion—or at least, that he hoped it would be—so he'd just have to hold his head high and ignore innuendo. Cissy's genuine happiness after the marriage would put a stop to wagging tongues. Or at least he hoped so.

* * *

Cissy Honoré stood at the head of the stairs in her parents' home. Below her, at the foot of the stairs, she saw her father waiting, his carefully brushed black frock coat pulled tight over the white tucked shirt beneath. Next to him, Ida was ready to carry out the obligations of the maid of honor. Beyond, in the spacious gallery of the home, some forty friends and family were seated in patient expectation. Her grandmother and other relatives had come from Louisville, though Eliza's mother, Mary York, was not charmed with the city to which her son-in-law had taken her daughter. "A flat city on a flat prairie by a dull lake," she had said bluntly after her servant took her about in the carriage. Cissy's four brothers, scrubbed and starched to the nines, sat beside the relatives.

When Cissy and Potter became engaged, Chicago society buzzed with anticipation. Theirs would surely be the biggest wedding of the year. Speculation ran wild on which church would be honored to host the event—probably not the Baptists and surely not the Catholics, so perhaps the Methodists.

Cissy confounded even her parents by announcing she wanted a small wedding at home.

"I can afford a big church wedding," Henry Honoré protested, "and I'd like to do that for my oldest daughter."

Eliza Honoré was more direct. "Everyone will think we've avoided the big wedding because of . . . of . . . uncertainty about the age difference between the bride and groom."

Cissy laughed aloud at that. "Well, I'll tell people that it was my wish. I want only people who care a great deal about me or about Potter to witness the marriage. You may invite the whole city of Chicago to a reception, if you wish."

Now, standing at the top of the stairs, the long anticipated moment having arrived, Cissy pictured in her mind Palmer taking his place next to the minister by the carefully constructed altar with its large bouquet of mock orange blossoms artistically arranged in a silver urn. He wore a black frock coat and certainly, she knew, the satin waistcoat she had fashioned for him as a wedding gift.

"Like carrying coals to Newcastle," she had fumed at her mother. "The man can buy any piece of clothing he wants . . . and ten of each if it pleases him."

"He will be pleased," her mother replied, "with the love that accompanies something from your hand."

"And the blood?" the daughter asked, sucking the finger she had just pricked for the tenth time. She wanted no more lectures on a wife's duties in relation to her husband. It was one of her mother's favorite topics lately.

During all the elaborate wedding preparations, Mrs. Honoré had not, of course, mentioned intimate relations—both mother and daughter would have been uncomfortable with that, even though both knew that Cissy's knowledge, if she had any at all, was slight and probably mistaken. No, pinning hems and planning menus, making up invitation lists and worrying about the bridal veil, Mrs. Honoré had talked of a woman's proper place, supporting her husband yet remaining strong herself.

Cissy was unable, in her mind, to move beyond the moment of the marriage. It was as though the ceremony, the culmination of all her wishes, would happen in a void. Everything led up to it—but what followed? When she thought of the future, of her life as Mrs. Potter Palmer, she could put no shape to it. In recent months, thoughts of the next time she saw him, when he was coming to dinner, where they might go to a party, had given meaning and shape to her days. She had planned her life around being with Potter Palmer. But now she would be with him day and night—she would, she vowed, think about that later!—and what would bring excitement to her life?

When the first strains of Vivaldi's "Spring" were heard from the gallery, where a string quartet played, Cissy started alone down the wide staircase. She moved confidently, never looking down at her feet, never reaching for the rail, the smile on her face steady and sure. The nuns had taught her well, and her inner confusion was hidden. Little did she know that no woman goes to the bridal altar without doubts. Yet doubts had assailed her all day, and she was indignant that this, the day she'd waited so long for, was marred by her thoughts, which ranged as far as, "Why am I doing this?" Deliberately, she smiled at Ida, who, watching, was touched with yet another pang of jealousy.

Ida proceeded into the gallery, where chairs had been set to approximate church seating. As Ida walked the length of a center aisle, heads turned away from her, toward the doorway where Cissy and her father stood.

Everyone thought Cissy Honoré would choose an extravagant and elaborate gown for her wedding. She could afford it, said the gossips. Again, she surprised them by choosing a simple silk gown that was fitted tightly at her waist and swelled into a wide skirt that swayed ever so slightly as she walked. The top was modest, rising to a banded collar, but without beading and elaborate decorations. The sleeves were long and appropriately modest, and Cissy was grateful that this June day was cool enough that the dress was comfortable. In contrast to the simplicity of the dress, her head was covered with a veil of intricate and old Spanish lace. As she entered the gallery, Cissy heard the gasps of delight, but her attention was on Palmer, who stood by the makeshift altar. She smiled slightly at him. Only he recognized the nervousness in the smile, but his in return was broad and unabashedly delighted.

The wedding vows were quickly said, one musical selection played—Cissy had carefully chosen "Ode to Joy"—and the couple pronounced man and wife. They held hands tightly when the minister intoned, "Whom God hath joined together, let no man put asunder." And then, when he said, "You may kiss your bride," Potter raised the veil, murmured "Cissy," and kissed her so soundly that she was sure she heard her mother gasp. She herself simply stood still while he kissed her—what else, she wondered, was she supposed to do?

Several hundred guests—"all of Chicago, just like Cissy said," her father had ranted at one point—had been invited for a wedding supper at Kinsey's Restaurant on Adams Street. Cissy, Potter, and the Honorés stood in the receiving line for two hours, but Cissy never faltered, never had to ask that a name be repeated, greeted each guest with a smile and a warm handshake. Next to her, Potter wilted visibly, and she knew he longed for the ordeal to end.

"You do business with them," she whispered to him at one point.

With a wry smile, he whispered back, "They damn well better do business with me after this!" Then, turning, he greeted a guest yet unknown to Cissy.

She had recognized many of the guests, friends of her parents and business associates of her father's. And she had been glad to see Marshall Field when he came through the line. Since he and Levi Leiter bought Potter's business, Cissy still shopped at the store often, even though she missed Potter's presence. Mr. Field was attentive, but it wasn't the same.

Somehow, this stranger that Potter turned to greet didn't look like the business associates of either her father or Potter. He was a large man, tall and heavy-boned, with a bushy beard and mustache. And his suit was, well, rumpled was the only thing Cissy could say to herself. But the man smiled easily and had a nice twinkle in his eyes.

"Harrison! Good of you to come!" The entrepreneur in him took over, and Potter was all smiles again. "Cissy, I want you to meet Carter Harrison, one of the most important men of this city. Carter's one of your fellow Kentuckians," Potter said, turning to Cissy.

"So glad to meet you," Cissy said. "I don't believe I've heard Papá mention your name."

"No, ma'am, but we're acquainted . . . and we'll be better acquainted."

Not knowing quite what the man meant, Cissy simply smiled and said, "I'm sure you will." Though he puzzled her, there was something about the man that attracted her—a good-natured honesty in his smile . . . maybe it was his eyes, which danced with laughter.

Harrison moved on through the line, but Cissy had no time to ask Potter about him.

The guests feasted on boned quail in jelly, chicken and lobster salads, escalloped oysters, Charlotte Russe, and various fruits. They toasted the newlyweds with champagne and soothed their palates with ices and frappes. Cissy and Potter Palmer ate as heartily as any of their guests. Palmer responded to the toasts with one of his own, gracefully thanking the Honorés for entrusting him with the well-being of their daughter and all the guests for celebrating this happy occasion with him. Cissy raised a silent glass toward him when he finished, and he leaned down to kiss her forehead.

It was, everyone agreed, the most impressive wedding yet seen in the city, even if the ceremony had been private. Chicagoans had shown that they were not the country bumpkins New York expected.

* * *

"You were magnificent, Mrs. Palmer," Potter said. He stood in front of the fireplace in which a small fire glowed, built in deference to a slight chill that had settled on the June night. "Are you exhausted?"

They would depart for Europe the next day, leaving Chicago in one of Pullman's fancy rail cars. But meantime they had simply returned to the farmhouse outside the city where Potter had been living until his hotel was complete.

His housekeeper, a woman named Margaret, had seen to it that sherry and brandy were neatly set out, the fire lit, the lights turned low—and then she had tactfully disappeared to the quarters that Potter had built for her next to the barn, so that he could have the house to himself in privacy. Now, with a young bride, he had even more reason to wish for privacy.

Cissy, seated on the sofa opposite the fireplace, laughed aloud for the first time. "No," she said, "I'm too exhilarated to be exhausted. It was a wonderful day." Her doubts were all banished, and she was truly happy. As she looked at her new husband, she thought how handsome he was.

Potter Palmer eyed his bride with a slightly bemused look. "Ah . . . did your mother . . . have a talk with you?" It was, of course, too much to hope that they had talked of the intimate side of marriage. Still, Potter had long thought that a mother was obliged to inform her daughter, for the husband's sake, if nothing else.

"Oh, yes," Cissy drawled, "about responsibilities. I shall have to stop being the carefree young debutante."

"No," he said expansively, "you can always be carefree. I'll see to that."

She shook her head. "It's all right when you're young, but it's not a way to live your life. I . . . I'll find my purpose," she said with a determination that sent a slight shudder through him.

"I thought," he said carefully, "that your purpose might be to ensure my happiness."

She looked at him with wide, innocent eyes. "Oh, of course, Potter. But that won't take all my time."

He sighed.

"Tell me, Potter," she said, "about that man named Harrison. How have I never met him before, if he's from Kentucky?"

Palmer shrugged, as if to say he couldn't account for it. But then, slowly, he said, "He's a different sort. Has a Yale education as a lawyer and has done very well in real estate. But he"— Palmer hesitated, uncertain how to continue—"he spends as much time with men in pubs as he does at places where you'd see him. Lord knows, though, he loves the city of Chicago."

She raised her eyebrows in question.

"Been known to refer to it as his 'bride,'" her husband explained. "I don't doubt that one day he will be mayor, which is his most fervent hope."

"Then we must entertain him," she said decisively.

"Well, now," he temporized, "we'll see about that. But speaking of brides, I suspect mine is tired in spite of herself. Why don't you go and make yourself comfortable? I'll give you time for your toilette, and then I'll join you."

She smiled, kissed him lightly on the cheek, and left the room, while he stared pensively after her. He had no idea what she expected of him that evening, and he—an urbane man in midlife— was nervous.

An hour later, he swallowed yet another sip of brandy and headed for the guestroom, which had now become his dressing room. A few minutes later, dressed in a nightshirt and robe, he found his wife, wearing a fine silk wrapper, propped up in bed, wide awake, waiting for him. She hadn't known he expected her to call to him when she was ready.

Cissy had, as a matter of fact, been sitting in the bed, propped up by the pillows, for the better part of the hour that Potter had given her. She had first brushed her hair until it shone, cleaned her face, and dabbed cologne on her wrists and earlobes. Then, uncertain what else to do, she climbed into the bed—and waited. The longer she waited, the more her uncertainty grew.

This was, she knew, the moment no one talked about—not her mother, certainly not her father, and not Ida, who knew even less than she did. She wished desperately that she'd had a confidante who might tell her what was expected of her, for that was Cissy's great concern—that she would not know her role. Her knowledge of intimate relations was indeed limited—she had once seen the family dogs copulating, and she'd heard snickers and whispers among her brothers, but how did that apply to men and women?

She had little idea, and her only consolation was that Potter should have had experience equal to his age. He would know what she didn't, and because she had absolute faith in him, he would show her what to do. The thought that the only reason he'd know what to do was that he had slept with women he was not married to did not occur to her.

Cissy was not afraid, but it would be fair to say she was very apprehensive. So she waited in anticipation of hearing his step. It was a long hour.

Discreetly, Potter turned the gas lamps off, took off his robe, and pulled aside the covers on his side of the bed, keeping his nightshirt carefully pulled down.

"Cissy," he said softly, moving toward her in the vast expanse of the bed.

"Yes, Potter?"

"I . . . I . . ." Words failed him, and he simply pulled himself over so that he leaned above her, reaching down to kiss her, not gently as he had at the altar, but with a certain demand, a need that was his alone and that she knew nothing of. To his surprise, she reached her arms around his neck and held him. As his tongue explored her mouth, his lips working on hers, he felt her answer back—timidly, gently, but a response.

He moved his mouth to her ear, her neck, down toward her bodice, and his hands began to move gently over her body, carefully avoiding any of the places that might cause her alarm and yet trying to relax her. She lay still, but when he would return to kiss her on the mouth, she answered with a kind of surprised questioning. Her hands stayed locked around his neck, though one finger began to twirl a bit of his hair at the nape of his neck.

Slowly, his hands reached under the wrapper—someone, thank heaven, had told her not to wear undergarments, or maybe she had figured it out by herself—and then carefully pulled it up to bunch about her waist. Did he feel a slight shudder as his hands moved lightly over her inner thighs?

As he pulled his own nightshirt up—damn the inconvenience of clothes!—he pressed his mouth, working against hers, and was rewarded with more response. He felt her twist and turn, her body pressing closer to him, her tongue meeting his.

Palmer was as gentle as he could be until need overcame scruples, and he exploded inside her. She never moved her arms from his neck, never cried out in pain—and never joined him in pleasure. That, he told himself, would come later.

"I'm sorry," he said, when his panting was gone enough to allow him to speak with some dignity. "I . . . I hope I didn't hurt you." He lay on his back, spent, one arm still beneath her neck.

She turned toward him, studying him. "I didn't know what to expect," she said.

He wanted to prod, to ask "And?" but one didn't discuss such matters, and he was quiet, comforted by the thought that his convent-educated, sheltered bride had been more responsive than he had any reason to expect.

Without another word, Potter Palmer turned over on his side of the bed to sleep, and Cissy rose to tend to herself. Finally, they slept on separate sides of the bed, a wide world between them.

The next morning at breakfast, Cissy, sipping a cup of coffee, said, "I'm surprised someone hasn't invented a nightgown that splits down the middle. Having it all bunched up around your waist is really uncomfortable."

Palmer choked on his coffee but said not one word.

The Great Fire

Chapter Five

Chicago was bone dry in the fall of 1871. Only one inch of rain had fallen in four months, and the unbearable heat had only made the need for rain greater. Men stood on wooden sidewalks talking of the worst drought of their lifetimes, shaking their heads and peering at the sky.

The city now had a population of over three-hundred thousand, and it boasted marble hotels and stores and brick residences. But it was still a wooden city. In the late 1860s, immigrants had begun pouring into the city, and by 1871 the German, Irish, Bohemians, and Scandinavians accounted for half the city's population. They lived in pine shacks and shanties, and the smell of Chicago was with them—the stench of pools of sewage and dead animals in the streets.

Leaves had fallen from trees by midsummer, as brown as though it was October, and buildings shifted and cracked as wooden walls dried and bent. The river had pulled back from its banks so that it was like a narrow ribbon within the channel it usually filled, and the banks had dried and cracked. The prairie had turned brown early in August and stayed that way. Prairie fires raced across the land, burning crops and graze alike. Waterholes dried up, and farmers bemoaned lost livestock. Henry, who tended to

Potter's farm for him, watched the livestock closely, but even so Potter had lost several of his cattle.

Fires broke out in the city as though by spontaneous combustion. A pile of dry leaves here, a bone-dry wooden fence there, and, too often, a wooden shack, its boards warped from heat and drought. In a city where one shack butted up against the next, the threat of spreading fire brought terror to poor and rich alike.

Carter Harrison was at home with his family that Sunday in October. He rarely spent much time with them, the press of his ambition for the city and his dedication to some of its less fortunate citizens taking precedence over his fatherly feelings. But this fall day, hot as it was, he was throwing a baseball with young Carter IV. What he really wanted was to go to sleep in the middle of the day. He was exhausted from having worked most of Saturday with the Johnson Volunteer Fire Company to put out a stubborn fire in a lumberyard on the South Side. When the fire bell rang again, he groaned. "Not another one," he said aloud. The city's firefighters, all volunteer, were as tired as he was, and water supplies were running low. With a muttered, "Please, God, let it be small," he told his son he had to leave, shoved his hat on his head, and went to saddle Kate.

Outside, he was puzzled. The bell rang three times for the Third Ward. He could have sworn that just minutes earlier it had clanged twice, the Second Ward. Fires in both places? It was a nightmare not to be believed.

Driven by panic, he ran the mare too fast to his office and stabled her in the barn there. Then he began running down LaSalle Street only to meet a fire wagon heading west.

"Hop on," one of the men called.

"How bad is it?" he panted, as he swung up on the moving wagon, tearing the pants of his good suit.

"Bad," Buck Johnson answered. "Already spread to the Third Ward. Wind's blowin', and I . . . I don't know what we can do."

Carter looked down at his suit ruefully and wished he had on work clothes. It would be the last time he even thought about his clothes for forty-eight hours.

* * *

Cissy Palmer spent a long day home alone on that Sunday. Potter had left early in the morning, after a breakfast that would, he said, have to carry him through the day.

"City's restless," he told her. "All those fires lately, and that big one in the lumberyards last night. People are scared."

Cissy knew the fire the night before had been bad. There were cinders on the ground outside their house, some three miles from the lumberyard that had burned. When Potter cautioned against trying to attend church that morning, she walked outside with him just to be out of the house. But the porch was gray with cinders, and the hot, dry wind carried the stench of fire about it.

"Why must you go?" she asked.

"I'm worried about the hotel . . . the store . . ." Potter paused as though distracted.

Cissy knew that Potter had invested not only his money but his soul in the hotel he was building. It was, she sometimes thought, her only rival for his affections. "You have a watchman there. And what could you do by being in town yourself?"

He shrugged. "I'm not much given to intuition," he admitted, "but something tells me—no, urges me to go into town. I'll go to the hotel first." He kissed her gently on the forehead, then straightened and said, almost sternly, "Stay in the house now. Herman and Margaret are here with you. But I don't want you to go into the city, even to see your family."

His intuition again! Cissy stifled the urge to reply sharply and followed him to the barn. When he rode away on Banner, the gelding he most trusted, she stood on the porch and watched until he was almost out of sight, shading her eyes to see better, though there was no glare from the sun. The smoky air floating toward them from the city dulled it.

The day stretched endlessly before her. Much as she loved her husband and loved the idea of being Mrs. Potter Palmer, Cissy found life on the country acreage boring. She was used to her parents' house, where her siblings were always up to something and visitors came and went frequently. At Potter's house—"our house," she had to remind herself—she was alone all day with Margaret and Herman.

By evening, she was almost unbearably restless, picking at the dinner of cold chicken and asparagus that Margaret prepared for her, sipping a little claret, which failed to soothe her, and pacing the parlor floor behind closed doors, so that Margaret would not know. Finally, she settled herself with a copy of *Self-Effort*, a book Potter had recommended. But she stared at the pages without comprehension.

"Madam? Madam!" Herman's voice took on an urgency that roused her from her daydream. Herman was Potter's—what? chauffeur? foreman? jack of all trades? It amused Cissy to think how many roles that man filled, all of them indispensable.

"Yes, Herman?" She rose from the chaise and went to the door of her sitting room.

"You better look out the windows to the northeast, madam." Herman, in spite of his good democratic German background, had learned the manners Potter requested of him. He never addressed her as "ma'am" or "Mrs. Palmer."

"The northeast?" she repeated vaguely, not understanding.

Almost impatient, he said, "Toward the city, madam."

She crossed the hall to Potter's sitting room, on the north side of the house, and drew aside the heavy velvet curtains. The sky, which should have been gray with dusk, was a strange yellow, streaked here and there with crimson as columns of fire flashed skyward.

"Fire!" she exclaimed, giving voice to the obvious.

"The worst yet, madam. I was outside and heard the fire bells. They're far away, of course, but I thought I heard them ring for three wards."

Her throat was dry, parched as though she herself were breathing smoke. "Which three?" she asked.

"The Third Ward and the Second . . . and then north of the river, the Fourth Ward, at least I think that's what I heard." He was almost apologetic about it.

Her parents' home was in the Fourth Ward, and Potter's beloved hotel was in the Second, the downtown ward. Cissy held her breath, as though if she could blot it all out for a moment, it would go away and nothing would have happened. Her strategy did not work, of course, and she was forced to breathe again, open her eyes, and face Herman.

"I . . . Mr. Palmer is at the hotel. He will do what he can. But I must go to my family. Hitch Golden Lady to the small carriage, please, Herman."

The young man hesitated slightly. "Mr. Palmer told me, madam, that—"

She interrupted him almost rudely. "Mr. Palmer is not here, nor could he have anticipated this circumstance, Herman. Hitch up the horse!" Cissy had been schooled never to show anger, but two spots of red flared in her cheeks when she was truly angry or frustrated. Now, her cheeks were burning. She put a hand to her face, as though to will the red away.

Looking at her once, quickly, as though he wished she'd change her mind, Herman murmured, "Yes, madam," and left to do her bidding.

He must, though, have passed through the kitchen, for Margaret appeared within seconds. "Now, madam, let me fix you some chamomile tea to settle your nerves. No need for you to go rushing off to that fire." She glanced over her shoulder in the direction of the city. "Just cause your poor folks to worry more . . . and their plate is probably already full."

Cissy willed herself to be civil. Margaret, she knew, spoke from concern—and with some truth about the Honorés. If her father thought she was setting out alone at night to chase a fire, he, like Potter, would have ordered her home. "I have to go," she said, her voice as quiet and low as she could make it and still convey her determination.

When Herman brought the carriage, Cissy had a moment of uncertainty, indeed almost a moment of panic. She could drive Golden Lady as well as Herman or Potter, but she'd never set off by herself alone at night. Her father had never allowed it, and since her marriage she had not gone anywhere at night except with Potter. She should wait. Potter would come soon and either reassure her that all was safe or take her to her parents. That was the logical course of behavior.

And then she thought of the long day she'd waited, and she envisioned sitting alone, far into the night, watching the sky glow red and not knowing what had happened. "Nonsense," she told herself, "I'm as capable as anyone else. I can go to the city . . . and I will."

* * *

Harry Collins was telling a story to Juliet when he first smelled smoke. The storytelling hours, in which he repeated stories he remembered from his childhood, were precious to both father and daughter, and Sheila often used the time to sew or even nap a little, leaving them alone. She recognized that these days the only time anger truly left her husband's eyes was when he was with Juliet.

The child snuggled in his lap, raptly listening to her father's version of "Little Red Riding Hood," when he suddenly stopped talking.

"What then, Papá?" she demanded.

"What?" he echoed, his thoughts elsewhere. Then, almost abruptly, he stood, sliding her onto the floor. Juliet began to wail.

Her wailing and Harry's loud cry of "Sheila!" brought the young mother out of the curtained-off sleeping area in a hurry. "Whatever is the matter with the two of you?" she asked, eyes flashing to see which one she should lash first with her tongue.

"Smoke," he said, "and not far away. I'm going outside to look. You best begin to gather whatever you want to take with us."

She looked doubtful. "It can't be that serious."

"It can," he said forcefully. "We may have to leave in a minute. Now do as I say, and gather what you'd take with you." His voice was stern, the tone of an order given.

Even before he reached the street, Harry heard the commotion. People were yelling, cursing, shouting at each other, issuing orders. The streets were jammed, and probably not three blocks away he saw flames shooting in the air.

"Gotta get outta here, Collins," a neighbor shouted. "Mrs. O'Leary's cow kicked over a lantern in the barn, and the whole thing went up in flames. It's spreadin' fast."

Harry bolted back into the house, said to Sheila, "We're goin' now," and put Juliet on his shoulders, where she grabbed his ears for handholds and crowed in delight.

Within minutes, they found themselves in the midst of a crowd that jammed the street and milled about as though without purpose. No one knew which direction to go, which direction would be safe. Harry grabbed Sheila's hand and pulled her back toward their house, over her loud protest.

"Just trust me," he whispered, taking the tied-up blanket into which she had hastily thrown some clothes, her family pictures and who knew what else. At the side of the street, they were free of the worst of the crowd and could move slowly ahead.

"Where are we going?" Sheila asked, grabbing onto the back of his shirt so as not to be separated from him.

"South," he said. "I think that's safest. Fire looks to be north of us and downtown too."

And so they began their long and desperate walk, always jostled by the crowd. They had not gone two blocks before Juliet began to wail that she wanted to go home to bed. Neither of her parents could silence her, so they plodded on, her cries ringing in their ears.

* * *

Even as she turned out of their own lane onto the road, Cissy met people coming toward her. Some rode in wagons laden down with household goods, and a few were in carriages that seemed to be crammed with clothes and belongings. But most were on foot—men pushed wheelbarrows and perambulators piled high with goods or carried bundles of clothing and dishes. Some even had chairs or small tables strapped to their backs, and women carried crying children, while other youngsters clung to their skirts and struggled to keep up. The nearer she got to the city, the thicker the oncoming traffic.

"Turn around, lady!" "Quit blocking traffic!" "Turn around, miss, you can't get to town!" and "You don't want to be there!" A few of the calls seemed helpful, but mostly they were angry, hostile, finally even threatening. Then someone grabbed at the horse's bridle.

"Turn this horse around and get out of here 'fore you hurt someone," a gruff masculine voice said. "Can't you see you can't go against all these people?"

Panic rose in Cissy's throat, and she could taste her own fear. She looked at the faces around her, their strained expressions clear even in the dark, their shapes outlined by the distant light of flames. What if one of these men decided he wanted her horse, her carriage? What if Golden Lady were to bolt, out of fear of the people who surrounded her? Cissy saw the horse's nostrils flare and tightened her grip on the reins.

She longed for Potter, for her father, for someone to tell her what to do. Instead, here was a total stranger, almost threatening her. Wryly, she thought it was too late to realize that Herman and Margaret had been right: she should have stayed at home and waited, ever the good wife.

The gruff-voiced man was also right. She could not go against the traffic. Neither could she abandon the horse and carriage and proceed on foot, though many would have leapt at the chance to take the horse. No, she would go back to the farmhouse.

The decision, once made, was not so easily put into effect. There was no room to turn the horse and carriage without trampling on the people who thronged the road. At last, a man, seeing her predicament, stepped up to the side of the carriage.

"Ma'am," he said, "if you'll let my wife and child ride with you, I'll turn that horse for you."

Gratefully, Cissy said, "Of course." She got no more than a bare glimpse of him, but his voice sounded educated, and she decided—with no evidence—that he was trustworthy.

They were Sheila and Harry Collins and their daughter, Juliet. "I saw the play once," the woman said by way of explanation of the child's name.

Cissy introduced herself as Mrs. Potter Palmer and then added, falteringly, "Call me Cissy."

The woman called her Mrs. Palmer.

Harry put the bundle he carried in the back of the carriage. A rolled and knotted blanket, it appeared to hold clothes. Later, Cissy would learn that a few precious family pictures were tucked in among work shirts and linsey-woolsey wrappers.

They lived near DeKoven and Clinton, the area where the fire had started, and they were sure their house—a wooden shack—was destroyed, though they hadn't actually seen it go up in flames.

"It was Mrs. O'Leary's cow, you know," Sheila said knowledgeably. "Stupid of her to put a lantern in a barn and then walk away."

Cissy supposed it was stupid, but she said nothing. She saw that her hands held tight to the reins, even though Harry was leading Golden Lady, and she relaxed them. Harry turned the horse gently, slowly, and carefully, calling out to the crowd, "Make way, now. Let's leave the horse a little room." There were catcalls and jeers, and a few pitiful cries of "Can't you take my child?" or "The wife needs to ride." Cissy shut her ears, because she could help no more than the Collins family.

"How far are you going?" Harry asked.

"A mile, maybe a little more. There's a lane off to the right. I'll tell you."

He nodded, and they began to move slowly with the throng, inching their way along. No longer occupied with guiding the horse, Cissy had time to look around and study the people in the crowd. The women appeared to be in wrappers, as though they'd just jumped from their beds, and the men wore hastily pulled-on work clothes. A few were even in nightshirts. All were blackened by dust and smoke, so that their eyes shone eerily white against black faces.

"Where . . . where are you going?" Cissy asked Sheila.

The woman shrugged, absolute hopelessness written on her face. "Far enough away so we don't have to breathe that smoke and heat," she said. "It's bad for her." She nodded at Juliet who, curled against her mother, had not spoken since they climbed into the carriage, though she shot quick, furtive looks at Cissy.

Cissy nodded, her mind whirling with questions. Where would these people go? Would they camp alongside the road, wait for the fire to die out, and return home? Would they flee Chicago forever? And beneath all those questions, the two most important: where was Potter, and what had happened to the Honoré family?

Behind them the sky glowed as red as ever.

At last, they reached the lane to the farmhouse. Cissy suspected it had been but an hour since Harry turned the horse, though her whole body felt as though an entire night had passed.

"This is it," she called as loudly as she could, and he nodded, gently turning the horse out of the road. Once they were well onto the lane, he pulled the horse to a stop and came back to the carriage.

"All right, my pretties," he said, addressing his wife and child, "time to hop out. You've had a nice ride."

"Hop out?" Cissy asked blankly.

"Yes, ma'am. You've taken us as far as you need to." He stared at her with appreciation—and perhaps a little calculation. "We won't trouble you anymore."

"Nonsense. You'll come to the house with me. Juliet needs a bed."

Harry started to protest but was interrupted by Sheila. "She's right, Harry. Don't say no more." There was an edge of desperation in her voice.

So Harry went back to the horse and began leading it down the lane toward the dark house that stood before them.

The warning came out of nowhere, or so it seemed to Cissy. "Stop right where you are!" And then, before Harry could react, a shot was fired over their heads. Golden Lady squealed in fright and would have reared if Harry's hand had been any less firm on the bridle.

"Herman!" Cissy called. "It's all right. It's me!"

He walked slowly toward the carriage, shotgun still trained on Harry. "Who's he . . . madam?"

"He helped me," Cissy said. "I . . . you were right, Herman. I shouldn't have gone. Mr. Collins rescued me . . . and his family is with me."

Herman looked at the newcomer and managed a grim, "We're beholden to you." He lowered the shotgun just a bit. "I apologize if I frightened you. All those people," he explained, "I was worried about the house."

"Thank you, Herman." She took the offered hand and alighted from the carriage. "Now we must feed these people and settle them for the night."

"They can have my room," Herman said, almost too quickly. "I'm sleeping on the floor in the house, Mrs. Potter, since the gentleman is not here." Herman's "room," like Margaret's, had been carved out of a corner of the barn, but it would be warm and cozy enough for the Collins family, and it was clear that Herman did not want them sleeping in the house.

"Follow me," Cissy said to the bewildered parents and child who stood looking first to her, then to Herman. She led the way into a dark and empty house but soon had lights glowing in several rooms. Sheila Collins stood, open-mouthed. Clearly, she had never seen such elegance as the marble-topped walnut tables with pineapple decorations and the horsehair sofa, nor such niceties as the library lamp with its dangling crystals and rose-decorated glass globe or the walnut mantel clock with inlaid wood. As she stared, it struck midnight—an ominous sound that startled all of them.

Cissy led them into the kitchen. Margaret had long since retired to her private apartments. While Herman put wood into the Superior stove, Sheila stared openly at the lavishly decorated range with its high closet, and Cissy bustled about, finally settling for eggs, which she could scramble, a tad of meat pie, which could be reheated, and this morning's loaf of bread, which would go down smoothly with some of Margaret's wild plum preserves.

Even the child ate ravenously, though her mother kept slapping her hand to remind her of her manners. With each slap, Juliet would wail and Sheila would suddenly remember herself and look guiltily at Cissy, who always managed to be looking elsewhere.

With Herman's help, Cissy carried fresh linens out to his room, along with blankets to make a pallet for Juliet, and got the family settled. Nothing would budge Herman from the foot of the stairs, where Cissy built another pallet for him out of thick blankets. As she spread out the blankets, Cissy mentioned, as casually as she could, that she'd prefer that Mr. Potter not know that she had taken Golden Lady out. She made it sound as though Palmer's concern would be for the horse, because she did not want Herman to know that she had been ordered not to go to the city.

"Yes, madam, I understand," he said in most proper tones, and she was sure he did.

At long last, Cissy, tired to the bone, climbed the stairs to her bedroom. She would never let anyone know that once out of her stays, she fell asleep in her chemise and stockings, too exhausted to complete the undressing process. She would make her toilette in the morning.

The next day brought no news and no relief. The air was still hot and acrid with smoke, cinders still flew about, carried on a capricious wind that turned from south to north but never stopped blowing, and even in daylight the sky over the city glowed red, first in one spot and then another.

"They must be running out of water," Harry said.

"I reckon so," Herman agreed. "They can only pump it so fast out of the river and there's not much there to begin with. The river'll go dry."

The road beyond them was still clogged with people, a sight from which Cissy periodically had to turn her head.

"Where're they all comin' from?" Sheila asked curiously.

"New areas must be catching fire," Herman explained, "and more people have to leave their homes."

"That's sad," Juliet said solemnly.

"Yes, it is," Cissy agreed, reaching for the child's hand.

Harry Collins stared into space but said nothing.

As children will, Juliet forgot her sadness almost instantly and was chasing after Herman as he headed for the barn, laughing happily as the barn cats ran from her in mock alarm.

"She's never been in the country," Sheila said wistfully. "I hope . . . well, I hope she doesn't bother him." She nodded her head in Herman's direction.

"I'm sure he's pleased for the company," Cissy said and wondered if it was true.

The adults could not brush sadness away as quickly as the child. They sat on the veranda—Herman had seen to it that there were chairs enough for all. Sheila tended to speak little and occasionally burst into small sobs, until Harry told her sternly to "let it be." Cissy was more composed, but she was solemn, made quiet with worry. Where was Potter, and what had happened to his wonderful hotel? What about the store? Was there looting? What about her family?

No one could answer her questions, and she sat through the long day staring at the red glow in the distance and keeping her thoughts to herself. Had she been alone, she realized, she probably would have given in to panic and bouts of sobbing worse than Sheila's occasional outbursts, but the presence of these strangers gave her strength.

Cissy and the Collinses picked at their supper that evening, while Juliet began to cry out of sheer exhaustion. They all retired early, and sometime during the night, it began to rain. Listening to the sound of rain on the roof, Cissy knew the fire was over.

Potter Palmer came home that night, late, after Cissy had gone to bed. He bent over her, whispered, "Your parents are safe and so are their things, but their house is ruined . . . and the hotel is gone," and then collapsed fully dressed on top of the covers. He smelled so strongly of smoke and sweat and grime that Cissy rose quietly from the bed, gathered an afghan and spent the remainder of a restless night on the chaise in her sitting room. The sky, when she peered out the window, was less red.

Potter slept until well after noon, and he and Cissy talked briefly while he drank the coffee that Margaret had sent up. He described the fire as he'd seen it, confirming that it had indeed started in a barn on DeKoven owned by the O'Learys. But no, no one knew if the cow kicked over a lantern—and never would know.

"How did it get out of control?" Cissy asked. "Fires don't usually spread like that." She knew the city had been plagued with small fires for weeks, but the volunteers had been able to keep them in check.

"They've always caught them early. This time the spotter in one of those observation towers gave the wrong location," he said, shaking his head in despair. "The wind," he said, and then, repeating himself, "the wind . . . it sent the flames in all directions, carrying burning brands and sticks and hurling them at buildings. And the fire itself whipped up a new kind of wind—whirls of flame and heated air that carried great bundles of flame through the air a half mile or more. Fire devils, they called them."

"Surely," Cissy said, and felt the naiveté even as she said it, "the firefighters—"

"Outdone from the first," he said. "They'd been fighting fires all weekend. They were already exhausted, and their equipment simply wasn't enough for what they were facing. It kept breaking down. I watched a wall of flame—literally a wall, Cissy, twice the size of your parents' house—coming toward the square."

"The people?" she asked.

"It hit everybody, not just the poor. It was an awful moment when the fire jumped the river and took homes on the North Side, homes we all thought were safe." He shook his head, as though unable to continue his description of devastation. "I was up there, checking on your family, and we saw people standing in the lake to stay clear of the fire. I saw a man, holding his child, standing almost waist deep in the water, his hand around his wife's shoulders. And I heard of men burying their families in sand on the beach to keep them safe."

Cissy shuddered and decided, privately, that there was something to the old saw about the fates knowing what was best for one. The isolated farm, against which she had inwardly railed, had been her salvation. "My family is safe." She made it a statement, and yet there was a hint of question in it.

"Your father's probably ruined financially. His new building, the Honoré Block, is gone. But they're safe."

She nodded and bit her lip. Another statement that was a question, even though she knew the answer: "The hotel is gone."

He nodded his head. "So are the buildings I put up on State Street. But others suffered equally—the Sherman Hotel and the Tremont, the courthouse, all the stores on State and Wabash. Field saved the store by hanging wet blankets over all the windows. Took all the merchandise to the lakeshore and then up on Prairie Avenue, by Leiter's house. No fire there. But we've still had to protect against looting."

All the while they talked, Cissy's mind was whirling with thoughts of the Collins family downstairs. She had to tell Palmer, before he simply descended the stairs and found them, but what to say. At last, she blurted it out.

"There are strangers downstairs," she said.

"Strangers?" he asked, his voice rising in question, as though he'd not heard her correctly.

"A family—husband, wife and child. I . . . they were so pitiful on the road that first night, I gave them shelter."

"You took strangers into our house?" Potter was still having a hard time believing what he was hearing. A part of his mind told him Cissy would never do any such thing. She would know that it would be against his wishes. But here she was, calmly telling him that she had done it. "Why?" he demanded.

Cissy looked warily at her husband. "It's a long story," she said. She was not at all reluctant to admit she had picked the Collins out of the mass exodus and brought them home, but she didn't want to confess her attempted trip into the city when everyone else was fleeing. She had, after all, disobeyed her husband, which her mother had told her never to do.

"I'll hear it later," Palmer said. "I'm famished." He would not then, however, hear the full story, not know that his wife had disobeyed him and driven to the city—or at least, tried to drive there.

Downstairs, he did indeed find the strangers seated at his table, eating his food. His manners frayed by exhaustion and worry, he barely managed to extend his hand to Collins, saying, "I'm Potter Palmer. I . . . I guess I'm your host."

"Yes, sir," Harry replied, "I guess you are. This is my wife, Sheila, and my daughter, Juliet. We're . . . well, we're obliged to Mrs. Palmer, who brought us here."

"Glad she could help," Potter muttered, helping himself to a hearty portion of eggs and mounds of fried potatoes.

"We're running out of some provisions." Cissy cleared her throat a little as she spoke.

His mouth full—he hadn't, after all, eaten for two days—Palmer shook his head. Finally, he muttered, "Nothing to be done about it. Gather eggs. Milk the cows. Kill some of the chickens. Have Margaret bake lots of bread. If need be, Herman can slaughter a calf. You'll find nothing in the city."

Cissy thanked heaven for Margaret's propensity for canning. She had put up preserves that summer at such a rate that Cissy asked if she foresaw a disaster, and Margaret had primly replied,

"You never can tell, madam, when the need will arise." Now Margaret's disaster was at hand, and they would be eating tomatoes and green beans and pickles, perhaps without much else.

As he ate, Potter Palmer eyed Harry Collins. A private man, it disturbed him greatly to find strangers in his house, and he was reluctant to leave his wife alone with these people. In the last day Potter had seen what the others had not: the desperation of the people that led to looting and even, occasionally, violence. Harry Collins looked to be a respectable sort, but there was something about him that made Potter uneasy. He was torn between admiring Cissy's charity—he himself would not have thought of giving succor to any of that mob on the road—and anger that she had robbed him of total control over his home and castle.

"You want to see if anything's left of your house?" he asked Harry.

"Yes, I do," Harry replied, while Sheila began to sob again.

"What will we do?" she wailed.

Harry put an arm about her and said, almost gruffly, "Shhh! You'll scare the little one."

Potter ignored the sobs and said to Harry, "Fine. Come with me."

Herman saddled Banner for Potter and River Boy, a serviceable but not striking gelding, for Harry, who, it turned out, sat a horse like a gentleman.

"You sit a horse well," Potter said, his statement really a question.

"Thank you," was all the answer he got. Having expressed his gratitude, Harry Collins was now somewhat put off by Potter's distant air and his obvious disapproval of Harry and his family. He was not about to admit that he had been raised in wealth, with horseback lessons part of his youth.

"Keep Herman close by with that shotgun," Potter warned as he left. "They're looting private homes in the city. I don't think you'll have any trouble, but you best be prepared."

The men trotted away, and Sheila began her quiet sobbing again, this time without a husband to solace or quiet her. Cissy had no time for sympathy. She knew her mission.

First, she told Margaret that the bedclothes Mr. Palmer had slept in were ruined and should be burnt, along with the clothes he had worn. Then she scoured the house from top to bottom, pulling clothes out of closets, linens off shelves, even dishes out of the kitchen, and sorting all into various piles, each intended for a household.

"Land's sake, Mrs. Palmer, what are you doing?" Margaret stood before her, hands on her hips.

Cissy, on her knees before a cedar chest, replied, "I'm sorting out clothes for those who need them more than we do."

"You'll have nothing left to wear yourselves," Margaret predicted ominously.

Cissy managed a faint smile. "We'll have plenty, Margaret. Plenty." She realized that now that she had something to do, a goal toward which she was moving, she was happier than she had been since her wedding.

"Don't be givin' away Mr. Palmer's clothes without his leave," Margaret warned, to which Cissy airily replied, "He won't mind. After all, look how pleased he was that I had given the Collins shelter."

Margaret looked at her and wondered if Mrs. Palmer was trying to fool her—or herself.

* * *

The fire had lasted thirty hours, burned eighteen thousand buildings, killed three hundred people, and left ninety thousand homeless. It cut a swath across the city one mile wide and four miles long, destroying seventy-three miles of streets and one-hundred ninety million dollars' worth of property. After all the small fires were finally put out, the firemen could rest. But not the policemen. Looting was widespread. Men looted liquor stores until liquor flowed in the streets. Then they took anything they thought they wanted.

Carter Harrison almost killed a man that night. He was exhausted, he told himself later, and not in his right mind. And he was disgusted with some elements of the citizenry, including some that he had tried in the past to protect. He had spent much of the fire near the river and had seen even the water on fire as burning sparks that fell like rain ignite the grease and oil on its surface.

Across the river, residents of Conley's Patch thought it was a Fourth of July show put on for their benefit. They whooped and hollered and shouted, until firemen had to waste precious water turning the hoses on them. Then the patch itself began to burn, and its residents panicked, crowding the bridge to get across the river to what they thought was safety. In their exodus, they abandoned the elderly and the infirm, and the first deaths were in Conley's Patch, where a wall of flame simply ate the tent city.

No, Carter Harrison was not in the mood to be charitable toward his fellow man. His office had burned to the ground, and he had no idea of Kate's fate, could only hope that she had escaped the barn behind his office and headed for Ashland Avenue, which had remained safe. As he trudged south toward home, he passed the City Café, wondered briefly if Sheila and her family were safe, and then stopped dead still in anger.

Inside the darkened shell of the café, a man was punching cash register buttons. Carter could hear the noise of the drawer opening.

"Stop, thief!" he roared, rushing past the sagging doorframe and into the smoke-blackened ruin. Like most men of the day, Carter carried a small pistol tucked into his vest pocket. Now he drew it.

The thief looked up in amazement at this large, wild man lunging toward him, pistol in hand, and did the only thing a sensible man would do. He picked up a chair and hurled it toward Harrison.

Harrison fired a shot, but it went wild. Seeing that his opponent was more serious than expected, the thief ducked and ran. A second shot also went wild, and then an utterly ashamed Carter Harrison pocketed his pistol. He went to the cash drawer, saw that the cash had survived the flames—later, he would learn that money in bank vaults also survived intact—and scooped it up. He'd give it to Brownlee, the café's owner, later.

Carter Harrison continued his long walk home. He never told anyone about that night, especially not the anxious wife who greeted him when he finally reached Ashland Avenue. Kate, she told him, had returned home half a day earlier, and she and the children were convinced that Carter had died. She threw herself, weeping, into his arms, and he barely had the strength to hold her.

Chapter Six

Chicago was in a strong position to rebuild. The stockyards and packing plants, major railroad trunks, wharfs, lumber-yards, and mills had survived. So had some grain elevators, though others smoldered for a year.

The Collins' house was spared by the whim of the flames, as was the now infamous O'Leary home, although the O'Leary barn was gone. The rumor that Sheila Collins took for gospel and that had spread through the escaping crowd that Sunday night was that Kate O'Leary had gone to the barn to milk the cow and carelessly left a lantern behind. The cow kicked over the lantern and ignited the straw stored in the barn. After the fire, reporters crowded around her cottage but she refused to emerge. Eventually, the family moved from DeKoven Street. Years later a pair of reporters would confess they made up the story based on a burnt lantern found in the ruins of the barn.

The Collins family did not suffer the notoriety of Mrs. O'Leary, but they had only the possessions they'd carried on their backs—looters had carried everything else off.

"I can't imagine," Harry said when he returned that night to the Palmer farm. "There was nothing there worth hauling off, 'less you were to use it for kindling." He gave a kind of wry smile.

Sheila only clutched Juliet and murmured, "It's a good thing I brought those pictures."

Remembering how he'd been short with her, telling her to hurry, not to bother with the pictures, Harry shrugged and said, "Yeah, I guess so."

The next day Herman drove the family of three back to DeKoven Street in a wagon that Cissy had filled with clothes, linens, canned goods, and some lumber from which Harry could build furniture. "I'll come soon to see you," she said, grabbing Juliet's hand. The child responded with a spontaneous hug, and even Sheila lightened a bit to say, "I'd like that, ma'am. We're . . . well, I don't know where we'd have been without you."

Harry muttered, "We're beholden," but couldn't look Cissy in the eye. He'd been raised to give charity, not take it, and he was illogically angry with her for taking care of them.

When Herman returned that evening, he said enigmatically, "Something strange about that Collins fellow. I'm glad he's out of here. But now the wife and child, they were . . ."

* * *

Potter Palmer lost his hotel and ninety-two buildings, the rents of which had brought him two-hundred thousand dollars a year. But the plans for the hotel survived. Hotel architect John Van Osdel buried the blueprints in a hole in the basement and covered them with sand and clay. They were so perfectly preserved that Van Osdel would later use clay for insulation in buildings he constructed.

"Aren't you angry at fate?" Van Osdel asked him.

Potter Palmer was not of the temperament to rail uselessly at the gods. He was more inclined to take whatever he was given and use it for a starting point. "No sense in that," he said. "I'm actually excited, because you saved the plans. Now, my friend, we can rebuild. If we'd had to draw new plans, it would have taken that much longer."

"I'll stay tonight to keep the looters away," Van Osdel said. "You look exhausted. Go on home."

"No," Palmer replied, "a man named Harry Collins will be here soon to stand guard." Unbeknown to Cissy, he had hired Harry Collins as a night guard. Potter was a bit puzzled himself, given his uneasy feelings about Collins, that he'd suddenly blurted out the offer of a job, probably at much better pay than Collins was getting stocking shelves. There'd been no opportunity to tell Cissy about it yet, but he knew he wouldn't. His rationalization was that if it didn't work out, it would be better that Cissy not know. "I am exhausted," he said, "and I've barely seen my bride in days." The brief visit in the presence of the Collins family, he thought, did not count.

Van Osdel, brushing dirt from the plans and staring intently at them, waved him away with one hand. "Give her my best." Then he turned with a smile. "And tell her we saved the plans."

"You saved them, my friend, and I'm grateful." Potter unhitched his horse, climbed into the buggy, and turned west toward his home. He wanted nothing more than a bath, clean clothes, a good dinner, and time alone with his wife.

Two days after the fire, he left for New York to borrow money and rebuild his empire, starting with the hotel. His last words to Cissy cautioned her not to leave their property. "There's looting in the city still, and I think the mayor wants General Sheridan to declare martial law."

Cissy reasoned that if martial law were declared lawbreakers would be in trouble and an honest, law-abiding woman like herself would be doubly protected. She did not say that aloud to Potter, however.

Mayor Roswell Mason hired the Pinkerton Detective Agency to guard the ruins and did declare martial law as Potter had predicted, putting the city in the hands of General Phil Sheridan and six companies of regular infantry. Sheridan, in charge of the Army of the West, had his headquarters in Chicago.

Herman went into the city a day later and returned with word of these developments. After that, Cissy felt perfectly free to go to her family. She drove into the city alone the fourth day after the fire, in spite of Potter's stern orders that she stay at home with Herman and his shotgun nearby. Potter, she reasoned, was in New York and would never know, though her deception gave her a pang or two of guilt. She tried to think of disobeying Potter as acting independently. Herman had protested that he must accompany her, but she simply smiled at him and said he'd better stay to protect the property against looters. He brought the small carriage around.

Once again, she said, "I'd prefer that Mr. Palmer not know about this trip when he returns."

And once again, Herman murmured, "Yes, madam."

Cissy was totally unprepared for what she saw in the city, and she knew why Potter had discouraged her—indeed forbidden her—from going until he could escort her. Smog from still-smoldering ruins blotted out the sun, and the air was heavy with the smell of burned wood and flesh, the latter an odor she could not at first identify. When she did recognize it, it was with horror. Cissy wished for her scented handkerchief. Some streets were still damp, and to Cissy they seemed to be steaming. The branches of bare, blistered trees pointed to the northeast, the way the winds had drawn the fire.

To reach her parents' home north of the city, she had to go through the business district, where only an occasional pillar stood here and there, a chimney or an arch somehow left standing among the blackened waste. Some of the ruins south of the business district were unrecognizable, and with a sense of panic Cissy realized she wasn't sure where she was. She hoped she was on State Street, and soon she came to ruins she recognized.

Parts of two walls of the new Sherman Hotel stood, roofless, the windows gaping. The rest of the marble-fronted building had sunk into its own cellar. The pillars of the First Baptist Church lay in a jumble on the ground. The courthouse had crumbled, and the bell that had tolled the fire call for the various wards now lay, dented and quiet, among the ashes. For blocks, she could see nothing but stark black outlines where there had been busy commercial buildings. Cissy bit her lip to keep from weeping. Her heart pounded in her chest, and she could hear it echoing in her ringing ears.

On Washington, opposite where the post office had stood, she passed a new business: Some enterprising young men had turned a rescued mahogany sideboard into a storefront and were offering cigars, tobacco, grapes, apples, and cider. She smiled at their ingenuity and thought of Potter, who would have applauded them.

At last, she came to the river, its channel now more filled with debris than water. Here the burned smell joined the river's smell, until Cissy thought she might suffocate or become light-headed from shallow breathing, as she tried not to take in the nauseous air. She crossed the river on the one remaining bridge—two others had broken loose from their moorings and one had burned. People had died on those bridges, crowding across them trying to escape. She drove slowly north, passing burned shanties, fine homes that had been destroyed, and the occasional building that the capricious fire had left standing. When she finally reached her parents' home, she stopped outside and realized it was a miracle that the house still stood, since many near it had been destroyed. The Henry Farnum home and William Brown's elegant mansion, where he'd once entertained president-elect Abraham Lincoln and his wife and had never let anyone forget since, were both gone, but those houses were wood and the Honoré home was built of brick. It had been spared because the fire stopped only a few houses from it and took one of its unpredictable turns, off in another direction.

Cissy's reunion with her family was brief. Her brothers were wandering the neighborhood, looking at the damage and probably, Cissy thought, getting into mischief.

"Bertha!" her mother exclaimed when she walked through the front door of the house. "Did Herman bring you? I know Potter's gone to New York."

"I came by myself, Mother. I had to see."

"By yourself? Your father will be beside himself with worry." She began to wring her hands.

"Don't tell him. I'll leave before he comes home. Where is he?"

"Off to do whatever he can. He's set up business in a shed somewhere, and he swears he'll rebuild the buildings he lost."

"Potter says the same thing," Cissy said, "and I believe they both will."

"I'm not sure how," Eliza Honoré said. "Your father's got nothing left to start with. But neither," she said philosophically, "does anyone else. We're not as bad off as some."

Eliza and the children were camped out in the shell of their ruined house—what wasn't scorched and smoked beyond repair was water damaged. A flying cinder had burned a good-sized hole in the roof before Henry Honoré was able to extinguish it, and the rain then came directly into the house, streaking down the walls to the first floor.

Cissy looked around with dismay and then put her arms about her mother. "You . . . you can come to the farmhouse," she said. Once again, only after she spoke, did she wonder what Potter would say. The offer was only partly generosity—if her family came to the farm, Cissy would have company besides Margaret and Herman every day.

Eliza Honoré hugged her oldest child and brushed her hair from her forehead, as though she were once again ten years old. "You know we can't do that, Bertha. We must stay here and protect what we have—and fix what's left." She looked around the parlor in which they stood with a shrug.

"What is left?" Cissy asked with disbelief that anything was worth saving.

"These walls," her mother said, looking around. "And the silver and china. We carried the important things to the beach," she explained matter-of-factly, "and buried a few in sand." She and the family butler had stood guard over their possessions and the younger children at the water's edge, while Henry Honoré did what he could about the house.

"What about food?" Cissy asked.

"What I had put up is gone. What's left is ruined, but I think looters got most of it when your father's attention was on something else. And food's not easy to buy—stores don't have any left to sell."

"I'll send some of Margaret's canned vegetables and preserves with Herman tomorrow," Cissy said, "and Potter suggested we might have to slaughter a calf. We can see that you have food."

"I . . . I'll go home with you, Cissy," Ida said, her face streaked with tears. "I just can't bear to be here in this awful mess."

Cissy's voice was almost stern. "Ida, Mother needs you here to help her."

Ida turned away. She would never have reminded Cissy that it was easy for her to say that because she had a comfortable and undamaged home to return to.

Cissy and Eliza sat in the overstuffed chairs in the bay window of the living room, while Ida perched on a footstool and used a foot to kick away the floor cushion. "It smells bad," she said.

Cissy thought the chair on which she sat was damp and musty, but she said nothing.

Then, as though it just occurred to her, Eliza Honoré asked her daughter, "Did you hear about Colonel Grosvenor?"

"No, what about him?"

Colonel Thomas Grosvenor was a friend of her father's, a man she had known since her childhood, one who had been at her wedding. Potter had told her the other night that Grosvenor was a member of the citizens group that went to General Sheridan to ask him to take control of the city and stop the looting.

"He was shot and killed last night," her mother said and genuine sadness crossed her face.

Cissy gasped. "Looters?"

Eliza shook her head. "He'd been visiting a friend—apparently they had a little brandy. Too much for his own good. He was walking home when a sentry told him to halt and identify himself. The colonel refused and said something to the effect of 'Go ahead and shoot,' and the young man did. He had no idea he was shooting a prominent citizen. Your father says Sheridan's going to dismiss the martial law to prevent any more tragedies like that."

Martial law, Cissy thought, *didn't last very long.* But she was saddened for Colonel Grosvenor's family.

As she left, almost as an afterthought, Cissy told her mother and sister the tale of the Collins family. Eliza and Ida were both appalled that she would take perfect strangers into her home. Cissy wished they didn't sound so much like Potter.

She had not told her mother and sister that she was next going to the Collins' shanty on DeKoven Street. She went back to the courthouse square and then headed west, passing through shanty areas that had burned to the ground. Wisps of smoke still rose gently from some of the piles of lumber. Here, the smell of death was even stronger. Many animals had died in the fire—pigs in their pens, cattle in their barns, even flocks of chickens—and not all the carcasses had yet been hauled away. But if she had expected the quiet, deserted air of the business district, she was wrong. There was life and activity everywhere. The Chicago Relief and Aid Society had miraculously furnished materials for countless families to build small wooden houses—"shelter houses" they were called—and men and women were building new shanties, throwing up rough lumber walls and covering them with thin sheets of wood. Some stopped their work to call and wave cheerfully to her, and she was struck with how the mood differed from that the night of the great flight, when she'd been scorned and threatened.

She felt perfectly safe driving through some of Chicago's immigrant neighborhoods on the West Side until a huge hand reached out and grabbed her marc's harness. Before she could react in alarm, an equally large face appeared from in front of the horse, and Carter Harrison said jovially, "Mrs. Palmer, what are you doing alone in this part of the city?"

Carter Harrison had been riding the streets of his city on his mare, Kate, talking to the people who were so desperately trying to rebuild their lives. Harrison felt it was his duty, his civic obligation, to encourage the workers. He had not yet thought with great certainty about a political career, but he wanted the people to know he was one of them. So he traveled the streets of the burned West Side, stopping here to talk with that one and there to offer advice on a board roof that was being roughly nailed on.

Lost in thought, pondering the future of his city and admiring the energy of its less fortunate citizens, Carter Harrison didn't see the carriage until it was almost upon him—or at least next to him. His first reaction was surprise that anyone in a carriage that fine would be traveling through this part of the city. But when he looked closer and saw that it was Potter Palmer's wife driving the carriage, he was truly alarmed. If ninety-nine out of every hundred citizens were bent on rebuilding, there was always that hundredth that didn't care how he restored his fortune.

Besides, this woman had fascinated Harrison at her wedding—so young and so attractive to be marrying a man so much older. When he reached for the bridle, it was an instinctive, protective gesture that he hadn't thought out. Certainly, he hadn't thought about her reaction.

In a brief moment Cissy recovered her senses and quieted her beating heart. "I'm going to pay a call," she said formally.

He roared with laughter. "I don't think anybody out here is serving tea this afternoon," he managed to gasp through his laughter. But beneath his laughter, he was impressed with her dignity and curious about whom she might call upon in this neighborhood.

She pulled herself up indignantly—and then was caught. It began as a quiet chuckle, and soon she, like him, was laughing aloud. Later she would wonder if it was the absurdity of expecting tea on DeKoven Street days after the Great Fire or if it was a release of tension for both of them that had something to do with the fire, nothing to do with tea, and perhaps a little to do with each other.

Being a lady and properly trained, Cissy sobered first. "I'm not expecting tea," she said quietly. Her air of formality and a distant civility had, however, given way to a softer tone.

Matching her change in tone, he said quietly, "I didn't think you were. But I am a little worried about you out here. Not all of Chicago's citizens have done her proud in the last forty-eight hours."

She nodded toward a group of men hard at work building a shanty. "They're too busy to bother with me," she said.

"But some," he answered evenly, "are not busy enough."

As if to prove his words, two men, obviously drunk, lurched into sight, and one called aloud, "Look at the swell come slumming to see if we survived. Can't burn us out, can they?" He poked his companion in the ribs with an elbow, and the two collapsed in besotted laughter.

"Been looting a tavern," Harrison said, shaking his head. "There's no way they could afford enough liquor to get that drunk."

He held her bridle in one hand and Kate's in the other and found controlling both horses difficult. "Wait just a minute," he said. He let go of her horse's bridle and walked to the edge of the street, calling to a man who was putting a roof on a shelter house. "Friend, can you tie my horse here for a bit? There's a reward if I come back and she's safe."

"Don't worry, Mr. Harrison," the young man said cheerfully. "I know who you are, and your horse is safe with me."

"Thank you kindly," Harrison said, stepping back to the side of the carriage. "Now, tell me who you're visiting in this part of town," he said, the question a demand.

She didn't hesitate. "A family that lives near DeKoven and Clinton—a block beyond, on DeKoven. The name is Collins."

"Harry Collins," Harrison said, and it was not a question. He was too polite to ask how a lady such as herself knew Harry Collins and his family, though curiosity burned in him. "I'll see that you get there."

She moved as though to make room for him in the carriage, but he shook his head. "No, I'll lead the horse. It's only a few more blocks."

And so she rode almost helplessly while this puzzling giant of a man led her horse. He never said another word to her until they reached the house—to which he went unerringly. Cissy wondered how and why Carter Harrison would not only know the strangers she'd picked up off the road, but know exactly where they lived.

"Here you are. I think if you go straight out Clinton when you leave, you'll be safe. I won't intrude on your business inside." He swept his hat off and bowed low, the best imitation of fine manners she had yet seen from the man.

Getting out of the carriage, she held out her hand. "Mr. Harrison, I'm very grateful for your help."

"You just let Mr. Palmer know that I took good care of his lady," he said with a smile, holding her hand just an instant longer than was necessary. He couldn't help but wonder if Potter Palmer knew his beautiful young wife was wandering around alone in Chicago's burned-out slums. Doubtful. Palmer wasn't the kind of man whose charity extended to risk. He was the kind who gave when it didn't hurt him. At least, that was Harrison's perception. But Mrs. Palmer, she was different.

Softly, she answered his unspoken question. "Mr. Palmer will not know I was here."

"Yes, ma'am," he said and turned wordlessly away. But his mind filled with joy at the thought that this woman was strong enough to do what she wanted and not tell her husband. Carter Harrison did not want his Sophie wandering around the city alone. But in someone else's wife—particularly someone as powerful as Potter Palmer with a wife Harrison admired so much—it was a wonder to behold.

Sheila Collins greeted Cissy with an incredulous question: "Was that Carter Harrison what brought you here?"

"I met him a few blocks away and he was concerned to see that I found you without difficulty."

"He's a fine man, that he is," the other woman said.

Cissy nodded and asked, "How are you, and how is Juliet?" To Cissy the puzzle grew only deeper. Not only did Carter Harrison know Harry Collins but Sheila Collins thought Harrison was a "fine man." Deliberately, she did not ask about the connection.

"We're gettin' on, thanks to you. I'd offer you a cup of tea . . ." She smoothed the dress she wore, a cotton wrapper that Cissy had sent home with her.

Without meaning to, Cissy chuckled, remembering her conversation with Carter. "I wasn't expecting tea," she managed to say with a straight face.

Sheila Collins was troubled by her guest's slight laughter. She was already more than a little flustered to have Mrs. Potter Palmer in her shanty, and now she feared she had done the wrong thing by even mentioning tea. With Mrs. Palmer, she very much wanted to do that right thing.

Cissy looked around. The house had apparently once had curtains, for tattered fabric hung in one window, and there was a rod that apparently held something to curtain off a sleeping area, though now it dangled empty.

"I had to throw out the curtains," Sheila said, seeing her look. "They were all soot and smoke. But I'll make some new. I thought to use some of the linens you sent with us."

"Oh," Cissy stifled a gasp, and then said gently, "Let me send some calico or something—" She wanted to say "something less fine than the linens" but couldn't quite bring herself to frame the words.

"Never you mind, Mrs. Palmer," Sheila said. "My Harry can bring me something, now that he's got a better job."

"A better job?" Cissy asked, thinking that probably no one could find employment in Chicago right now.

Sheila eyed her speculatively. "Mr. Palmer didn't tell you? He's hired Harry as a night guard at his hotel. Keep the looters away."

Cissy laughed just a little. "Not much there even for looters," she said.

"Harry takes his work real responsible," Sheila said.

"I . . . I brought some supplies," Cissy said, somehow not wanting to talk about Sheila's Harry.

"You've done plenty for us," Sheila said, her voice just a trifle haughty, as though to say she would take no more charity.

"I wondered if any of your neighbors were in need."

Sheila Collins eyed her carefully. "You are a good woman. You . . . you don't expect a return, do you?"

Cissy shrugged. "Yes, I do. I expect my city to be rebuilt, better than ever, and I want to do what I can to help. So far, I can think of nothing else beyond providing food and clothing." Mentally, she was already raiding the shelves of Field and Leiter for more supplies and canvassing those friends who had not lost everything.

"You could help down the street. They're rebuilding some houses. I don't suppose you've had any experience with a hammer and nails."

Cissy's cheeks flamed momentarily. Was the woman mocking her? Cissy decided not. "No," she admitted, "I've not." She knew the word "houses" meant "shanties" but more than that, she knew who she was and what her limitations were. She would give generously; but she would not build houses, just as she would never muck barns nor curry horses. There was, however, no sense making that point to Sheila Collins.

She left, thinking the visit had ended badly because she would not help with the physical work. But Sheila called to her as she climbed into her carriage: "Mrs. Palmer, I'm grateful for all you've done for us . . . and now Harry's job at the hotel. Someday I hope I can do something for you."

"Perhaps you can. I'll keep in touch."

Cissy was dirty and tired, with soot coating her hair, face, and clothes. She knew she smelled as bad as she looked, and she longed to be home.

* * *

Harry Collins came home from his watchman's job the next morning in a nasty frame of mind. "Building those wooden houses all over," he said in disgust. "Just fuel for another fire. You watch, it'll happen all over again. The rich'll build brick, and the rest of us will get burned out."

"We're luckier than most," Sheila said, a touch of defiance in her voice. "You got a job, and we got a place to live. People are livin' in camps, boilin' their water over a fire, standing in line for food. We're a lot luckier."

"Just because Palmer gave me that job," Collins said, his voice angry. "Some job! I've got nothing to do except run punks off, and I can do that with my hands tied behind my back," he complained to Sheila. "Do you know what it's like to sit up all night in a burnt-out shell of a building?"

"I'm sure it must be awful," she murmured and then put her fingers to her lips to shush him. Juliet was still asleep.

Sheila had much earlier decided not to mention Mrs. Palmer's visit. Sixth sense told her that Harry would only get angrier. She also decided not to remind him again that men were looking for work all over the city and being turned away. Harry knew that, but it would do no good to make him face the fact that he was luckier than most. She didn't understand why good fortune only made Harry angrier.

Wordlessly, Harry Collins held out his cup for more coffee. He couldn't say to Sheila what was really going through his mind: it wasn't fair of the world to expect a man of his education and up-bringing—and, yes, intelligence—to serve as a night watchman. That damned Potter Palmer may have thought he was doing him a favor, but it was . . . well, it was demeaning. And with that thought, he slammed his fist down on the table so hard that Sheila jumped. And then, to his absolute amazement, she burst into tears.

"What's the matter with you?" he asked.

She began to sob. "I think . . . I think . . . we're gonna have another baby."

He just asked, "You sure?"

Harry reached out a hand and took hers and said the only thing he could think of. "We don't have enough to feed the three of us as it is. We'll be hard put with another mouth around here." Then he wondered why Sheila sobbed all the harder.

* * *

"Field and Leiter are back in business," Potter told Cissy soon after his return from New York as they sat before a fireplace of warm coals. "They've got a full staff and their stock is as good as it ever was."

"It was probably no problem to find salespeople," Cissy replied. "I hear everyone in the city is looking for work."

"Marshall Field's a smart man," Potter mused. "Three days after the fire he posted signs notifying cash boys where to get their back pay and announcing the resumption of business, with hiring open. Most businesses didn't offer back pay. Made Field some loyal employees. I think he'll be a big name in this city."

"With your help," Cissy murmured.

Potter shrugged. "It was good business for me to help them reopen the store. I expect Field will be the merchant king in Chicago one day, now that I'm no longer in the mercantile business."

"What about Levi Leiter?" she asked. She liked Leiter, who was large and jovial. On the other hand, Cissy found Marshall Field remote and distant. He never looked her in the eyes when he helped her at the store.

"They're splitting the operation into retail and wholesale. Leiter's going to be in charge of the wholesale warehouse. He'll send drummers into rural areas. Field will run the store."

Cissy would rather have Levi Leiter wait on her, but she recognized that Marshall Field had the taste and polish to cater to the carriage trade.

They both sat silent, pondering the fate of the city. Finally, with a sigh, Cissy said, "I still wonder that the city can build again," and then added, almost fiercely, "yet it must, it simply must."

"It will," Potter said complacently. "Fate works in funny ways, and there have been some odd bits of help. For instance, Queen Victoria is sending a carload of books to start a new library."

"A library!" Cissy was torn between anger that books were the last things needed and an appreciation that the city would not rebuild without culture. "Maybe," she said, "it would have been better if she sent cash."

Potter smiled at his wife. "We need cash, that's true. But everything in the bank vaults all over town is safe. The vaults protected people's belongings. They've were just been too hot to touch until now."

Cissy thought with gratitude of her great-grandmother's jewelry that Eliza Honoré had insisted in keeping in a bank vault, over the protests of her husband, who told her to hide it in the pantry.

"The pantry!" her mother had scoffed. "Why that's the first place a self-respecting thief would look."

With a deliberately casual attitude, Potter said, "I've borrowed two million to rebuild the hotel and some other buildings."

After her initial startled echo of "Two million!" Cissy realized this was where Potter had been directing the conversation all evening. "Who," she asked, "has that kind of money to loan?"

"Not here," he said. "I borrowed from Connecticut Mutual in New York. I think it's the biggest loan made yet. New York business knows Chicago is crucial to the national economy. They're willing to lend money for the recovery because it's in their best interests." Then, with pride, he added, "They didn't ask for collateral. My name was enough. It's the biggest loan I've heard of."

"Biggest in Chicago?" she asked.

"Biggest in the country," he replied complacently. "My credit is good, even though my circumstances are, at the moment . . . ah . . . strained."

"What about Papá?" she asked.

"He'll be able to borrow," Potter said. "I'll see to it."

Cissy stared at the coals in thought. Her father was fond of Potter, very fond, but he would never want to be in his debt that way. She hoped he could borrow on his own, or, if Potter helped, that her father never knew it.

* * *

"Mrs. Johnson? I'm sorry for your loss." Carter Harrison stood with his hat in one hand and reached the other toward the woman in front of him.

Eunice Johnson raised her head and looked at the man who had invaded her sister's parlor. So many people had come and gone since the fire that she had lost track.

"I only now heard that Frank was among the missing," the man went on. "He and I . . . well, we fought fires together. And truth to tell, we played a little poker together." He smiled tentatively.

Eunice smiled a little herself. Frank had loved his poker, and she had spent many a night at home, doing what Frank called her "infernal needlepoint," while he dealt the cards. Sometimes he won, and they celebrated; more often, he lost, and there was little grocery money. But Frank Johnson had been a good husband for twenty years, and Eunice had loved him as though she had no choice.

"Your sister tells me you've lost your house, too, ma'am."

Eunice nodded and murmured, "Yes. Yes, I have." He seemed so caring that, without thinking she put into words the worry that she'd harbored since the fire. "I . . . I don't know what I'll do."

Carter Harrison gave her his most sympathetic look. He knew the Johnsons had not been rich, not even what you'd call comfortable, but Frank had managed to support his wife. They were the people caught in the middle, not desperately poor but by no means rich enough to ride out this disaster.

"The insurance . . ." she went on, "well, there is none of course. Wouldn't have been even if an insurance company could pay. And the house was the only thing we have. I . . . I don't know . . . ."

Carter Harrison knew without being told that Eunice Johnson had never worked in her life and would not know how to go about supporting herself. Probably, she could take in sewing—but who in

Chicago now could pay for such work, except perhaps Cissy Palmer?

He looked again at the woman before him. She was perhaps forty, and she was now pinched and worn with grief and fear and worry. But beneath the temporary grimness he saw an attractive face, strong cheekbones, and dark gray-green eyes, hidden when she looked down by long lashes that fluttered to hide her sadness. Her hair was brown, not mousy but a deep, dark brown, and it shone from the hundred daily strokes she must be giving it even in her grief.

"It would be my pleasure, ma'am, to be of whatever service I can," he said. Harrison didn't know quite what he meant, but Eunice Johnson was one of the large mass of people he wanted to help, the people for whom Chicago didn't work right.

"Thank you," she said, the eyes lowering and the lashes fluttering again. "My sister and her family, they have been so good, so kind . . . ."

"And they will continue to be, I'm sure," he said.

Harrison and Eunice chatted for a few minutes more, he sympathetic and concerned, she restrained in her grief. Occasionally, one of her two nephews peeked around the doorway and giggled, and then the hand of an unseen adult pulled them back. Finally, Harrison took his leave.

"Miss Eunice, it's been a pleasure to visit with you. I'd . . . I'd like to call again, if I may. Just see how you're gettin' along."

"That would be very nice," she said softly.

Harrison Carter walked away deep in thought. How could he help all the people who needed help?

* * *

Chicago celebrated the first anniversary of the fire with the dedication of its new Board of Trade Building, a granite structure that mixed architectural styles wildly and featured a three-hundred and ten-foot Gothic clock tower. In the 1880s when Frank Lloyd Wright arrived in the city, he took one look at the building and decided not to keep his appointment for an apprentice position in the office of the architect who had designed it. But to Chicago in 1872, the building stood for rebirth.

Railroads underwrote much of the resurrection of the city, and the economy grew in 1872. A great deal of rebuilding was done, although the process was not smooth. The poor suffered the most, for the "Great Rebuilding" consisted of removing shanties from the business district and erecting fireproof buildings. Too many citizens were homeless. Even Conley's Patch disappeared. The poor stood in food lines and boiled drinking water, while the Relief Aid Society delivered food to the wealthy. The gulf between the haves and the have-nots in Chicago grew.

Most rebuilding was done within two years, and by 1874 downtown Chicago looked as it had, only bigger and with taller buildings made of brick and stone. The buildings were designed and constructed by the same builders who had built the structures destroyed in the fire. Chicago's architectural renaissance was still to come.

Chapter Seven

Ida Honoré sat on a window seat, her nose pressed against the glass, watching the steady rain outside. She was in her sister's sitting room, and Cissy was busily ruffling through the pages of Harriett Beecher Stowe's *The American Woman's Home, or, Principles of Domestic Science, Being a Guide to the Formation and Maintenance of Economical, Healthful, Beautiful and Christian Homes.* The fire was now almost two years behind them, and Ida's thoughts were clearly on matters other than disaster, but Cissy barely paid attention to her sister's talk until she said,

"Cissy? Fred is going to ask Papá for permission to seek my hand in marriage." The younger girl spoke hesitantly, as if uncertain of how she herself felt about the news she was delivering.

There was no such hesitation in the response she received. "Fred Grant? The president's son? Ida, that's wonderful news!" Cissy had been pleased ever since Fred Grant, son of Ulysses S. Grant, Civil War hero and now president of the United States, had begun courting her younger sister. Fred Grant, stationed in Chicago with Sheridan's command in the Army of the West, had graduated from West Point.

Cissy was up from her desk and beside the window seat in a second, grasping her sister's hand. "When will the wedding be?"

"Cissy! Papá has not given his blessing yet . . . and I have not said yes."

"Oh, but you will," Cissy said confidently. Then looking at her sister's expression, she added, "Won't you?"

Ida's face took on a dreamy expression. "Oh, yes, I shall. But I . . . it's just such a big thing to do, getting married."

Cissy laughed and went back to her desk. "I guarantee you'll like it," she said. "I do. Now, let's see. A June wedding at the hotel would be charming . . . ." Her mind was whirling with plans. Cissy had moved her into an arena where she felt supremely confident, that of social arrangements.

"It won't be June," Ida said decisively. "Fred is going on a scout to the Black Hills this summer with General Custer."

"General Custer!" Cissy said scathingly. She had met the man once when he'd been in Chicago to confer with General Sheridan, and she'd thought Custer too much "sold on himself," as she later told Potter. Those ridiculous long blond curls on a grown man! She had rather liked his wife, though she wondered how the woman could be so dotty about that unpleasant man.

"I wish," Cissy said, "that Fred would give up this army business. I'm sure Potter would find suitable work for him."

Ida anticipated her sister's thought. "The army is his career, Cissy. He's been at battle since he was thirteen and went all through the Civil War with his father."

"I know, I know," Cissy said impatiently, "and he was wounded twice. Of course, it makes you proud, dear, but it's no way for a grown man to live, running off to chase the poor Indians around every few months. What kind of family life can you possibly have unless he resigns from the army?"

"I won't even ask him that," Ida said decisively. Then she added, "The wound in his leg still bothers him. He limps when it rains. I think he must have been very courageous during the war."

"I'm sure he was, dear," Cissy said. She vowed to talk to Potter and see if he couldn't persuade Fred to leave the army.

The two women talked of wedding plans—Ida was firm that she would be married in her father's house, though she was gracious about Cissy's suggestion of the hotel.

"We are rather getting the horse before the cart," Cissy laughed, "since Fred has not even talked to Papá yet, but I am certain how it will all work out. Oh, Ida, it will be wonderful!"

"Which?" asked Ida. "The wedding or the marriage?"

"Both," Cissy answered without hesitation.

After a few minutes, Ida spoke again, this time in a timid voice. "Cissy? What was it like? Your wedding night?"

Now it was Cissy's turn to hesitate. "My wedding night? Well . . . Potter and I talked about who had been at the wedding. There were people I didn't know, and some he didn't . . . and we . . ." She was babbling, because she remembered her own uncertainty and her wish that someone had been there to talk to her. Especially, she guessed, she had wished for her mother. But she pretended not to know that was what Ida was asking about.

"That's not what I mean." The usually diffident Ida was now direct. "Your wedding night. How will I know what to do?"

Cissy understood why her mother had never had that talk with her, why the subject of intimate marital relationships was never talked about. In spite of her sympathy with Ida's uncertainty, she was embarrassed.

"You won't have to know what to do," she said slowly. "Fred will know." She almost added, "and he will do it all," but thought better of that. And then she hoped to heaven that it was true that Fred would know. Potter had known, but he had been more worldly—and older. Early on in her marriage she had privately decided that was an advantage to marrying an older man.

"Is it . . . is it unpleasant?" Ida asked. As a child, she had been more squeamish than Cissy about everything from playing in the mud to trying new foods.

"Unpleasant? Oh, no. Oh, Ida, you mustn't worry about that. It's not unpleasant . . . it's something you do for your husband."

She thought a minute and then added, boldly, "And you'll come to find pleasure in it."

Beneath the desk she rubbed at her gently rounding belly and thought of the pleasure she had known the moment that her child had been conceived. No doctor would have believed her, but she knew without a doubt that the two were connected. Beyond that instant cry of joy on her part, Potter as yet knew nothing about the baby, and she would soon have to tell him—and then the rest of the family.

"Well," said Ida, "if I don't like it, I don't have to do it very often, do I?"

"Ida," Cissy answered, somewhat in exasperation, "you really are putting the cart before the horse now. Fred hasn't talked to Papá since we started this conversation, I presume, so it is still far too early for you to worry about a wedding, let alone your wedding night."

Ida looked unconvinced and stared pensively out the window once more, as Cissy gathered the papers together on her desk and prepared to move on to the next item on her day's agenda.

As she left the room, Cissy said softly over her shoulder, "But, Ida, don't wear underclothes beneath your nightgown." And she was gone.

Potter Palmer was overjoyed when Cissy told him of the impending arrival of their firstborn. "I'm sure it's a boy," she said, though she would never explain to Potter that it was that moment of high joy she'd experienced that convinced her the infant would be a boy. Girls, she reasoned, were conceived in calmer circumstances.

"I don't care if it's a boy or a girl, as long as it's healthy," he had said, his voice rising in pride. Nearing fifty years of age, Potter Palmer long thought he would die without an heir. Before he married Cissy, he sometimes wondered why he worked so hard, if he had no one to leave his fortune too. Now it seemed that all his wishes were coming true.

"Cissy," he said in a preachy tone of voice, "you must take very good care of yourself—and of our baby."

A slight shudder of alarm struck her at the words, but she smiled and said, "Of course I will, Potter." To herself, she voiced a hope that he was not about to order her to curtail her activities and once again confine her to the farmhouse.

* * *

Carter Harrison heard the rumor making its way through Chicago that Mrs. Potter Palmer was expecting. The rumor was carried in the words of Palmer's business associates, who treated the news as yet another accomplishment on Palmer's part. And Harrison himself thought it was. By himself, he raised a silent hand in salute to a man nearing fifty who fathered a child. But the news made him think of Sheila Collins and the all-but-forgotten news Harry had delivered that she was in the family way.

"Can't afford to feed the family I got, and she's got herself knocked up again," Collins had said. Carter resisted the urge to punch him and remind him that it wasn't something Sheila did alone—and no man should talk about his wife that way. But he kept his peace.

Now he went to the City Café early one morning, where he found her, as usual, behind the counter, only now she was obviously swollen in the late stages of pregnancy. "Sheila, my love, you shouldn't be on your feet," he exclaimed.

"Posh," she said. "I'll be fine. My shoes get a bit tight at night, but moving around is good for me."

He thought of Cissy Palmer, who was, no doubt, cosseted and cared for. Maybe Sheila was right—the active life is better.

"You looking forward to having another young one?" he asked.

"Oh, yes," she said, and her face glowed. "As me mother proved, you can't have too many children." She was thoughtful a minute, and then added, "Harry's not pleased. He says we can't afford to feed another mouth."

"Go on now," he said cheerfully. "He's got a good job at the Palmer House. You need to leave this place, though."

"I will when the baby comes," she said. "And I know he has a good job, it's just that he doesn't believe it." She put both elbows on the counter and leaned toward him. "You know what I think?"

"No. What?"

"I think Harry was raised to be rich. He's so . . . so educated. And I don't know what happened to make him like he is, but he thinks he's too good for the work he does now. And I don't know how to change that."

Carter looked long at her, marveling at her insight. Then he said, "I don't think you can change it, Sheila. He's lucky he doesn't work for the railroads, where they're laying off. But I doubt he sees that."

"No," she said slowly. "More and more, he hates the rich, the ones who have money and business. And that includes Mr. Palmer, which isn't smart of Harry."

Carter sighed. "No, it's not. Sheila, make me a promise. You ever need help, you come find me."

She reached her rough, coarsened hand out and held it over his hand. "Thanks, Mr. Harrison. I'll remember that." And then, "Why, I haven't ever gotten you any coffee."

"Coffee?" he roared. "I want eggs and bacon with that coffee."

* * *

As her pregnancy progressed, it became truly impossible—and unseemly—for Cissy to leave the farmhouse. Eliza Honoré came to see her daughter as often as she could get away from her busy family, and Ida came for a day or two at a time, but Cissy was essentially alone. She read everything she could get her hands on, from philosophical treatises to the latest on raising babies, and she was interested in none of it.

Sometimes in her loneliness at the farmhouse, when neither her mother nor Ida was around to distract her, Cissy's mind wandered morbidly. Too often, she worried about an imperfect child.

If anything were wrong with the baby, she would take all the blame herself. Potter would not sire a child less than perfect. She had finally, with uncharacteristic timidity, asked her mother how one knew if the baby was healthy.

Eliza shrugged, not realizing the depth of her daughter's doubts. "When they kick, they're healthy." It was a simplistic approach to prenatal predictions, but it was all Mrs. Honoré knew.

Some weeks before the baby was due, Potter arrived with the long-awaited news that their apartment in the hotel was ready for them. He didn't realize how desperately Cissy wanted to be away from the farmhouse and in the hotel, but still he expected a joyous reaction to the news. He was sorely disappointed.

She stood before him and smiled, "That's good news, Potter. We'll have plenty of time to move." Then she looked ruefully down at her swollen shape. "But I won't sneak into the Palmer House when no one can see me. I will wait until I can walk proudly through the front door, with my child in my arms." She wanted to add that he was the one who had drilled care of herself and the child inside her, but she kept that thought to herself.

Potter Palmer did not see the relationship at all between his edict that his wife not leave the farmhouse alone and her failure to rush into the hotel. His face fell in disappointment. For one thing, he thought the decision of when to move was his as head of the household. Later, he would recover from his disappointment by remembering that the move would be hard on Cissy. If anything were to be wrong with the baby, he thought, it would be his fault for insisting on the move.

"Margaret can begin packing the things we don't need," Cissy said, "and if you bring me samples, I'll choose drapery material and that sort of thing." She already felt better than she had in weeks, because she had a project. She was engaged in something, even if it was only decorating their hotel apartment from a distance.

They stood still, facing each other in the hall where she'd greeted him when he came home with his announcement. Now, he looked away from her and seemed to study the pattern in the rug at their feet. "The drapes are up, the furniture's in place," he said.

"What?" Her tone took on a frosty edge.

"It was best to do it while we were doing the entire hotel. The apartment . . . well, it matches the hotel rooms."

Cissy said nothing for a long minute and then only, "I'll tell Margaret to prepare dinner."

The Palmers ate a silent dinner that night.

The move was indefinitely postponed.

One evening, when the baby's arrival was momentarily expected, Cissy was particularly uncomfortable. She and Potter were in her sitting room, each occupied with a book, but she found it increasingly difficult to concentrate. Once, when the baby kicked with particular vigor, she grunted aloud in spite of herself.

"What is it?" he asked in alarm, ready to send immediately for the doctor.

"Your son is kicking me quite hard," she replied with a touch of irony. "Do you want to feel his kick? I should call it rather vigorous." She smiled, because she remembered what her mother had said about healthy babies and kicking. This was, she thought, surely a healthy baby.

Potter looked uncertain. Between husband and wife, it was not common to discuss the physiological details of pregnancy and childbirth. He was quite sure, though he had no previous experience, that it was also not common for a husband to feel his wife's pregnant belly. He had, of course, been careful to keep physical distance from Cissy—beyond a peck on the cheek and an affectionate hug—ever since the announcement.

"Are you sure?"

"It's your baby, too," she said, and then with the boldness that always caught him unaware, "and you had a part in putting him where he is."

Potter Palmer would never have admitted to blushing, but Cissy saw the faint pink rise across his cheeks to his forehead.

He put his hand where she directed and waited patiently, as she told him. In a few minutes, he felt a thrust so strong it caused him to pull away in surprise. "Does it hurt?" he asked foolishly.

"Yes," she said, "it does. I told you it's a boy. He's pounding to get out."

Honoré Palmer "got out" a few nights later. One morning, after Potter had left for the city, Cissy was seized with a pain so violent that it nearly doubled her over in the chair where she sat. It passed quickly enough, and with her customary efficiency, she began to order things, sending Herman for her mother and then her husband, in that order. She instructed Margaret to prepare the bed in the guestroom and to begin to heat water. Then she dressed in a clean wrapper of soft white cotton, brushed her hair thoroughly, and moistened her wrists and earlobes with perfume.

The second pain was even stronger than the first, and by the time Eliza Honoré arrived, her daughter was in bed, with pains only five minutes apart. The mother brought with her Charity, a black midwife who had followed the family from Kentucky all those years earlier and now served as cook and maid in the Honoré household. But Charity had delivered Cissy herself and in the years since she had not forgotten her midwifery skills.

"I'm glad you're here," Cissy said, reaching for Charity's hand. Somehow she found the old black woman more comforting than her mother—and she knew Potter would be no comfort at all. With Charity there, though, Cissy found that she had no fear.

Charity wasted no time rigging rope handles from the posts of the bed. "When you get a pain, you pull hard on these," she instructed, "and you bite down on this, so's you don't scream and scare Mr. Palmer half to death!" She handed her a piece of leather.

When a pain came, Cissy followed Charity's orders, pulling on the handles, biting down on the leather, and riding the pain until it subsided.

Potter had arrived at home, according to Mrs. Honoré, and wanted to take up watch outside the bedroom door. "I sent him down to his parlor and recommended brandy," she said. "I don't know why men expect babies to come within five minutes."

As the pains grew more frequent and stronger, Cissy felt herself retreating into a cocoon where the only thing real to her was the vise that gripped her abdomen. She heard the voices around her as though in a fog and was only dimly aware of Charity's repeated assurances. "You're doin' fine, Miss Cissy, just fine. We're gonna have us a healthy baby any time now."

She was not aware that Potter knocked on the door frequently, each time demanding, "Shouldn't you send for a doctor? I don't like this. It's taking too long."

And each time Mrs. Honoré reassured him in soothing words, telling him the birth was progressing normally and in good time and that Charity had delivered all the Honoré babies.

"I don't care if she has," he at last said angrily. "She can watch for this one. I'm going for the doctor."

"You'll be gone when the baby arrives," his mother-in-law said in her sweetest tones.

That stopped him in his tracks, and he settled down again to waiting.

Toward evening Cissy let out the one and only cry of her labor, a long agonized scream of pain that brought Palmer to his feet again, determined this time to take charge. But before he could knock on the door, he heard the sound of a baby crying—and crying loudly.

Mrs. Honoré opened the door, knowing he would be there. "You have a fine, healthy son," she said. "Let us clean them both up, and you can come in."

Potter Palmer turned away before she could see the tears in his eyes. Later, though, at Cissy's bedside, he let tears of joy run openly down his face. "Are you all right?" he asked over and over, and each time Cissy smiled happily at him and said, "I'm fine, just fine. It was not hard at all."

"Not hard," he wanted to explode. Hadn't he waited all those long hours, hadn't he heard her scream? Not hard indeed!

For Cissy, the pain and memory of it vanished at the sight of her son, though she did make a mental note not to tell Ida much about the childbirth.

* * *

Across town, Sheila Carter gave birth just days later to a baby boy, with only her mother in attendance. Harry dropped Juliet off with Sheila's sisters and then retreated to O'Malley's. The infant was not healthy—he neither squalled nor squirmed but lay in his grandmother's arms like a limp puppy. When he died, some four hours later, Sheila turned her face to the wall and sobbed silently, her mother rubbing her back and saying "There now, there now. The good Lord knows what he's doing. There'll be more babies."

Sheila knew there would not be more babies, but she said nothing.

When Harry came in and heard the news, he was as tender as he'd ever been, wrapping his arms around her and holding her tight. "A son," he said, his voice catching, "I really wanted a son."

"We've got to name him to bury him," Sheila said between gulping sobs. "What will you call him?"

"Harry Collins Junior," came the prompt reply.

They buried the infant the next day, in unconsecrated ground, and the day after that, Sheila went back to the café.

* * *

In October 1873, as Potter's hotel was nearing completion, headlines in Joseph Medill's *Tribune* screamed, "Jay Cooke and Co. fails!" "New York Stock Exchange closes!" An unprecedented financial panic swept the country. Banks, businesses, and factories closed. Workers lost their jobs. Investors lost a lifetime of savings.

"Potter," Cissy asked, "what does it mean for the hotel?"

He looked up from the paper he was studying. "Nothing, Cissy. Don't worry about it." Potter often talked business with his wife, but he didn't want to worry her now with an infant to care for.

"Potter," she persisted, "I want to understand what happened." She held her sleeping newborn in her arms.

He put the newspaper aside with a reluctant sigh. He'd heard that tone in Cissy's voice before. "Jay Cooke and Company was the biggest bank in the country. When it failed, everyone panicked and other failures followed."

"Why did it fail?"

"It invested too heavily in the Northern Pacific Railroad. We've just built too many railroads too fast in this country since the war. And prices and profits have been too high. It couldn't last."

"And it doesn't affect the hotel?"

"No, my financing is secure. Not one thing will change about our plans and our lives."

Her fork clattered awkwardly against her dessert plate, and she asked, "Is my father in difficulty too?"

"I have not talked with him about it," he said slowly and carefully. "But if he has extended himself on loans, yes, he probably is."

"What about Chicago?"

His expression grew darker, and he shook his head. "I don't know. Field says he won't lay people off. Thinks his clientele will continue to spend. But McCormick—he may have to lay some people off at the factory and reduce their working hours. Field's sure if that happens they'll strike and we'll have rioting. It may not happen immediately, but I'm afraid there will be trouble with workingmen."

Honoré stirred in his mother's arms, and she cooed comfortingly at him. Then her tone changed completely. "What about President Grant?"

Potter was startled. "What about him? He didn't cause it, and he couldn't have prevented it."

"But will it, you know, damage his presidency?"

He was thoughtful. "His name has been associated with the scandal, and I doubt he'll be elected for a third term. He may not want it."

"Poor Ida," she said softly.

Now Potter was really confused. "How did Ida get into this discussion?"

"She is really looking forward to being the president's daughter-in-law."

Potter kept his next thought to himself. *And you are looking forward to visiting the White House, as a member of the family.* Aloud he said, "She still will be. He will always be President Grant. He just won't live in the White House after the next election. Besides, Cissy, the election isn't until 1876. Ida will have plenty of time to visit the White House."

Despite what Potter thought, Cissy was not worried about Ida or visiting the White House. She was worried about her father. "Margaret!" she called down the stairs as soon as Potter had left for the city. When the housekeeper appeared in the door of Cissy's sitting room, the young wife said, "Have Herman bring my carriage. I'm going to see my mother."

"I can't do that, Mrs. Palmer," Margaret said, wringing her hands in apprehension. "Mr. Palmer gave orders that you were not to drive yourself. Herman can take you."

Cissy remembered her ladylike upbringing barely in time to keep from throwing the book she held, although she reassured herself later she would never have thrown it at Margaret. Just in that general direction. "I am perfectly capable—" she began. It dawned on her that Potter must know—from Herman or Margaret—about her forbidden trips into the city at the time of the fire.

She sighed and said, "Please ask Herman if he has time to drive me to my mother's. And wrap Honoré against the cold."

Margaret was aghast. "You'll take that baby with you?"

"He might," Cissy replied evenly, "need to eat while I'm gone. And besides, he needs to visit his grandparents."

Margaret knew a rebuke when she heard one. "Yes, ma'am. I'll get him ready. It's best, you know, for Herman to drive you anyway," Margaret volunteered without having been asked. "There's so much trouble in the city and all, but you know that."

Now Cissy's voice was sharp. "No, I don't know that. I'm out here on the farm, and Potter doesn't tell me things he thinks will upset me. What kind of trouble?"

Margaret looked guilty, as though she'd given away a secret. "Well, of course, I don't want to be carrying tales—" Her voice dropped to a whisper.

"Margaret," Cissy demanded, "tell me what has happened."

"Well, the railroad workers haven't been paid, and they're striking. General Sheridan called out the troops to control them."

Martial law again, and it was such a disaster before. How could it happen again? "Troops to control the railroad men?" she said aloud. "I thought the troops were off fighting the Indians."

"They're just back," Margaret said, now proud of her knowledge.

Cissy eyed her. "Margaret, how do you know so much of the news that I don't?"

"Herman tells me," the housekeeper said. "Let me just go and call him."

After the housekeeper left, Cissy thought wryly that it was exactly like Potter to alarm her about national news and omit serious troubles in Chicago, which he knew would upset her even more.

Herman obligingly found time to drive Cissy and her infant across Chicago to her mother's house. On the ride he was, as always, silent unless spoken too. Cissy alternated between withdrawn silence and an urgent need to question him. She noticed that he rode with a shotgun in the carriage, not his usual practice. The thought flickered through her mind that she was foolish to have brought her child into danger. She did not even want to think about what would happen if Potter knew.

"Herman, are the railroad workers really striking in Chicago?"

"I . . . I don't think it's quite here, madam, although it may be. Where did you hear that?"

"Margaret," she muttered.

"Now, Margaret ought not to be upsetting you."

Cissy understood Potter's concern but she could not forgive him for shielding her from the world.

When they reached her parents' house, she said, "We won't be long. Do go in the kitchen and see if they have a cup of tea and some cookies or something for you."

Herman tipped his hat and drove the carriage around to the back of the house, after letting her out at the front porte cochère. Cissy carried little Honoré in her arms as she went up the steps, calling as she went, "Mother? Ida? Where are you?"

"Bertha!" Her mother came to the door, knitting in hand. "What are you doing here, dear? And that precious baby? You've brought him out in this fall chill! Is something the matter?"

"Honoré is fine, Mamá. He's bundled up, and he enjoyed the ride. Fresh air is good for him—I read that in a book. And no, nothing's the matter, and yes, everything's wrong," Cissy said, handing the baby to her mother and throwing her cape on the nearest chair. Without pausing to sit down, she poured out her tale of worry about finances, particularly her father's, and finished it by raving—later she realized that she literally had raved—about not knowing what was going on in Chicago. "It's my city! To think that troops have been called out because of strikes, and Potter didn't even tell me. He just lets me sit out there in the country!"

Throughout her daughter's discourse, Eliza Honoré had sat quietly, rocking the baby and cooing to him, her eyes avoiding her older daughter. At last, she asked, "Are you through?"

Startled, Cissy murmured, "Yes," and sank into a chair.

"Let me ring for some tea," Eliza said.

When the tea was delivered, with wonderful shortbread squares, Cissy nibbled and then asked, "Well, what should I do?"

"Turn around and go home so you'll be there when Potter gets home," her mother said serenely. "He would be terribly alarmed that you brought his son into the city. And he didn't marry you to have you run the world or tell him how to run it. He married you to love him and take care of him, as any wife should. What you've been talking about is men's business, not yours."

Cissy opened her mouth and then shut it again. *Mother just doesn't realize how lonely it is out there. She's in here with a big family and people in and out all the time, and I'm left to my own devices, tending to a baby and relying on Margaret and Herman for conversation, even when they hide things from me.*

As though she'd read her mind, Eliza said, "You're talking about two separate things. One is that you don't know what's going on in the world—you don't need to, as long as it doesn't affect you. And so far it doesn't. Potter and your father both have resources to weather this financial storm. They've built carefully and solidly since the fire, and we'll all be all right."

"But others won't," Cissy protested, even though she was relieved to hear that her father was not in danger—*if* her mother was telling the truth. It was on the tip of her tongue to ask what the Collins family would do, but she knew her mother still disapproved of that relationship and that act of generosity on her part.

"That can't be your concern," Eliza went on, still cooing to her grandson. "You must take care of yourself, your baby, and your husband. And that's all. Now, as for your loneliness, I can send Ida home with you. She's pining for Fred, and he's off somewhere, although I thought he'd be spending the winter in Chicago." She wondered fleetingly how her oldest daughter could be either bored or lonely with an infant.

"Probably off putting down railroad strikes," Cissy said with a touch of bitterness in her tone. Fred Grant had indeed asked permission to court Ida after he'd returned from scout the past summer, but the couple had decided that the wedding would be put off over a year, until after Fred had gone on yet another scout with General Custer. Cissy couldn't understand why Ida was so complacent about the delayed wedding. Maybe, she thought wryly, it was the thought of the wedding night.

Aloud to her mother, she said, "Maybe she could come for a few days. She'd be company." But she won't give a fig about railroad strikes and starving workers, Cissy thought.

"I'll talk to her when she comes home tonight," Eliza said. "She's out to tea with some friends. Now you best get Herman to drive you home."

Cissy clearly felt that her mother had dismissed her. As she rode home, she pondered her mother's advice that she didn't need to know what was going on in the world—or even in her city—if it didn't affect her directly. She knew she didn't believe that.

Just as they turned into the farm lane, Honoré began to demand feeding, and Cissy had other things to worry about than the financial panic.

* * *

Carter Harrison was a man of comfortable means but not wealthy like the men he dealt with on a daily basis, the bankers and merchants and men like Pullman and Palmer. The Panic of 1873 did not threaten him. He had no outstanding debts, he kept his money to himself because he feared bank failure like the country was experiencing, and his house was paid for. Like Potter Palmer, he did not panic about the Panic. But, unlike Potter, more like Cissy, he worried about others who would be affected. The poor of Chicago would suffer in the end, he knew.

He went one evening in early January of 1874 to O'Malley's Pub to take the temperature of his city. The place was less crowded than usual.

"Men can't afford to buy even a pint o' beer," O'Malley lamented. "Keeps on like this, I'm goin' out of business."

"Drinks on the house," Harrison said loudly, and the twenty or so men present crowded up to the bar, holding out their mugs.

"No need for that," O'Malley said. "I ain't askin' for charity. But I wish some of those swells, who made all that money for a while, could see what's happenin' with the ordinary folk."

"So do I," Harrison said, "so do I." He sat and sipped his beer, watching the men around him. Their very posture revealed their despair—hunched over their beers, propping their heads on their hands, sinking down in their chairs. *There ought to be some kind of national fund to help people like this*, he thought.

Just as Harrison was about to leave, Harry Collins wandered in. From the looks of him, he'd already had a beer or two somewhere else. He plunked coins down on the counter and said, "Pint." No please, no thank you, just the demand for the pint.

Harrison got off his stool and moved toward him. "Collins, how's the wife?"

Harry Collins shrugged. "She still cries a lot, but she'll get over it. I got other things to worry about, like earning a decent living."

Harrison looked directly at the younger man. "You've got a good job with Palmer. You're better off than most of these fellows." He jerked his head in the direction of the men gathered in the pub.

"Yeah," Collins spat, "doing chores for a man who's too good to do them himself."

A fellow named Blake who worked for the railroad had come close and heard the last comment. "Just be thankful you got a job, Collins," he said. "Me? Got laid off by the railroad this morning. Don't know how I'm gonna go home and tell the old lady."

Collins gave him a dirty look. "Try workin' for no money for a man who's got more than God."

"Believe me," Blake said, "I'd be glad to. I'd trade to be in your place in a minute."

Carter Harrison saw that Blake's last comment was about to cause trouble. "Come on, boys. Let me buy you both another beer," he said.

Collins was still glowering at Blake, and Carter thought he might take a swing at him. They were all distracted suddenly when a woman, dressed in black, pushed through the doors of the saloon.

With an awful start, Harrison realized it was Eunice Johnson. Two years after the fire, Carter Harrison was still calling on Eunice Johnson. He went because he found her sad and because he felt some loyalty to Frank Johnson. Sometimes he took the widowed lady for a ride in his carriage and once, before Sophie got so sick, he had taken her to his house for dinner. She'd seemed quieter than usual, though Harrison had never found her talkative.

Sophie, a good-hearted woman with an ample figure and a ready laugh, had tried to draw her out. But each question was answered with a monosyllable. Sophie did glean from Eunice that she did not do much during the day—"Just help my sister with the young 'uns"—and that she had almost no friends.

Eunice allowed that she appreciated Mr. Harrison calling on her, and she knew her Frank would be grateful, if he were here. Mention of Frank brought a tear to her eye that she wiped away with one hand, her eyes downcast.

"Aren't you fortunate to have such a good sister and her family to take you in," Sophie said cheerfully.

Eunice nodded. Then, unsolicited, she added, "But the children . . . they're noisy, and I have no privacy. They rush into my room whenever they want. And my sister—she expects my help all the time."

To herself Sophie thought, *and well she should, if you're living there free.* Aloud she said, "Perhaps you could find another place to live?"

"I don't want to live alone," Eunice said.

Sophie tried another approach. "Do you go to church?"

A sigh. "Me and Frank, we were Catholic. But it doesn't seem to mean much to me. I've been to confession, and the priest said I ought to join some ladies group or another. I've been attending another church occasionally."

Sophie Harrison got the feeling that Eunice was deliberately not saying which church, and she didn't push.

When Carter returned after taking Eunice home, he asked his wife, "Don't you think after all this time she should be getting back to some kind of normal life? I didn't know her much before Frank died, but I remember she was fairly happy. And Frank, he talked like she was a good woman, kept a clean house and cooked a fine meal—you know what I mean."

"She has nothing to give her life shape," Sophie said. "As withdrawn and depressed as she is, I can't imagine her meeting another man. She needs . . . well, if she were a man, I'd say she needs a job. But there's so little that women can do."

"She shouldn't work in a factory," Carter mused, "and I doubt she's qualified to teach." Then he had a thought. "Perhaps she could do some office work for me."

"Carter Harrison," Sophie exploded, "you don't pay enough attention to your law practice to be able to pay her. And what you earn from the legislature sure isn't going to pay for it. I'll do whatever work you need done."

But as Sophie's health declined, Eunice's spirits seemed to improve. Twice when Carter called, she was out, though her family did not explain where, and once, when he caught her at home, she seemed more animated. In fact, he detected a sort of fierceness in her eye, but no amount of cheerful palavering on his part could bring out the reason for the change.

And then one day in 1875 he knocked on her sister's door, only to be told, "Eunice doesn't live here anymore."

He remembered her comment about not wanting to live alone and asked aloud where she had gone.

The sister shrugged. "Some woman named Frances Willard took her in. The two of them, they're death on drinking and smoking, and they want to tell everyone about it. They belong to some kind of union or something." She rolled her eyes at the absurdity of telling men not to drink and smoke. Behind her, children giggled and screamed at each other.

Carter could well understand why Eunice had left the house, but he puzzled over the circumstances. He had, like most people, heard of the Women's Christian Temperance Union, organized a year before in some city in Ohio. But he had thought it distant from Chicago, unlikely to ever touch the city. Had it come to his town, to Chicago—the city with more saloons per man than any other in the country? He was so preoccupied that he didn't even ask where he could find Eunice and this Willard woman, and he doubted the sister would know if he had asked.

"Maybe she's found what she needed to give meaning to her life," Sophie said, when he reported the conversation.

Now, in O'Malley's Pub, Harrison watched in alarm as Eunice sank to her knees and began to pray in a loud voice, "Oh, Lord, deliver them for the evil of alcohol! Make them see the sins of their life! Cast out the grape and send them home to their wives and families."

The stunned men in the saloon were silent for a moment, but then they began to jeer at her.

"Go on, take your preachin' somewhere else."

"Leave us drink a pint in peace. We ain't hurtin' no one."

"Your husband know you're doin' this? I wouldn't let my old lady act like that."

Carter Harrison looked at O'Malley, who shrugged and said, "I been expectin' this. I hear sometimes they bring an ax and break things. Guess we're lucky this one only wants to pray."

Amid the catcalls, Carter Harrison rose and went to her, taking her elbow and almost forcefully pulling her to her feet. "Mrs. Johnson, you don't need to be in here. You're too fine a woman to be in a place like this."

If she recognized him, she gave no sign. "I have to save these men's souls," she said fiercely.

"Let me escort you home," Harrison responded gently. "Where are you staying now?"

She seemed to calm down some and come to her senses. "You're Carter Harrison, aren't you? Frank's friend."

"Yes, ma'am, I am, and I'd like to help you."

She jerked her arm away. "I don't need help! I've a mission."

"Then at least let me be sure you get home safely."

The men in the pub were watching in silent fascination. "Hey, Harrison, who is she?" one called out.

Harrison shook his head and made a motion for silence, and no more was said. Then he led Eunice Johnson out of the saloon. It turned out that Frances Willard lived on North Michigan, near the Honoré home, and Harrison had to hire a hack to take her home and then take him back to O'Malley's so he could retrieve Kate and ride home. The pub was then closed and shuttered, and Harrison rode home deep in troubled thought.

Cissy Palmer Emerges

Chapter Eight

The Palmer House had not yet had its grand opening when Cissy Palmer arrived, her son in her arms, just weeks after Honoré's birth. Potter drove her to the Ladies Entrance, with its two-story, elaborate metal porte cochère with lanterns built into its supporting poles and the words "The Palmer House" prominent across the front.

It would be the grandest hotel in Chicago, from its magnificent lobby to the barbershop with silver dollars embedded in the floor. The brick structure covered an entire city block and towered over the intersection of State and Monroe streets, with a turreted tower dominating the corner. It was billed as the only totally fireproof hotel in the United States.

In the lobby, fluted pillars supported carved and frescoed ceilings. Oriental carpets covered the floor and were bordered by inlaid strips of marble. Ornate furniture of dark wood decorated the public area, with fresh flowers on the tables. Sofas and easy chairs were deep and inviting, and gilded mirrors hung on the walls. Some of the paintings and tapestries on the walls had an Egyptian flavor, a taste that Potter had acquired when he traveled the world studying first-class hotels.

Once the hotel was fully opened, the lobby was a grand men's club, complete with tickers and news bulletins so guests could check the day's trade in comfort. There was a broker's exchange on the property, so visitors could trade pork or spring wheat without going to the Board of Trade Building. The air was heavy with cigar smoke and trade talk as Chicago's leaders debated and settled political and social issues. The hotel was also the unofficial headquarters for the Democratic Party, and national conventions were regularly held there for years.

This day, however, belonged to Cissy.

She paused just inside the door to take in everything. As she looked at the magnificence of the hotel's lobby, she forgot her anger at Potter for decorating their quarters without consulting her. It almost took her breath away—and Cissy Palmer did not lose her breath easily.

"Fresh flowers in March? What's the occasion?" Cissy asked, turning to Potter, quite sure that he would say the flowers were in her honor—and for young Honoré.

Instead, he shrugged and said, "We'll have them daily. It's one of the . . . what would you say—touches?—that I've put into practice. You can't stay in another hotel in this country, I dare say, and find fresh flowers throughout the lobby every day."

Nor could you stay in many hotels where the owner kept such a personal eye on operations. Off to one side of the lobby was a small glassed-in room in which Potter intended to spend much of his time, watching the comings and goings in his hotel.

"A man can't rely on his staff to make guests welcome," he would say time and again. "It's my responsibility, and I've got to see to every detail."

Cissy remembered how he had personally greeted customers at his dry goods store and what a success that had been.

The staff had lined up to greet Mrs. Palmer, and Harry Collins, wearing a smart uniform, was at the head of the line. "Good morning, madam," he said formally, his voice a little distant and his expression resentful. "It's going to be a real pleasure to have you and the little one with us." His tone was automatic, and Cissy hoped he showed more warmth to the guests. She had no way of knowing that he considered the position of chief bellman beneath him and the uniform an indignity.

She asked about Juliet and sent again her condolences to Sheila, even though she'd sent a hand-delivered note when the Collins' infant died. Now, Harry just muttered something and looked at the floor. He looked relieved when she moved on down the line to greet maids, clerks, receptionists, the chef from the dining room, even the chief barber, who declared it would be an honor to give "the little mister" his first haircut. Cissy noted that most of the employees were from the city's small African-American communi-ty and suspected Potter had deliberately avoided hiring European immigrants. Like many well-to-do Chicagoans, Potter distrusted the Irish, the Germans, and almost any Europeans except the French and English.

At last the family took the iron-cage elevator to their own suite on the top, or eighth, floor. The entire floor of the hotel had been given over to the Palmers, and Cissy consequently had more space than she had previously enjoyed in their country house.

"Couldn't you make more money by renting part of this out?" she asked Potter, only to be told that his family came first and he would subdivide the suite someday when they moved into a house of their own.

"A house?" Cissy echoed in amazement. "I've barely gotten moved in here, and you're talking about moving already." She tried to hide her disappointment. She so looked forward to living in the hotel and being in the midst of everything—and here was Potter talking about a house in the country. She'd had enough country living to last a long while.

Potter chuckled. "It will be years before we have a house, Cissy. When Honoré is older and needs space—you know, horses and all—then we'll talk about it." He kissed her quickly on the fore-head. "Could you enjoy touring your new quarters without worry-ing five or ten years down the road, please?"

She smiled at him, as though in recognition of her own fool-ishness.

Their parlor had an unobstructed view of Lake Michigan. Cissy would find herself spending more time than she cared to admit simply staring at the lake, particularly when it was in a wild mood, its waters stormy gray with breakers crashing against the shore.

The hotel's formal opening followed some weeks after the Palmers moved in. Potter invited the entire city of Chicago—well, at least, all those of a certain social status—to a reception at which they could view the luxurious appointments of the hotel and taste the finest its dining rooms had to offer.

Cissy floated through the rooms, dressed in a salmon silk faille gown with a small train and elaborate trimming of white chenille balls. Similar chenille ornaments formed a necklace and decorated her hair. She liked the way the train swirled behind her as she turned from one guest to another. She also liked very much the role of hostess, urging guests to try the escalloped oysters, sweet-bread patties, turkey, chicken salad, and boned quail in jelly. For the sweet palate, there were Charlotte Russe and fresh fruits, along with champagne, port, and sherry.

"You are urging escalloped oysters on our guests as you once urged them on me," Potter whispered in her ear. "Careful, or I shall be jealous."

"You have no cause," she said, smiling at him and then lowering her eyes so flirtatiously that Potter would, if he could, wave a magic wand and have all the people disappear. As it was, they both went about graciously greeting guests.

"A fine event," Marshall Field said in a soft voice. He said no more. Field easily earned his reputation as "Silent Marsh." Cissy inquired about his wife and was told that Nannie was not feeling well and had not accompanied him. His gray eyes revealed no emotion when he mentioned his wife.

The only other thing Field said was a muttered, "Glad to see Potter didn't hire a lot of immigrants."

Cissy let that pass without reply.

George Pullman introduced his wife, Harriett, who seemed, to Cissy, to look down her nose a bit. "It's very grand," she said. "Now in Pullmantown, we plan more simple things, more down to earth." Her tone was critical.

Cissy had heard of Pullmantown, the city out south that Pullman was building to house his workers. It would be, rumors said, a model city.

"You'll have to come when we celebrate the opening of the city," Mrs. Pullman said.

What Cissy thought was left unsaid was, "You'll see the right way to do things." Aloud, she said, "Mr. Palmer and I will look forward to it," and turned to greet other guests.

Palmer pointed out a man named Aaron Montgomery Ward. "Used to be a clerk when I still had the store with Field and Leiter," he said, "and then went on the road selling things. Now he tells me he wants to start a mail-order business."

"Mail order?" she asked, only vaguely interested.

"Everything from barbed wire to paper dolls. Cash only. Rural customers."

"No competition for Marshall Field then," Cissy murmured. She couldn't imagine buying something without seeing it first.

With unabashed pleasure, Levi Leiter told her how good the refreshments were and went back for seconds, while General Phil Sheridan—"Little Phil"—remarked that he doubted he could put his army officers up in such grand quarters without spoiling them, but the Palmer House would be a perfect place for President and Mrs. Grant to stay when they visited their son, Fred.

Potter pulled her in another direction. "Cissy, have you met our new state representative, Congressman Harrison?" Potter was at her elbow, and beside him was Carter Harrison, the man who had shepherded her through the West Side days after the Great Fire, an association she still did not want Potter to know about.

Extending her hand, she said smoothly, "Of course. Weren't you at our wedding reception?"

Harrison bowed low over her hand, but he was the kind of large, bluff man from whom the gesture was slightly incongruous. "Yes, ma'am, I had that privilege," he said. "You are kind to remember."

She could have sworn that he winked ever so slightly at her as he raised his head. Fortunately, Potter was behind him and saw nothing.

"And now you are a member of the state legislature?" Cissy asked, her tone implying that she was much impressed—which she was.

"Ah, yes, but I'd rather be serving my city," Harrison said with a wink.

She didn't realize she had just heard a declaration of his eligibility for mayor, but she was aware of Potter's sudden frown. Just as the conversation was about to grind to an embarrassing halt, someone pulled Potter away to greet another dignitary. Once her husband was safely out of hearing, Harrison whispered conspiratorially, "I trust you've not been wandering about the wrong parts of the city by yourself anymore."

Cissy drew herself up, prepared to take offense at such familiarity, and then she looked into his face, the eyes glinting with laughter, and she began to laugh herself. She remembered this man had had that effect on her once before, and then it occurred to her that Potter, who did many things for her—from showering her with gifts to making her feel sensually alive—rarely made her laugh. She dismissed that as a disloyal thought.

"I won't tell if you won't tell," Harrison said, and Cissy, laughing again, struck that bargain with him.

"Is Mrs. Harrison with you?" she asked politely.

His expression changed. "My Sophie's been feeling poorly lately. I'm worried about her. I thank you for asking. That will please her."

"You must bring her to the hotel when she's feeling better," Cissy said.

When he turned away, she stared after him speculatively. Carter Harrison was apparently a happily married man and yet he was attracted to her, no doubt about that. She found it even more puzzling that she felt herself drawn to him. Asked to reflect, Cissy would have said he was none of the things she found attractive in men and several of those she found unattractive. But Carter Harrison had caught hold of her imagination.

* * *

Harry Collins heard rumblings about layoffs and cutbacks in time at O'Malley's Pub. These days, he rarely looked at the newspaper, so he hadn't heard about the Panic. "What'd ya mean, layoffs?" he asked, taking a large gulp of his pint.

"Where you been?" asked one of the men from McCormick's factory. "Banks are closin', and factories are goin' bust all over the country. We have no way to protect our jobs."

"Factories are closing?" He was having a hard time grasping the idea.

"Yeah," said another man. "No money to pay us or buy supplies or anything."

If factories are closing, Harry thought, *what about the Collins Woolen Mill in Connecticut?* He cared not a fig for his father or his brothers, but thoughts of his mother could still bring a tear to his eye, after all these years. He thought now about the grandson she would never know, the grandson who had not lived to bear the family name. Abruptly, he shoved the unfinished pint away and stood up to leave.

"Collins, what's the matter with you? You haven't even finished your beer."

"Don't feel like it tonight," he said in a surly tone. "Goin' home."

"Well, you won't lose your job. Nothin' can touch Potter Palmer and his charmed hotel."

Harry considered punching the man, clenched his fist, and then thought better of it. "You never can tell," he said as he pushed through the swinging doors.

Sheila greeted him with a hug, which he barely returned, and then helped him out of his shoes, a chore she gladly did each night.

"What's to eat?" he asked.

"Corned beef and cabbage," she said, with no little pride.

"Where'd you get the money for corned beef?" he demanded angrily. She knew they couldn't afford that, even if he did complain constantly about her penny-saving meals.

"Ma gave me some of a large one she cooked at home," Sheila explained nervously. She knew Harry didn't want to take charity, but she also knew he wanted good food. This time he simply scowled at her.

As he ate, he said, "Harrison still come into the café now and again?"

Sheila nodded. "Most mornings, even if just for coffee. His wife, she's doin' real poorly, and it upsets him. I worry about both of them . . . and those children."

"You know the wife?"

"No, just through him. But I can still worry." There was a touch of defiance in her tone.

"Tell him I want to talk to him," Harry said curtly.

"Sure," Sheila said. "What about?"

He took another mouthful and thought how his mother would feel if she could see him shoveling corned beef and cabbage into his mouth. He was eating food she would disdain, and he was doing it without one bit of the manners she'd so carefully drilled into him. "Men's stuff," he said gruffly. "Tell him to come by O'Malley's tomorrow night."

"I'll *ask* him," Sheila said, but the change in words was lost on Harry.

Carter Harrison did as Sheila asked and showed up at O'Malley's the next night. Men crowded around him, clamoring for attention, demanding to know what he could do about their jobs.

"You'all belong to the union?" he asked.

The men from McCormick's chorused yes, but mutterings and curses from Pullman employees informed him that they'd lose their jobs if they joined a union.

"Why'd you join the union?" he asked.

One man stepped forward, a self-appointed spokesman. "For better pay and better hours."

"You willing to strike if McCormick cuts your hours?"

The spokesman became less sure of himself and looked to the others, who looked at the floor, their feet, the ceiling—anywhere but at Harrison.

"See, fellows," Harrison said, rising to his feet, "that's what I wanted you to figure out. Striking isn't going to help you. It's just gonna cost you your livelihood. If you have to take a cut in hours, it's better than not working." Harrison had been worrying for weeks about how to prevent strikes in "his" city. He hoped he'd made his point.

Finally, he singled out Collins. "You wanted to see me?"

"Yeah. Outside. I don't want anybody to hear." Collins led the way, carrying what appeared to be his third pint of beer. He was steady on his feet, but his speech was a little slurred.

"I don't unnerstand this panic business, but I hear a lot o' factories all over the country are closin'."

Puzzled, Carter Harrison nodded.

"How can I find out about a certain woolen mill in Connecticut?"

Harrison shrugged. "I could make some inquiries. Might take some time."

"Do it," Harry said, "but don't tell anyone. 'Specially don't tell Sheila. It's the Collins Woolen Mills." With that, Harry turned away and headed—Harrison hoped—for home.

Carter Harrison stood outside for several minutes, trying to make sense of this request. He finally puzzled out that it gave him a clue to Harry Collins' background—and perhaps to his anger.

Then Harrison turned and went back into the pub to talk to "his" men and soothe them. Sophie, he told himself, would be asleep. She'd started taking laudanum to help her sleep these days.

* * *

If Cissy Palmer had been depressed and lonely during her pregnancy, she was now riding a crest of happiness. She was the wife of a successful man, she had a beautiful and perfect young son, and she was mistress of the grandest hotel in Chicago. She loved what was called "the ladies' half mile," a string of stores anchored at one end by Marshall Field's emporium and at the other by the Fair, whose slogan was "Everything for Everybody." Field denounced the Fair as a department store, while his store, he insisted, was a dry-goods business.

State Street was loud, noisy, and windy enough to blow a person off his feet when the winds came off the lake and were funneled down the street by the tall buildings. Wagons and trolley cars thronged the brick-paved street, and people crowded along the sidewalks. Cissy frequently put on a sensible double-skirted walking suit, one that didn't sweep the ground, and a firmly anchored hat to hold her hair in place and then set off from the hotel to walk the half mile, usually ending her trip at Field's. But for her shopping was only part of the pleasure. She liked being in the midst of the turmoil, the people all around her, the excitement and vitality. Sometimes she stood by a store window and just watched the people for a few minutes.

"Cissy," Palmer said one night. "I don't think it's appropriate for you to walk alone on State Street. Perhaps Harry Collins could escort you."

"Potter! Whatever could happen to me? I'm perfectly safe. And they don't call it 'the ladies' half mile' for no reason. I meet many women I know on State Street." She most emphatically did not want to be escorted by Harry Collins, who grew more withdrawn by the day.

"There's also a reason," he said, "that they say you take your life in your hands if you cross the street at State and Madison."

"I'm very careful," she said primly.

In the end, Cissy continued her solitary trips up and down State Street. She longed to ride the horse-drawn trolleys, but she knew that would seriously displease Potter. One day, watching a crowded trolley, she saw a man fall off. As if landing on the cobbled street wasn't enough, a passing carriage hit him, and bystanders carried the man away. Cissy did not tell Potter about the incident, but it stayed vivid in her mind for a long time.

"Ida, I can't believe you expect to be married in October! Why, this is July, and we can't possibly plan a wedding that quickly!" Cissy took a sip of lemonade and stared at her sister, her look almost a challenge. Ida and Cissy sat with their mother on the veranda of the Honoré house. It was one of those summer days in Chicago that are hot and sticky to the point of immobilizing residents. Cissy fanned herself languidly with a fan her father had once brought from Paris.

"I can plan it," Ida said calmly, "and Mamá will help. I know exactly what I want. And we'll be married then because Fred will be back from his scout. We would marry in September, but his sister has already spoken for that date."

Cissy straightened in her chair, as though aware of her responsibilities. "Well, the hotel will be yours, I'm sure." She conveniently forgot that they had discussed this before, hoping Ida would relent about being married at home now that she saw how grand the hotel was.

"I don't mean to offend you, Cissy, but I don't want the hotel. I want to be married here at home, like you were."

"Well, of course, when I married, a grand hotel wasn't a choice—there wasn't one like the Palmer House. But now . . ."

"Ida wants to be married at home," Eliza Honoré told her older daughter firmly.

Cissy thought for a minute. "Well, the reception will have to be at the hotel. You can't possibly fit all those guests in here. Ida, think about it—you're marrying the son of the president of the United States!" Even as she said those words, Cissy felt a rush of excitement—she herself would be related to the president. Of course the wedding would have to be perfect.

"That's not why I'm marrying him," Ida said with the same calm she'd shown all afternoon. "I'm marrying him because I love him . . . and I don't want to invite half of Chicago to the wedding reception, like we did to yours."

"But Papá will have so many business associates he'll want to invite."

"Those are his business associates, Cissy, not the people I care about. And Fred doesn't have business associates in town like Potter. Your wedding was a very different kind of thing. Fred will invite army officers."

Probably, Cissy thought, *that bothersome, vain General Custer.* She stared at her lemonade, wishing briefly that it were a glass of claret to soothe her nerves. She could see that she was not making progress with Ida or with her mother, and yet she was so sure she was right. Suddenly, she felt as though she and Ida had been transported back ten years to the time when they were quarreling teenagers, though Ida never was much to hold up her side of the quarrel. Now she was doing herself proud.

Eliza Honoré stared off in the distance, Cissy studied her lemonade, and Ida sat patiently watching her sister. Finally, after a long silence, Ida said, "You will stand up with me, won't you, Cissy?"

Slowly, Cissy set the lemonade on the wicker table. She stood up and crossed to Ida, who stood up to meet her, and the two sisters hugged. "I'd be honored," Cissy said, "and I'll do whatever you want me to with the wedding." It was a difficult compromise for Cissy, but she made it gracefully.

Presidential expectations were at least met in lodgings. The Grants were given the hotel's finest suite and the entire seventh floor was closed to other guests except members of their traveling entourage. Cissy was surprised by President Grant. She had expected a forceful, determined man—after all, hadn't he led the Union to victory? Wasn't he a soldier by career? As president, however, he seemed tentative. She overheard him talking with Potter about the ongoing problems of Reconstruction in the South. "I just don't know what to do about it," he said. And that was Cissy's general impression of him. Uncertain of what to do, he waited for others to tell him, even if it was Potter suggesting it was time for a libation—Grant did seem to take comfort in his bourbon—or Fred telling him that as president he should not wear his military uniform to the wedding.

Julia Dent Grant also gave her husband more than a few directions, but they had been married nearly fifty years and were devoted to each other. "Ulys," Mrs. Grant would say, "you need to rest." Or, "You cannot have another bourbon, Ulys."

Best of all, Julia Grant was enthusiastic about Ida and the marriage. "I do adore that girl. I'm so glad she's marrying Fred. I just hope she can put up with army life."

They were having tea in Cissy's private study, seated in adjacent reed rockers. The room was softly lit by a gaslight with a painted glass shade. A canary in a hanging brass cage chirped occasionally.

"Ida seems to be prepared to accept Fred's career. I mentioned something about him possibly turning in another direction, and she said the army was what he wanted. I believe she's strong enough."

"Oh, heavens, yes. She's a wonderful girl. I just hope they give me a grandchild fairly soon. I would so love to rock and cuddle a baby again."

Cissy smothered a grin.

Ida chose a gown even more simple than Cissy's had been. It was of peau de soie, cut rather straight instead of with a dramatic wide skirt, with cap sleeves and a rounded neckline that would showcase the pearls that Potter gave her for a wedding present. She would wear Cissy's veil. Cissy's outfit as matron of honor was more dramatic. Ida had given her a free hand to choose her dress and its color, so she wore pearl gray with facings of soft pink and a gray sash with a pink fringe. Fresh pink roses were scattered among the diamonds in her hair, which was fixed in an elaborate concoction of puffs and ringlets.

"Careful, my darling," Potter said when he saw her, "or you'll outshine the bride."

"Potter, I am an old married woman," she said scornfully. "Ida is young and beautiful and will carry the day." But secretly she was pleased at his compliment.

It was a 7:00 P.M. wedding, at dusk on a fall night when the Chicago sky turned crimson with one of the prettiest sunsets anyone remembered. Guests coming into the Honoré home speculated aloud that it was a sign of blessing to the marriage. "And good weather tomorrow," Cissy thought wryly, remembering the childhood saying that began "Red at night/sailors delight."

Peeking over the stair railing as she waited her turn to descend, Cissy saw a few Chicago businessmen and their wives—the McCormicks, the Medills, the Pullmans, the Fields, and others—dressed in cravats and long coats. They mingled with army officers in full dress uniform, while the ladies were in elaborate gowns and highly built coiffures. Beside them, Cissy thought, Ida will be a beautiful contrast for the simplicity of her gown and hairdo.

Potter, dressed in a gray frock coat with gray topper and one perfect pearl in his gray cravat, was nervous about taking little Honoré to the ceremony. "He's only eight months old," he protested.

"He has a right to see his aunt married," Cissy replied serenely. She had dressed the baby in a long, embroidered sacque of white mull with a pale blue ribbon sash. Potter had a satin cushion on which to carry him, but the child's father was not pleased.

"What if he fusses?" Potter asked nervously. "You'll be at the front with Ida."

"Mrs. Worthington will be watching and will come get him," Cissy replied. "And I'll join you the minute the ceremony is over. Remember how brief the actual ceremony is, Potter."

He shook his head and picked up the cushion and baby, but his grip looked awkward to Cissy and she put a hand over her mouth to keep from giggling. As it turned out, Honoré slept during the whole ceremony, and afterward Potter gloried in the profuse praise given his skill as a parent.

The wedding had enough of a military atmosphere about it that Cissy was sure the president was pleased. Fred arrived in an open wagon drawn by army mules with bells on their harness. General Phil Sheridan and his staff in full dress uniform followed him. During the ceremony, President Grant stood beside his son, beaming. Cissy cast an occasional furtive glance at him and thought to herself, "That is the president of the United States! In my parents' house!" She liked the way that thought made her feel.

Potter came to her bed that night, as he often did, though she had not expected him because of the lateness of the hour.

"Cissy?" he asked tentatively, and she, by way of welcome, reached her arms out to him. They lay comfortably coiled together, talking of the wedding.

"It was a grand affair," Potter said.

"Your friend Carter Harrison was there. Why does he always show up at our state occasions?"

"Because I do business with him, and so does your father." He paused for just a moment. "I saw you talking quite a bit with him." Then, before she could respond, "Do we have to talk about Carter Harrison?"

She laughed softly. "One more question. How is his wife? He told me at the hotel opening that she was ill, and I always see him alone."

"I don't believe she's doing any better." Potter Palmer had other things on his mind than the health of Sophie Harrison.

"He doesn't act like a worried or grieving man . . . I mean, he isn't forlorn or sad. He . . . he seems to love life."

Palmer murmured, "Uh huh."

"Would you be like that if I were seriously ill?" she asked.

"I'd be devastated," he said and then firmly cut off conversation with a kiss that meant far more than affection.

Some minutes later Cissy felt herself transported by pleasure, a peak of experience beyond what she normally knew with Potter. Briefly, she felt as though she soared beyond their bedroom, beyond the hotel, even beyond the city of Chicago. She knew then that she had conceived her second son, though she dared not tell Potter, who would, of course, be gratified at her pleasure but skeptical of the importance she assigned to it.

As she drifted off to sleep in Potter's arms, Cissy wondered about Ida's wedding-night experience and hoped it was as pleasurable, though she doubted it.

Chapter Nine

Cissy and her sister Ida gave birth days apart, though Cissy had refrained, ever since Ida's pregnancy became known, from making whispered comments to her sister about wedding nights. Since Fred had been called to duty shortly after the wedding, it was clear that Ida had become almost instantly pregnant.

Ida's child was a girl, Julia. Cissy, true to her unspoken prediction, gave birth to another son, Potter Junior, soon to be called "Min" because of his fragile air.

"The Grants will be back any time," Cissy predicted to Potter. "Julia Grant will want to see that grandchild."

After Min's birth, Cissy settled into life at the Palmer House. Some of her time was spent in social engagements—she shopped, she visited with friends for tea, gave dinner parties, attended the opera and theater. But Cissy Palmer also devoted a great deal of time to what she, with a touch of sarcasm, called her "good works."

"Cissy," Potter asked one night, "have you spent any time with Min today?" The child was then about a year old.

She shook her head. "He cries unless he's with Mrs. Worthington. And I've been working on this paper I'm to present."

"What paper? To whom?" Potter Palmer was dumbfounded.

Cissy had deliberately kept this bit of news from her husband. Now she said airily, "Oh, a paper for the Fortnightly Club."

"The Fortnightly Club," he repeated thoughtfully. "Isn't that the thing founded by Kate Newell Doggett, the one who wears her hair so short? I've heard her opinions are quite radical."

"It's a literary club," Cissy said calmly. "I'll go see Min right now." She rose from the desk where she'd been seated.

"Wait," he said, waving a hand in the air. "What's your paper about?"

"It's titled 'The Obligations of Wealth,'" she said over her shoulder as she disappeared from the room.

And just what book, Potter wanted to ask, is that from? He'd heard that the Fortnightly Club did much more than read books. They discussed social issues such as education, aid to the poor and the like, all things he thought were men's business that women should not concern themselves with. But until that night, he had no idea Cissy had joined the organization. He was not pleased, but he would not say that to Cissy.

She had worked long and hard over this paper, figuring out her own belief as she wrote. If one was as blessed as she, then one had an obligation to share one's wealth—and energy—for the benefit of those less blessed. Laboriously recalling her convent training and looking up relevant passages in the Bible, Cissy strove to prove her argument in theological terms. Little did she realize that she was simply putting into words a philosophy that had seen its first flowering in her the night of the mass exodus from the Great Fire. Harry Collins and his family were proof of her conviction.

Potter was tolerant of this activity, although not totally in agreement with Cissy's philosophy about the obligations they bore. He teased her gently: "I gave a hundred thousand dollars to the YMCA," he said. "Have I satisfied my obligation?" He had, indeed, been generous since his finances had once again recovered from the national panic.

"Not forever," she told him.

"You're not going to cut your hair short or start protesting for the vote, are you?" he asked nervously when she expressed ideas he thought too liberal, such as the importance of working to end child labor in the factories. Potter would have given money for the funeral of a child who died in a factory fire, but it wouldn't have occurred to him to change the child-labor system.

"No, but I do think women should be paid as much as men if they do the same work," she replied.

Potter Palmer shuddered inwardly, because he was afraid one day he and Cissy would come to a philosophical difference they could not easily solve . . . and he knew his wife would not bend. Whether or not he would, he was not prepared to say. Surely charitable obligations could not become the breaking point in a wealthy and successful marriage.

In spite of her many activities, Cissy did spend much of each day with her sons, reading to them, encouraging their first attempts at play, seeing that they learned manners early. Both well behaved, the boys had the run of the Palmer House at an early age, for they were the pets of the entire staff. Honoré, the more outgoing of the two boys, was by the age of three standing at the great front doors of the hotel, greeting guests in the manner he'd seen in his father, his hand solemnly extended. Following the fashion of the day, when he greeted guests Honoré wore a Little Lord Fauntleroy suit of velvet. Both Cissy and Potter were very proud of him.

* * *

Sophie Harrison died in the early spring of 1876. Cissy read a notice in the morning paper that the funeral would be at First Methodist Church in two days. "Will you go?" she asked Potter.

"Of course," he replied. "I must, even though Harrison and I are more likely to be at odds than joined on any one cause. But you've no need to attend."

"I want to," she said slowly. "I like him. He's brash, but he loves Chicago. I enjoy seeing him at various receptions and the like."

Potter frowned but said nothing. He had made it clear to Cissy that while he admired much about Harrison, he was not personally fond of the man

At the funeral, Cissy raised her voice with the others in singing, "How Great Thou Art." Next to her, Potter sat silent. He never sang the hymns, self-conscious about his aging and cracking voice, but Cissy thought it proper for a person to mouth the words when not singing. She had never, however, ventured this opinion to Potter.

At the reception following the service, Cissy stood for a moment, watching Harrison greet visitors. He looked, she decided, tired and sad. Then she realized that the unthinking part of her expected this man always to be happy and gregarious, because that was the face he put on for the world.

Harrison's children cowered in a corner, protected by a woman Cissy thought was probably their aunt. There was a young man who looked to be about sixteen and who was trying hard to be stoic, another boy about eight or nine, and a young girl of only three or four years old. The aunt frequently picked up the sobbing young girl and held her in her arms. Cissy had to suppress a fleeting thought of her boys without her if something happened to her and Potter. And then she wondered how Carter Harrison was as a father. She had never before seen him in public with his children, which now struck her as odd.

When she went through the line, he said, "Thank you for coming," and his voice was more subdued than she had ever heard it. "I am truly grateful. I wish you'd met Sophie. She was a wonderful woman." He held her hand clasped in both of his for a fraction of a minute too long.

"I'm sure she was. I . . . I am truly sorry for your loss."

He nodded, and she moved on to make way for others behind her to greet the bereaved husband. As she turned away from

Harrison, she spotted Harry Collins across the room and smiled at him. He glared back.

"Potter," she asked softly, "is something wrong with Harry Collins?"

Potter followed her eyes across the room and saw the still-glaring Collins. "He's gotten worse. He was never an ideal employee, and I regret hiring him. But every day he gets worse, surly, rude . . . I don't know how much longer I can keep him on at the hotel, the way his attitude is." Potter had never told Cissy that hiring Collins had been his way of telling Cissy he admired her charitable gesture toward the family.

Cissy thought about Sheila and Juliet and wondered if they were also suffering from this surly change of attitude.

When she saw an opportunity to speak privately with Harrison, she excused herself quietly from the knot of people in which she was entwined and made her way to his side.

"I . . . well, I said it before, but thank you for coming," he said.

"I have missed you lately," she said honestly, "and Potter told me it was because of your wife's illness that we hadn't seen you at any gatherings."

"That's part of it," he said ruefully, "but I've been out of favor, you know . . . I guess the saying is 'out of office, out of favor.'" Harrison had been defeated when he ran for re-election to the legislature. Privately, he was philosophical about it. He wanted to work toward being elected mayor of Chicago. She laughed lightly. "I can hardly believe that. Everyone in Chicago knows you're the city's biggest booster. You should be included in everything."

"Thank you," he said and was about to add more when Harry Collins barged up.

"They'll get you every time, Harrison," he said, his voice loud and strident. "No matter what you do, the sons a bitches will get you."

Harrison looked blankly at him and finally said, "I . . . I don't know what you mean, Harry."

"Well, man, your wife's death. I mean, if it ain't one thing, it's another. And them big businessmen—begging your pardon, Mrs. Palmer—they'll do whatever they have to."

Cissy noticed how the man's language had deteriorated. He had once spoken in a proper, educated way, but now he sounded like a factory worker, an angry factory worker. No wonder Potter was distressed to have him in the hotel lobby.

Cissy resisted the urge to ask Collins if that meant that big businessmen, her husband included, had caused Sophie Harrison's death. She saw the absurdity of his argument, but she was afraid of inciting him further. She wondered if the man had suffered some sort of mental breakdown.

Harrison threw a long look at Cissy as though asking for her help. Finally, he said, "I appreciate your sympathy, Collins. It's good to know that my old friends care about me . . . and about my wife."

Cissy bet that Harry Collins had never met Sophie Harrison.

Collins confirmed her suspicion. "Never met her," he said brusquely. "You was grown too fancy by the time I came to town. But I know, nonetheless, what you're up against, and I'll do what I can to help."

"Thank you," Harrison murmured, and this time the look he gave Cissy was frantic, seeming to ask, "What will he do next?"

To their relief, Harry Collins moved on. He said neither good-byes nor final words of condolence. Instead, he just left the conversation hanging in midair and disappeared. Cissy and Harrison stared after him.

"Could you . . ." Harrison's voice was tentative. He knew he was asking for the forbidden. "Could you walk out in the courtyard with me?" The church courtyard adjoined Fellowship Hall, and although it was cool that day, the freshness of the air was tempting. Tired to death of people fawning over him, Harrison appreciated the straightforwardness with which Cissy Palmer faced him and his loss.

She looked around quickly and saw Potter deep in talk with some bankers. "Yes, surely," she said, and then added, "for a moment." Potter, she knew, would frown.

"I won't keep you long," he promised, offering his arm in an almost formal manner.

As she took his arm, Cissy told herself there was nothing wrong in offering comfort to a grieving widower. But she knew she was fooling herself. Even in grief, something about Carter Harrison fascinated her.

Nor did Carter Harrison fool himself. Sophie had been ill a long time, and he'd done his grieving long ago, though now he put on a good public show. He would never tell Cissy, but he just wanted to enjoy her company for a few minutes.

"I just need," he said, as they began to walk the paths of the courtyard, "a woman's point of view. Sophie, she never talked to me much about how women feel." He was dissembling to keep her with him, but he felt not one bit of guilt.

"Oh, we don't feel that much differently than men," she said, and regretted it instantly. She and Potter were polar opposites in their approach to life.

"I know I shouldn't be talking about meeting someone else when Sophie is not yet cold in the ground . . . and yet, I can't bear the thought of living alone the rest of my life."

She was emboldened. "You won't have to. You're an attractive and vital man. There will be many women anxious to share your life. And your children need a mother." Then she was amazed at herself for having been so forthright. "Potter," she said. "Potter will be looking for me. We must return."

"Of course," he said, again offering his arm. "And thank you." To himself, he was savoring the words "attractive" and "vital."

Potter spotted them immediately when they entered Fellowship Hall. He came toward her, bowed politely, and said, "Cissy, I've been looking for you."

"Mr. Harrison asked me to walk out with him"—what an unfortunate choice of words, with its implication of courtship!—"for the fresh air," she said smoothly, and then, more softly, "I was trying to offer my condolences."

"I'm sure they were appreciated," Potter said urbanely, "and I hope, Harrison, that you will accept my condolences along with those of my wife."

"Of course, Palmer," the bereaved husband said quietly. "I am grateful to both of you for your support." He kept himself from looking at Cissy.

As they rode home in their carriage, Potter said bluntly, "The man is infatuated with you . . . even with his wife newly in the ground."

"Nonsense," she replied. "He is devastated at having lost his wife, and I was trying to be of comfort. I doubt any of us can understand the depth of his grief."

"Or the shallowness," Potter replied nastily. Then his tone softened, "I'm sorry, Cissy. I just get so damned mad when I see other men fawning over you in public."

"Then," she said, "you should go in public with me more often."

They said nothing more until the carriage pulled into the porte cochère at the ladies' entrance to the hotel.

* * *

Harry Collins stopped at the pub before he went home after the funeral, and he was in a foul mood when he finally stumbled into their shanty.

Sheila's mood was not much better. She had intended to go to Sophie Harrison's funeral with Harry, and she'd told him that. He'd promised to come get her before the service, and she'd gotten off early from the café, arranged for a neighbor to keep Juliet, and dressed in her very best. Now, hours later, she was back in her wrapper, Juliet was asleep in her own bed, and the dinner she'd fixed Harry had congealed on the stove.

"And where have you been?" she demanded.

"I don't have to report to you," he said angrily. "I went to the funeral."

"Without me!"

"You could've gone yourself. Besides, I think you're too fond of Harrison. He'll be wanting you to take his wife's place, if you catch my drift."

Sheila raised a hand to slap him, but even drunk Harry was too fast for her. "You'll not be hitting me," he said, pushing her backward until she fell against the door he'd left open. She'd have a black eye in the morning, she knew. And besides, the neighbors had all heard the commotion, though not as many were listening as she suspected.

Sheila Collins retreated to bed. Lying there, trying to muffle her sobs, she heard Harry banging in the kitchen. Finally, she heard him exclaim, "Slop! That's what it is, slop!" And then he came to bed. When he tried to approach her, she knocked him away with her fist, and he was too drunk to protest. Within seconds, he was snoring loudly.

Potter Palmer gave Collins his notice the next day, without explanation except that his presence in the hotel lobby was "no longer satisfactory."

Collins went straight to the pub, where he downed three pints and began to rant about Palmer's lack of gratitude for all he'd done for him.

"I'd have thought," muttered one of the men, "that it was the other way around."

When Harry went home that night, he blamed it all on Sheila. "Your fine friend," he mumbled in anger, "fired me. Said I no longer behaved appropriately for the lobby of his damn fine hotel."

Sheila tried to control her temper. "Perhaps because you drink so much you're angry all the time," she said.

Harry Collins found work with the railroads. He joined The Brotherhood of Locomotive Engineers, even though his job, much more lowly, was to load boxcars with wheat.

* * *

Cissy was in the apartment on July 2, unaware that news of the massacre at Little Big Horn had reached the city. The desk called to announce Mrs. Grant, and Cissy went to the elevator to greet her sister. But Ida's distraught appearance took her back for a moment. Ida carried little Julia in her arms, and the child was howling. Ida's eyes were wild with fright, and her color was pale enough to alarm Cissy.

"Ida, what's the matter? Here, give me the baby." She took the infant and began to whisper softly to it, trying to calm her.

Ida led the way into the parlor and stood staring out at the lake, which this day was sparkling, bright blue. "General Custer," she blurted out. "He's been killed. And all the men that were with him. Nearly two hundred."

Cissy sank onto a sofa, still clutching Julia. "Killed," she repeated dully. "Indians?" She asked the question she dreaded, for Fred was on scout in the West again. "Fred?"

Ida shook her head. "I don't know. I think he was on the *Far West* with General Terry, but I can't be sure. He might have gone ahead and joined Custer. Cissy, I'm scared . . . I'm so scared." She began to sob.

Cissy tried her best to comfort Ida while holding Julia. Finally, she rang for tea, and the two women sat in silence for more than an hour.

Potter came in, having heard the news of the battle on the ticker in the hotel lobby. "Ida! Are you all right? Fred wasn't with Custer, was he?" He looked at his wife and sister-in-law with horror written on his face.

She shook her head. "I don't think so, but I can't be sure."

"I'll get in touch with Sheridan," Potter said decisively. As always, he was sure he could solve whatever problem was at hand.

Wires flew across the country as news spread of what became known as "Custer's Last Stand." But it was two days before Ida had confirmation that Fred was alive and safe.

"Now I want him to leave the army," she told Cissy. "I can't go through that again."

For Cissy, the Indian Wars were so remote she could barely comprehend them. But Ida's fright had been too close and too real.

The railroad riots, on the other hand, were close to home. They began in Chicago in June 1877, and Harry Collins was in the midst of them. Workers protested their living conditions: families lived in cellars and drank infested water, and children became ill in great numbers. These poverty-stricken workers were drawn to the Workingman's Party, which urged workers to unite on the idea that workmen should rule. "The working man made this country, and what a man makes belongs to him," exhorted one speaker.

The riots actually began in West Virginia, but they swept across the country with a frightening urgency that alarmed civic leaders. Railroad workers were among the poorest paid in the country, and their work was dangerous—two hundred workers died each year and as many as thirty thousand were injured. Management called these accidents "acts of God," attributable to worker carelessness. Workers targeted reduced work forces, which required men to work with inadequate sleep and rest.

In Chicago, rioters closed down packinghouses, lumberyards, rolling mills, and foundries. They attacked strikebreakers, set fire to railroad property, and fought pitched battles with police, local militia, and federal troops. Wives of railroad workers formed an army of their own, brandishing clubs and stoning police who tried to disperse them. Finally, they retreated in the face of gunfire.

The city closed its saloons and pubs, sent for federal troops, and rang the fire bells to summon militia. In the newspapers, it was called the "Battle of Chicago" and dire predictions of "Mob Rule" frightened respectable citizens.

"Cissy," Palmer said in his most commanding tone of voice, "you and the boys will not venture from this hotel until I say it is safe."

"My family," she protested.

"I trust that your family is safe, and I'll do what I can to be sure of that. But you will not leave. Marsh Field has organized a neighborhood vigilante group on Prairie Avenue to sure the rioters don't try to loot the homes of those of us they resent."

The next day Potter brought word that no neighborhoods had been attacked and her family was safe. Cissy sighed in relief but fretted at what was happening to her city.

Predictably, gunfire ended the crisis. In Chicago, thirty workers were killed, another two hundred wounded. Nationally, a hundred people were killed, a thousand or more went to jail, and half the nation's railroads stopped running. The railroads took back some wage cuts and made other concessions, but the working people were not satisfied.

Harry Collins was among the wounded, though his was a superficial bullet graze to his arm and Sheila treated it at home. Collins had been so busy protesting and rioting in the streets that he had not been drinking.

"Thank you," he said, as she bound up his arm. "I'm beholden to you, Sheila, as always."

She bit her tongue to keep from saying she wished he would realize it more.

"The railroads—the sons of bitches—they're lettin' us die of starvation, while they make millions for their owners."

Sheila sighed. "It's true, Harry, the owners are gettin' rich. But look at it this way, you have a paycheck—or did until now—and we can feed Juliet. It could be a lot worse."

"It isn't right," he muttered.

Across town Cissy Palmer was having a very different discussion with her husband. "Don't these riots mean that the city fathers need to listen to the workers?"

Startled, Potter asked, "Listen to them? Why?"

"Because they aren't being paid living wages, and if that continues the riots are going to happen again and again."

"Cissy," he said patiently and a little paternalistically, "the workers have got to learn their place. They need to do their jobs, accept their wages, and live their lives."

"But, Potter, they don't live like we do."

"Not everyone can expect to live this way," he said haughtily.

The Potter Palmers did not share a bed for several nights after that discussion.

* * *

As the boys grew older, Grandpapá Honoré became concerned about their sheltered existence. "What those boys need," he scoffed one day when he stopped at the hotel, "is to run barefoot in the grass and feel mud between their toes."

Cissy remembered running barefoot in the grass as a child, of course, but she had never much liked the mud and she could not see that the experience had anything to do with developing her character. She simply smiled at her father and said, "It's winter."

"I tell you, Potter, it's not natural for boys to grow up in a hotel." Henry Honoré sipped brandy in his son-in-law's sitting room, while Potter enjoyed a cigar.

"They're fine boys," Potter said defensively, "and they have the run of the hotel. Besides, you take them home with you every time I turn around, and Mrs. Worthington takes them to the park."

"Mrs. Worthington takes them to the park!" the elder man mimicked. "Yes, and makes them walk next to her and stay on the pathway. They need freedom, Potter. They need to be boys." He was silent a long while and then, finally, said what had been on his mind for six months or a year. "You need to build your family a home."

"We have a home," Potter responded mildly, "have had for five years now. We like living here." The men were not far apart in age, so it was not a question of Potter Palmer respecting his elder. But he did respect Henry Honoré as his father-in-law and as a man of uncommon good sense.

"I won't intrude on your family," Honoré said, "but I can't help but make my opinion known. You give me those boys for the summer, and I'll show you new lads—fatter, healthier color, livelier." He waved his hand as though dismissing the thought. "I know,

I know. My daughter would never 'give' her sons to anyone else. It was just an example."

"I'll think about it," Potter promised. "I always intended, of course, to build a house. I just hadn't thought about it so soon."

"Well, if you'll think about it, I'll be quiet from now on," the other man promised.

They sat a long while in companionable silence.

Potter Palmer was accustomed to discussing his business affairs with his wife. He used to say, with a laugh, that she could run the hotel as well as he, for when he came upstairs at night he told her the day's problems—an unhappy guest, a difficult staff member, supplies that did not arrive on time. She asked intelligent questions and made even brighter suggestions, though Potter found she tended to be even more demanding on staff than he himself was. But, as a man who conferred with many business associates but confided in none, Potter found his wife invaluable as a confidante and supporter.

Strangely, though, he never reported to her his conversation with her father, nor did he involve her in his thinking about a house. Potter himself was uncertain as to why he didn't confide in Cissy. It could be, he thought, that she is so pleased to be here, in the center of things, that I am afraid she will be reluctant to move. Or, and he realized this with a sudden start, it could be that I simply want to provide a home for my family myself.

Cissy Palmer, who believed women should not be denied the right to better themselves in the workplace, no doubt also believed that women should have an equal voice in choosing and planning a home. And Potter Palmer, some twenty-plus years older and of another generation, believed that a man should provide for his family and a woman should receive.

He never made it a conscious decision, but he knew he would present Cissy with the house as a *fait accompli*. It almost worked out that way, but not quite.

"You're preoccupied tonight," she said, while they lingered over after-dinner coffee, port for him and Madeira for her.

"No, no. It's nothing. Just some business downstairs." "Downstairs" was how he always referred to the hotel in their conversations.

"What is it? Usually you tell me what's bothering you."

"Oh," he waved a hand, "it's nothing. Come, tell me what the boys did today."

Several evenings followed this pattern, but Potter Palmer kept his counsel, and Cissy wondered what was on his mind. Where some wives would have suspected a mistress and gone on guard, even attack, Cissy was not one to borrow trouble. She simply shrugged off Potter's preoccupation and assumed that sooner or later she would know the cause.

She found out on a spring night in 1880.

"I've started work on the land where we'll build," Potter said at dinner without any preliminaries.

"Pardon me?" Cissy took a quick swallow of water. "What did you say?"

"I've started work on the land where we'll build . . . on the north shore."

"The north shore!" The words exploded from Cissy with more force than she intended, and she rushed on without stopping. "It's all sand dunes and stagnant water, a wasteland. The only thing it's good for is to let young boys hunt mallards and canvasbacks. Potter, that's the bleakest land in the whole city. Why there?"

He stared at his wife in amazement. Never had he seen her so vociferous, so indifferent to the manners the nuns had carefully drilled into her. When he spoke, after some time, his voice was almost frosty. "Because I own the land. I got it some time ago, and I intend to develop it—starting with our house." His tone brooked no disagreement, and he closed the subject by saying, "Excuse me. I believe I'll take my brandy in my sitting room." Afterward, he realized he could have added a barbed comment about the fact that though the land might be suited to young boys hunting mallards and canvasbacks, she would never allow her sons to do such.

Stunned, both by her husband's announcement and his anger, Cissy sat unmoving at the dining table for a long time before she rang for the table to be cleared. Then she went slowly to kiss her boys goodnight and sit, thinking, in her own darkened sitting room.

She realized that she had acted badly. Potter was less angry than he was hurt, because she had scorned his idea instead of praising his provision for his family. Eliza Honoré would never have reacted that way, and her oldest daughter knew it. Ruefully, she remembered her own words to Ida about doing what brought pleasure to your husband. The advice applied, she realized, out of the bedroom as well as in it.

When the servants had retired, Mrs. Worthington was safely snoring, and the boys dreaming of whatever hotel-raised children dream, Cissy did an unprecedented thing. She left her own room and walked silently through the darkened suite to Potter's bedroom where, without a word, she disrobed and slid beneath the covers.

Potter lay tense and awake, and it was Cissy who made the first wordless advance. After a few minutes, he turned toward her and took her in his arms with only a muttered, "Cissy."

Afterward, as she left him for the night, she said, "I'll like living by the water. I like watching the lake."

To herself, she was grateful that there had been no transporting moment of passion. She did not want another child now.

The next day Cissy ordered Golden Lady hitched to the small carriage. When the doorman inquired solicitously if Herman was not driving her, she said lightly, "Oh, I'm just going up Michigan Avenue to my family home. I'll enjoy driving myself."

She headed the carriage north on Michigan but once across the river, she veered to the east, following dirt paths until she came to a spot where she could see the lake. There were no buildings in sight, only a few stunted willows and a pool of dirty water. The wind swept across the bleak, low-lying land, and she held one hand to her hat to keep it firmly in place. The wind, she knew, would always blow off the lake like this.

She saw what she had come to see: a scow was anchored off-shore and pumps were sucking sand from the lake bottom and throwing it by shovels on the shore. This was to be her home.

Cissy breathed deeply, taking in the familiar smell of the lake—fresh and watery but always slightly fishy. Just one element of the smell that defined Chicago.

"It will be fine," she said aloud, "just fine."

In the coming weeks, fellow businessmen scoffed at Palmer for building so far north—a mile beyond the river—and on the swampy wasteland. Unknowingly, they echoed the sentiments that Cissy had given voice to but now silenced forever.

"You've gone too far, this time," Henry Honoré cautioned. "I fear you'll take a bad beating financially."

Potter Palmer thanked him for his concern and proceeded with his plans.

"Who's designing the house?" Honoré asked.

"Two new young architects—Henry Ives Cobb and Charles S. Frost."

"And what kind of plans have they shown you?" The older man pushed.

Palmer shrugged. "It will be three-story," he said, "but beyond that . . . I'll just surprise you." He didn't add that it would cost ninety thousand dollars.

"I suppose you'll surprise your wife, too."

Palmer answered that by changing the subject. "They've begun work on the roadway. It'll be called Lake Shore Drive. Several men have come to me about buying lots. You'll never blast McCormick off Prairie Avenue, but others have admitted that they think it's a delightful location."

"Are you going to sell?" Honoré asked.

"Only to those I choose to," was the reply. "If you want a lot, you may have it."

Honoré chuckled. "I'm afraid the neighborhood will be too rich for my blood. We'll stay on Michigan Avenue."

Chicago's Gold Coast was born with the building of Lake Shore Drive and christened when Potter Palmer decided to build there.

* * *

Cissy reluctantly accompanied Potter to the grand opening of George Pullman's model town. "Each time I see either of them," she said privately, "I like them less. He's vain, and he always seems determined to get his way. And Harriett is smug about how wonderful his accomplishments are."

Potter smiled wryly, "He's an important man in this city. You can't really blame him if he's a little pompous." That was as close as he would come to admitting that Pullman was cold, a loner who cared for no one else.

"See!" she triumphed. "You do think he's pompous. Potter, you're an important man in this city, and if you were that pompous about it, I'd . . . I'd . . ."

"You'd what?" he asked, laughing.

"I'd bob my hair and wear bloomers," she retorted.

They took the train, the White City Express it was called, along with a small select group—the Swifts, the Fields, with Nannie present for once, the Medills, and a few others who Pullman had invited for the opening ceremonies. The train pulled into a small station on a tree-bordered boulevard. Across from the station was a landscaped park with a lake and a small waterfall. The Pullman Palace Car administration building across the lake was distinguished by a tall clock tower.

George Pullman himself led the group on the tour, pointing out the church, the post office, bank, library, theater, and offices for the *Pullman Journal*. "We can house twelve thousand here," he bragged. "We'll have the greatest schools, a boathouse, track, ice-skating rink, and rowing on the lake. There will be no saloons."

The houses and apartments Pullman showed them were of red brick, with slate roofs—they matched the car works where the men toiled daily. "Running water," Pullman said expansively, "inside toilets, gas street lights, macadam streets—it's a worker's paradise."

"Will the workers be able to buy their houses?" someone asked.

"No, it will all be a lease arrangement. The city will be managed by a town agent of my appointment."

"No elections?" came the query.

"None." Pullman looked annoyed by the question.

The group was escorted back to the hotel, where they were refreshed with sorbet ices and petit fours. Most of them fell all over themselves telling George and Harriet Pullman what a wonderful place they had created.

"We think so," Harriett said, without a trace of modesty, while her husband stood and beamed.

Potter Palmer congratulated Pullman on his ability to plan for the future of his workers, and Cissy added words of praise about the opportunities he was giving to less fortunate people than himself. Pullman beamed again.

On the train back to Chicago, Cissy whispered, "I didn't mean it. He's going to run their lives with an iron fist."

Potter sighed. "I think you're right, Cissy. If anyone disagrees with him, his lease will be cancelled immediately. And Lord helps anyone who even thinks of joining a union. I wouldn't be surprised if his factory superintendents were . . . well . . . eavesdroppers." For Potter, who was always on the side of management, this was a big step in defending workers.

"No elections," Cissy said, her voice rising. "Can you imagine that?"

"Shhh," Potter cautioned, looking around the train. "He has many friends in this group."

"Or many who pretend to be," she said. "You know, I feel sorry for the people of Packingtown. Sometimes I worry about them. But they have much more freedom than George Pullman's employees."

Packingtown was the stockyards district, sometimes called "Back of the Yards," where employees of the Swift and Armour meatpacking plants congregated. The families were poor, but most heads of the household had a job. It was the kind of work they did that made it a depressed area. The men of Packingtown dealt in death and violence every day . . . and they brought the smell home with them on their clothes. The smell of death and animals and feces always hung over the community. There were more saloons than houses, in contrast to Pullman's pristine town.

"The only thing to do about Packingtown," Potter replied, "is to tear it down and start over again."

"I think I'd like to have a tour of it," Cissy said. "I want to see how those people live and figure out what we can do about it."

"Nothing, Cissy," Potter said firmly. "I don't want you in Packingtown. And you can't do anything for those people."

He looked stern, but Cissy kept her own counsel. They were soon at the downtown Illinois Central station, where Herman waited to whisk them back to the luxury of their apartment on the top floor of the Palmer House.

Palmer's Castle and
Labor Troubles in Chicago

Chapter Ten

"Good morning," Cissy said. "Is Mr. Harrison available?"

"I'm sure he's busy. I'll see how soon he might be available," the receptionist replied somewhat haughtily.

"Thank you," Cissy said, seating herself on a straight wooden chair and taking note of the plainness of the office furnishings. Harrison's law certificate hung on the wall, next to a calendar advertising Montgomery Ward's mail-order house.

"I'm available right now," Carter Harrison roared, striding out of his office. "Mrs. Palmer, how nice to see you. Come into my office." He stood aside for her to precede him.

When they were seated—Harrison at a scarred and battered rolltop desk, his chair turned toward Cissy, and Cissy in another plain wooden chair—he asked, "To what do I owe this unexpected pleasure?" Pray God, he thought, she's after a divorce, but he knew that was impossible.

"I've been to Pullmantown," she began.

"Ah yes, the guided tour. I was not on the guest list and wasn't very disappointed," he said, laughing.

He was about to make her laugh again. "You'd have found it instructive," she said. "Mr. Pullman has built himself quite a kingdom."

"So I've heard, so I've heard."

"I want you to take me through Packingtown," she said bluntly.

"Packingtown?" he echoed. "Oh now, Mrs. Palmer, you don't want to go there. It's not a place for the likes of you."

"I just want to see it, and with you as my escort I'll be perfectly safe." She paused. "I do not want Mr. Palmer to know of this, of course."

"Of course," he replied, his eyes dancing with laughter. "When would you like to take this trip?"

"Is now convenient?"

Carter Harrison would have dropped anything for this woman, but unfortunately he didn't even have enough legal work to pretend that an immediate excursion would be a hardship. "Now," he said carefully, "would be fine."

He had ridden Kate to town that morning, so he borrowed a horse and carriage, and they were soon on their way. Harrison turned north toward the river and then west along the river before turning south.

Cissy realized he had gone the long way around to avoid going near the hotel.

"I hear you're building a house," he said conversationally.

"Potter is building a house," she said archly. "On the North Shore."

"Been under construction a while, hasn't it?"

"Over a year," she said, "but I'm in no hurry to move. I enjoy the hotel and the closeness to downtown."

"The ladies' half mile?" he speculated.

She smiled. "Yes, especially Field's."

Cissy smelled Packingtown before she saw it. The stench was so overwhelming that she took out her lace-trimmed handkerchief and held it to her nose, wishing she'd thought to douse it in cologne as her mother used to do.

"Put that away," Harrison said mildly.

"What?" Cissy could not believe she had heard correctly. She didn't like Potter telling her what to do, and she certainly wasn't going to follow orders from Carter Harrison.

"Put it away," he repeated. "It makes you look prissy. These people live with that smell day in and day out. You can stand it for half an hour."

The stench was worse when they passed the Stone Gate, the main entry to the Stock Yards. Three limestone arches formed the gate, with a bull carved over the central arch.

Cissy would never know that she was smelling what Potter smelled when he first set foot in Chicago. Sewage ran in open ditches. She saw a dead dog in a ditch and, further on, two dead cats. Women in long faded dresses sat on the steps of small wooden houses, children playing at their feet. The children too wore long clothing, even long sleeves.

"It's summer," she said. "Children should be wearing play clothes."

"They're trying to keep the mosquitoes from biting them," Harrison said. "They come from Bubbly Creek."

"Bubbly Creek? That's a nice name for a river."

"It's not a nice river," he said tersely. "It's an arm of the Chicago that goes nowhere, and decaying garbage bubbles to its surface. In summer these people roast because they have to close windows and doors to keep mosquitoes and flies out. In winter they freeze. There's no way to heat these shanties."

The air was hazy with smoke from the plants and the trains that took away their produce. "Too many children are killed or injured at these railroad crossings," Harrison said as they drove across a set of tracks. "They're totally unprotected."

They passed a saloon and could hear loud voices, even in the middle of the day. "The night shift is in there," Harrison explained.

"What do these people do for . . . well, relaxation."

"Mostly they don't. They just try to survive. Oh, there's some horse racing and dog racing. And the saloons do a big business."

"It almost make you support the temperance movement," Cissy mused, "to think that men whose families live in such poverty spend their money on drink."

"They're not all that poor," Harrison said. "Almost all the men are employed, and I suspect they make more than Pullman's rail car employees. But it's a totally different kind of work. Demoralizing. Depressing. They never get the blood and the smell out of their skin, out from under their fingernails. And they bring it home with them. It's not poverty. It's hopelessness."

Cissy was silent. She had no reply.

"You interested in statistics?" Harrison asked.

"Of course."

"The packing plants employ twenty-four thousand men, women, and children . . . ."

"Children!" she exclaimed. "Whatever do the children do?"

He shrugged. "Whatever needs to be done that they can manage. They slaughter fourteen million animals here a year."

"There aren't enough people in Chicago to eat that much pork."

Harrison chuckled. "It is mostly pork," he conceded, "but there is some beef, and there are always chickens. Since Mr. Swift developed his refrigerated railroad car, they can ship meat east without any danger of spoiling."

As they left Packingtown, they passed the drying field, where hides were put out to cure. Flies swarmed over the area and attacked Cissy and Harrison. Cissy, batting them from her face, was horrified.

"See why they wear long sleeves?" Harrison asked mildly.

Cissy was silent on the ride back to downtown. At long last, she said, "If you were mayor, what would you do with Packingtown?"

"If I had a magic wand? I'd tear it down. No one will ever be able to improve it."

"That's just what Potter said," Cissy murmured.

Carter Harrison wanted to escort her back to the hotel, but Cissy insisted on walking. She knew Potter would be displeased if she showed up with Harrison, but more than that she wanted to think. She also desperately wanted to bathe and wash her hair and throw away the walking suit she wore. She was afraid the smell would haunt her forever.

* * *

The Palmers moved into the finished mansion in 1884. Built of Wisconsin granite, it had facings of contrasting Ohio sandstone, which created a striped effect.

"The appearance will soften with time," the architects assured an unhappy Cissy Palmer. "We'll plant English ivy."

Cissy couldn't believe ivy would do much to tame the structure's wild appearance. She never told anyone—certainly not Potter—that she was overwhelmed and uncertain about the mansion. She'd heard from her father, on the promise of absolute confidentiality, that people were calling it "Palmer's Castle" and laughing over whether it was early English battlement style, castellated Gothic, or Norman Gothic. What captured everyone's attention was the four-story tower that rose eighty feet above the ground and ended in a turret, towering over the smaller turrets at the corners of the house.

"They think he's flaunting his money, don't they?" she asked her father.

"Now, Bertha, don't you worry about that. Man makes as much money has Potter has, he's got a right to build whatever he wants." But then he chuckled. "That tower sure is something. One fellow said to me it looks like they're gonna fight a battle and throw boiling grease over the edge."

"That's not funny," Cissy said. "Well, at least the boys have the room to run and play as you always said they should. They've got trees to climb and grass to run barefoot in."

"True, if they don't get lost in the house," her father replied.

"That's not funny either, Papá." She was thoughtful a minute. "It's a jumble of styles, as though Potter put every style in it that had ever interested him—the drawing room is French, the music room Spanish, the dining room English, the library Flemish

Renaissance. And those Gobelin tapestries—they're too much, too big."

"Potter says Gobelin was the greatest tapestry-maker ever," her father reminded her.

Cissy just sighed.

The day they moved in, Honoré looked at her and asked, "Why do we need so big a house, Mamá?"

"Because, my darling, we're going to give grand parties and fill the house with lots of people." It was the only justification she could think of.

"My room is too far from yours," Min said gently. "I'll be lonely in the night."

"I'll tuck you in every night, and you'll have Mrs. Worthington sleeping right next door to you. You'll be fine, Min."

The frail child clutched her hand all the tighter and looked up at her with some doubt.

To Potter that night, Cissy said, "I'm the luckiest woman alive. Potter, we'll raise our children and grow old together in this magnificent house. And thank you for putting my bedroom at the front of the house, where I can look at the lake."

"I'm glad you like it," he said and experienced real relief. He was the king in his castle, unaware of the jokes going around town using that very word.

"Potter," she said, "I need my own keys to the house. I come and go at different times than you do, and—"

"Cissy, have you not noticed? There are neither doorknobs nor locks on the outside of the house. You don't need keys."

"No doorknobs?" she echoed. "How will I get in?"

"There will always be servants to let you in," he said smoothly. "I planned the entire house that way."

Servants to let me into my own house, she thought, and keep track of my comings and goings. I can never on a whim go anywhere . . . or come home, without the entire household knowing. "Potter, is this a security measure? For safety?"

He shrugged. "Only in part. I think it fitting that we always have servants waiting on us."

Cissy felt trapped in her own keyless home, amazed at the irony in the fact that the grandest home in all of Chicago had no locks and no keys—and no doorknobs.

* * *

"Now, Mrs. Stripling, you will have complete authority over the staff," Cissy said to the older, rather stern-looking woman. "I will consult with you about menus, but I expect you to deal with the staff and to tell me when linens and such are needed. There are quarters on the third floor for you and the maids. The maids are to have one day off a week. You decide everything else."

"Yes, ma'am," Mrs. Stripling said. "I'm looking forward to the challenge. It's . . . it's an unusual home, and I'll make sure it runs smooth enough to equal its beautiful appearance."

Cissy looked at her a long minute but said nothing.

A few days later, as she sailed through the grand entry on her way to an appointment, Cissy noticed a young maid sitting quietly on a bench near the front door.

"Are your duties all done?" she asked.

"Yes, ma'am. I dusted everything in the entry." The young woman rose to her feet and almost made a curtsey.

"And that's your assignment?"

"That and answering the front door, should anyone ring."

The girl was young—maybe twenty—and blonde, probably one of the recent immigrants from the Scandinavian countries. Cissy detected an accent to her English.

"Tell me your name," she said to the girl, and was answered with, "I'm Martha, ma'am."

"Fine, Martha, I'm glad to make your acquaintance." She went on to her appointment, but Martha stayed in her mind. In the next few days, she frequently went out of her way to go through the grand entry and greet the girl or at least put her head around the corner to say, "Good morning."

Some days Martha was industriously dusting the furniture, down on her hands and knees to get legs and rungs of the one bench in that hall. Other times she used a mop on a long pole to dust the walls as high as she could reach. But too many days she simply sat on that bench near the door, her expression plainly one of boredom. The doorbell did not often ring, except, of course, when there were parties.

Finally, Cissy spoke to Mrs. Stripling. "Could she not be mending or something while she sits there?"

"Oh, no, ma'am," replied the horrified housekeeper. "How would it look if someone should come to the door and she had needlework in her hands? No, Martha is one of my most trusted workers. That's why I've given her the front door. It's a big responsibility." She drew out the last words for emphasis. "And, of course, she must be available to admit you or the mister, whenever you arrive."

The damn keyless doors, Cissy thought, using a rare cussword in her mind.

Whenever Cissy came home during the day, Martha sprang to open the door and greet her. Cissy was always cordial, and she fancied that Martha appreciated her efforts.

* * *

The 1880s were a period of general prosperity in Chicago and the United States. There were no wars, no natural disasters, and no income tax. It was the decade when skyscrapers began to dominate the landscape, particularly in Chicago. The city's downtown was hemmed in by river, railroads, and lake—the only logical place it could expand was upward. But it took two innovative architects to make that possible.

Daniel Hudson Burnham spent most of his youth in Chicago. He left periodically to follow a variety of unsuccessful careers, finding himself one of those who soon got bored with whatever he was doing. Then in 1873, he went to work as a draftsman—a skill he had long had—for a Chicago architect. In the offices of Peter

Wight, Burnham met John Wellborn Root. The two men clicked immediately, and by 1874 they had their own firm. They would build Chicago's first skyscraper, then defined as a building of ten or more stories.

"Daniel Burnham wants me to build a new hotel, a skyscraper," Potter said one night to Cissy.

She looked up from her book. "Will you?" She wasn't sure how she felt about this idea. She had met Burnham once, briefly, and been impressed by his charm and, yes, his good looks. But architecture and skyscrapers were foreign to her.

"No," Potter replied calmly. "I like the hotel I have. Bigger would be . . . well, less personal."

Skyscrapers, cliff dwellers, and rich men who got richer were only one small part of Chicago. A majority of Chicagoans were laborers, working in McCormick's reaper factory or Pullman's factory or the stockyards. They worked long hours, six days a week, and barely made enough to support their families. Labor unrest plagued Chicago. When Carter Harrison was first elected mayor in 1879, fulfilling his lifetime ambition, the scions of Chicago industry—Potter Palmer, Marshall Field, Joseph Medill, George Pullman, Gustavus Swift, Philip Armour, and others—shook their heads in disbelief and anticipated doom and gloom.

"He is," Potter told Cissy, "too much a friend of the working man. He'll turn the city over to labor, mark my words." And then he added, "And to the Irish."

Harrison was known to have firm ties to the Irish in the city, Chicago's largest ethnic minority and the people who were slowly taking over Palmer's beloved Democratic Party. There were whispered rumors, too, of Harrison's supposed ties to shady activities and places—gambling dens, pubs, and the like. Some even hinted that he was a friend of the prostitutes, though few went that far. Potter, of course, would mention none of that to Cissy.

As if he knew he had been the subject of conversation, Carter Harrison appeared at the Palmer mansion one day, having unsuccessfully looked for Potter Palmer at the hotel. Cissy came down from her sitting room—the White Room, Mrs. Stripling called it, because of its color scheme and delicate French decor—to hear voices in one of the small parlors off the main entry hall.

"I tell you, Potter, it's a different world. Man can't expect to get ahead like he could twenty years ago. Then he went to work for one man, knew his employer. Man worked hard and saved some money; he could go into business for himself, like you did. Today, it takes a fortune to go into business for yourself, and most men work for owners they don't know and never meet."

"I don't care," Potter replied, "a man can still get ahead by hard work. It's what built this country. And we can't have all these foreigners telling us how to run our businesses, how much to pay our workers."

"They're not all foreigners," the other voice said patiently, and Cissy recognized that it belonged to Carter Harrison. "Some of them were born on farms right here—just like you and me—and they believe what you said: a man can get ahead by hard work. Only they see it's not true anymore. The foreigners tend to be more violent in their demands and threats, I'll grant you that, but they're only part of the problem."

Chicago was the American center of socialism and trade unionism, both forces that men like Potter Palmer feared. The Socialist Labor Party, made up mostly of Germans, was active in the city. When a socialist candidate for city office had the election stolen from him in 1880 by ballot stuffing, the party lost faith in the ballot box as a mean of reform. They began to agitate for social revolution. Carter Harrison thought the city had good reason to fear them and sensed that trouble, big trouble, was ahead for Chicago.

"Well," Potter said stubbornly, "the railroad workers struck in '77, and it didn't do them any good. Rest of the city was against them—Field and Leiter even armed employees at the store. And Sheridan finally called in federal troops."

"Killed men unnecessarily and left a lot of men out of work, their families homeless. That's not what I want for my city, Potter.

But I warn you, wages get cut again, there's going to be trouble in this city."

Wearily, Potter said, "But I don't know what I can do about it. I haven't cut wages."

"You have influence," Harrison said. "You can talk to others—talk to Pullman, McCormick, those who employ a lot of men. Try to get them to see the importance of this."

"It's hard to get a man to see another man's needs when his own pocket is threatened," Potter replied.

"More than their pockets will be threatened if they don't listen," Harrison warned him, "and besides, most of them have more money than's decent for one man to have." Immediately, he regretted saying that as he thought of the mansion in which he sat. Harrison considered the Palmer Castle an exercise in bad taste—too much money and not enough sense—but he would never have offended Potter Palmer, especially when he needed his help.

Palmer had indeed taken offense at the quick comment. His response was stiff and formal. "A man's entitled to as much as he can gather honestly."

Cissy, who had been eavesdropping, decided this was a good time to intervene. "Excuse me, gentlemen, I heard voices and wanted to make sure you'd been offered coffee or brandy."

Both men rose to their feet to greet her.

"Thank you, my dear, we have no need of refreshment," Potter said, a clear sign that he was not happy with his visitor.

"I'm just leaving, Mrs. Palmer," Harrison said, "but I appreciate your hospitality. Lovely home you have here." It never hurt, he thought, to lie through your teeth if it made someone feel good and did no harm.

"Well, you must come back often," she said cordially. "I'll excuse myself and let you men finish your discussion."

"We're finished," Potter said shortly.

Later, when she asked about the discussion, Potter dismissed Harrison's fears as alarmist. "He thinks there's going to be more rioting if we don't find a way to deal with the living conditions of working people. I don't see it. I don't think workingmen are any worse off today than they were ten years ago. They can't complain that they don't succeed if they won't help themselves. And don't worry about Harrison, Cissy. He's dedicated to Chicago, but his loyalties are in the wrong places. He's letting the town run wide open. There's no check on gamblers, and they're selling liquor on Sundays. I even hear he's had maps printed that show the . . . uh . . . houses of ill repute." He paused to see if Cissy was appropriately horrified. She wasn't, so he went on, "He won't be elected again. Besides, it's men's business, not something you should worry about." He regretted the last sentence as soon as it left his mouth.

"Men's business!" she said and stalked from the room. But Cissy did not easily nor quickly forget the overheard conversation between her husband and Carter Harrison. Her head told her to listen to Potter, the husband she had promised to obey. But in her heart, she agreed with Carter Harrison, sensing that a city as divided as Chicago could not survive. There seemed no middle ground between the very rich and the very poor. The old saying was right: the rich get richer and the poor get poorer.

* * *

Across town, Harry Collins stood in the bar at O'Malley's Pub, surrounded by men who, like him, wore soiled work clothes. It was the end of the day, and the men had come for a pint on their way home. Most worked for the railroad, and their bodies were tired, their minds numb from twelve hours of hard labor. When Harry Collins began to talk, however, they gathered around.

"It can't go on," Collins said. "We can't be expected to feed our families on the wages these big shots pay. But our day is coming, wait and see. We're going to rise up against the railroad kings and the bankers and all those who grind us under their heels." Subconsciously, Harry Collins was probably rising up against the father who had disowned him.

There were murmurs of agreement, cries of "You're right, Collins," and the like. But one man spoke up and said, "Why are you workin' for the railroad, when you used to have a soft job at that grand hotel? You aren't one of us. You didn't used to talk like us."

He ignored the man. "I live in a shack like you do, my old lady"—he had learned to say that instead of "wife"—"working her hands to the bone in that café and at home. I know what we're up against," he finished ominously.

"What we're up against, me boy," said a jovial voice, "is too much talk and not enough beer. Sammy?" Carter Harrison strode up to the bar and motioned the bartender over. "A round for my friends. On me, of course."

Murmurs of appreciation shot through the crowd, and Harrison began greeting the men individually, calling them by name, asking about their families. "How's that new baby, Gus? Got any teeth yet?" And, to another man, "When's that fine daughter of yours gonna take a husband? I were younger, you'd find me at your door." He joked with them, clapped them on their shoulders, and generally left them with smiles on their faces.

"Collins? I talk to you a minute?" Beer in hand, he approached Harry Collins, his mood now more somber.

Collins shrugged and followed him to a table well away from the crowd.

"Harry, my friend," Harrison said seriously, "you've got to stop trying to stir up trouble. Sounds to me like you been listening to those Germans too much. You're goin' to make the wrong people angry."

"Mr. Palmer?" Harry asked derisively.

"Among others," Harrison agreed. "But take Potter Palmer. He was good to you, man, and his wife's been more than good to your family."

"He gave me the boot," Collins said angrily, "and what Mrs. Palmer does is charity, and that don't count."

"Harry," Harrison said, his tone still somber, "you're barkin' up the wrong tree. And I am warning you, as a friend, to quiet down."

Without replying, Collins rose and stalked away from the table, but he had lost his audience. Their bellies full of beer, they had drifted toward home.

Carter Harrison watched Harry Collins depart and wondered what had gone wrong with the man, where and why he had turned sour. When he first met Collins, he thought he showed promise, really seemed about to rise through the ranks. Carter knew his family background, at least sketchily, after he'd checked on the Collins Woolen Mill. He'd reported to Harry that the mill was in good shape. "Owner must be treating his workers right," he'd said. Harry had sneered and turned away, muttering something he refused to repeat. Carter Harrison could only surmise that Harry Collins was the black sheep of a respectable family. As he uneasily watched him over the years, growing angrier, Harrison thought of contacting the family. He knew he'd never do that.

"Harrison? There's a game in the back. They're holdin' you a seat," Sammy the bartender called.

With a wave, Harrison got up and said, "Can't keep 'em waiting. I'm lucky tonight, feel it in my bones."

* * *

Cissy Palmer, having thought long and hard about Carter Harrison's words with her husband, decided it was not only the working men who needed a chance to get ahead. It was just as much the factory girls. She sought out Kate Doggett. "What can I do?"

"You really know how factory girls live?" Kate asked by way of reply. "Why not make it a project to find out. Then we'll know how we can help them. It's a place to start."

Cissy went to Carter Harrison, once again without telling Potter. Harrison was in his mayoral office at City Hall.

"Mrs. Palmer, what a pleasant surprise . . ." He rose from his seat and rushed to hold the chair for her, all the while reflecting that he had almost called her Cissy.

Cissy did not waste words on pleasantries. "I want to meet some factory girls, say about ten or twelve," she said without preamble. "I want to have them in my home for a meeting."

"Whoa, Mrs. Palmer. You're going too fast for me." All the polite comments he'd intended—"What brings you to City Hall?" etc.—fell from his mind as useless. He stared at the fashionably dressed woman before him, his look frankly admiring. *If I'd met her before Palmer . . .* He envied Potter Palmer many things—his wealth, his power—but none so much as the beautiful and strong woman he had married.

"I want to talk to some factory girls," Cissy repeated almost impatiently, sensing that his thoughts had wandered. "If I can find out how they really live, I can begin to think about what we can do to help them. Who do you know who owns a factory and will introduce me to his workers?"

"No one," Harrison said flatly. Then his smile broadened. "But I'll have ten women at your house. You name the time and date . . . but it has to be after their working hours. The bosses will hardly excuse them to meet with Mrs. Potter Palmer."

Was he being sarcastic? Laughing at her? Cissy studied his face and decided he was not. She set the time for ten o'clock in the morning on the following Saturday and hoped that Potter would be at the hotel as was his Saturday custom.

A stunned Martha opened the door of the castle Saturday morning to ten awkward, shy young women who were obviously overwhelmed by the house and uncertain about their presence there. Without a word, Martha led them to the gallery.

Cissy strode into the room, dressed in the plainest dress she owned—a simple navy blue chambray that she had not adorned with any jewelry. Her hair was swept plainly back from her face and caught in a twist at the back. But the girls smelled her perfume and knew it was expensive.

"Good morning," she said. "I'm Cissy Palmer. Thank you for coming. There's tea and fresh muffins on the sideboard over there. Please help yourself, and then we'll have some introductions."

They looked uncertainly at each other until one girl boldly got up and crossed the room to the sideboard. The others followed one by one, and Cissy saw them fingering the fine linen napkins she had asked Mrs. Stripling to lay out. When they returned to their seats, she said, "Would you each please tell me your first name and where you work. Here, let's start with you." She chose the girl who'd been courageous enough to take food first.

"I'm Rachel," the girl said and grinned boldly at the others. They went around the circle, some speaking so softly that Cissy could barely hear them. But when they were through, she knew which one was Esther, Ruth, Eleanor, and so on. They worked in millinery factories.

Asking direct questions of one girl and then turning to the others and saying "How about the rest of you?" Cissy found out that they were all unmarried and lived with their families in one or two unheated rooms, they had little or no education, and most had gone to work at the age of ten or thereabouts. They worked a twelve-hour day and were paid by the piece; they saw little future ahead of them except to keep on working as they were.

"I'd like to marry me a fine man," Rachel offered, "but I won't live like me ma has, with all us kids and no money. No sir, I'd rather keep on sewing feathers on hats for ladies like yourself, begging your pardon."

"Ah," scoffed Eleanor, "you know you'll marry that Mike what's courting you, and the two of you will have ten brats before ten years is up."

"I will not!" was the indignant reply.

Cissy let them banter back and forth, learning more from their talk with each other than she did from questioning them directly. Finally, she spoke. "The way you live is not right, when I can live like this." She gestured around her as though to take in the whole house, and she heard them gasp at her honesty. "I want to see what I can to do help you." She thanked them for coming and dismissed them by rising from her seat. As each girl left—to be seen out by the still puzzled Martha—Cissy greeted her individually.

"You're a fine lady," Esther said. "You ain't gonna' do nothing to change the factories, but we like knowin' you'll try."

Eleanor said, "Thanks for showing us someone is our friend."

Cissy felt like weeping when they were all gone.

That was the first of many such meetings. Cissy had shopgirls and factory workers into her home, listened to them describe their lives, asked them what would help them. Then the Fortnightly Club met there to hear her explain what she had learned and what she thought they could do by bringing pressure on the owners. One of her recommendations: contribute to the Women's Trade Union League.

Potter learned of the meetings when Honoré unconsciously mentioned "Mother's meetings with those women from the factories."

"Were you going to tell me about this?" he asked one evening as they sat talking over the day's events, as was their custom. Inwardly, he was seething, and he wasn't sure if his anger came from her activity or her deception. That she had "forgotten" to tell him clearly meant she didn't want him to know.

"Of course," she said. "But the meetings are an experiment. I saw no reason to bother you with them until I saw how they were progressing." She spoke with calm and convincing assurance, but behind her back she crossed her fingers, for it was a gentle lie. She did not believe in white lies, and it surprised her that the childhood habit of crossing your fingers came back so quickly.

"Cissy!" He threw his hands up in the air in exasperation, but his tone was one of mock good humor. "You're becoming a reformer! Next thing I know you'll show up in bloomers." He had unconsciously given vent to his greatest fear: that she would become one of those raving feminists. He had married a well-bred, educated young lady from a cultured, upper-class family; he could not bear it if she turned into a ranting liberal.

She laughed lightly, matching his tone. "No, and I won't cut my hair."

He knelt before her chair and took both her hands in his. Now his tone was serious. "Cissy, you have no need to take on all these . . . these causes. You have this house to run, your sons to raise, your friends, your organizations—and I don't mean that Doggett woman's club. I mean things like the Tuesday Art and Travel Club or the Saddle and Cycle. Why must you involve yourself in problems that don't affect you?"

Cissy gently withdrew her hands and answered quietly, "They affect all of us, Potter. I can't live like this and ignore the terrible way so many other women live. I promise I won't embarrass you, and I promise I won't become a suffragette, but I feel certain obligations strongly."

The next day Cissy received a hand-delivered note: "Mrs. Palmer, Thank you for the work you do for our beloved city. Yours for Chicago, Carter Harrison."

She couldn't help but contrast the two men's attitudes.

Chapter Eleven

As Potter Palmer rose from the breakfast table and his newspaper to head for the hotel, Cissy said, "Don't forget the Arnolds' dinner tonight."

"The Arnolds?" he asked blankly.

"They're fairly new in town, but he has a thriving hack business, and she's active in the Tuesday Club. Several people you know will be there." Cissy said all this in a straightforward manner, but she knew what was coming next. It was a variation of a conversation repeated many times in recent years.

"Oh, Cissy, do I have to go? If I stay home, can you find someone to escort you?"

She wanted to laugh. There were always men who would escort her with great propriety, though it somewhat offended her that she was to make those arrangements herself. It seemed to her that if Potter did not wish to accompany her he should see that she was properly escorted.

Until Fred Grant mustered out of the army in 1881, he used to escort both Ida and Cissy to social events. But they had moved to New York now, and Cissy missed her sister much more than she thought she would. "Phil Sheridan is in town," she said. "I'll send a note and see if he will escort me." Carter Harrison would be more than willing to escort her, she knew, but she saw no sense in unnecessarily angering Potter.

There was no rift between the Palmers. Potter Palmer still adored his wife—in spite of her liberal tendencies—and she was still in love with him. "Like a schoolgirl," she told Ida, who looked away nervously when her sister spoke. Potter's hair was receding just a bit and had turned a true silver, matching his goatee and mustache and making him, in Cissy's eyes, a striking and sophisticated man. But sophistication was not something he sought. Potter Palmer had never been totally comfortable in the world of formal social events— "I wasn't born to the social life like you were," he once explained to his wife. And now, in his late fifties, he played poker with a group of men, including Marshall Field, once a week, and he found a round of golf with his father-in-law relaxing, but in the evenings he much preferred a glass of brandy, a good book, and a roaring fire.

"Go, my bird of paradise," he told her. "Enjoy yourself, flirt with all the men . . . but come home to me. I shall be here waiting."

She kissed him passionately and said, "Be sure that you are. I may wake you if you're not."

"I'll count on it," he said, laughter lighting his eyes. Potter Palmer still believed he was a lucky man.

"Papá," Honoré once asked, "why do you not go out with Mamá in the evenings?"

"Because I am an old and tired man," Potter responded in good humor, "and she is young and full of life . . . and she likes to dance all evening."

Honoré considered for a moment and then said, "When I am old enough, I shall go dancing with her in your place."

Enormously pleased, Palmer replied, "I'm sure she will look forward to that . . . and I shall be grateful that you can look after your beautiful mother."

"Maybe next year," said the fifteen-year-old Honoré.

Phil Sheridan was more than glad to escort Cissy to the Arnolds for dinner. It was a large, seated dinner, and as Cissy predicted, there were several people she and Potter knew. But the Arnolds, being new in town, were not as rigid about their guest list as the longtime upper crust residents. Among their guests this night were Kate Doggett, who did not hesitate at all to arrive unescorted, and Mayor Carter Harrison, who looked somber to the point of being out of character.

When she had an opportunity, Cissy approached him, a glass of claret in her hand.

He had been watching her from across the room, thinking as always how lovely she was but also wondering what her reaction would be if he told her all the troubles that were on his mind. Perhaps she'd think her work with the factory girls superficial or meaningless, and he didn't want to imply that at all.

"You're looking particularly unhappy tonight, Mr. Mayor," she said. "It's . . . it's not like you. What's troubling you?"

She asked it with such sincerity, that Carter almost told her. Then he said, "Nothing for you to worry about, Mrs. Palmer. City business."

"It's my city too," she replied calmly, "and I like to know what's going on in it."

Harrison remembered that something she said once led him to believe that her husband did not share "men's business" with her and that irked her. "Of course," he said, nodding his head. "There's a man by the name of Johann Most recently moved to town, a German anarchist."

"And he's most objectionable," she said, making a play on the man's name.

"Yes, he is. He came to America by way of a London jail," Harrison continued. "He's a co-founder of the International Working People's Association, and now he's traveling the country urging social revolution. Says the best thing to do with men like Jay Gould and Vanderbilt is to hang them from the nearest lamppost. Unfortunately, he's an effective speaker."

"And he's gaining converts in Chicago?"

Harrison nodded. "I tried to tell your husband some months ago that Chicago is ripe for revolutionary violence, but he wouldn't listen to me. There are too many men in this city who will listen to Most and join his cause." He paused. "But this is a party, not a time for me to burden you with mayoral concerns."

Just then General Phil Sheridan joined them. The two men shook hands, but it was clear they were not fond of each other.

Trying to include the General, Cissy said, "Mayor Harrison has been telling me about a revolutionary anarchist who's going around the city preaching open violence."

"Johann Most," Sheridan said. "My men are watching him."

The mayor turned a steady stare on the army man.

"We're ready, waiting for him to lead his first riot," Sheridan continued. "It won't last long."

"That kind of confrontation is just what I hope to avoid," Harrison said quietly.

"They've got bombs, man," Sheridan said heatedly, forgetting the social setting for a moment. "Bombs small enough to carry in a man's pocket and destroy whole armies. I tell you armed conflict is coming."

"I pray you're wrong and we can prevent it," the mayor said. "Too many innocents will die."

"We're going to have to deal with it sooner or later, Mister Mayor. And I hope it's sooner." The military anticipation was clear in this voice.

Dinner was announced, and General Sheridan held out his arm to escort Cissy to the table. Harrison bowed, and Cissy gave him a fleeting look as she turned away. This time, neither of them was threatened with laughter.

As she often did, Cissy came home to a quiet and darkened mansion. She went silently into Potter's bedroom to tell him of the evening's events. It was an outrage to which she delighted in treating him—an outrage only in the conventional attitudes of the day toward women and sex and their enjoyment—or tolerance—of it. The order of events rarely varied.

"How was the evening?" he would ask, sliding back the covers to make room for her.

"Wonderful! I must tell you about it," she would say as she stood fully clothed before him. "But wait . . . ." And then she would begin the slow process of undressing. First jewelry—hairpins, necklaces, earrings, stomachers, even rings went in a heap on Potter's bedside table. Then the shoes went, usually carefully placed under his bed—"To leave the toes pointing toward the bed invites bad dreams," she told him time and again, carefully pointing the toes toward the door. And then whatever gown she wore landed on the floor at her feet, where sometimes she kicked it aside in a wild, carefree gesture. Then came all those undergarments and corset covers, until she was down to a chemise, at which point she always chastely said, "Turn your head," and he did.

United under the covers of his bed, they rarely discussed the evening until much later. Potter Palmer was proud of his continuing prowess in the bedroom and delighted with the response he was still able to evoke in his wife. And Cissy, who had come ignorant to the marriage bed, had grown into an accomplished lover who delighted as much—more?—as her husband in physical pleasure.

"Shhh!" he would whisper. "The boys will hear you."

"They're in their own wing," she would pant, "and they're asleep. Don't stop."

And he never did, until both lay exhausted in each other's arms. Then, and only then, would Cissy describe at length the event she'd attended —who was there, who danced with whom, how the ladies looked.

"Don't you think, Potter," she asked one night, propping herself up on one elbow to look down into his face, "that you are missing business opportunities by not escorting me? I saw Marshall Field tonight talking to . . . ."

He silenced her by pulling her toward him for a long, deep kiss. "Marshall Field is not doing what I am right now," he said, "and I venture his wife was with him all evening."

They spoke no more of that evening's ball.

Usually, morning's rays found the two curled together in sound sleep. Cissy, wakened by first light, would frantically pick up her clothes and jewelry and shoes and run for her own room before the maids brought coffee and the newspapers. Once she left behind her jewelry—when it appeared in her dressing room later in the morning, Cissy didn't have the nerve to look Mrs. Stripling in the face.

This night she said, "The mayor was one of the guests tonight." She deliberately avoided mentioning that Kate Doggett was also there. "He looked very somber. I talked to him a moment, and he said he's concerned about the growing number of anarchists in the city."

"Phil Sheridan is ready to handle any uprising in whatever way necessary," Potter said, "and Field has funded a civilian militia."

"Militia? Untrained men?"

"They're drilling in riot-control techniques," Potter said, his impatience creeping into his voice. "Cissy, you really needn't bother yourself about this."

"Mayor Harrison is truly afraid of violence, like there was in 1877. He's says innocent men will be killed."

"Mayor Harrison," he said archly, "should not have been discussing such matters with you, especially at a dinner party. He won't be re-elected you know." He was silent a moment, then reached over, kissed her cheek, and said, "Good night, Cissy. Sleep well."

That night, she went back to her own bed. During the night, Potter reached over toward Cissy and found an empty space. Cissy awoke alone in her bed with a nagging unpleasant thought in her mind, though it took a few minutes to remember what it was. When Potter asked, she said that she was sleepless and restless and didn't want to disturb him.

* * *

Carter Harrison still stopped by the City Café from time to time, mostly to check on Sheila. He suspected that life—or Harry—were hard on her. As she poured his coffee one blustery November day in 1884, he studied her. Now in her forties somewhere, he guessed, she had thickened through the waist and was no longer the bright young thing she had been when Harrison first started going to the café. Her face was fuller, and the blonde of her hair had dimmed. What worried Carter was the look in her eye, though he couldn't precisely define it—fear? Despair? All he knew for certain was that it was not a happy look. But whatever bothered Sheila, she usually put a good face on things.

"And how's our city, Mr. Mayor?" she asked with a grin as she placed a steaming mug of black coffee in front of him.

"Troubled," he said. "You know that, Sheila. Most men are content to go about their work, but there are too many trouble-makers, and workingmen listen to them. We don't have many anarchists as such, maybe two or three hundred, but they're noisy."

"And don't I know that," she sighed. "I'm married to one of the troublemakers, and don't think I don't know it."

Harrison stared at her. "I don't know that I'd call Harry an anarchist. He's just . . . well, discontent, angry. Have you ever thought of leaving him?"

"Leave Harry? I'd just as soon cut off my right arm!" She was indignant, and Harrison almost regretted speaking. Then her voice softened, "I remember Harry as he was when I met him, right here at this counter—handsome, charming—and I carry that picture with me in my mind all the time."

"What makes him so bitter?" Harrison asked, fishing to see how much she knew about her husband.

"Sure, and I don't know. He's never talked about his family back east, but I think that's where all his anger comes from. He's talking now about some sort of parade on Thanksgiving Day. I don't know if he's joinin' it or not, but it doesn't sound good to me."

"A parade?" Harrison echoed blankly. Usually, if a parade was planned in the city, the mayor knew about it. Thanksgiving was only about ten days away.

"Maybe I misunderstood him," Sheila said quickly.

Carter Harrison wanted to explore further, but he could see that Sheila was nervous. Changing the subject, he asked, "How's Juliet? She must be—what? Fourteen?"

Sheila nodded. "Me mother says I was difficult at fourteen, too. Something about girls and their mothers. She won't do a thing I tell her, unless Harry tells her to listen to me. And . . ." She hesitated. "And he's not always gentle about tellin' her. One day, she's gonna turn on him . . . and I don't know what will happen. I worry about her. I want something better for her than I've had."

Carter nodded and thought about his own children, all happily launched into their own lives. He tried to think what he could do to help Sheila and Juliet, but Sophie had raised his girls. He had no idea what to do. Maybe he'd speak to Cissy.

"Sheila, my girl, you might as well own this café, you worked here so long." He looked around at the empty café. The room hadn't changed in twenty-five years—the tables and chairs were still battered and scarred, the walls coated with a thin layer of grease and grime. The only new thing was a current calendar from Montgomery Ward, which reminded him he needed to update the one in his office. But the cotton curtains that hung from rods halfway up the front windows were clean and sparkling. No doubt Sheila had taken them home and plunged them in her washtub.

"Go on with you," she said. "I can't afford to be owning a café. But Mr. Schmidt that bought it, he treats me fine. Even gave me a raise."

"Schmidt? I thought Junior Robertson owned it."

"He sold it, oh, three, four months ago. Mr. Schmidt, he's newly come to Chicago from Germany."

Harrison's ears picked up. "You get a lot of Germans in here now?"

"In the evenings. They come to drink beer, which we didn't use to serve. Sometimes they have meetings of some sort, and Mr. Schmidt sends me home, says he'll take care of things."

Carter Harrison made a mental note to come by the café some evening, rather than his usual early-morning visit. "You let me know if you need help," he said, reaching a huge hand to cover her calloused and rough one that rested on the counter.

She blinked away a tear. "I will, and I thank you. You've been a good friend to us, and Harry . . . he'll come to realize that someday."

When Carter Harrison left the café his mind was not on the Collins family. It was on a Thanksgiving Day parade. In the next days he mined his sources but could find out nothing. As Thanksgiving approached, all he knew was that Chicago's upper crust and middle class were not planning a parade. Neither were the Irish.

* * *

Thanksgiving Day found Daniel Burnham in a rare moment of relaxation. He sat in his study, a cigar clenched in his teeth, the newspaper in his hand. His reverie was cut short by the sounds of shouting outside. Prairie Avenue, the most fashionable street in Chicago, was known for its peace and quiet, and Burnham couldn't imagine what was disturbing that atmosphere. He strode through the parlor to the front door and looked out its glass pane.

He was looking at men wearing crimson sashes and carrying huge black flags marching up this quiet residential street. Burnham was savvy enough to know that crimson and black were the colors of hunger, and he recognized one of the men at the front of the parade—August Spies, editor and publisher of the German-language newspaper, *Arbiter-Zeitung*.

One of the crimson-sashed fellows pointed at his house and then pushed a homeless man, urging him toward the front door. Burnham stood rooted to the spot.

The man approached the door and rang the great bell that echoed throughout the house. He did not open the door. As the man approached, he could see that he was nearly toothless and his eyes were wild with—Burnham did not know with what.

"C'mon, mate," the man shouted through the glass. "Give us a bit of food or some coppers."

Burnham did not shake his head in the negative. He simply did not move. The man continued to stand and shout for what seemed an eternity and then, muttering an oath that ended with "You bugger," he turned and left.

Later he learned that several of his neighbors on Prairie had been similarly disturbed—but no one dared to ring Marshall Field's doorbell.

* * *

Carter Harrison's enemies blamed him for the Thanksgiving Day parade or, at the least, for not preventing it. The blame didn't bother him. That the parade took place bothered him a great deal. But he had no contacts in the German community, beyond a religious leader or two, one of whom sometimes translated articles from the *Arbeiter-Zeitung*. Frequently, Spies published articles on Alfred Nobel's new invention, dynamite—how to build bombs, use hand grenades. The articles became known in the German community as "bomb talking." To Harrison, they exaggerated the strength of the anarchist movement in Chicago.

Carter also knew that his city, like others across the nation, was in trouble. Factories and laborsaving machinery had cost many skilled workers their jobs. In the early 1880s, unemployment in Chicago was at about thirty thousand, and that probably included as many Irish as it did Germans and other European minorities. But the Irish had no socialist tendencies, and they had lighter dispositions, a fact not lost on Harrison.

The Germans were a tight-knit ethnic minority. What began as daylong picnics celebrating their heritage, with traditional music, dancing, and food, grew into a movement of men united against the factories which forced them to work long hours under appalling conditions and for little pay.

Carter Harrison thought the remedy for the anarchist situation was to raise pay, shorten the working day, and improve working conditions. To his eye, that was what the daylong labor rallies and even the parade were intended to accomplish. So far it had been peaceful, but the threat of violence hung over the city.

When Marshall Field stormed into the mayoral office, his face pinched in an expression of displeasure, and demanded that Harrison stop allowing the anarchists to congregate, Harrison replied calmly, "It's their right. I have no power to stop them, unless they break the law."

"Then it will be too late," muttered Field.

"And Mr. Field," Harrison said, his tone polite and deferential, "if your militia attacks unprovoked, they will have broken the law, and I will hold you responsible."

Field left without another word.

Harrison began drifting by the German picnics, introducing himself to people, drinking beer and eating bratwurst and sauerkraut with them—he developed a real fondness for the food—and listening to what they had to say. He told them he thought their working conditions were not to be tolerated, and he asked what he could do to help them. He began to make friends and to develop some sources in the community.

A year later, he thought it was all useless. A group of anarchists carrying banners and crudely painted signs marched around the Board of Trade Building, effectively imprisoning those inside who had come to trade in wheat and pork. Men in business attire peered out of windows, watching the marchers. Harrison, who had no advance warning of the demonstration, called out the police, and armed officers stood nearby. But he had given specific orders that they were not to act unless violence occurred. The tireless anarchists marched for hours, and several prominent businessmen were late for dinner that night. At last, in groups of two or three, they began to emerge from the building and cross through the lines of marchers, all under the watchful eyes of the Chicago police.

Once again, Carter Harrison was blamed and vilified. But that year he was re-elected to yet another term as mayor, in spite of Potter Palmer's prediction to his wife.

"It was the Irish vote," Marshall Field complained to Palmer. Field refused to recognize that men who thought like he did, though powerful and with loud voices, were very much in the minority in Chicago. And he quite likely was right about the Irish. The German anarchists, bent on destroying the system, probably didn't use it to their advantage. The Irish voted, and Carter Harrison was their man.

Re-election meant that Carter Harrison was mayor in 1886, when the Haymarket Riot occurred. If the Chicago Fire was the first great shaping event in the city's history, the Haymarket Riot was the second.

Chapter Twelve

The Haymarket Riot might well be traced back to the strike against the McCormick reaper plant. Cyrus McCormick had died the year before, and his wife, Nettie, presided at business conferences and unofficially directed the Harvest International Company, even after her son, Harold, was named president. In 1885, McCormick workers demanded an eight-hour day and went on strike. Harold McCormick used three hundred Pinkerton agents to protect his non-union new hires, further enraging the workers.

By 1886 the number of anarchists in Chicago had grown to twenty thousand, and they were organized, led by a man named Albert Parsons, leader of a local group fighting for better wages and editor of a newspaper called *The Alarm*. Parsons was the political candidate who had been defeated by ballot stuffing in the 1870s, turning attempts to work within the existing system into bitter determination to destroy it. Parsons was a strange revolutionary—a descendent of Plymouth Rock pilgrims, he fought for the Confederacy and then married a former slave in Texas. Hounded out of that state by prejudice and threats, the couple came to Chicago, where Parsons began preaching anarchy. In 1886, twenty-six craft unions supported his IWPA plan to replace organized government with voluntary producers' cooperatives.

In the spring of that year, workers across the country were demanding an eight-hour day. The IWPA saw this discontent as a way to recruit more members and adopted the eight-hour-day crusade, even offering free rifle lessons at German beer halls on the city's north side. The Federation of Organized Trade and Labor Unions called for a nationwide strike on May 1.

George Pullman sought out Potter Palmer in the lobby of the hotel. "Have you heard?" he demanded.

"Heard what?" Potter asked mildly. "The stock market?"

"No, no! That damn strike. Workers think they can work eight hours a day for ten hours pay."

"That's union stuff," Potter replied, "and you don't have any union workers. You won't allow it." Pullman had made good more than once on his earlier threat to fire any employee and evict him from Pullmantown who even showed an interest in joining a labor union. "I don't have any union employees, either, so I'm not sure why we're talking about it."

Pullman harrumphed impatiently, as though he were talking to someone not quite bright. Palmer bristled but kept his temper and his tongue. All around them men sat in leather chairs, smoking cigars, checking market futures. Palmer wished Pullman would lower his tone.

"We're talking about it," the other man said, his voice rising in anger, "because there's going to be blood running in the streets of this city."

"That's what the anarchists want," Potter replied, "but I doubt that most workers will be violent. As I hear it, they're just supposed to lay down their tools in a sort of symbolic gesture. Then they'll go back to work in a day or two—they can't afford not to."

"The anarchists are giving men free rifle lessons," Pullman exclaimed, "and that blankety-blank mayor of ours isn't doing a thing about it."

"The mayor," Potter said calmly, "supports the idea of an eight-hour day."

"And you agree?" Pullman was incredulous.

"No, I don't. I didn't vote for him and won't if he runs again. I think Chicago would be better off without him in many ways." Why did he think of Cissy as he said that? "He's too closely tied to gambling and . . . other corruption." He knew Pullman prided himself on moral righteousness.

"We ought to impeach him!" Pullman snapped and walked away without as much as a "Good day."

* * *

On May 1, August Spies led eighty thousand workers up Michigan Avenue, where they ceremoniously laid down their tools. Chicago's factories were silent. Carter Harrison had police on alert and had called out Pinkerton's men—they were on the roofs of buildings, Gatling guns at the ready. But there was no violence.

Chicago breathed a collective sigh of relief, and Carter Harrison treated himself to an extra pint at O'Malley's Pub that night. But the city celebrated too soon.

On May 3, Cyrus McCormick Jr. used Pinkerton's men and armed strikebreakers to keep the strikers from returning to work. They cracked the skulls of strikers with billy clubs and rifle butts, and several men were badly injured. The uninjured gathered in a crowd some distance from the factory entrance, and August Spies began exhorting them about their rights. When the shift bell rang, protestors drove the strikebreakers back into the plant and began smashing its window.

Captain John "Black Jack" Bonfield arrived with two hundred of Chicago's finest policemen. Bonfield and Harrison were enemies. In 1885, when city trolley workers went on strike, Bonfield had issued a "shoot to kill" order, in direct contradiction of Harrison's order. Now, his men, under his orders, attacked the strikebreakers, killing two. Spies called for a meeting the next night in Haymarket Square, to "destroy the hideous monster that seeks to destroy you," he yelled at the strikers.

Chicago was on edge, fearing a bomb attack. "Anarchists to rally" screamed the headlines of Chicago's papers, while Spies put out a special edition of *Arbeiter-Zeitung* urging workers to attend. He expected as many as had marched up Michigan Avenue with him two days earlier. He got only twenty-five hundred men and moved the group to an alley off the square.

Carter Harrison had asked for riot troops to be on alert at the Des Plaines Street station, a half mile from Haymarket. His order to Bonfield was clear: "Do not order your men to shoot." But Harrison went further. He attended the rally himself, standing near Spies and Parsons as they spoke, repeatedly lighting his cigarette to draw attention to the fact that the mayor was there. The meeting was peaceful, and after an hour or so, Harrison stopped by the police station to tell Bonfield to send his troops home. There would be no trouble this night. As he left, rain was threatening, and the meeting was beginning to break up as men drove away. Harrison rode his mare to Ashland Avenue and went to bed, assured that all was well in his city.

But Bonfield disobeyed Harrison's orders and marched a force on the meeting, though by this time no more than three hundred men lingered to hear the last of the speeches. As Bonfield ordered Spies and the other speakers to clear the area, someone threw a bomb. A sudden terrible burst of light, sound, and vibration shook all of them.

Bonfield yelled "Fire," and the police fired wildly in all directions into a mass of shrieking, running, stumbling men, some of whom crawled on their bellies in a desperate attempt to find safety. One policeman was killed, six died later, over fifty civilians were wounded. The debacle became known as the Haymarket Riot.

Cissy and Potter Palmer learned of the tragedy the next morning when an arriving worker brought word. They quizzed the man, a gardener, but he insisted that a bomb had been thrown.

Potter was still dubious. "I cannot believe a bomb would be thrown in Chicago. But I'll warrant one thing—if a bomb was thrown, it was an anarchist that threw it. That man will pay."

Cissy was less concerned with revenge than compassion. "Think of the wounded men," she said, "and their families. They must need help."

Potter's answer was so harsh it startled her. "They should have thought about the consequences before they went to that meeting." Shortly afterward, he left for the city, saying, "I'll find out the truth of what happened and send word."

Cissy did not intend to sit around and wait for him to send word. She called Mrs. Stripling, enlisted the curious Martha, and began collecting clothes and blankets.

"Mrs. Potter, you'll run our supply too short!" protested the housekeeper.

"We can buy more," she said. "Those people cannot. Tell the kitchen to prepare bundles of food—bread, meat, cheese, whatever you have. Wrap each in a towel if necessary. I don't suppose we have enough baskets."

"No, ma'am, I'm sure we don't," said the disapproving Mrs. Stripling.

A mound of bundles, both clothes and food, began to appear in Martha's entry hall. "Ma'am?" she asked in a tentative voice. "What are you going to do with all this?"

"Take them where they're needed," Cissy replied without hesitation.

"You yourself, ma'am?"

Cissy paused. She hadn't thought that far. "I . . . well, I'll ask Herman to drive me."

"I . . . I'd be pleased to accompany you, ma'am, should you want another lady along."

Cissy stopped in midmovement. "Martha, how very kind of you. You know, of course, that we could meet an . . . unpleasant reception."

"You mean folks might be ugly? That's why I think I should go with you."

In the long run, Martha was saved from making this sacrifice by the arrival of Carter Harrison. The usually jovial man was a picture of distress, his shoulders slumped, his smile gone, his eyes missing their usual sparkle. He barely made the necessary polite preliminaries, so great was his anguish. "You hear?" he said to Cissy, and she assured him they had.

"I . . . I came to see if Mr. Palmer would throw in with me to help calm the city."

Cissy doubted that, but she replied, "He's gone to town to find out what really happened. What did happen? Was there really a bomb?"

"Must have been, from the descriptions I heard. But if Bonfield had done what I'd told him and sent his men home instead of sending them to that meeting . . . ." He shook his head in despair.

"Who's Bonfield?"

"Police inspector. Or was, until today. He's lost his job for disobeying the mayor, but that doesn't bring those men back. I went to him last night, told him it was a peaceful meeting and to send his men home . . . and instead he marched on them." He looked at the mound of things on the floor. "What's all this?"

She hesitated but only a moment. After all, Harrison had caught her taking provisions before. "I thought to take these to the families that would need help after last night."

"Police families?" he asked.

She shook her head. "No. Other police families will take care of them. I thought to go to the wounded men's houses . . . if I could find them."

"You know who needs help?" he asked.

"Too many people," she murmured.

"Yeah, but right now, the families of the men who were arrested. No one else will help their families."

Cissy thought long and hard. "You want me to take food to the families of the men who caused this tragedy?"

"They didn't cause it. The police did. This is America, and those men have a right to express their opinions. Now, if there was a bomb, then someone acting on those opinions broke the law. But just talking isn't against the law, no matter how much we hate it.

And those men who were arrested aren't ever going back to their families—take my word for that. Those women and children need help worse than anyone I know."

"Will you take me?"

"Of course," he said. "Let me load this up."

Honoré came into the hallway just at that moment. "Where are you going, Mother?"

"To deliver supplies to people who need them," she said. "You go on back and work at your studies."

"I don't want to do that," he said. "I want to go with you."

She looked at Harrison, who shrugged and said, "Let the boy come. Maybe he'll learn something."

After brief introductions, Honoré helped Harrison load his carriage with all that Cissy had collected, and then they pulled away from the castle. Cissy left no message for Potter.

They headed for the Parsons' shack on the West Side first. It wasn't in the area where the Collins lived, but it might as well have been. "Fifteen years after the fire," Cissy said, shaking her head, "and these people are still living in shelter houses that were supposed to be temporary."

"They've no place else to go," Harrison said. "And they're . . . well, they're kind of used to it. They can't imagine much better. They probably think this is where they belong."

"How could anybody think they belonged here?" asked a wide-eyed Honoré. And then he said something that made Harrison regard him with renewed respect. "They don't accept this, because if they did they wouldn't riot for better wages."

Harrison grinned and looked at Cissy. "Boy's right. You've done a fine job with your son, Mrs. Palmer."

She wondered if Potter thought so.

Harrison went as straight to Albert Parson's shack as he had years before to the Collins' quarters, and Cissy wondered if he knew every poor person in the Third Ward. He was greeted with dull politeness—a nod of the head from Lucy Parsons and curious looks from the teenage children who sat around. But when he introduced Cissy and Honoré, there was open hostility.

"What's she doin' here?" Mrs. Parsons asked, while one of the boys spat in Cissy's direction, though he was far from hitting the mark. It was a gesture, not a determined effort. One of the others cocked his fist in Honoré's direction, causing the younger boy to move swiftly behind Carter Harrison. The boy with the clenched fist gave a bitter laugh.

Honoré noticed and would later ask about the family—the mother was obviously a woman of color, and the children had honey-colored skin and dark, curly hair. He had never heard of a mixed marriage and wondered if that was the whole problem with Albert Parsons. Carter Harrison later agreed with him that Parsons might not have fought so hard against oppression if he had not been married to someone who had experienced it firsthand.

"I brought some provisions," Cissy said in a determined voice, "to help until Mr. Parsons is returned to you."

This time, a long, unfriendly look. "He ain't comin' back," Lucy Parsons said. "I know that, and you know that."

But her scorn was not deep enough to keep her from accepting what Cissy had brought. Mrs. Parsons reached for the food almost greedily, a gesture that prompted Cissy to look around the shanty, beyond the rickety table and chairs in the middle of the room and the curtained-off sleeping area to one side.

A wood stove, crudely vented, sat in one corner, next to a scarred and dirty smaller table on which sat a dishpan, full of cold and dirty water. Open shelves held scant supplies—a tin of tomatoes, a small sack of flour half full, a mesh bag that appeared to have only five or six potatoes in it. She saw no sugar nor coffee, no icebox. When and if they ever got meat, Cissy realized, was something she could not even worry about. The fresh air Cissy so loved by the lake had not made it this far west through the cracks of this dark and dank shanty, and the air was heavy and stale.

"Mrs. Parsons," she said, reaching for the woman's hand, which was almost withdrawn but then reluctantly given to her, "I will hold you in my heart . . . and I will send more supplies."

The other woman managed an awkward, "You are kind," muttered with a heavy southern accent.

They left, their contribution of bread and vegetables and meat piled high on the table, the family staring after them silently.

"Well," Honoré said with some indignation, "they weren't very nice about saying thank you." For a boy drilled in fine manners, the Parsons' behavior had been unforgivable.

"It's not about 'thank you,' son," Harrison said. "That's not why your mother does things for other people."

"Well, I know, but still . . ." His words trailed off.

This time Cissy spoke slowly, with thought. "It's all right, Honoré. I . . . I know these people resent us, but that doesn't stop me from wanting to help."

"I don't know that I'd want to help people who hated me," he said, still angry.

"They don't hate, Honoré. They fear."

August Spies was a bachelor, so there was no one for them to visit. But they went to the homes of George Engel, Adolph Fischer, Louis Lingg, Michael Schwab, August Neebe, and Samuel Fielden, where their reception was much the same as it had been at the Parsons' shanty. Except these people spoke to them in a guttural voice, heavily tinged with German.

A weary Cissy slumped in her seat—something Mrs. Potter Palmer never allowed herself to do in public! Behind her, Honoré was silent and pensive, digesting the day's events.

"You all right?" Harrison asked, glancing at her.

"Discouraged. How can I make a difference? How can I help these people?"

"You helped today. It's like you told the boy there, you just can't expect thanks. And I guess you can't expect instant results either. It's not like you give some people food and their lives turn around instantly."

She smiled slightly. "I'm not that naive."

"But close," he said and reached a bold hand to cover hers ever so briefly.

* * *

Whether Potter Palmer learned of the day's expedition from the poor confused Martha or from Honoré was never certain, and Cissy never asked. But learn he did. His displeasure was immediately evident. Cissy knew that he did not want her working with the poor, let alone going to their houses, and the fact that she would not honor his wishes was a sadness to him. But taking his son into the Third Ward was an entirely different matter.

"Why did you take Honoré?"

"He asked to go."

"Didn't you know it would displease me? That I don't want my sons put in danger?"

"He was in no danger. Carter Harrison drove us. We were never in any danger. And the day made a great impression on him."

"I don't put the faith in Harrison that you do. Oh, I know"—he raised his hand to forestall her objections—"he loves this city. But he is not a man of sound judgment. He's made friends in low places . . . ."

"That," Cissy said, "is what makes him an effective mayor."

"It is rumored," Potter went on as though she had not spoken, "that he has used his shady accomplices to gain his political ends."

"Ah," she said, "Machiavellian. The means justifies the end. It seems to me that philosophy is fine when someone like Cyrus McCormick employs it but suspect when it is used to benefit the workers."

Potter Palmer wished briefly that his wife were not so well educated. "I won't argue with you, Cissy. But I don't want Honoré in Harrison's company again. And I'd prefer that you not be either."

After that, Potter Palmer took Honoré to the hotel with him on Saturdays and any other day the boy was not occupied with school. "It's good training for him," he explained.

Cissy knew that it was Potter's way of keeping her son out of harm's way.

* * *

The bomb thrower was never identified, so the arrested anarchists could not be charged for that crime. They were charged, instead, for the violent insanity of their speeches. The jury foreman was a salesman at Field's, and there were no workingmen on the jury. Carter Harrison testified, at length but to no avail, that the meeting had been peaceful until the police intervened.

Michael Schwab and Samuel Fielden officially asked for mercy and were given life sentences, from which they were later pardoned by a governor who then lost all his political credibility. After a bitter trial, Albert Parsons, Louis Lingg, August Spies, Adolph Fischer, and George Engel were sentenced to be hanged.

Lucy Parsons began a campaign to seek clemency for her husband. She was aided by Nina Van Zandt, a Chicago socialite who had attended the trial out of curiosity and ended by marrying August Spies by proxy. Chicago civic leaders protested that clemency would do far more to restore order in the city than executions, but their pleas fell on deaf ears. Potter Palmer agreed with this position, but Marshall Field remained vengeful, and few would contradict the most powerful man in Chicago. Louis Lingg cheated the hangman by killing himself with a small bomb smuggled to him in jail. The remaining four—Spies, Parsons, Engel, and Fischer—were hanged, dying with the words "Let the voice of the people be heard!" on their lips.

The funeral of the four was the largest Chicago had ever seen, with twenty thousand people boarding special trains to a German cemetery in an outlying part of the city.

The day of the funeral Chicago was nervous. Armed guards were posted at the homes of those who had helped with the prosecution, and several prominent businessmen—including George Pullman and Marshall Field—left town with their families.

The Potter Palmers remained within their castle.

"I cannot believe it," Cissy said in despair. "Those men did not kill anyone. They simply voiced their opinions. This is America, and we're supposed to be allowed to say what we think. That's the whole purpose of democracy."

For once, Palmer, who often disagreed with his wife and frequently kept his disagreements to himself, agreed with her. "This is a black day in the history of Chicago," he said. "But perhaps it will stop other anarchists from protesting."

Cissy didn't think one could sit back and rely on that thought. She was resolved that action was necessary, but she didn't say that to Potter.

Cissy Palmer did not see Carter Harrison, except on formal social occasions, for five years after the Haymarket Riot. When they met, they barely acknowledged each other, as though they were strangers.

The Columbian Exposition

Chapter Thirteen

"We have secured a large house on Halstead Street, and we will call it Hull House, after the former owner, Charles Hull." The speaker was a young woman, plainly dressed, her hair drawn severely away from her face. Her back was remarkably stooped for her age, and she held her head at a strange angle as though she had a painfully stiff neck, but her eyes were intense, and her voice was strong and sure.

Cissy Palmer leaned forward in her chair, intent on the speaker's words. She was one of about fifty women from the Chicago Woman's Club who had invited Miss Jane Addams to speak to them. Cissy looked about and saw many faces she recognized. What had begun as a reading and self-study group had developed into an organization aggressively working to better life in Chicago, especially for women. Cissy was not the only "swell" to believe in the idea of obligation for the wealthy, though she would never convert Potter to her point of view.

"Halstead is an area of immigrants—mostly German, Bohemian, Italian, Polish. These people need help to live in this country, to learn our customs and way . . . and that will be the mission of Hull House. We'll give classes in history and English and provide some basic manual training. We plan a clinic for children and a clinic to monitor people's health, although we will not be able to treat any severe illness.

"Five of us will live in the house and be available at all hours. But we need your help. We need volunteers to teach classes, and we, quite without shame, need money and supplies."

For a fleeting moment, Cissy wished she could be one of the five to stay at Hull House, so that she could be a real part of the volunteer effort. Then she laughed inwardly at herself. Give up Potter and the boys so she could help immigrants? Her charity didn't extend quite that far.

Jane Addams, on the other hand, was single with physical disabilities from a bout of spinal tuberculosis. Even worse, she had suffered for several years from a sort of malaise brought about by not knowing what to do with her life. College educated, she had tried medicine, only to be forced by her health to turn away. She had traveled in Europe extensively, which did little to relieve her dissatisfaction until she visited a pioneer settlement house in London. Suddenly, she had direction in her life. With her college friend Ellen Gates Starr, she moved to Chicago, leased the Hull mansion, and began planning a settlement house for women.

When Addams called for questions, Cissy's hand was one of the first raised. "Will you address the problem of child labor?" she asked.

"Not at first," was the reply. "The mission of Hull House will be to help people learn to live in America. It's our belief that were they more familiar with our country, these families would not have to send their young children to work nor would they have to live in poverty and hunger and squalor. We believe education is the answer as much, if not more, than legislation."

"I'd like to help," Cissy said promptly.

Addams nodded. "I'll see you afterward."

They met in a tearoom. Cissy found Addams, close up, to be straightforward and businesslike, unconcerned about her appearance or her awkward, pigeon-toed gait. She was neat and clean, but there were no frills. For just a moment, Cissy was self-conscious about her splendid jewelry, but she straightened her back and spoke in her own direct manner.

"I'd be glad to help with cooking classes," she said. "I've had young girls into my home for cooking classes before."

"I've heard," Addams said, without mincing words, "factory girls. You've made great contributions, Mrs. Palmer."

Cissy nearly asked the young woman to call her by her first name but then thought better of it—at least for now. "I will, of course," she said with a smile, "make other contributions—specifically monetary—to your program."

"We will be appropriately grateful," Addams responded, her tone so slightly ironic that Cissy was not sure if she had heard correctly.

Cissy was always on guard against charity workers who solicited the rich for contributions and then scorned them for their wealth. She had long been fed up with the old business of damning the rich for their good fortune. If that were Addams' attitude, she would withdraw from the Hull House project. But she had heard that Addams herself had put a lot of private wealth into Hull House, and Cissy decided to wait a bit and see.

She began to spend one day a week at Hull House in the spacious but poorly equipped kitchen. The first day she offered a cooking lesson, she faced five expectant women who spoke only broken English.

"We will make a hearty vegetable soup, with vegetables that are available locally," she said, speaking as distinctly as possible. She had chosen soup as an economical dish. Most women could buy the ingredients at the local market.

Busily she showed them how to scrub the vegetables. Then she put the cleaned vegetables—carrots, potatoes, turnips—in some broth in the kettle, trying hard to explain that in growing months they could add peas, corn, tomatoes, whatever struck their imagination. If they have any imagination, she thought. She didn't realize that these women had scrubbed thousands of potatoes and carrots in their homeland, and her little exercise was amusing to them.

"Meat!" one said. "Must have meat. My man not eat if no meat."

"You don't always need meat," she explained patiently. "You must tell him that the vegetables can provide the nourishment he needs. And you can make a meat stock by boiling bones." Cissy had no concept of the physical effort that these women's husbands put out in their long days and the fact that they really did need meat to sustain them.

When Cissy began to add herbs to flavor the soup—"a little thyme, bay leaf, salt and pepper, and maybe some basil"—another woman shouted out, "Paprikah!"

Cissy thought a minute, and then said, "Paprika! Of course, we must have paprika."

But when yet another woman called out, "Kraut!" she threw her hands up in the air and began serving bowls of soup. The women ate cautiously.

When she arrived at Hull House the next week, a strong smell filled the building's halls. "What do I smell?" she asked Ellen Starr.

"Kraut and sausage soup. The ladies wanted to show you how they eat."

In the kitchen, Cissy found the five ladies of her class huddled around the soup kettle on the stove. "We fix," one lady said proudly, pointing to the kettle.

The smells, though strong, were not unpleasant. But when Cissy looked in the pot, she saw grease floating on the top. When they served her a bowl, she decided it would not be tactful to spoon the grease off. She dipped a tentative spoon into the soup, took a sip, then a bigger taste, and soon the bowl was empty.

"More?" they asked delightedly.

She shook her head. The soup was wonderful. As far as she could tell it had sauerkraut softened with tomatoes, chunks of potato and sausage—the latter the source of the grease. But how could she tell them about nutrition and American ways?

Cissy tried English-language classes and let others worry about the immigrants' nutrition. She worked one-on-one with the women on pronunciation and sentence structure. The results were much more satisfactory, for if the newcomers were anxious to cling to their food ways, they were equally anxious to lose their accents. They knew that speaking a pidgin German-English marked them forever as outsiders, and their children, trained in Chicago's schools, would be ashamed of them.

Potter Palmer was uncertain, to say the least, about his wife's days at Hull House. He thought she would do better to stay home with their boys. But one night, as she recounted her day at the settlement house, he reached over to cover his wife's hand with his own. "It's a good thing you do there, Cissy, even if the cooking didn't work out." He grinned a little as he said that. "If these people can learn to break the bad habits they brought with them, why any one of them can live like we do."

Cissy looked around at the elaborate room in which they sat, but she bit off the words that sprang to her tongue—"I hardly think so." Besides, Potter wanted everyone to abandon the customs of their homeland, those "bad habits" they had brought with them. But didn't he recognize that her own parents had clung to their southern heritage and yet prospered in this northern city? Potter, she realized for the umpteenth time, had little understanding of those whose way of life differed from his.

To her surprise, he went on, "I'm very pleased with your work at Hull House, Cissy. It makes a real contribution and yet doesn't put you in line with the anarchists or feminists or any of the extreme groups that cannot appreciate the opportunities of America."

Cissy knew that meant that Hull House had attracted society matrons, and it was now fashionable to be involved with the settlement house. She was doing something socially acceptable—far different from attending the Fortnightly Club. Potter also applauded her membership in the Woman's Club, not realizing that Cissy and other society matrons worked for the protection of women and children. They had done investigative work in asylums, hospital, poorhouses, and prisons. The result was that a woman physician had been assigned to the local asylum, and a matron appointed to the jail, to prevent male jailers from abusing the female prisoners.

Cissy's work with the Woman's Club and with Hull House did exactly what Jane Addams intended such work to do—it relieved women of "high society" of the feeling that their lives were useless.

But Cissy found a new meaning to her life with the World Columbian Exposition.

* * *

By the late 1880s, when the nation began to plan an exposition, Chicago was a city of over a million people, the second largest in the United States. It was a city of circles, with the retail and financial institutions clustered in the central districts. Factories and tenements ringed the downtown. Beyond lay the suburbs, from the North Shore to Hyde Park. Chicago was a segmented city, with inner city poverty and affluent suburbs. There was some effort to landscape the city—a park program designed to surround Chicago with a green belt resulted in Washington and Jackson parks, which were considered healthful areas. Excursion trains took workers to these parks and even farther out in the country to listen to polka bands. Green boulevards were planned, such as Drexel Boulevard on the city's South Side. Somewhere along the way, the Palmers' old farm was swallowed up and became part of the city.

Chicago was probably not in many minds when the United States began to plan an international exposition, ostensibly to celebrate the 400th anniversary of Columbus' discovery of America but really to showcase America's wealth and achievements. Several cities—St. Louis, Philadelphia, New York, and Chicago prime among them—were in fierce competition to host the event. Delegations crossed the Atlantic to attend the Universal Paris Exposition in 1889 and returned to swear that America could do it better and bigger. Other delegations lobbied Congress, where the locale would be decided. Men not only boosted their own city, they tried their mightiest to run down the competition.

New Yorkers scoffed that Chicago would put on a "cattle show." Determined to prove their sophistication, Chicagoans fought back by forming committees, raising money, and acting as though their city had already been chosen. The usual civic leaders—Field, Palmer, McCormick Jr., Medill, Pullman, and others—formed a citizens' commission in 1889 to secure the fair, but everyday citizens were part of the effort. Clerks and shop girls bought ten-dollar shares in the World's Exposition Corporation. Over thirty thousand Chicagoans subscribed.

On the day in February 1890 when the announcement was expected, hordes of people gathered outside the *Chicago Tribune* and at the offices of Western Union and the Postal Telegraph Company. At the *Tribune* offices, results were posted as they came in by wire. On the first congressional ballot, Chicago led New York by forty-three votes, both cities well ahead of St. Louis and Washington. But Chicago lacked the majority it needed to win. Ballot followed ballot. By the fifth vote, New York had gained fifteen votes, but Chicago only six. Throughout the city, people asked each other, "Have you heard yet? Have they decided?" Potter Palmer sat in his glassed-in cubicle in the hotel lobby and frequently sent a bellboy to check the tickertape. At O'Malley's, men drifting home from work gathered in knots and derided the fair as a project for "the swells." But they still wanted to know if their city had won.

When the final results were posted in the *Tribune* window, the crowd was struck silent for a moment. Then pandemonium broke loose, with yelling and shouting and cheering. Congress chose Chicago. Messenger boys raced off with the news to many destinations, including the Palmer House and the offices of architects Burnham and Root. The city celebrated for two full days—pubs and fancy restaurants alike did a booming business, people stopped each other on the street to rejoice. The mood of the city ran high. Chicago, they told themselves, had been chosen because it was a railroad hub and because it had shown that it could produce events—no one mentioned that the major events in the city's history were a disastrous fire and a tragic riot. Nor did they mention that the over four million dollars the city promised had some influence with Congress.

In April 1890, President Benjamin Harrison signed the bill designating Chicago as the site of the World's Columbian Exposition. The date was pushed back to 1893 to give the city time to prepare. Now they had to choose a location.

* * *

"I've been named second vice president of the Chicago Fair Corporation, which means I'm a member of the board of directors," Potter said one night in April of 1890, pulling his glasses down a little on his nose and looking at Cissy over the top of the paper he was reading.

Cissy had been a member of a large group of women who called themselves the auxiliary executive committee to the citizens committee. The women had raised almost as much money as the men. Now, hearing Potter's announcement, she asked idly, "How many directors are there in this corporation?"

"Forty-four. Mostly people you know. Lyman Gage of First National is president, Thomas Bryan is first vice president . . . ."

She interrupted his list. "How many women among the forty-four?" she asked, knowing the answer full well.

"Now, Cissy . . . ." His tone was patient. "You know that men can accomplish more. You women will get your share of this exposition before it's all over. The national commission has the authority to appoint a board of lady managers."

"They'll be managers in name only," she predicted, "and the name is unfortunate. It makes them sound like a group of idle women with nothing more on their minds than the latest fashions from Paris."

"I know some women feel that way," he admitted, "but they're too sensitive."

"Some women," she said, echoing him and drawing out the words, "would rather be part of the general planning than shunted off by themselves."

"Hah!" he scoffed. "You know who they are as well as I do. Feminists like Susan Anthony. Thank God you're not like that, Cissy."

"I may still cut my hair," she said, using the teasing tone of voice by which she sometimes worked around Potter's disapproval.

He ignored her. "I think you'll get your separate pavilion. Wasn't that what the auxiliary wanted?"

She nodded. "But, to paraphrase Mr. Lincoln, you'll find you won't please all the women all of the time . . . or even most of the time. And you haven't heard the last of the Isabellas by any means."

The Isabellas were a group of women who operated almost at counter-purposes to the auxiliary. Where the auxiliary was interested in charitable works and the exhibition of women's industries, the Isabellas were dedicated to the causes of equal rights and suffrage. They were mostly professional women—doctors and lawyers.

They had taken Queen Isabella of Spain as their symbol. When they announced their name, Cissy reminded Potter that all Isabella had done was to send Columbus to the New World. "I can send you to the exposition," she suggested.

He shook his head. "No, you want too badly to be part of the planning."

Now she asked, "Have appointments been made to the board of lady managers yet?"

"No. I imagine," he said dryly, "that you'll be one of the first to know."

She was open and honest. "I hope so."

"I hope," Potter said, "that your friend Harrison will no longer be mayor when the exposition comes. "We need a mayor with polish, sophistication . . . not just a genial, good-hearted—"

"Don't," Cissy said, not wanting to hear him slander Harrison. "You told me before the last election that he would never be elected again, but he was," she said. "Is he a member of the corporation for the exposition?"

"No, he's a director. There's a difference, but it's all too complicated. Next they're going to appoint a board of control, to sort of coordinate between the national commission and the local corporation. Too many chiefs and not enough Indians."

"Harrison wants to be an Indian," she said, "as mayor."

Potter stood up suddenly and began pacing the room. "I wish the blasted thing had been given to St. Louis," he said at last, with a vehemence that surprised her. "We don't need the whole world visiting Chicago."

She was tempted to remind him it would be good for businesses, including his, but he already knew that. He had done his civic duty and helped bring the exposition to Chicago, but she knew he dreaded being part of it. Just as he dreaded attending dinner parties. *The difference in our ages is showing more and more every day.*

"I'm going to walk along the lakeshore," Potter said, turning and striding out of the room.

Cissy Palmer sat for a long time, thinking about the fair and what part she could have in it. If Carter Harrison had anything to do with it, she expected a big part, and she expected to hear from him soon. She smiled to herself and got up to see if the boys were doing their studies.

Six months after the president signed the decree, the exposition committee had still not decided where the fair should be built. Daniel Burnham, bemoaning the lost time, suggested several sites. The dedication of the grounds was scheduled for October 12, 1892, just twenty-six months away. *How,* he stormed, *can they schedule a dedication before they choose a site?*

Meanwhile, he had to tend to the firm's other projects. The WCTU building at LaSalle and Monroe, a paean to temperance, was one of the city's tallest buildings when built. In October 1890 the ladies held a cornerstone ceremony. The building was complete, except for the cornerstone. The women tried to overlook the fact that the nearby Masonic Fraternity Temple, at twenty-one stories, overshadowed theirs and was the tallest building in the world.

Mrs. Frances E. Willard presided over the ceremonies. Carter Harrison was there, part of his campaign to regain the mayoralty. Burnham appeared, representing his architectural firm, though everyone knew he enjoyed a good glass of wine as much as Harrison liked his pint and his Kentucky bourbon.

To Harrison's alarm, when Burnham passed the silver trowel to Mrs. Willard—after all, they couldn't put a bottle of champagne in the cornerstone—Eunice Johnson leapt from the crowd, fell on her knees, and began praising the Lord God in a loud voice. Even Mrs. Willard looked embarrassed.

Harrison went to her. "Eunice? Let me help you up."

She raised wild eyes toward him. "I am praising the Lord for this great edifice," she shouted.

Frances Willard had regained enough composure to command in a soft voice, "Go with him, Eunice. I'll talk to you later."

Carter Harrison, sighing over lost opportunities to gain votes, took Eunice Johnson back to the Willards' North Side home. There he waited with her until Frances Willard returned, triumphant, from the ceremony. It was some four hours, because there had been a reception—with apple juice, of course.

Eunice was so distraught—crying out, "Why did you bring me here? Don't you know my place is at the ceremony?" and then bursting into sobs—that Harrison was afraid to leave her. On the other hand, he was impatient to be among "his" people, not stuck here with an emotionally disturbed woman.

When Mrs. Willard sailed in under a full steam of self-satisfaction, he rose immediately, barely making the polite acknowledgments before he said, "Well, I must go. An appointment I'm late for, you know."

Within a week, he heard that Eunice Johnson had been committed, against her will, to the county insane asylum. His guilt haunted him the rest of his life, but he could not imagine what he could have done differently.

* * *

In September 1890, Carter notified Cissy Palmer that she was one of two delegates from Illinois to the Board of Lady Managers of the World Columbian Exposition. The board would meet in November to choose a president.

"I want to be president," she told Potter as they shared a late-night drink in front of the fire.

"Harrison assumes you will be," her husband assured her.

"But the ladies will have to vote," she protested. "And I don't know any of the delegates."

Potter cleared his throat and spoke slowly and deliberately. "Although I don't always approve of them, Carter Harrison has his ways. It would be unseemly of you to appear to be campaigning. I think you'll just have to bide your time."

Biding her time was not something Cissy did easily. November seemed a long time away.

Chapter Fourteen

Cissy sat in her new office waiting for Daniel Burnham, the architect for the exposition. She'd met Burnham a time or two and liked him, but now she was prepared for a difficult meeting.

"Mrs. Palmer," Burnham said most correctly, "I have good news for you."

She rose from her desk and extended her hand. "I'm delighted, of course, Mr. Burnham. Won't you have a seat?" She indicated the armchair across from her small desk.

Even as she took her own seat again, Cissy was aware of the increased interest on the part of Phoebe, her assistant, whose ears had literally perked up and whose eyes were riveted on the visitor. Phoebe had been dumped on her—there was no other word for it—and Cissy suspected she had strong ties to the Isabellas. She wished there were a way to dismiss the woman so she could have private meetings.

"I want to talk to you about the ladies' building," Burnham said without wasting any time on pleasantries.

"Good," Cissy replied, reaching for a sheaf of papers. "I have some pencil sketches here of what I envision." She had spent long hours over these sketches, first formulating in her mind what type of building would work best and then committing her ideas to paper. She had excelled in drawing in school, and she felt her sketches were clear enough to serve as a guide to any competent architect. They showed a building with a central two-story gallery surrounded on both floors by exhibition rooms. "Here," she said, handing them to Burnham.

He took them without much notice, merely holding them in one hand without examining them. "We have," he said smoothly, "secured Richard Morris Hunt as the architect for the ladies' building. He is, as I'm sure you know, an expert on neoclassic architecture and one of the most honored architects in America. It is a real triumph that he has agreed to add your building to the list of those on which he will work. I'm sure you will be more than pleased with his plans." Only then did he glance at the sketches in his hand. It simply did not occur to him that Cissy was serious about her rough sketches.

Cissy's mouth twitched in amusement. Behind her, Phoebe fell into an exaggerated posture of indignation. "He is also, I believe, a man." Cissy spoke softly.

"Well, of course he is a man," Burnham replied, his expression showing confusion.

"To meet women's needs and show off women's produce to best advantage, the building must be designed by a woman," Cissy said, her voice still soft but now with an added degree of firmness.

"A woman!" He was amazed. "There are no women architects, at least not licensed, in all of Illinois and damned few—pardon me—in the entire country." He paused for a minute. "Let's see, there's Minerva Parker Nichols—"

At the mention of that name, Phoebe became even more distraught and was visibly anxious.

Cissy ignored the woman behind her. "I believe," she said smoothly, "that Mrs. Nichols is at work on plans for a building for the Isabella group." She badly wanted to add, "Although they say they do not want a separate building . . . and they will never be granted permission for one." Instead, she said, "My informants tell me it is of Moorish design and not suited to the neoclassic theme of the exposition."

Daniel Burnham was nobody's fool. "What do you propose, Mrs. Palmer?" he asked.

"A competition," Cissy said immediately. The plan had been in her head for weeks. "There will be a first prize of a thousand dollars, with second and third prizes of five hundred and two hundred and fifty. The winning design will be chosen by a panel of architects—perhaps Mr. Hunt would like to be one of them?—and will be used to erect the building." She paused. "I would suggest . . . but not insist . . . that my sketches be given to the entrants as guidance. The winner will be brought to Chicago and her expenses paid to be present while construction proceeds."

Burnham sat silently, apparently processing this idea in his mind and not pressured to answer quickly.

Cissy knew only too well that her plan for a building would come to a total cost of one thousand, seven-hundred-fifty dollars, considerably less than Hunt's fee would have been. Burnham could save a great deal of money on the ladies' building and apply it to another project. And yet her plans satisfied the goals of the lady managers.

"I think," he said slowly, "that we might consider that plan. I'll discuss it with the board of control." He made his farewells to Cissy, nodded to Phoebe, who glared at him, and left the office a little dazed.

"It's not a good idea," Phoebe said darkly after he left. "The men will end choosing our building, even if it is a woman who plans it."

"I think it is a grand idea," Cissy said.

Phoebe left without another word, gathering her things in rather noisy and obvious anger.

The call for architectural plans was issued in early February, with the closing date as soon as late March. Interested lady architects had only six weeks in which to develop drawings.

* * *

Carter Harrison called on Cissy a week or so after her meeting with Daniel Burnham. She had seen him only occasionally since her appointment, and Cissy was disappointed he did not take more interest in the women's projects.

"You've done a smooth bit of work," he said, sinking, uninvited, into the chair opposite her desk. She looked, he thought, more vibrant than ever. Responsibilities agreed with her, energized her. He had missed her, but he had deliberately not come to see her, for being with Cissy Palmer only reminded him how much he was missing in his life.

"I'm sure I don't know what you mean," she said demurely, lowering her eyes.

He roared with laughter. "Burnham, that's what I mean!"

Phoebe Couzins pounded the keys of that newfangled machine—called a typewriter—all the more loudly, as though to make it clear she was not listening—which she was. Ironically, it had been Carter Harrison who had so proudly presented the machine to the office.

"Mr. Burnham and I," Cissy said, "came to an agreement. I was able to help him see the ladies' point of view."

"And to save him a lot of money," Harrison chortled.

"I'm afraid," Cissy said with a slight grin, "that I tend to think of quality before cost. Apparently, at least in this case, I have not been a spendthrift."

"Far from it," Harrison said, still amused at her wily ways. "A coup, Mrs. Palmer, a great coup!" He stood and bowed before her.

"I am glad, Mr. Harrison, that I have been able to make an important savings."

He was still laughing when he left her office. Cissy sat, thoughtlessly twirling a pencil in her hands, her eyes off in space, unaware for once that Phoebe Couzins was again watching her closely.

* * *

Cissy expected that John Root would be part of the judging process, and she looked forward to meeting the man about whom she'd heard so much. Root did not go about in society like Daniel Burnham, and Cissy had never met him but she knew that he was musical—he played the organ at the Presbyterian Church on Sundays—and that he was a lively and skilled conversationalist. But John Root died before the plans for the woman's building were submitted.

In January, when the new board of architects was meeting for the first time in Chicago, Root came down with pneumonia. The illness at first seemed mild, and Root used his confinement to sketch and to joke with his wife, Dora, and with Burnham, who stayed quite close to his partner's bedside. But his breathing became more labored, and his dreams strange and shapeless. In his last moments, he ran his fingers over the bedclothes, playing an imaginary piano.

* * *

The plans submitted for the woman's building were opened at a formal meeting in early March. Cissy went to the opening with a sinking heart. There were thirteen sealed bids, to be opened at 2:00 P.M., and by noon Cissy was beset with doubts: what if her idea had failed and no plan was acceptable? She had asked to take the plans back to her executive committee, but Burnham insisted decisions had to be made on the spot. Hunt would be there, and of course Burnham would have an opinion—probably a strong one, Cissy thought ruefully. She was able to take two of her committee with her—Frances Shepard and Amey Starkweather. Suddenly, intensely, she wished Carter Harrison were at the meeting, though he had no reason to be there.

"The three of you," Burnham had said, "will be able to make the decision, along with Hunt and myself. I have confidence."

Mrs. Nichols had submitted the same Moorish plans she had drawn for the Isabellas. There was little consideration of her effort, but of the others, five had real merit.

"I like this one," Cissy said boldly, pointing to one drawing and all the while sure that Hunt would immediately show her the flaws in it.

Hunt was a man of medium build, with an iron-gray mustache and goatee. He spoke so cordially to Cissy, upon meeting, that she thought she had been wrong in her negative reaction to him. Now he stroked his goatee in consideration and did not speak for several minutes, while the others waited in expectation.

Finally, Amey Starkweather could stand it no longer. "I like that one, too," she said.

At last Hunt spoke. "It is," he said sonorously, "by far the most suitable. The balconies, the loggias and vases for flowers—all of it is light and gay and indicates a building meant for a joyous and festive occasion."

"Why," Amey whispered to Cissy, "that's just what I was saying. I just didn't use exactly the same words."

Cissy breathed a sigh of relief. She would mention to no one that the plan followed her own basic sketches, with wings forming exhibit halls around the large main hall.

Sophia Hayden submitted the plan chosen. She received an architectural degree from the Massachusetts Institute of Technology. Second prize went to Lois Howe, a colleague of Miss Hayden from MIT, and third to Laura Hayes, a government clerk with no architectural training but a good eye and a good sense of the use of a building.

As she left the judging, Cissy knew that Phoebe Couzins' response to the Hayden plan would be negative. "Too expensive," the secretary would shrill, "and too casual. It won't give significance to what women have done."

And an ersatz Moorish temple would?

* * *

Matters between Phoebe and Cissy came to a head shortly after the architectural competition. Phoebe Couzins knew that she was not well that morning in early April when she dragged herself into the office, but she felt obligated to get out the minutes of the November meeting. To her practical mind, it was a disgrace that the meeting, now some five months past, had still not been legitimized by properly published minutes.

Head aching, throat raw, vision almost blurry, she sat at her desk and pounded out the last paragraphs on the typewriter. The darned contraption made so many mistakes—even, she was sure, when she hit the correct key—that she thought it would be better to write the minutes in longhand and send them to the printer. But Mrs. Palmer insisted she use the typewriter, since Mayor Harrison had been good enough to donate it.

Phoebe's hands paused above the keys, and she wasted a moment's thought on Carter Harrison. Big and loud he was, an offensive man. Cissy surely seemed to butter up to him, though. They would both have their comeuppance, Phoebe thought, when the inner workings of the board of control were made public—and publication of these minutes was the first step.

At last, she laid the minutes on Cissy's desk and put with them a note explaining that she was ill. Would Mrs. Palmer be so kind as to send the minutes directly to the printer once she'd read them? In a day or two, her health recovered, Phoebe would see to their distribution.

Mrs. Palmer did no such thing. Aghast at the mistakes, innuendoes, and accusations in the minutes, she slashed at them with her pen, marking this out, adding a phrase of explanation there, and working almost the entire afternoon on them. Still, they were in no shape to be published, and Cissy left a note to that effect. Then she took the offending minutes home with her.

Phoebe Couzins almost succumbed to influenza. Sicker than she had ever been in her life, she truly believed that she was about to die. Her one regret: her work for the Columbian Exposition would go unfulfilled, and she would have failed the Isabellas.

Thanks to the ministrations of her mother, who came from St. Louis, and to a naturally hardy constitution, Phoebe slowly began to regain her health. In late April she was beginning to feel strong enough to think about going to her office—those minutes? Where were they?—when her brother was taken ill with the same disease. Mother and daughter immediately left Chicago for St. Louis. By the time her brother recovered, it was mid-May.

* * *

"Where's your sidekick?" Carter Harrison had asked one day when he dropped by Cissy's office,

"She's been ill, and now her brother is very ill," Cissy said.

"Gives you some privacy anyway," Harrison said. "I'm sorry about this tiny office, but there's just no space . . . ."

Cissy shrugged. "I'll do what I have to. It's just that Miss Couzins and I disagree on almost everything . . . ."

He laughed aloud. "I can imagine, after one look at her." Then he sobered. "I've missed seeing you, Cissy, something I could never have said if she"—he jerked his head toward Phoebe's desk—"were here."

She noted his use of her first name. "I've missed you, too. I hope you're doing well," she said formally.

He caught the unspoken message. "Fine, thank you, just fine. I . . . well, I miss Sophie but I'm getting on." He paused a moment. "I didn't mean to get out of line just now. It's just that you have always . . . well, you seem to understand me. Not all the big shots in this city do."

Cissy was at a loss what so say. *I'm not a big shot? I don't really understand you at all? But you intrigue me?* None of those seemed right. She settled for an impersonal, "I'm glad I've been of some help to you. And . . . and I'm grateful that you put me in this position."

Harrison studied her and wondered what was going on in that beautiful head. He sensed that she kept him at a distance out of a sense of propriety—didn't he hear she'd been trained by nuns?—but that she was sorely tempted to a closer friendship. He had never hoped for intimacy with Cissy Palmer—that, he knew, was beyond his grasp. But Carter Harrison had known enough women in his life to sense when one was attracted to him. He was also smart enough not to push his luck. So he rose, bowed, and said, "I worked to secure your election because I knew you were the best person for the job."

As he left, she said, "Potter and I are going to Europe in May."

He turned, surprised. *Why would she travel, when there was so much to be done?* "My best wishes for an enjoyable trip."

"It's business," she said. "We're looking for items from various countries for the ladies' building."

"Then my best wishes for your success." And he was gone.

Cissy relived those moments in her mind a thousand times as she sat at her desk. What could she have said differently? Was she cold and formal? Did he think she put herself on a pedestal? Wishing he could come back and she could live those moments all over again, she decided to give up for the day and go home. The thought that Potter would be waiting for her was cold comfort at that moment.

* * *

Potter Palmer accompanied his wife to Europe, but not without some reluctance.

"What will you do while Cissy makes calls?" Henry Honoré asked his son-in-law. Honoré was delighted that the Palmers were going on this trip, for it meant that the two boys, young Honoré and the frail Min, would spend the summer at their grandparents' home. Their grandfather intended to make it an outdoor summer of healthy exercise for them, and he smiled blandly every time Cissy mentioned continuing their lessons. The grandfather planned a summer of riding bareback and diving into a swimming hole. He was particularly worried about Min and intended to "toughen" him over the summer.

Now, in response to his question, Palmer sighed. "Well, I shall have to accompany her to evening events where titled noblemen will roll their eyes at this country bumpkin from Chicago. I can hear them now: 'Chicago? Can't say that I've been there, old chap. In the West, is it?'" His imitation of a British accent was perfect.

"You can tell them it's next to California," Honoré laughed. "But you're not exactly a country bumpkin, Potter. You can hold your own with the most sophisticated."

"If I have to," Potter agreed, "but it won't be pleasure." Then he hastened to add, "Don't tell Cissy I said that."

Honoré nodded his head in agreement.

"Actually," Potter went on, "I intend to spend my days looking at horses and art. Horses in England, art in Paris. I promised the Art Institute that I'd bring back some of the best of the new impressionists . . . maybe some Degas. Who knows? I'll see what's available."

"Lord knows you have an eye for art," the father-in-law admitted. "You make me feel the country bumpkin in that regard."

The two men shared a chuckle and poured themselves more brandy. But Potter Palmer sat thoughtfully over his brandy long after his father-in-law had gone in search of Cissy. A man of action who measured his life by direct results, Potter was not given to brooding. Yet he was troubled by this forthcoming trip to Europe.

One evening just days before they left, Potter and Cissy sat in the smaller, more intimate drawing room. He sipped a brandy, she claret, and they talked companionably about their trip.

Suddenly changing the subject, Potter said, "Have you heard about the election?"

Cissy shook her head. Elections were men's business, and she often didn't get word until Potter brought her the news. Some wives, she knew, never got word and were blissfully unaware of who their elected officials were.

"Harrison was defeated again."

She gasped and said, "I am so sorry. He wanted the office so badly."

Potter gave her a long look. "Yes, he did. And he might have been best for Chicago. Who knows? Certainly he's enthusiastic about the exposition." It was the closest Cissy had heard her husband come to saying something good about Carter Harrison in a long time.

"I wonder if he'll travel again," she mused, "as he did the last time he was defeated."

"No, he's apparently talking of buying the *Times* and turning himself into a newspaper editor."

* * *

Cissy and Potter sailed in May, once winter storms were well past in the Atlantic. They went on the *USS Victoria*, an ocean liner fitted with every conceivable luxury from walnut-paneled walls to a master chef. Their stateroom was large and comfortable, and Potter prepared for a restful crossing during which he could read and sleep and ignore what lay ahead.

Cissy, however, was a one-woman machine, making lists, planning her days aloud, pacing from one end of the stateroom to the other, often with a sheaf of papers in her hand. Sometimes she would suddenly begin to talk to Potter, as though they'd been having a conversation on the subject.

"If only Secretary Blaine had done his job and notified the various ministers that we were coming . . . ." she began one day. James Blaine, the secretary of state, had fallen seriously ill, just after Cissy had notified him of her travel plans.

Potter put down his book. "You know Blaine was ill, Cissy. It's not as though he didn't do his job," he said patiently. "You can call Robert Lincoln. He can make appointments for you."

"And young Stanton—Eliza's son—is in Paris as resident commissioner for the exposition," she went on. "He surely can help me there."

"You're not exactly in the same political camp as his mother," Potter said mildly.

"But we all want the exposition to succeed, Potter," Cissy flared. "We'll have to put aside these petty differences."

"Of course we will," he said, picking up his book again.

* * *

Potter Palmer found himself driving a barouche with high-stepping chestnut horses through Hyde Park on a Sunday afternoon. Beside him sat Cissy, stiffly regal.

"Look at that gilded coach," he said. "You don't see that on Lake Shore Drive."

"Potter," she said softly, "we are not in Chicago." Cissy knew that her husband was uncomfortable about this trip. She knew Potter Palmer well enough to see the signs: a tendency to withdraw, an absent look in his eyes, a lack of ardor at night. But not quite as astute about her husband as he himself was, she was bothered by his discomfort. He should, to her mind, have been boastfully proud of her important mission. Instead, he had a slight hangdog look about him and insisted on comparing everything to Chicago, something he'd never done before in Europe, where he'd always recognized each country and sightseeing wonder for its own uniqueness.

"I can tell that from looking around," he said, appreciatively studying the horses. "We don't have horses like these in Chicago."

Bother the horses! Cissy, ever planning her strategy, was studying the people. She was sure that if she watched them and learned their ways, she could enlist them as supporters of the exposition.

"There," she said, "that's the duke and duchess of Teck, with Princess May. And there, that lady who just stepped out of her carriage, that's the countess of Warwick."

"Which one?" Potter asked, for all around them ladies were seated in the shade, while men on the most wonderful horses Potter had ever seen stopped to talk to them.

"I shall have to get a white China silk carriage gown," Cissy murmured. "That's what most seem to wear."

"And those clanking things around the waist, with all those trinkets hanging from them," Potter said in disgust. "The women are liked belled cats."

"Those are chatelaines," Cissy said frostily, "and they're all the rage. I must have one." She lowered her eyes and then looked sideways at him flirtatiously.

"Of course, my darling," he said, reaching for her hand. "You shall have three or four of the damn things if you wish."

Cissy used their outings in the park to settle in her mind the people she needed to see and to make her presence in England generally known. Within days, she herself sat in a chair in the shade, and various people stopped to talk to her, while Potter drove the barouche around the park, admiring the other horses and carriages and making notes of the fine things he would take home to Chicago.

Cissy met with Edward, the prince of Wales, and the British Royal Commission. These men were enthusiastic about her proposals for a women's exhibition. But, they said, shaking their heads, she would have to secure the Queen's backing.

"The Queen?" Cissy said. "I cannot get an audience with Her Majesty."

The prince of Wales shook his head but the smile that emerged through his walrus mustache was genuine. "No, I doubt that you can. But I can arrange for you to see my sister, Princess Christian. She heads the South Kensington School of Art Needlework and the Hospital School for Training Nurses. Sometimes, to her majesty's dismay, Christian makes a study of the effects of industry on the lives of women. But the Queen listens to her."

Cissy felt a slight bit of awe that she should be talking to the son of the Queen in such casual terms about what his mother— Her Majesty—did and did not like. But as she always did, she gathered herself into composure. "Does the Queen . . . well, is she likely to approve of our goal of demonstrating women's work?"

The prince twirled his mustache and spoke very carefully. "Her Majesty is offended by the—what to you call them—suffragettes? They infect both your land and ours, and she is horrified at their outrageousness. But she is also proud of the work that women do, and she recognizes that many women of very poor circumstances turn out wonderful handiwork. She would not want the British Empire to be excluded from such an exhibition."

Cissy smiled, thanked him for his help, and waited for her appointment with Princess Christian.

When the two women met over tea, Cissy was struck by the princess' beauty. *She's much prettier than her mother, the Queen,* Cissy thought. Cissy had decided from a distant glimpse that the Queen was actually not a very attractive woman, even disregarding her now advancing age. But Cissy kept that thought to herself and didn't even share it later with Potter.

"It is kind of you to see me, your highness," she said.

"I am anxious to hear about your work," the princess replied, leading the way to a pair of Louis XIV chairs with a small tea table set between them. The table held a silver teapot, creamer and sugar bowl, and a small platter of finger sandwiches, all on an elaborately detailed silver tray. The princess poured, and Cissy put milk in her tea. She had learned it was the British way.

"I want the exposition to display the things women make, from art to literature, and the things women do—medicine, law. I want to show the full range of how much women have developed in the four hundred years since Columbus discovered America."

"Oh, my," the princess said, setting her cup down so vehemently that Cissy heard the clink of china meeting china. Looking straight at Cissy, she said, "I believe that women should be trained to care for their families, beautify their homes, and nurse the sick. They don't need so-called careers like medicine and the law."

"But women must have a place in whatever profession they choose," Cissy insisted, never flinching, "and they must be paid equally for the work they do."

"Ah, Mrs. Palmer," the young princess said philosophically, "I am afraid you have been influenced by those women of extreme opinions and loud voices—the suffragettes. I believe they are much more active in your country than ours, thank goodness."

Well, Cissy thought, the prince had warned her. She began hesitantly. "No," she said thoughtfully, "I have not. Those women believe that women should not be separated from men, that all is equal. I do not think that, but I am aware that not all women are given the opportunities that you and I are . . . and that those women who of necessity must find gainful employment should have more fair opportunities."

"And better training," the princess agreed readily.

"I have worked with some women much less fortunate than myself," Cissy said and went on to describe her work with the factory girls, her days at Hull House.

The princess paid close attention. "You had these women in your home?" she asked incredulously.

"Yes. It seemed the logical place to meet with them."

The princess permitted herself a small smile. "Mamá would never agree to that," she said, "but I very much admire what you've done."

In the end, Princess Christian agreed to head a committee in Britain that would put together items for the women's exhibit. The committee included the Countess of Aberdeen, who was developing cottage industries in Scotland and Ireland and who wanted very much to set up an Irish village at the exposition. There was also Lady Jeune, who had once maintained a literary salon frequented by poets Alfred Lord Tennyson and Robert Browning.

"We will get a good contribution to the exhibit from England," she told Potter that night. "The princess will appoint a committee that includes mostly traditional Victorian women but one or two free spirits. I think they will send some fine things for display, like the sweaters the Irish women knit." Then, with real interest, she asked, "What did you do today?"

"Went to the races," he said happily. "They really have fine horseflesh in this country, Cissy." In fact, the horseflesh—and the fact that he could go off on his own during the day—was adding greatly to Potter's enjoyment of the trip.

And that night, in the drawing room of the Marchioness of Salisbury, Potter Palmer talked easily with duke of this and marquis of that about horses, while Cissy charmed the gathering with her soft, feminine ways and never once mentioned equal rights for women.

"You were charming tonight," she said to him when they returned to their hotel suite.

"No, my dear," he said drolly, "you were the one who was charming. I saw the men's eyes glaze over with boredom if I mentioned the exposition, so I simply talked to them about horses. It worked for both of us."

Potter Palmer found himself desperately wanting his wife, but as he lay beneath the covers, waiting for her to join him in the bed they of necessity shared in this hotel suite, he wondered if that were his way of exerting his dominance. He hoped not. Then he said silently to himself, "Balderdash! A man could think himself into a lot of trouble."

When Cissy slid demurely into her side of the bed, he was instantly next to her, kissing her neck, whispering in her ear, stroking her belly until she rose to meet him.

* * *

In Paris, Cissy met with Madame Carnot, wife of the president, and found her as conservative about suffrage and women flaunting their powers outside of the home as Princess Christian had been. Although there was an active group of women who had served on the Paris Exposition of 1889, Madame Carnot had kept herself aloof from that effort. Still, with Cissy's gentle persuasion, she agreed to head the women's work in France for the Columbian Exposition.

Cissy moved on to talk with other wives of government officials and, one by one, enlisted them in her cause. But her real triumph came when she met the Minister of Commerce.

"Why should women stand apart in an exhibition?" he asked with a Gallic shrug. "I cannot see the need for a separate building."

Speaking in perfect French, Cissy said, "If women's work is displayed with men's, it will be overlooked. It is important to demonstrate how much women of the world have learned in the four hundred years since Queen Isabella sent Columbus to discover the Americas." She cut her eyes demurely, deliberately flirting with the man, and then, raising her gaze again, handed him a sheaf of papers. "Here are preliminary drawings of the building. They were done by a woman architect."

The minister accepted them with another Gallic shrug. Monsieur Jules Roche had never had a woman so fashionably dressed in his office, nor one who spoke with him in such a businesslike fashion, nor, especially, an American who spoke his language so well. He had expected halting, schoolgirl French. And, secretly, he had worried that Mrs. Palmer would, well, wear bloomers—who knew what these American women would wear?—and be somewhat spinsterish, her hair perhaps in that awful bob that some rebellious women were sporting. Cissy overwhelmed him.

"There will be a women's commission appointed in France," he assured her, "with a budget of . . . oh, let us say two-hundred-fifty thousand francs." He waved his hand expansively in the air.

Cissy smothered a gasp. That was larger than the budget given the board of lady managers by the U.S. Congress.

"You are most kind," she said, rising to leave. The minister bent over her hand and murmured, "You are most persuasive, Madame Palmer."

Cissy could feel herself blushing as she swept out of his office.

* * *

"Cissy," Potter said that evening in their suite at the Grande Hotel, "someone is joining us for dinner tonight."

"Oh? Who?"

"A surprise, my darling," he said, looking secretive and pleased with himself. Then he drew a hand from behind his back. "Here, a little something I picked up for you today."

Happily, she took the box he offered and in slow, drawn-out gestures untied the ribbon and unwrapped the paper.

"Can't you hurry?" he asked impatiently.

"I like to prolong the suspense," she said, smiling at him. At length, she opened the box, pulled back the tissue, and lifted out a parure—a matching set of jewels for her hair, ears, and neck. These were diamond-encrusted gold roses, with rubies adding highlights—a single rose would lie on a gold chain at the base of her throat, perfect roses would adorn each ear, and a string of roses would be pinned into her hair.

"Potter! They are the most beautiful things I've ever owned. How did you . . . I mean, they're so perfect . . . ."

"They remember you at Tiffany's," he said, "and they know your taste."

"They do . . . and you do," she said, rising to kiss him.

The surprise guest that night was Sara Hallowell, an American who operated on behalf of artists and dealers in Paris. The Palmers had known Hallowell in Chicago, when she saw to it that six works by Monet, four by Pissarro, and one by Degas were hung at the 1890 Chicago Interstate Industrial Exposition. Potter had been on the art committee for that event and was much taken with the Impressionists, though not everyone in Chicago shared his view.

"The colors are blotchy and they clash," wrote Harriet Monroe in *Art Amateur*. Potter had not yet forgiven Monroe and had privately scoffed at the "Columbian Ode" Monroe had been commissioned to compose for the exposition.

"Sara Hallowell should be director of fine arts for the exposition," Cissy had fumed at Potter months before they left for Europe. "The only thing that holds her back is that she is a woman."

Potter had shrugged at the time. He knew the post was going to a man—Halsey Ives—and another gentlemen—Charles Kurtz of New York—would be named his assistant. Sara was to be appointed secretary to the director, at a much-reduced salary.

"See," Cissy had fumed, "Sara will do all the work, and the men will get all the pay! It's simply not to be borne." She pounded her fist angrily on the table in front of her, and Potter sought to soothe her.

"Sara will bear the responsibility of choosing the art. The exhibit will reflect her taste," he said.

"But her pay and her position will not reflect her responsibility," Cissy had said, with real anger in her voice, though she realized it was not Potter specifically at whom she was angry.

Now, in Paris, which was home ground to Sara and tourist turf for Cissy, the two women greeted each other cordially. Cissy was relieved that Sara bore no ill will over her diminished appointment.

"Sara and I have spent the day together, prowling galleries and studios," Potter said over claret in the hotel's dining room. "I found some interesting pieces to take back to the institute—the Degas I'd hoped for, a Manet, another Monet, but, unfortunately, I found no suitable Pissarro."

"For the institute," Cissy said in a tone that she supposed confirmed what she knew to be true.

Potter smiled broadly. "No, my dear, for your gallery at home."

"Potter, I thought you were buying for the institute!" Cissy was pleased at the prospect of adding to the collection of fine paintings already in her own home—most purchased with the help of Sara Hallowell—but troubled that perhaps Potter had been untrue to his mission.

"I shall loan them from time to time," he said grandiosely, and both women laughed. "And, of course, they will be on exhibit at the exposition."

After they ordered—fois gras for Potter and salmon mousse for the ladies, as starters—Sara spoke directly to Cissy. "I want to recommend the work of two women to you for the murals proposed for the Woman's Building."

The murals would be large—twelve by fifty-eight feet—and curved to fit the barrel-vaulted glass roof. One would be called *Primitive Woman*, while the other would be titled *Modern Woman*.

"Who are they?"

"One is Mary MacMonnies . . . she goes by her full name, Mary Fairchild MacMonnies. She's married to Frederick MacMonnies, who's already at work on a wondrously beautiful fountain for the exposition. MacMonnies work tends to be rather classical . . . . I think she should be given the commission for the primitive woman piece."

"And the other?" Potter inquired curiously.

"Mary Cassatt," Sara Hallowell replied simply. "You know her, an American who's been taken under Degas' wing, lived here most of her life." Sara looked at Cissy. "A woman considerably older than you."

Cissy smiled, for she knew that there was probably not even ten years difference in their ages. Sara was delightfully tactful.

"We own a Cassatt painting," Potter said, "and admire her work greatly. I think she's an excellent choice."

Sara opened her mouth to speak, seemed to think better of it and closed it, then, at length—with Potter and Cissy looking expectantly at her—said, "They don't get along, you know."

Cissy's heart sank. All she needed were more women at each other's throats. "Who doesn't get along?" she asked cautiously.

"MacMonnies and Cassatt." When she began to explain, the words tumbled rapidly, nervously, from Sara. "It's mostly Cassatt . . . she's . . . well, the British term is prickly. Doesn't get along too much with anyone. But she's fabulously talented . . . and she wants to do this project."

Potter mused aloud. "Their work wouldn't exactly have to complement each other's—they'll be so far apart."

"And," Sara added, "if I envision the projects correctly, far above people's heads."

"That will put a burden on the artists, no doubt of it," Potter said. "I, for one, am anxious to see what these ladies will come up with."

In her most businesslike tone, Cissy said, "I would like to see preliminary sketches from both of them." Then she added, "But I will brook no fighting—if we contract with them, that must be made clear. And so must the deadlines."

Sara, on behalf of her clients, readily agreed, and Potter and Cissy left the meeting well satisfied that they had made great strides for the woman's building. The contracts, she told Sara, would be mailed as soon as she returned to her office. But they would stipulate preliminary sketches.

"I cannot believe it's all falling into place so smoothly," Cissy said to Potter one day on the voyage home, as they sat in deck chairs, staring at a peaceful Atlantic Ocean.

"My dear," he said, "never count your chickens before they hatch . . . or until you're sure they won't come home to roost again."

Cissy threw him a wry smile, but she was serenely confident about the direction of the women's exhibit.

Chapter Fifteen

Cissy presided over a catfight when the board of lady managers met the day before the exposition opened.

"I think the state of Florida should be represented prominently with the duchess," called one shrill voice. "After all, that's where the Spanish first landed." The speaker referred to the duchess of Veruga who, with her husband, the duke, would be the honored representatives of Spain at the opening ceremonies.

Cissy resisted an urge to tell the woman that Columbus never made it to Florida, indeed probably never got beyond some of the obscure Windward Islands in the Caribbean.

"I demand that Isabella Hooker ride with the duchess, so that the elderly among our cause are represented." This voice belonged to Phoebe Couzins, who surprised Cissy with her vehemence. Of late, Phoebe had been content to let others speak for her, while she sat smugly in their midst. The ridiculous idea of Hooker riding with the duchess brought a twitch to Cissy's lips that she did her best to hide.

On all sides, voices called for this one and that to ride with the duchess, to entertain the duchess at tea, to have a private meeting with her. Almost every lady refrained from asking for herself—they were too well bred. But their requests usually involved someone who would have included the asker in the meeting. Cissy thought they were all transparent—and horribly behaved.

"Ladies," Cissy reminded them, hitting her gavel smartly against the podium, "our structure provides for a committee on celebrations to cover just such occasions. Those ladies, whose responsibility it is to show hospitality to visitors, will greet the duchess tomorrow."

Cries of "Unfair!" and "We all want to meet her!" rose around Cissy like the swell of an ocean so that, briefly, she thought she might drown in discord.

"Madame President, Madame President!" One of the women clamored for Cissy's attention. Turning she saw that it was Miss Katherine Minor, a crony of Phoebe Couzins.

"Yes, Miss Minor," she said with a sinking heart.

"I would like to propose that the standing committee on celebrations be abolished, to be replaced with a revolving committee. That way, more women would greet the guests, and the entire board would not be summoned together again during the whole summer. A great savings of the government's funds," she ended with smug satisfaction.

Cissy considered for a moment. In her heart, she knew there were some women in this room she simply did not want greeting the duchess and other important guests. It wasn't exactly snobbishness, she told herself, but a straightforward recognition of the facts.

"I believe," she said slowly, "that would be more costly in the long run, bringing different people to Chicago throughout the summer, paying them a per diem plus their lodging . . . no, I think we must stay with the standing committee that I have appointed."

Now the cries changed to "favoritism!" and "only your friends!" Cissy noticed, though, that the protests came from the same small group—with Isabella Hooker's voice loud and Phoebe Couzins sitting amid the group, nodding her head in agreement.

Mary Cantrill, once one of Cissy's good friends, rose. "I specifically requested to meet the duchess, but I am not on the committee . . . ." So great was her disappointment that the poor woman broke down in tears and was unable to continue.

Heaven deliver me, Cissy thought, from weeping women. Aloud, she said, "The board will now go into executive session. The marshals will please escort all visitors from the room."

Several women were ushered out, huffing indignantly as they went. As soon as the doors closed, pandemonium broke loose, women shouting and screaming at each other. Someone suggested a separate luncheon for the women, to which Cissy, unable to make herself heard, simply shook her head in the negative. Out of the babble, the words that stuck in Cissy's mind, were "favored few."

Finally, she pounded the gavel on the podium with all her might, raising her voice well above ladylike tones to call almost stridently, "Ladies, Ladies!" Slowly, the shouting diminished into a hostile murmur punctuated by occasional unpleasant comments. At last, she had their attention enough to speak, and she faced the lady managers squarely. "I presume," she said, "that all this discontent reflects badly on me. I will make neither excuses nor defenses. Good intentions count for nothing. Congress is already paying all of you a per diem, and I felt that we had no right to submit a bill for a separate ladies' luncheon. We have thought we were working together as a band of women for something fine, for the interests of women everywhere. If I am mistaken in that, and we are all torn up and pulling hair over an introduction to a duchess, I have nothing to say to this board except that I am deeply humiliated."

The ladies sat in stunned silence for a moment, and then there was a great rush for the podium, as weeping women hovered around Cissy, full of apologies. Over their heads, Cissy caught a triumphant nod of the head from Susan Gayle Cooke, who stood, called for order, and then asked for a vote of confidence for the president.

It was resounding, although Phoebe Couzins remained silent.

* * *

"I fail to understand why a man can't ride to the opening with his wife," Potter fumed early the next morning. "The duke's a pleasant enough fellow, but Carter . . . I've about had enough of him." He gave Cissy a long look.

"It's the price of fame, Potter," she told him with a smile, ignoring his implication.

"If that's it, you should be in the second carriage, not me. You're the one who's worked for this exposition."

"Ah, but women could not ride so near the front of the line," she said, a mischievous smile flitting across her face. "It would not be considered fitting."

"Balderdash!" He threw his napkin down, then rose and kissed the top of her head lightly. "Women should lead the parade, and they would if I had my way."

"If I had my way," she said pensively, "the duchess would ride in a carriage that held a hundred women, so that none could be offended by not being asked to ride with her. There is simply not enough of the duchess to go around."

"Who is riding with you?" he asked. "I see you had quite a row yesterday." He waved the morning paper in her direction.

"Oh," she said with a startled gasp. "I had hoped to keep it from the papers."

"It's not much of a piece," he replied, "just indicates that there was a row because there's not enough of the duchess to go around."

Cissy nodded and decided not to look at the paper. "No one else is riding with us," she said quite simply.

Cissy and the duchess rode to the exposition grounds in a long line of carriages. Theirs was the twentieth; ahead of them, second only to Cyrus McCormick's monogrammed carriage, which held President Grover Cleveland, the duke of Veruga rode in the Palmers' most magnificent carriage with Potter and Carter Harrison.

After they alighted from their carriage, Cissy and the duchess stood on a bridge, looking west at the Grand Basin. The duchess gasped and then murmured softly in Spanish. Cissy missed most of what she said but caught the words *magnífico* and *incredible*.

At the far end of the huge lagoon, bronze horses plunged and dolphins frolicked, and water jets sent streams heavenward. It was Frederick MacMonnies' statue, the Columbia Fountain, with rowing maidens at its center. Everything, Cissy decided, was allegorical. At the east end, close to where the two women stood, Daniel French's gilded statue of the Republic towered sixty-five feet high. Around the basin, the white buildings of the Court of Honor gleamed, reflecting the early morning sunlight so strongly that Cissy shaded her eyes.

Beyond the MacMonnies statue, at the far end, sunlight danced on the golden dome of the Administration Building. "The next one," Cissy said to her guest, "is the Machinery Hall, with its tall towers and those enormous statues of women." She spoke slowly and distinctly. The duchess was fluent in English, but one could never, Cissy thought, be too careful.

The duchess nodded appreciatively.

"The Woman's Building is over there"—Cissy pointed to the left—"and the statue on top is Diana. Augustus St. Gaudens sculpted it. You know his name?"

The duchess nodded and murmured, "Muy grande."

Cissy continued her verbal tour. "The Manufactures and Liberal Arts Building is the largest building in the world under one roof—Potter says it could hold the standing army of Russia." Cissy herself was never sure whether that was a joke on Potter's part or a verifiable fact, but she found it an impressive statistic to quote.

"And the one with the enormous arched entrances—it's the Mines and Mining Building. And the one that looks like it is all columns—the one with huge spires at each corner—that's the Electricity Hall. You shall see the inside of all these soon."

In slow, careful English, the duchess said, "These buildings will be monuments to Columbus for years to come. They are magnificent."

Cissy shook her head unhappily. "No," she said, "they are temporary buildings. They will not last for years to come." Should she explain about staff, that stuff that looked like marble but was really more like plaster of Paris? She decided against it.

"Temporary?" the duchess echoed. "One puts so much money into temporary buildings?"

"It is to honor what your country did for ours," Cissy said with great tact. Somehow her rapt wonder at the beauty of the scene had dimmed.

Neither woman could know that hours earlier, just as daylight broke and the first rays of sun hit the golden domes of the buildings and the smooth, still waters of the basin, Carter Harrison had stood almost at the same spot where they now stood. He had come to revel in the accomplishment of it all, to enjoy in perfect solitude the fruition of his dreams and his work.

As he stared at the scene, he was indeed overcome by its grandeur. But he could not erase nagging thoughts about its temporary nature. Where, he wondered, would it all be a year from now? What would it look like? And then he laughed aloud at himself. Talk about crossing your bridges before you got to them! He had the whole long exposition to look forward to, and he intended to enjoy every minute of it, now that he was mayor once again.

The duchess turned to look behind her, and once again Cissy heard her prominent visitor gasp. "What is that?" she asked.

Behind them, some distance away, the shell of the Ferris wheel towered over the entire grounds of the exposition. To Cissy, it was a great wooden monolith that contrasted badly with the richness and elegance of the Court of Honor.

"It's . . . it's a wheel," Cissy said, at a loss to explain the monstrosity. "It was invented by a man named Ferris—George Washington Ferris—so it's called a Ferris wheel."

"And the little cages?" the duchess asked.

"People ride in them, or so I've been told. But you won't have to, your ladyship. It's not on your tour." She hesitated a moment. "It's not finished yet."

The duchess' eyes sparkled. "Oh, I am so sorry. I should very much like to ride around that wheel."

Cissy simply nodded, remembering Carter's vow that he would insist that she ride the blasted wheel. Turning to her guest, she said, "We'd best get back in the carriage and arrive at the opening ceremonies in style. There's an escort waiting for you."

The duchess followed her obediently to the carriage, and Cissy stood back to let her guest enter first. Just as she herself turned to get into the carriage, she glimpsed one of the groundsmen for the exposition—they were easily identified by the distinctive uniforms they wore, a touch Carter had insisted upon. This man, though, looked familiar to Cissy. When he saw her looking at him, he turned hurriedly away, but not before she recognized Harry Collins.

* * *

President Cleveland pushed an electric button and the flags of forty-seven nations broke out simultaneously, whipped by the breeze off Lake Michigan. Gondolas appeared on the waterways as if by magic. The crowd in the plaza cheered, and people poured into the exposition grounds. The greatest world celebration to date was underway, quivering with life.

At the luncheon following the ceremonies, Carter Harrison leaned over to whisper in Cissy's ear, "You're playing with your food. Are you not hungry?"

The lunch was sumptuous—consommé, soft-shelled crab, julienne potatoes, cucumbers, filet mignon, French peas, celery and potato salad, strawberries and cream, cheese and crackers But Cissy indeed was not hungry. "I'm just worried about the opening ceremonies in the Woman's Building," she said. She put her hand briefly on his, a way of thanking him for his consideration, and then removed it quickly as though she had touched something burning hot. Too late, she looked up and saw that Potter had watched her.

"It will be fine," Carter said, basking in the warmth of his closeness to her.

* * *

"Your ladyship," she whispered to the duchess, just before the cheese was served, "I think it's time that we left for the Woman's Building." Intent on the forthcoming event, it never occurred to her to notice that the president was still enjoying his filet.

"Yes, of course," the duchess replied willingly, and the two women rose.

Immediately, the members of the committee on celebration also rose, so that the atmosphere was one of confusion and even mass exodus. The president took one last bite of his steak and then gallantly rose, took Cissy's hand, and bowed low over it.

"I understand that you must leave us too quickly," he said. "Will you forgive me for returning to my plate?"

Flustered, Cissy realized her gaffe. The president had not signaled that the luncheon was over, and it was an unforgivable breach of manners to arise before he did so. His own graciousness only made her lapse more painful, but Cissy recovered nicely.

"You are most understanding, sir, and I regret my haste already."

His eyes twinkled as he said, "Not at all, not at all. Ladies must not be kept waiting." With that he sat back down and applied himself to his filet.

As she turned to leave, Cissy saw Potter raise an eyebrow at her and then, slowly, give her a broad wink. He knew she was mortified, and he was trying to tell her it was all right.

* * *

Even Cissy gasped in delight and forgot to worry about the duchess or the president when she saw the Great Hall of Honor in the Woman's Building. Palms and potted plants were grouped between arches and on the temporary speakers' platform. The mingled colors of Spain and the United States were draped overhead.

"The presentations—poetry and music—have all been composed by women," Cissy whispered to her guest as they made their way to the platform.

When she rose to speak, thunderous applause greeted her, and Cissy let out a sigh of relief, sure now that it would all go smoothly. Isabella Hooker and Phoebe Couzins had lost out, at least for the time being.

The presentations were mercifully brief, especially Flora Wilkinson's "Ode to Isabella" and the dramatic overture composed by Frances Ellicott of London. When Cissy rose to speak, she too was brief but touched on the issue of equal pay and the folly of insisting that women's supreme calling was in the home when only the "favored few"—there, she had turned the enemies phrase against them—could afford such luxury. "What," she asked, "of the widow with dependent children, the wife of the drunkard? Shall we condemn them to their homes or shall we help them clothe and feed their families by paying them honestly for their work outside the home?

"This exposition—and these women—seek not to destroy the home, but indeed to enable more women the privilege of focusing their attention there. Freedom and justice for all are infinitely to be more desired than pedestals for a few," she concluded to thunderous applause.

Ceremonial gestures followed. Cissy used a silver hammer to pound a golden nail into a symbolic block of cypress—into which a hole had been drilled so that her effort would not go amiss—and she was presented with a silver laurel wreath and a piece of fringe from the silk flag carried in the parade by the women, along with the scissors used to cut the fringe.

Then, to the strains of Mrs. Beach's "Jubilate," it was over.

"Well done," a masculine voice said in her ear, as she received congratulations from the women who flocked around her. "I . . . uh, I was worried . . . after I read the paper this morning."

"You might," she whispered to Carter Harrison, "still worry. I may have won the battle, but the war is not over."

He squeezed her hand. "I must return to our honored guest. I snuck away only long enough to hear your speech . . . and I'm glad most of the other men did not hear it."

"Why?" She pretended surprise.

He laughed aloud. "You toe the line nicely between placation and rebellion . . . and I've never known you to mince words—even if you are on one of those on pedestals."

When she opened her mouth to protest, he said, "Well, my pedestal, anyway" and walked away before she could reply.

Watching Carter Harrison leave, Cissy realized that Potter had done his duty and stayed by the duke, no doubt giving him the grand tour of the exposition. He had not heard his wife at her most triumphant moment toward which her life had been building for well over two years now.

* * *

Harry Collins stumbled a little as he entered the wooden shack his family called home. This had been his first day working at the exposition, and Harry's resentment that he was a groundskeeper had driven him to the bar, where he expounded on his anger at Carter Harrison until the other men turned their backs. "Got ya the job at the expo, didn't he?" one asked.

Sheila Collins watched him come through the door with both apprehension and a studied detachment. In part, she saw a stranger, the lines of his face no longer crisp and clean as they had been when, as a young man, he'd loved her—or she had thought he did. Now there was a puffiness about him—not just bags under the eyes but a general blurring by softness. And he who had once stood ramrod straight now stooped his shoulders, as though always tired. His eyes most disturbed her: they had always been hard, but they had once softened with love for Juliet and even Sheila herself. Now they burned constantly with an indefinable anger.

He sat at the board table, slumped in his chair, and propped his feet on the chair opposite him. "Juliet!" he called. "Come take my boots off my feet. I've had a long day."

The girl pushed aside the curtain that created a makeshift bedroom and stared at him. When she was little, taking his boots off at night had been her special chore, and she had thought it a privilege. It had been years, though, since she'd done that, and she was both puzzled and angered by his request.

"Aren't you swell in that uniform?" she asked, sarcasm edging her voice.

He looked down at the exposition uniform he wore, now wrinkled and stained with sweat and dirt. "Your ma'll have to clean it tonight. They only give us two, and I got to wear a fresh one tomorrow."

"Why don't you clean it?" Juliet asked, as her mother rushed to hush her.

He stared at the girl, his bleary eyes making out the fact that her face was painted. In fact, heavily painted. "What the hell you lookin' like a whore for?" His voice was harsh.

"Maybe," she said flippantly, "I am one. I'm goin' out to meet friends. You'll have to take off your own damn boots."

He rose as though to threaten her, but he was unsteady on his feet, and she easily pushed him back into the chair as she passed.

"Don't wait up," she said to her mother as she left, but there was almost as little tenderness for her mother as for her father.

Sheila could do nothing but stand there in agony. Harry, however, roared, "If you don't come home at a decent hour, don't be comin' back here!"

"All right," the girl agreed, almost too willingly.

"Harry!" Sheila protested, but he stood and raised an arm as though to strike her.

Juliet took a step toward him, and he lowered the arm. She watched him sink back in his chair. Without another word, she left.

"Take my boots off?" he asked his wife in a weary tone.

"Sure, and I'll be glad to," she said, as though nothing had ever happened in that room in the last ten minutes. "I've a good stew for you."

"Stew," he said, almost spitting out the words. "Can't you cook a damn thing but stew?"

It would do no good for her to tell him that she could barely afford stew on what he gave her and what her work in the café brought in. She considered, briefly, asking how the first day of the exposition had been and then discarded the idea. Instead, she pulled off the boots, put a bowl of stew before him, and took herself behind the curtain.

Tomorrow, Sheila Collins told herself, she would go to the exposition. Hadn't none other than Cissy Palmer herself invited her? Hugging that thought to her, she finally slept.

Harry Collins' face fell forward onto the table, barely missing his stew, and he slept half the night there, slumped over his dinner.

Juliet Collins did not come home that night . . . nor the next.

* * *

The Ferris wheel opened fifty-one days late. The first passengers rode in mid-June, with Mrs. Ferris among them. Rumors had floated around the fairgrounds that there would be accidents, even suicides. The wheel could simply collapse under the weight of its passengers. The motor could stick, leaving some people stranded at the top. Cissy's mind whirled with awful possibilities.

What was intended as a trial run, with one car occupied, soon brought a throng of fairgoers, all crowding onto the remaining cars. In some instances, cars were grievously overloaded, but even guards were unable to stop people from climbing aboard the car. At long last, the crowds emptied the cars only when the engineer threatened to run them to the top and leave them there overnight.

George Washington Ferris had created a marvel.

* * *

"You've visited the Midway?" Potter asked his wife. They sat, sipping aperitifs, in the roof garden of the Woman's Building.

Somewhere on the grounds below them, their two sons wandered the exposition, exploring the exhibits and fairgrounds. Potter had turned them loose with a simple admonition or two, though Cissy worried about them in the crowds.

"Cissy, Honoré is nearly twenty years old!" Potter had exploded, and she'd said no more.

Now she turned toward him. "No, I haven't been to the Midway. I think I should like to avoid it forever, if I can."

"I doubt that," he said dryly.

"Well, you can't imagine the stream of women through my office today, with one thing or another to say about the Midway, especially the performance at that place they call Little Egypt."

"The belly dancers?" he asked, and grinned mischievously when she said, "Potter, please!"

"That area was to be educational, with ethnological exhibits, and yet it's turned into the lowest form of entertainment, something they call the 'Hootchy-Kootchy.'"

"That's an unfortunate name someone tacked on to it," her husband replied, "but the dance at Little Egypt, for instance, is of some religious significance in the dancers' homeland. *Danse du ventre*, they call it—unfortunately, it translates literally into belly dance. Probably better if the public had never heard that, but I understand the dance is as graceful and as carefully choreographed as our own ballet, which indeed may well horrify Egyptians."

Cissy said tightly, "I've had some of the Isabellas telling me it was a 'religious memorial that inculcates purity and self-control.' I . . . I think it's debasing, and so do most of the other board members I've talked to."

"Ah, but my love, you can't say that until you've seen it."

"And I never shall!"

He raised an eyebrow at her and then continued. "Now the Ferris wheel . . . you could learn a great deal about physics from that. I understand it weighs a thousand tons and has underground supports of forty feet."

Cissy was rather bored by the Ferris wheel, considering that everyone talked about it. "I forbade the boys to go to the Midway," she said. "I suggested Wooded Island."

"With Oriental curved bridges and teahouses," her husband said. "Just what will intrigue two young men! My bet is that they're on the Midway." And then, under his breath, he added, "At least I hope so." More loudly, he said to his wife, "The breeze is coming off the lake. Let's take a walk on that pier with the movable sidewalk."

"Don't you mean take a ride on the movable sidewalk?" she asked, then hesitated. "What about the boys? We told them to meet us at my office."

"In another hour and a half," he told her, holding out his arm.

So Chicago's most prominent couple—the president of the board of lady managers and her highly successful entrepreneurial husband, himself an exposition official—glided in a large loop on a long pier built over the lake. Beside them were drovers and shop girls, foreign exhibitors and janitors.

As they walked back toward Cissy's office, a short young man with dark hair and piercingly dark eyes greeted them. "Palmer! It's good to see you!" He placed himself almost directly in front of Palmer.

"Good to see you, Sol. How're things on the Midway?" the older man asked, genially holding out his hand.

"Couldn't be better," Sol replied. "I've made it work, and now we're packing in crowds. I just wish the Buffalo Bill people had been allowed inside the grounds—it would have meant more revenue for the exposition."

Cissy kept a gasp to herself. Inside the grounds was exactly where she didn't want any such entertainment.

"My dear," Potter said smoothly, turning toward her, "I don't think you've met Sol Bloom. The Midway is entirely his doing, his project."

Politely, Cissy extended her hand. "You must be very busy," she said. There was a restlessness, an energy about the man that disconcerted her.

"Always busy," he said. "Today, it's ostrich egg omelets."

"Pardon me?" Cissy thought that surely she'd misheard.

"Ostrich egg omelets," he repeated. "We've run out of eggs at the ostrich farm—a delivery problem, and people really like those omelets. Say they've got a subtle taste."

"You make omelets of ostrich eggs?" she asked incredulously. Vaguely, Cissy was aware that Potter was watching her with amusement.

"Of course not," Bloom said, his tone implying naiveté on her part. "We use chicken eggs, but we don't tell people that. This week we've used turkey, duck, and goose, anything we could get our hands on."

Potter grinned. "I bet those omelets really did taste different."

The smaller man just shrugged. "Wouldn't know. I never try them."

"I don't think I would either," Cissy murmured, appalled at the man's brashness.

"You'll visit our exhibits one day soon?" His tone made it a demand rather than an invitation.

"Of course," Cissy said crossing her fingers behind her back, in the age-old precaution against lying. Potter hid a small smile.

"Just tell anyone to call Sol. I'll give you the personal tour."

Cissy smiled again, but nothing would have induced her to express pleasure in the prospect.

When the man was safely out of earshot, Cissy asked incredulously, "Wherever did he come from?"

"California," Potter replied. "He's a show organizer by trade. Owns the Algerian Village but manages the whole Midway. It was a mess until he got here."

"I'm sure he's improved it," she said sarcastically.

"He has," Potter said, "and it may very well make some much-needed money for us. Now, I, for one, am ready to find the boys and go home for the evening. But tomorrow, I think I'll look up Sol and visit the Midway."

If she'd been carrying a parasol, Cissy would have stabbed him with the sharp end.

In the carriage on the way home, Min, now eighteen and stronger than he'd been as a child, said exultantly, "We rode the Ferris wheel. Wait till you try it, Mother! You can see clear from the south side way past our house."

While Honoré rolled his eyes and Cissy debated reminding her sons that she had ordered them away from the Midway, Potter said heartily, "That wonderful, eh? I think I'll try it tomorrow. You boys want to come with me for a repeat ride?"

"I sure do," Min said without hesitation, while Honoré, after a glance at his mother, muttered, "Me, too."

Potter almost hid the newspaper the next morning, for a "Special Exposition Report" contained the announcement that Mrs. Potter Palmer, president of the board of lady managers, had been seen at Little Egypt and was quoted as saying she thoroughly enjoyed the performance.

"Such trash!" Cissy exclaimed, raising her voice so that even Potter was startled. "How can they?"

"I'm afraid," Potter said, "they saw your sons there and assumed you were with them."

"I will write a letter of protest this morning," she said decisively, though even then she wasn't sure to whom she would address such a letter.

* * *

If Cissy Palmer had not been at Little Egypt that night, Carter Harrison had, although he didn't cross paths with the Palmer boys. He had escorted Annie Howard to dinner at the Japanese teahouse, where they dined on exotic dishes neither of them recognized nor hoped ever to eat again. Then, telling her he had a surprise, he took her to Little Egypt, just in time for the second evening performance.

Carter Harrison did not make this move blindly, assuming that Annie was so grateful for his attention that she would appreciate any entertainment he provided. No, he did it calculatingly, almost as a test—though he would have admitted that to no one else and had a hard time admitting it even to himself. He wanted to see how she would react.

She stared at the performance thoughtfully but without comment, and Carter cast sideways looks at her occasionally as though he could read her mind. But her face was inscrutable. When the performance ended, however, she was straightforward.

"I never thought I would see anything like that . . . most women raised in my circumstances would feel the same way . . . but I admired their grace. I . . . I guess we cannot judge propriety, because they're from a different culture . . . but in terms of dance, it's an amazing accomplishment."

Carter Harrison's heart soared at her openness, but his tongue was less facile. "I . . . it's supposed to have religious meaning . . . of course, I don't know that it does."

"Carter," she asked, "are you nervous about bringing me here? After the fact?"

"No," he said, "I guess I'm not as nervous now as I was before."

"Then why did you bring me at all?" She smiled as she asked the question, and lights of amusement glinted in her eyes.

He shrugged, as though he himself did not know the answer. But it was on the tip of his tongue to ask her to marry him right then and there. He didn't.

Two days later he heard that Cissy Palmer had demanded that the directors close down Little Egypt. The directors, instead, issued a statement proclaiming that concessionaires must "restrain exhibits within the limits of stage propriety as it is recognized in this country." That was as much a slap at Sol Bloom as anyone, but the next time Harrison saw Bloom he thought him particularly unfazed by the reprimand.

* * *

"You upset about Little Egypt?" Carter Harrison edged cautiously into Cissy Palmer's office. He found her sitting at her desk with a murderous expression on her face, and, for a long moment, he thought she wasn't going to speak to him. She simply stared, anger in her eyes.

"I said, are you upset about Little Egypt?"

"Why not?" she replied, her voice deadly quiet. "I'm upset about everything else. You might as well add Little Egypt to it."

He began to fumble in words. "Well, I mean, the commissioners' statement—"

"Have you read this?" She thrust a newspaper toward him.

The offending passage had been underlined in red, no doubt by Cissy herself. "The building," Carter read, "is practically a white elephant." The statement was from Secretary Hovey of the commission, and the article went on to quote Secretary Hovey's opinion that women artists of the highest rank had refused to have anything to do with the Woman's Building. "I think we should turn the building into a large kindergarten," he concluded.

"Do you wonder I'm not upset over continued performances at Little Egypt?" she asked as he raised his eyes from the article. "They don't care that we exist, let alone that an exhibit on the Midway is offensive to us." Then, after a moment, she said, "I suspect Phoebe Couzins . . . or one of her cohorts . . . got to him. I will never be free of that woman!"

"And St. Gaudens' 'Diana' on our building—now I'm hearing that women are offended by its so-called immodesty. Good heavens, Carter, we get a renowned sculptor like St. Gaudens practically to contribute a magnificent work of art, and women quibble because of its drapery!" She threw her hands in the air in impatience.

He could, he knew, placate her, point out the success of the building, the prestigious works it housed, the crowds who had poured through it in the first week. But she would counter that Ellen Richards had kept her Rumsford Kitchen out of the building, putting it in the liberal arts building. Throughout the fair, women were exhibiting in other categories, so that Cissy's dream—a building where visitors could see the produce of women all in one place—was shattered. And she would counter, rightfully so, that no matter what she did, she was criticized.

"Get your hat," he said quietly but with determination.

"Pardon me?" She had expected him to argue against her anger, persuade her of the importance of her work and the building, cajole her out of her mood. She had not expected to be ordered about.

"Get your hat," he repeated, "and your purse, unless you feel comfortable leaving it here."

"Where are we going?"

The first hint of a smile crossed his face. "Never mind. Just do as I say." Then, as an afterthought, "It's past noon. Are you hungry?"

She'd been too angry to think about food, but now that he asked, she admitted, "Maybe. A little."

"Good," he said, holding out his arm, "I wasn't planning to feed you one of those fancy twelve-course meals you're used to."

With her arm safely tucked in his—he put his big hand over her smaller one, so that she could not gracefully escape when she saw where they were headed—Carter Harrison escorted Cissy Palmer from the Woman's Building. Once outside, he turned directly west, toward the Midway.

She hesitated. "Carter . . . ."

"I won't listen," he said. "I'll drag you if I have to."

She looked to see a smile on his face, but he seemed deadly earnest, staring straight ahead.

They paraded past most of the concessions—the Algerian Village, the ring where John L. Corbett challenged any and all comers to a boxing match, even the infamous Little Egypt. Cissy, now feeling incapable of rebelling, kept her eyes straight ahead.

They stopped in front of the Ferris wheel.

"Two," Harrison said to the ticket-taker, who smiled and said, "No tickets for you, Mr. Harrison. You and your friend go right ahead on. Boss' orders."

Cissy tried to pull her hand away. "No. I won't set foot in that thing."

Looking at her, Carter saw the slightest sign of fear, an emotion that Cissy Palmer would never publicly admit.

"It's perfectly safe, Cissy. Thousands of people have ridden it already."

Something—her fear, perhaps?—loosened her tongue. "That only means it's about to crash," she said, her anxiety totally uncharacteristic of the controlled woman he knew. "I've heard people talking . . . predicting a horrible accident from this monstrosity."

"Nonsense," he said. "They had a problem at first with the brakes—not strong enough to stop it once it got going—but they've got air-powered brakes now, and they've not had one problem. Come on," and he walked determinedly into the cage, which sat at ground level.

Cissy's choices were to accompany him or create a scene, and she was too much the lady to do the latter, no matter how horrendous the situation.

She was astonished at the size of the cage they entered. Made of wood and iron, it had swivel seats to hold forty people—Cissy did a quick rough count—and along one end was a counter where food and drink could be purchased.

Carter saw that she was seated in a chair near the counter—he did not exactly shove her, but his touch was firm as he helped her into a chair. "Stay here," he said.

She nodded.

He returned in a moment with two plates of cold chicken, fresh fruit, and glasses of champagne.

She ate more hungrily than she had expected, and she felt the tension ease away from her as she sipped her champagne. But as the wheel began to move again and the car lurched with movement, she grabbed the sides of her chair convulsively.

Carter stared at her. "Cissy? You're afraid of height, aren't you?"

"I don't know," she managed to say. "I've never been higher than the third floor of our house."

"You lived on top of the Palmer House," he reminded her.

"Oh, but that was inside, different," she said.

He reached out and took one of her hands in his. "You'll be fine," he said, "and you'll love the view."

At first she wouldn't look, but as the car climbed higher—with frequent stops while other cars, below, were loaded with passengers—she began to steal glimpses straight ahead. Then she would look to one side and the other, and finally she stood to get a better view.

"Better sit back down," he said. "It's safer."

"But look, you can almost see our house."

He followed her pointing finger and thought he saw the absurd turrets of the Palmer mansion, miles away on North Lake Shore Drive. Between them and the mansion lay the city, spread out like a relief map. They began to point out this place and that to each other—"Look, there's State Street" and "Isn't that Prairie Avenue?"—until they were giggling like schoolchildren.

To the east, the lake glistened and shimmered. "I can see clear to Michigan," she told Carter, who smiled and shaded his eyes as though to see farther.

Cissy grew silent, and he watched her surreptitiously. But the look on her face was one of rapture as she gazed out at *her* city and *her* lake, spread out before her in a way that, previously, only birds had seen them.

"Carter," she said, turning to him with such enthusiasm that she, without thinking, took his hand in hers, "It's the most wonderful thing I've ever seen! And to think I'd have missed it if you hadn't bullied me into going."

"I didn't bully you," he protested, but he never moved his hand.

When their cage began its descent, Cissy complained, "I can't see as far." And when it reached ground, she sat unmovable for a moment.

"You want to go again?" he asked.

"No," she said, laughing, "not now. But later, yes."

"You liked it?" He beamed with pleasure.

"Yes, Carter, I loved it." Her mood, she realized, was lighter than it had been since before the controversy over who would ride with the duchess of Veruga had put her in a frenzy. But even as she spoke, she remembered that Potter had said he was going to ride the wheel days ago . . . and she had never asked if he did, nor with whom.

Sol Bloom met them as they disembarked from their cage. "I heard Mrs. Palmer was on the Midway," he said, "and I didn't want to miss a chance to be of service. What else may I show you, madam? Little Egypt?"

Cissy didn't know if the man did that deliberately or if he were truly ignorant of the minor row she had caused over the *Danse du ventre*. But her mood shattered. "No, thank you," she said. "I must get back to my office."

Harrison threw Bloom a black look, then offered his arm to Cissy, and they began their promenade from the far end of the Midway back to the Woman's Building. Before they got very far at all, a deeply masculine voice called, "Harrison! Harrison!"

Cissy and Carter both turned to see an older gentlemen, tall and thin, with long hair and a pointed white beard, dressed all in white, except for his cowboy boots. While Cissy looked with a question in her eyes, Harrison said, "Cody! How's the Wild West business?"

So this, Cissy thought, is Buffalo Bill. Other than his outlandish outfit and the trim of his beard, he looked an ordinary man.

As the men shook hands, Harrison said, "Mrs. Palmer, I want you to know Colonel William F. Cody."

Cissy somehow had never imagined herself shaking hands with Buffalo Bill, and she'd never expected to hear him called "colonel."

She extended her hand but was uncertain what to say and settled for nothing.

"You been to my show?" he demanded.

She shook her head in the negative.

"Well, Harrison, you bring this lady on over and let us show her what the Wild West was really like." In an almost automatic gesture, he reached into the breast pocket of his coat and withdrew two tickets.

"She's got sons," Harrison said, "and a husband. I suspect they'd all like to see your show."

Before Cissy could protest, more tickets were thrust into her hand.

"Bring friends," he said, "bring anybody you want."

"I . . . I thought you were not on the Midway," Cissy said, having recovered her wits to a slight extent.

"I'm not," Cody said, without a trace of anger. "Said my show wasn't good enough. But I set up just outside the fairgrounds, and I expect I get more folks than all the other shows here put together, more even than that Little Egypt everyone's talking about."

Cissy forced a smile. Was Little Egypt going to haunt her all summer? She and Harrison thanked the colonel for his generosity and started to move on.

"Harrison," Cody said, "I do have one problem. My Indians—they're getting so drunk they can't stay on their horses during the performances. I think they're getting liquor here on the Midway."

"Probably so," Harrison said. "Talk to Bloom. Tell him next time the Indians get drunk, all the Algerians go to jail. He'll make it work out."

"Thanks," Cody said.

"Will you use those tickets?" Carter asked her as they walked away.

She shrugged. "I don't know."

"I could bring Annie, and you could bring your family, and we'd all go together," he said.

To Cissy, that sounded like an unmitigated disaster, but she smiled and said, "Maybe we can arrange that."

They parted at the Woman's Building, and Cissy was sincere in her thanks. "I'm not going to throw darts at anyone now," she said with a smile.

"Good, and I'm going back to the affairs of the city with a lighter heart."

But, watching him walk away, Cissy's heart was anything but light.

* * *

For Cissy Palmer, every day at the Columbian Exposition brought a new discovery, a new excitement. She watched and listened when Alexander Graham Bell made the first long-distance call, ringing up a colleague in New York City. She was in the audience when Frederick Jackson Turner announced his theory that the American frontier had closed forever in 1890, a theory that was to dominate historical interpretation of the American West for the next century. In the Hall of Machinery, she met the morose historian Henry Adams, who talked almost frenetically of his belief in the opposing powers of the Virgin and the Dynamo. Her heart raced as she listened to John Philip Sousa conduct his marching bands, and she felt a calming quiet at the concert by Paderewski, where the famed pianist captivated the ladies with his long locks, which he swung dramatically as he played.

She marveled at a life-size knight on horseback, made entirely of prunes, and she scorned the folly of a map of the United States fashioned of pickles. She refused to ride the ice railway, though both her sons did and reported it a marvel; neither realized that in another thirty years, the ice railway would lead to the ever-popular roller coaster.

Cissy expected everyone to share her enthusiasm for the exposition, and it came to her as a shock when not all did. When she asked one of the lower housemaids on her home staff if she were planning to attend the exposition, the woman replied, "No, ma'am,

I think not." Her words were accompanied by a curtsey. "I've nothing suitable to wear."

"Nothing to wear! Why wear what you've got on now," Cissy said in an instinctive reply that she immediately regretted as thoughtless.

"No, ma'am, I won't be going to a fair in a uniform."

Without another word, Cissy strode from the parlor where this encounter had taken place, leaving behind an open-mouthed parlor maid. Within minutes, she was back, carrying one of her own gowns.

"I'm not liable to need this again," she said, thrusting it into the maid's hands. "See if you can adjust it to fit . . . and then come let me see you wearing it at the exposition."

"Yes, ma'am!" The maid's low curtsey was accompanied by a broad smile. She had never worked for anyone before who would have done such a thing for her.

Cissy went to Hull House, where she was directed to an efficient, brusque woman who sat behind a desk and didn't even rise when Cissy came into the office.

"I want to donate a dozen dresses . . . for the express purpose of giving women in this community suitable attire so that they will feel comfortable attending the exposition. They may pass the gowns about among themselves, so that each gets several wearings." Cissy spoke directly and without hesitation.

"Oh, now, our ladies . . . they aren't interested." The woman looked annoyed, as though a troublemaker had interrupted her.

"Let me introduce myself," Cissy said. "I am Mrs. Potter Palmer, president of the board of lady managers at the exposition. I want the women of Chicago to be able to come and see what women around the world have accomplished . . . and what they can do."

"Yes, Mrs. Palmer." The woman was on her feet, smiling. "That is most generous of you, and I know the ladies will be grateful."

"I expect to see them on the fairgrounds," Cissy said as she left the office.

As she directed Herman to unload the dresses, Cissy had one sudden and unexpected thought. "Leave one dress in the carriage, Herman," she directed.

When the dresses were unloaded and she was settled in the carriage, Cissy told Herman where she wanted to go.

"Are you sure, Mrs. Palmer? That's the Third Ward."

"I know where it is, Herman. It will be all right."

And so, she drew up in front of the Collins' shanty, a place she had not visited in many years.

Sheila Collins, startled by a knock on the door that no one ever knocked on, opened the door a crack and peered out hesitantly. Then the door flew open, and she said in amazement, "Cissy!"

"How are you, Sheila?" Cissy asked, and then, at a gesture from her hostess, followed the woman into the shack. Behind her, Cissy could almost feel Herman's disapproving glare.

Inside, she saw that nothing had changed—the table was still rickety and scarred, the other furnishings scant, the supplies on the shelf above a cooking counter also slight. She turned again to Sheila. *She looks defeated and worn down,* Cissy thought.

"I'm all right," Sheila said, a statement that conveyed that she was not really all right and yet did not ask for pity. "Won't you sit down?" She indicated a chair that wobbled when Cissy sat in it. "May I make you some tea?"

Cissy shook her head. "No, I can't stay long. I was . . . ah, I was in the neighborhood . . . and it occurred to me—have you been to the exposition? I know Harry's working there."

Indeed, Cissy had seen Harry Collins almost every day since he started working there. She got the odd feeling he was watching her, and it made her uncomfortable. His expression was baleful.

Sheila shook her head. "No, I haven't been there. I . . . I don't think Harry wants me to, but I guess that shouldn't stop me."

Cissy spoke forthrightly. "I've found some women—indeed, some in my own household—are staying away for fear they haven't the proper clothes. I've just taken some dresses to Hull House, but I saved one back for you."

"Harry, he won't let me take charity." Her voice dropped, and then she added, "especially not from you."

"Harry," Cissy said, "need never know where you got the dress."

"I'd . . . I'd like to go, that I would."

"Good. I'll have Herman bring the dress in." She rose, and then turned to ask, "Are Harry and Juliet getting along better than the last time we talked? I . . . I did what I could, but I'm afraid it wasn't much."

The other woman lowered her eyes briefly, then raised her chin and looked Cissy in the eye. "They're not getting along. They don't have to. She's left home."

"Left home? Is she married?"

"No, ma'am. I . . . well, I believe she's workin'." Now Sheila's chin quivered and she chewed her lower lip nervously.

Cissy said nothing but simply waited, and within seconds a great wail arose from the distressed woman. "I think she's livin' in a crib."

Cissy held out her arms, and Sheila came willingly to her. They stood together, arms locked about each other, while Sheila cried tears that probably should have been shed years earlier. At length, she drew away, dabbed at her eyes, and said, "I'm sorry . . . I shouldn't have done that."

"Yes," Cissy said, "you should. What can I do to help?"

Sheila shook her head. "Nothing. None of us can help Juliet now. And Harry . . . I've about decided we each got to help ourselves, and these days I'm thinkin' what I can do for myself."

"And?" Cissy prodded.

"I been thinkin' of tryin' to get a place at the exposition myself. Do they . . . is there anything I can do?"

"Yes," Cissy told her, "there is. Come to my office in the Woman's Building when you're ready." She knew that taking work at the exposition would be an enormous step for Sheila Collins . . .

and a real slap at Harry Collins. Cissy didn't ask about her job at the café. Apparently, Sheila wanted to move on to better things.

With another quick hug, Cissy was out the door.

Chapter Sixteen

"The infanta can be . . . ah . . . difficult." The round face of the consul of Spain glistened with nervous perspiration, and he barely kept himself from wringing his hands in front of the self-possessed woman across from him. He was in Mrs. Potter Palmer's office in the Woman's Building of the Exposition, trying to prepare Mrs. Palmer for the forthcoming visit of the Spanish infanta, who would be representing the queen regent.

"Difficult?" Cissy raised her voice in a question and stared directly at the uncomfortable man.

He took a deep breath. "She will expect deference . . . the utmost deference."

"Well," Cissy said, rising briskly, "we shall certainly see that she gets it then." She felt almost sorry for the consul and his attack of nerves. "I believe, sir, that we understand royal protocol and will handle the infanta's visit to your complete satisfaction." Cissy had no idea how much she would regret her smug sureness within days.

He managed a slight smile. "To my satisfaction, I am sure. But the nfanta . . . she has no satisfaction."

Cissy resisted the temptation to smile at his small joke. "How does she pronounce her name? Tell me again so that I get it absolutely right."

"She likes it said Ay-oo-lay-lia."

"Ay-oo-lay-lia," Cissy repeated. "I shall of course refer to her as your highness."

The consul sighed in relief. "You are very understanding, Mrs. Palmer. My country is already in your debt."

Ushering the little man out of her office, she made a list of points to be checked with Potter that evening: the table silver and gold plate from the Palmer household had been taken to the Palmer House for the infanta's personal use; an Egyptian parlor and a huge bed, inlaid with mother-of-pearl, had been installed in the royal suite—Cissy had learned that the infanta adopted the current craze for Oriental furnishings; a small staff had been specially coached to serve the royal visitor; pansies had been ordered thrown on the carpet for her arrival at the Spanish Building. It was, Cissy thought, all in order, but she would review it one more time with Potter. And then there was the reception at the Palmer mansion . . . .

* * *

"I declare this building open," the infanta said, her tone bored, her eyes wandering around the crowd as though she desperately hoped she would find something of interest. She had stormed from her carriage into the building, literally crushing the pansies beneath her angry footsteps, never even seeming to notice the flowers.

Cissy's only thought as she watched the arrival was, "I wish she were my child. I'd not tolerate such behavior!"

Standing next to her, Carter Harrison made a "harrumphing" noise in his throat, and Cissy saw that Carter's face had turned red in a rare sign of anger from a man who was genial almost to a fault. Today a silk topper replaced his usual slouch hat, and Cissy thought he looked strange to begin with. She had barely stifled an amused smile when she saw the hat. The Spanish consul's advice, no doubt.

At the reception that followed, Eulalia barely acknowledged introductions, giving each dignitary a limp hand and managing to look over the person's left shoulder instead of directly into his or her eyes in greeting. Then, outrageously, she lit a cigarette, as casual as though women all around her were smoking.

"She can't do that!" Susan Gayle Cooke whispered to Cissy.

"I fancy she can do what she pleases," Cissy murmured in reply. "I, for one, wouldn't think of stopping her."

But all around, dark glances were cast in the infanta's direction.

Cigarette still in hand, she sauntered toward Cissy. "I hear," she said, her voice ripe with condescension, "that you are the wife of an innkeeper."

Cissy looked levelly at this challenger. "Yes," she said, "I am. And I rather like the innkeeper. You're staying at his inn, of course."

The infanta did not dignify the last statement with a reply. After a long and appraising look at Cissy, she turned away without another word.

The Palmer reception in honor of the royal visitor was scheduled for that evening. At five, when Potter arrived from the hotel, he reported that there was some kind of scene in the royal suite.

"We heard raised voices," he said with a shrug. "The Spanish ambassador was with her."

"Hobart Taylor? I didn't know he'd come from Washington." Then she said thoughtfully, "Good for Hobart. I know the local consul would never have nerve to raise his voice to Ay-oo-la-lia," Cissy said, her drawn-out pronunciation mocking the princess ever so slightly.

Potter looked at her with amusement and suddenly decided to tell his wife the whole story. "She's refusing to come to the reception," he said. "She refuses to go to the home of an innkeeper." He rolled his eyes in the way he often did to show his amusement.

"Refusing?" Cissy echoed. "I've a guest list of Chicago society, exposition officials, foreign ambassadors . . . I've even set up a dais in the ballroom . . . and she's refusing? She needs to be thoroughly scolded."

"Spanked, I'd say," he replied, and Cissy laughed briefly to hear her husband echo her own earlier thought. Then she turned sober.

"Shall we cancel the reception? What shall I do about all the guests . . . and the food?"

"Of course we won't cancel it," Potter said, rising to put his arms around her. He was nearly insensitive to any slight to himself, but inwardly he was furious at anyone—royalty or not—who insulted his Cissy. "We'll have a party without her."

The appointed hour came, guests arrived, butlers saw that they had refreshment . . . and everyone stood around nervously talking, glancing now and then toward the door as if hoping the infanta would suddenly materialize before their eyes. Outside, a sudden summer storm raged, drenching the city in a downpour.

"It's the rain," Cissy said calmly to Vice President Adlai Stevenson, who had been elected in 1892 with President Grover Cleveland. "I'm sure we can't expect her royal highness to venture out in a storm like this. It will pass shortly, and then she'll be here."

"The rest of us," said the vice president, "ventured out in it for her sake."

"Potter says she might not come at all," Marshall Field whispered in Cissy's ear, as though he were a naughty child delivering bad news.

"She will be here," Cissy said serenely, though inwardly she was not at all sure of her conviction.

Eulalia arrived an hour late, in a fury, almost borne on a bolt of thunder from the storm. The hem of her white satin gown and the matching slippers were wet and soiled from the storm, though an aide nervously held a large black bumbershoot over her head. It simply didn't protect the infanta all the way down.

Before she left the entry hall, she said haughtily to Potter, "I require a carpet and a canopy at the hotel entrance. They were not there, and I very nearly didn't go out the door at all because of it."

Potter began profuse apologies, but Cissy—knowing him too well—could see amusement dancing in his eyes. He was delighted to have caused the ill-tempered woman discomfort, even if it had been inadvertent.

Behind Eulalia, Hobart Taylor pulled a finger across his throat in the traditional death sign. But he, too, had a glint in his eyes, and a smile for both Palmers. No one pitied Eulalia.

Cissy began a round of introductions—Stevenson, General Nelson Miles, Marshall Field, Cyrus McCormack, George Pullman, Julia Ward Howe, painter Andrew Zorn, the governors of several states, an assortment of Russian princes, and representatives from other countries. The infanta glared at each and acknowledged no introductions.

Finally, the infanta took physical hold of Cissy by the arm and pulled her aside. "I will not stay here," she hissed. "I'm not being given proper honor."

"You, my dear," said Cissy, pale but determined, "are being given far more honor than you have earned."

"I will leave," Eulalia threatened.

"Let me have the butler show you out," Cissy responded.

Taken aback, the infanta shook in anger. "You can't . . . ." she began in protest, but Cissy had turned her back and left in search of one of her house staff. Within minutes, the infanta was ushered out the front door, to the amazement and delight of a large crowd of distinguished visitors who had been shunned. Once the woman was gone, they laughed, talked, ate lavishly, drank champagne, and tried to pretend that they had not seen an unbelievable insult delivered to Cissy Palmer.

Cissy was the gracious host—"May I get you a dessert?" "More champagne?" "Are you having a lovely evening?" "So good of you to come"—and Potter was ever at her side, adding his hospitality.

"You all right?" Carter Harrison asked her at one point.

"Of course," she said too brightly. "Why shouldn't I be?"

"Cissy, this is me—your old pal, Carter. You've just been insulted in the worst way, and I want you to know I'm concerned."

She let down her guard just a bit. "Thank you, Carter. Tomorrow I may collapse . . . or go stark raving mad in anger. But tonight, I have guests to attend to."

"My hat's off to you," he said with a grin, hiding the fact that he longed to reach down and kiss her then and there, onlookers be damned.

"Is it a silk topper?" she asked mischievously.

It was near midnight when the last flabbergasted guest left. "Thank God," Potter moaned, sinking into the nearest chair. "I thought they'd never leave."

"They were so . . . what would you say—keyed up?—by what happened, that they couldn't leave, they didn't know how to end the evening."

"But you were magnificent, Cissy. You've made me proud on many occasions, but none so much as this. You kept your dignity, you entertained your guests."

"And you almost laughed at Eulalia," Cissy retorted, her eyes laughing. "I saw you, when she arrived mud-spattered and complaining about the canopy."

"Guilty," he said with a grin.

"Mother?" A quiet voice came from the stairwell. It was Min, peeking around the balustrade. "Is the rude woman gone?"

"How did you know she was rude?" she asked.

"I watched from the balcony."

"You are old enough to have attended the party," Potter said sternly.

"Oh," he said airily, "I didn't want to do that. It's much more fun to watch. But she was rude to Mother."

Potter's laughter was gone. "Yes, son," he said, "she was indeed."

The incident made the front page of the Chicago papers the next day. Cissy and the infanta shared front-page space with the collapse of Ford's Theater in Washington, where twenty-two people died, and a violent strike in the rock quarries outside Chicago. "Can two queens share one ballroom?" blared one headline.

Cissy, who had maintained her composure throughout all of Eulalia's antics, broke down at the suggestion that she was equally at fault with the Spanish woman.

"I will *not* attend the concert in her honor," she told Potter, raising her face from the newspaper as they sipped early morning coffee.

"We have box seats," he said mildly, "and our absence will be most conspicuous."

"You may go without me," she said, but then, again, firmly, "I will *not* go."

He shook his head and reached across the small table to take her hand. "Neither will I, Cissy, neither will I. I would not think of going without you."

By evening, the dailies had a better picture of the situation. Now the headline declared, "Chicago's Queen outclasses Spanish Royalty" and the story detailed the infanta's rudeness to Mrs. Palmer and to all the most important people in Chicago. Public sentiment had turned.

* * *

The following day was to be the infanta's last in Chicago. With her fingers crossed that nothing else would go wrong, Cissy went into her office. She found Carter Harrison waiting for her.

"You didn't appear in public yesterday," he said, accusation in his voice. "It's not like you . . . especially to miss the concert, an official function."

Cissy firmly deposited the notes she was carrying on the desktop and turned to face him. "Surely, you know why I did not attend the concert, Carter."

He grinned. "Of course I know. The empty seats were most conspicuous, though."

"Good. Where is the *enfante terrible* today?"

Carter laughed aloud at her transposition of languages. "Hobart Taylor is showing her through the Midway."

"Good," Cissy said, afterward muttering, "perhaps she'll fall out of the Ferris wheel."

"Pardon, Cissy? I didn't hear you?"

Cissy merely shrugged her shoulders.

"Will you attend the farewell dinner the infanta is giving tonight?" he asked, and when she nodded in the affirmative, he pursued with, "Will Potter escort you?"

Cissy stood perfectly still and looked at him, this man who intrigued and yet frightened her, because he raised unfamiliar feelings. "Of course," she said. "Potter is wonderful about letting me drag him to official functions."

Now it was Harrison's turn to shrug. "Just wanted to be sure," he said with an effort at casualness. "I'd have volunteered if you needed an escort."

Her instinct was to go to him, take his hands in hers, look him deep in the eyes, and tell him she appreciated his thoughtfulness. Instead, Cissy Palmer stood perfectly still and straight, and muttered a soft "Thank you." Then, "Are you not escorting Miss Howard?"

"I fancy I will," he said, picking up his slouch hat and preparing to leave.

As she listened to his footsteps echo down the corridor, Cissy found that her hands were trembling ever so slightly.

* * *

The infanta had turned charming, even if her charm was a little late in coming. She had, she told everyone who would listen, "adored the Midway. It's the most exciting place in this whole festival . . . or whatever you call it. That Little Egypt . . . I mean to have them teach me how to do that dance."

Women gasped in embarrassment, and men shook their heads in amusement and then turned solemn if their wives looked their way. The infanta relished the outrage she caused and went merrily on her way describing the wonders of the Midway.

"And the Ferris wheel—I rode it three times, is that not so, Señor Taylor?"

Hobart Taylor nodded, albeit not with a great deal of enthusiasm.

"And the fistfight . . . what you call it?" She turned to Taylor for help.

"Boxing," he supplied.

"Yes, boxing. Where they've put a floor over a swimming pool. I see the great Jim Corbett fight a . . . what you call it?" Again she turned to Taylor, while the circle of men and women around her stared mesmerized.

"A kangaroo," he said. "From Australia." He did not know and would not have explained if he had that the Fleischman's Yeast Company had built a swimming pool to accompany their restaurant. Their theory was that people would work up large appetites swimming and then order huge quantities of food in the restaurant. Nobody swam—although people did order huge quantities of food.

"Oh, yes, a kangaroo." She pronounced it kan-gá-roo. Then she laughed aloud. "It knocked him down with its tail."

"Wonderful," Cissy murmured to Potter. "She will tell everyone in Spain that the most interesting thing at the exposition was a kangaroo who went a round with a boxing champion and beat him."

Potter whispered back, "There's nothing we can do but put our trust in Hobart Taylor to carry the proper message back to Spain. Surely the duke and duchess of Veruga will have given a different report."

Cissy nodded, and Potter went on, "I have declined to drive her to the rail station tomorrow. Your friend Harrison has agreed to do the honors. I shall let him use the coach-and-four."

She imagined that she heard undue emphasis on the words "Your friend," but she merely said, "He'll have to wear that silly silk topper again."

The infanta left an indelible impression on Chicago, and Cissy breathed a sigh of relief when she was gone.

* * *

"Ladies and gentlemen, I have the honor of introducing to your attention a man whose record as a servant of the government, whose skill and daring as a frontiersman, whose place in history as the chief of scouts of the United States Army . . . and whose name as one of the avengers of the lamented Custer, and whose adherence throughout an eventful life to his chosen principle of 'true to friend and foe,' have made him well and popularly known throughout the world . . . . The honorable William F. Cody, Buffalo Bill!"

Mounted on a prancing buckskin horse—the color of his own clothing and hair—Buffalo Bill swept into the arena, shouting "Wild West, are you ready?" A roar went up from the crowd.

Cissy and Potter, their two sons, and Carter and Annie sat in the stands of the outdoor arena, though the Palmers were there as reluctant guests of Carter.

"Buffalo Bill?" Min had asked. "Who's he?" while Honoré said with a yawn, "Is this about cowboys and Indians?"

"Your mother has accepted an invitation for all of us," Potter said, "and we will attend this . . . ah . . . performance."

Cissy thought he might well have gritted his teeth and added, "And we *will* enjoy it, whether you like it or not!"

Now, seated in the audience, she remembered what Cody had said to her the day she'd met him briefly on the Midway. "It's not a show," he insisted. "It's a re-creation of the Wild West for informative purposes, not to entertain."

"How could he have said this is not a show?" she asked Carter incredulously. "It's all . . . bigger than life. There's no history here."

Harrison shook his head. "There's history, Cissy. Wait till you see the act he calls 'Custer's Last Stand.'"

Potter and the boys were soon, to her amazement, swept up in the spirit of the performance. They elbowed each other like schoolboys, repeating, "Look at that!" and "Think of living back then!" The usually talkative Annie Howard sat silently beside Cissy, occasionally giving the older woman a questioning glance.

Cissy watched the performance spellbound and did not speak to any of her companions until it was over. She saw Indians attack stagecoaches, Indians attack settlers' cabins, Indians murder soldiers and innocent women. When the Indians massacred General Custer and his troops, the audience hissed as the Indians rode away in triumph, leaving crumpled bodies scattered over the arena floor. She watched the cavalry ride to the rescue and heroic cowboys fend off attacks. Cowboys were heroes when they rode bucking horses, but Indians were simply savages when they shot bow and arrow from horseback. The whole thing puzzled her, so sure was she that it was distorted history.

"Wow! Can we come again, Father?" Min asked. "That's the best show I've seen in a long time."

Cissy, who had taken both her sons to several performances during the fair, including that by Paderewski, shuddered just a bit at his enthusiasm.

"Well," said Annie Howard with her usual forthrightness, "I'm grateful I did not live among the savages. But they'd have had a hard time getting my scalp!"

Carter smiled at her and with some admiration said, "I bet they would, Annie. But I'm glad none had the opportunity to try."

"Too much action for me," Potter said. "What was it Cody told us? 'A thrill a minute'?"

"That describes it," Harrison said heartily. "A part of me . . . oh, I don't know, but a part of me longs to have been there, to have fought for the frontier. It's . . . well, like Cody says, it's heroic."

The conversation swirled around her, and at length Cissy spoke softly. "They remind me of women," she said.

"Women? Who?" Potter said incredulously. "Cissy, whatever do you mean?"

The others all looked at her in amazement. She shrugged, "The Indians. They are seen altogether, as though everyone were exactly like the next . . . and not much good about them. All Indians are savage. All women are troublesome, demanding their rights. Neither contributes to the common good much." She rose from her seat and walked away from them.

"She's had a long, difficult day," Potter said apologetically, hurrying after his wife and beckoning the boys to follow.

Cissy was amazed at the things that happened during the exposition. For instance, a woman with a delegation from the State of New York nursed her baby openly in her office. "And they say our manners are provincial," she said, describing the incident to Potter. She happily served as godmother to an Eskimo baby born on the fairgrounds. She paid for folding wicker chairs to take the elderly and infirm through the exposition, and she fed the girl guides luncheons of beefsteak, strawberries, and cream. She set up dormitories for young girls from foreign countries—and loaned them money when they came to her in despair.

Sheila Collins, wearing the dress Cissy had delivered to her, came to her one day in triumph rather than despair. She had, she announced, taken a job serving meals in the Illinois building.

"How does Harry feel about that?" Cissy asked curiously.

"He's more than a little against it, but I'm no listenin' to him anymore," the woman said tartly. "Harry thinks the mayor, Mr. Harrison himself, got me the job, but he didn't. I got it myself." There was pride in her voice.

When Cissy asked about Juliet, Sheila shook her head and looked downward, and Cissy assumed that Juliet was still living in a crib.

* * *

Every day at five o'clock, Potter Palmer called for his wife in the coach-and-four and drove her home. Occasionally, she emerged from the Woman's Building on the arm of Carter Harrison, and Potter frowned a little as they approached, but he said nothing. Invariably, he greeted Cissy with a light kiss on the cheek and a concerned, "How was your day?" It struck him he sounded like a housewife welcoming her husband home at the end of the day.

All during the exposition, Carter Harrison ruled the city of Chicago from the grounds of the World's Fair, keeping an office there and rarely appearing at City Hall. "There's too much going on here," he explained with a grin. "If I went downtown, I might miss something."

On the day before the fair closed in October, Potter sent word that he and Cissy would have to attend a dinner at the hotel. Important clients, he wrote, and added a note that the boys had gone to their grandparents for dinner, and he had given the household staff the evening off.

Carter Harrison was in Cissy's office at the end of the day, and he walked out of the building with her, gallantly offering her arm as they took the two steps down from the building entrance to the street level. "Will Potter be coming for you?" he asked.

"No. We have to meet important clients at the hotel tonight. Herman will drive me home so that I can change clothes and freshen up."

Without Potter glaring at him, he felt free to suggest that they stop on the bridge over the canal. The White City looked as it had that morning all those months earlier, when Cissy had shown the scene to the duchess of Veruga, except now it was busier, the water filled with more boats than ever, the sidewalks covered with people.

"If you and I hadn't been in this city at this time, this would never be quite the same," Harrison said, staring at the scene.

Startled, Cissy protested, "Someone would have done what we've done. I never believe one person is indispensable."

"Oh, but you must believe it. Some are." He looked directly at her. "You are. Without you, the Woman's Building would have never been built. The whole concept would have fallen apart in the midst of bickering women."

She smiled. "They have been fractious at times, but now . . . now it's almost over."

"You know what they say," he said philosophically, "it's never over until it's over."

They were both silent for a moment, feeling the sense of dread at the end of the dream that had become the center of their existence. They were not the only ones. A sense of nostalgia had already settled over the fairgrounds.

"And what kind of a story will they tell when it is finally over?" Cissy asked, looking up at him with a twinkle.

"One of triumph," he said. Then, after a long pause, "You and me, we're a good team . . . . Would you run away with me? I'd give up the city of Chicago for you, and, believe me, that's not an offer I make lightly." A broad grin did little to hide the fact that he meant what he said in dead earnest.

Cissy Palmer knew for a heady moment that if she said "yes" to him, they would both be gone from Chicago within twenty-four hours, embarked on new lives of which neither one had ever dreamed. She smiled at him, "The nicest offer I've ever had . . . and the most self-sacrificing. But of course not. I won't."

He shrugged. "I knew you wouldn't, but I had to ask. You and me, we're bound by the roles we've set for ourselves, including the one of being honorable people. So you'll go home with Potter to that gilded cage he's built for you, and tonight I'll ask Annie to marry me, and we'll go on with our lives. But for me . . . and I hope for you . . . there'll always be that little 'what if' question in my mind."

Her eyes were just slightly damp as she looked up at him, and for the first and only time in his life, Carter Harrison kissed Cissy Palmer, not on the cheek, but full on the mouth, a kiss of sadness and longing for what could have been. If Herman sees, Cissy thought fleetingly, be damned with it!

"I hope you and Annie will be very happy," she said enigmatically and walked to her carriage without a backward glance. Carter Harrison would never know the turmoil that raged inside the calm, controlled Mrs. Palmer.

* * *

Harry Collins sat at the table in his small house, while Sheila pulled off his boots.

"Hard day?" she asked sympathetically.

"You damn well know it was! Every day's hard out there, when I'm doin' the kind of work the Lord didn't mean me ever to do."

Sheila wondered frequently exactly what the Lord had intended Harry to do. Surely not what he was doing, but her reasoning differed greatly from Harry's. "I'll just get you a bowl of soup."

"What I need," he said in disgust, "is another beer."

"We don't have any," she said flatly, thinking he'd probably already had at least four.

As she turned to ladle out the soup, she heard a loud, "Help! Somebody open the door!"

Immediately fearful, she sprang to the door. Harry, his senses dulled by drink, moved much more slowly, muttering, "What the hell? Man can't even have peace in his own home."

Sheila opened the door to find two neighbor men, one holding the limp body of a woman. At first she didn't recognized the shape, and then she screamed. "Juliet!" Her cry was long, loud, and agonized.

"She dead?" Harry asked, his voice for the first time showing some emotion.

"Half," said the man who held her. "Tell me where to put her."

Sheila quickly drew aside the curtain and motioned to a bed, her mind only half understanding the words of the second man. "We found her lying in the street outside. Somebody seems to have wanted her dead, but at least they brought her to her mum."

"Bring me a lamp," Sheila commanded, her voice now calm and controlled. In the dim light, she saw that her daughter had been beaten badly about the face. Her eyes were swollen shut, her lips puffed far beyond normal; blood was seeping from a cut on one cheek and trailing out of her mouth. It wasn't a fresh beating, Sheila knew, because blood was not flowing freely. How long had her child suffered like this?

Her voice soft, she whispered, "Juliet? It's me, Mum. You're safe now, darling. I'll see that you're just fine. You lie there and sleep." She waited for some slight sign of recognition and was rewarded when the unconscious girl moaned and stirred ever so slightly.

The two men—Tim Fisher and Ryan Green—stood awkwardly in the home's main room. "Can we . . . can we do anything else?" Green asked.

"Yes, please," she said. "Send for a doctor."

"Can't pay no doctor," Harry insisted belligerently. "She'll just have to figure how to get well on her own." He looked angrily at the men, as though it were their fault.

"I want a doctor," Sheila said, ignoring him. "I'll figure a way to pay him when I have to. And Mr. Fisher, would you be so good as to draw me a fresh pail of water, so I can bathe my child?"

Wordlessly, Fisher took the pail and disappeared out the door.

"I can draw water for my own child," Collins protested.

"You're drunk," Sheila said, her tone now harsher than he'd ever heard it. "Sit down and stay out of my way."

"Man that can't take care his own is a poor man," Harry muttered, while Tim Fisher looked away in embarrassment.

Sheila spent the next twenty or thirty minutes bathing her daughter with warm water, gently sponging away dried blood and dirt, all the while crooning to the young woman in loving tones. She gave not another thought to Harry Collins until she emerged from the sleeping area for a fresh rag.

Fisher and Green had long disappeared, and Harry stood in the middle of the room, wearing his exposition uniform, which he had discarded much earlier in the evening.

"And where might you be goin' when I need you here?" Sheila asked, her tone very much indicating who was in charge.

"If Potter Palmer had paid me a living wage all those years, my daughter wouldn't be a whore," he said, almost ignoring her question. "I'm goin' to settle scores." And he was gone. The stumble seemed to have disappeared from his gait, and he moved with such purpose that he was too quick for Sheila. She could not stop him.

Minutes later, as she stroked her daughter's forehead and waited impatiently for the doctor, Sheila had a horrifying thought. She rushed through the curtains, went to the room's one small chest of drawers, and began pawing through the top drawer. "Mother of God!" she exclaimed. "He's taken the pistol." But she had no one to send to warn the Palmers, and she could not leave Juliet.

Sheila Collins buried her face in her hands and sobbed, "Lord in Heaven, what's to become of us?"

* * *

The hour was nearing midnight when the Palmers arrived home that evening. Potter had asked Mrs. Stripling to be ready to admit them any time after eleven, so he was not surprised to find the housekeeper in the entry hall. He was surprised, however, at her distraught manner.

"Mr. Palmer, thank God you're here!" The older woman wore a housecoat and had a sleeping cap on—attire in which she would never have appeared before her employers except in the most extreme circumstances.

"Mrs. Stripling, whatever is the matter?" With real concern, Cissy placed an arm about the woman's shoulders and led her to the bench.

Wringing her hands, she said, "It was awful, just awful."

Palmer, thinking the woman hysterical for no cause, thought to himself that he was tired and wanted to go to sleep. He didn't have time for this uncontrolled behavior.

"What was awful?" Cissy asked in a soothing tone.

"Well, two of the girls and me, we didn't have any place to go even with the night off, so we were in our rooms on the third floor. I was doing some mending, when I heard this yelling outside. I . . . I couldn't make out the words, but a man was yelling at the house. Tildy told me she peeked out a third-floor window—mind you, she was cautious, but she saw a man pounding on the front door."

"Could she tell what the man was saying?" Potter asked, his interest now more than aroused.

Mrs. Stripling looked down at the floor, almost as in embarrassment. "He was calling for you, sir, for you to come out and get what you deserve." Her face flushed a little as she said it.

"Why didn't you call the police?"

Here, the housekeeper faltered. "We were afraid to come downstairs to the phone. And after a while, the man . . . he went away. So then I came down here to wait for you. I wanted to be sure you could get in right away, just in case . . . ."

Potter's voice was grim. "Now that we have a telephone, the proper thing in all such cases is to call the police," he lectured. "I will call them now and report this incident." He strode off toward the servants' hall, while Cissy patted Mrs. Stripling on the back and offered her tea. As they headed for the kitchen, Potter said, "The police are investigating a murder. They'll come inspect the grounds when they can."

* * *

Potter Palmer unfolded the newspaper, with a certain sense of apprehension. He had not again heard from the police, though he knew with certainty that no one now lurked outside his home. After all, it was daylight now.

Without glancing at the newspaper, Palmer thought how he had longed for this last day of the exposition. The damn fair had driven a wedge between him and his wife—she was busy all the time, going out in the evenings to events he didn't want to attend. And there was the troublesome but constant presence of Carter Harrison. Today should be one that he greeted with great pleasure . . . and yet, Potter Palmer was uneasy.

One glance at the headlines riveted his attention, and he quickly fixed his eyes on the article. Reading closely, he waved away the maid who came to ask what he wanted for breakfast. Then, in a sudden fit of movement, he threw down the paper and ran out of the room.

Upstairs, Cissy sat at her dressing table, still in her gown but with her hair fixed. She too was weary after a sleepless and worried night, and she had found it hard to summon up her usual enthusiasm this morning. The thought that it was the last day of the fair was far from her mind. And she was worried about the man who had attacked their home the night before.

Worried though she was, her thoughts kept straying to Carter Harrison. His face would pop in front of her vision, obscuring the mirror in which she was staring at herself. She was just beginning to pinch some color into her cheeks and consider whether or not a tiny bit of cosmetic help would be justified when Potter burst into her boudoir without knocking, a lapse in manners totally unlike him.

As she turned slowly to face him, Potter blurted out, "He's dead! He's been killed!"

"Who's been killed?" she asked, her mind leaping to frightening possibilities.

"Carter Harrison, that's who!" He was distraught to the point that he sounded as though he were blaming her.

Her first instinct was to reply, "Of course Carter's not been killed. Potter, what gave you this idea?" But then she remembered that the police had been investigating a murder last night—a fairly important one, she gathered, since they put it before Potter Palmer's request—and she looked again at her husband and knew that what he said was true. She also knew no matter how much he had railed against Carter's presence in their social lives—and, silently, in her personal life—this was a genuinely good man who was upset by the death of a colleague.

But all she could say was "Killed?"

Potter shook his head. "It gets worse," he said miserably. "Harry Collins shot him."

For a moment, just a moment, she thought she would faint, something she had never done before. But she steadied herself with a hand on the dressing table and said, "Tell me all of it."

"I don't know," he said. "I . . . I just read the paper quickly and came to tell you. But they've arrested Collins."

"Why," she wondered aloud, "would Harry Collins kill Carter Harrison?"

The answers came slowly throughout the day. Before Cissy could finish dressing, three newspaper reporters were at the door. A constable soon followed, insistent on talking to the Palmers while they huddled over their breakfast table.

"What do you know about Harry Collins?" he demanded.

"He was probably here last night," Palmer said, "creating a ruckus. We were not at home, but our staff told us of an unruly man demanding that I come outside."

"Did they call the police?"

"They were afraid to come downstairs. I called immediately when I returned home," Potter said calmly. "We didn't know at the time who the man was, but now I'm convinced it was Collins. Should have thought of that last night."

"How do you know he did it?" Cissy asked the constable.

Slowly, the story came out. Collins had been found, pistol still in his hand, sitting on the curb outside Harrison's house. Neighbors, hearing the shots, had sent someone for the law, but Collins had not bothered to leave the scene.

"I think he's bonkers," the constable said without feeling.

"I must go to Sheila," was Cissy's only reply.

* * *

Sheila Collins sat dry-eyed at her sagging, wooden table. When Cissy knocked, she called out a soft, "Come in," but she made no move to rise, and when Cissy put comforting arms around her, she sat still as stone, except that she cast a quick glance toward the curtained-off sleeping area.

Curious, Cissy followed the other woman's eyes, and then, un-bidden, went to draw back the curtain. The sight that met her eyes made her gasp in horror.

Juliet Collins lay on her parents' bed, asleep. It was her face that caused Cissy to gasp. Battered and blackened, it had swollen to twice its usual size.

"Sheila!" she said, whirling toward the woman.

"Someone brought her here last night, early in the evening," Sheila said. "'Twas that set Harry off. It was like the final straw that he couldn't bear. He . . . he blamed it all on your husband and left looking for him. I . . . I couldn't go after him and leave Juliet. I prayed that you all would be safe."

"Will she live?" Cissy asked, her concern now not on her own safety but on this poor battered young girl.

Sheila nodded. "There's been a doctor. She's badly hurt . . . someone wanted to kill her, but she's strong . . . always been strong. That's what got between her and Harry. He couldn't stand her strength, but he couldn't stand this either." She hung her head.

"Mr. Palmer?" Cissy echoed.

"Sure, he thinks it's all Mr. Palmer's fault for firin' him and not payin' him enough for years. If Mr. Palmer had promoted him, long ago, then he wouldn't have been so angry at the world, and we wouldn't be livin' in this shack, and Juliet, she would have had the advantages your sons have had. He's harbored hate for a long time, Mrs. Palmer, and it's been eatin' at him. Juliet's trouble"—she nodded toward her daughter—"it was just the final thing, the . . . what do they say? The straw that broke the camel's back."

Cissy's mind whirled at the thought of the anger and violence building up inside a man she had once befriended, anger that was directed against her family. She shuddered at the thought of what might have happened if Potter had not had his dinner, if she had gone home as usual, if—heaven forbid!—the boys had been home the night before.

"Mr. Harrison was his friend," Sheila said, her monotone continuing. "I don't know why he shot him. I'd have believed it more if he'd shot Mr. Palmer."

"We weren't home," Cissy said dully. "He must have come to our house. The housekeeper told us that someone pounded on the door, demanding to see Potter."

"I guess," Sheila went on, "Mr. Harrison was just the next person that came to his mind . . . and he had to shoot someone. He was resentful that Mr. Harrison got him that job. Thought he should have had some better job than groundskeeper." She shrugged, her gesture eloquent testimony to the fact that no one would ever know what really went on in Harry Collins' mind the night before.

Cissy barely kept herself from gasping aloud at the thought that Carter had died for befriending an angry man.

* * *

The closing ceremonies of the Columbian Exposition and World's Fair were cancelled, replaced with a memorial service for Carter Harrison. All of Chicago came. Flags flew at half-mast, and the orchestra played Beethoven's "Funeral March." Cissy, seated with Potter on the platform, watched dead leaves swirling in the corners of the buildings and knew that the fair was over, a thing of the past. A crack, sprouted three weeks ago in the outer wall of the Woman's Building, had widened, and she stared at it, as though calculating the length of time it would take the opening to rend a gaping hole in the wall. Debris floated in the lagoon, and the boats were all gone. The air was chilly, and Cissy pulled a wool shawl more tightly about her shoulders. Silently, Palmer reached over and laid his hand across hers, and they listened to empty words of praise for Carter Harrison.

"It started," she said to Potter that night, "with the fire."

Startled, he asked, "What started with the fire?"

"The whole thing," she said, "the whole chain of events. It began because I was headstrong and went against your advice. If I'd stayed at the farmhouse as you told me . . . ."

Alarmed, Potter said as calmly as he could, "And so it's your fault that Harrison is dead, because you brought Harry Collins into our world. If you hadn't, Harrison would still be alive. Is that what you're thinking?"

She didn't answer directly. "It makes the Exposition small," she said. "It's not important anymore." And then she smiled. "But it was important to Carter, and he enjoyed every minute of it. I guess he died at a high point. What if . . . never mind, one can't do that."

Potter Palmer never knew what would have followed that whispered "what if."

* * *

Two days later, Cissy Palmer presided at the final ceremony at the Woman's Building. "When our palace in the White City shall have vanished like a dream," she told the assembled women, "when grass and flowers cover the beautiful spot where it now stands, its memory and influence will still remain with those who have been brought together within its walls."

Cissy Palmer really believed that.

Epilogue

The fair, by everyone's standards, had been a great success. It had brought close to twenty-seven million people to Chicago. On October 9, it recorded its highest attendance—seven-hundred-fifty thousand people in one day. Among the many luminaries who appeared on its programs were pianist Ignacy Paderewski, the magician Houdini, inventor Thomas Edison, historian Frederick Jackson Turner, lawyer Clarence Darrow, and feminist Susan B. Anthony, who irritated Carter Harrison by proclaiming loud and long that the fair should open on Sundays.

Official studies proclaimed that there had been some petty crime, mostly pickpocketing incidents, but no real problems. They overlooked the fact that a serial killer named H.H. Holmes operated a hotel nearby from which several women—and his business associate—disappeared. But that's another story. Twelve firemen were killed when the cold storage tower caught fire and then exploded, but officials glossed by that too. The exposition hospital treated over eleven thousand patients for everything from indigestion and diarrhea to exhaustion. One man was known to have panicked on the Ferris wheel and broke glass and bent iron in the protective siding before he was subdued by a woman who unfastened her skirt, stepped out of it, and threw it over his head.

The world outside the insular fairyland created by the exposition went on. The financial panic in the country continued, and the number of unemployed people grew at a frightening rate. Carter Harrison predicted riots, if federal aid was not forthcoming. Society, he said, was changing. But the city fathers of Chicago were too pleased with their creation to listen to his dire warnings. Harrison enjoyed the fair as much as any man, probably much more, but he saw beyond the end of a beautiful and successful dream.

When the fair closed, the many who had worked there were out of jobs, in a world where there were no jobs. Winter came, and crowds of hollow-eyed men and hooded and shawl-covered women filled the streets of Chicago. Had the exposition gone on forever, one voice pointed out, they would have found employment. Now they had in common their anger and their hunger.

An army without a leader, they migrated to the now-vacant and crumbling buildings of the exposition and took up residence in those cavernous halls. Small fires did their damage, and vandalism destroyed the decorative elements. Then, on July 5, 1894, when strikers and police clashed violently, someone set fire to the entire grounds, and all of Chicago watched as the buildings of the Colombian Exposition burned. Two hours after the first flames were spotted all that was left behind were twisted beams of steel and piles of dark ash.

* * *

Harry Collins was found not guilty in the death of Carter Harrison, by reason of insanity, and committed to a local asylum. Sheila moved into the Palmer mansion when she was offered the position of front entry hall maid. Juliet recovered her health, eventually married a railroad worker, and seemed set upon repeating the patterns of her parents' life.

Cissy Palmer left for Europe immediately after the closing of the exposition. Chicago would always be her home . . . but it would never again be the same.

Author's Note

As a young child growing up on Chicago's South Side in the Hyde Park neighborhood, I wandered the land that once boasted the World's Columbian Exposition. My mother took me out in rowboats around Wooded Island, and I learned to ice skate on the Midway, which still cuts a swath of green through the city for more than a mile west from the lakeshore. My friends and I made countless trips to the Museum of Science and Industry, the only exposition building that survives. Much later I attended the University of Chicago, which sits almost on the exposition grounds. That part of the city was "my" Chicago.

My love for that part of Chicago more recently became entwined with a fascination for Bertha Honoré Palmer, frequently known as Cissy. Raised to be a socially prominent and financially secure wife and mother, she moved far beyond those roles to demonstrate her strength, individuality, and civic concern. Where she could have spent her days, as the saying goes, eating bonbons and reading frivolous novels, she became one of the first to combine wealth with civic responsibility. Active in Chicago's Hull House—a pioneer settlement house in an immigrant community—she also strove to improve the lot of workingwomen and played a major role in the Woman's Club, an organization devoted to civic concerns.

Her crowning achievement was as president of the board of lady managers of the 1893 Columbian Exposition. Against the backdrop of an artistic, intellectual, and showmanship event never rivaled in the twentieth century, she managed to call international attention to the achievements of women throughout the world while mediating between extremists among both her sisters and the male population. No small feat, and the real Cissy Palmer has my utmost admiration.

But I am a storyteller, not a historian, and as so often happens, my characters took over the story and dictated the direction it would take. Explanations are thus in order: there is no evidence of an attraction between Chicago's mayor, Carter Harrison, and Cissy Palmer. Indeed, evidence points to a long and very happy marriage between the Palmers. And, although Carter Harrison was killed the night before the exposition closed, it was one Patrick Prendergast who shot him, because Prendergast, who almost hero-worshipped Carter, had not been given the expected appointment as corporation counsel for the city. Harry Collins, the villain in these pages, is of whole fictional cloth: no such man existed. Other, smaller incidents and characters within the story are also of my own making—for instance, in preparation for the exposition, Mrs. Palmer made two trips to England; for simplicity in storytelling, I combined them into one trip. If readers enjoy the story, I hope they will forgive my slight tampering with history.

I have tried to be faithful to the era of this story and to the major events—the Civil War as it was experienced in Chicago, the Great Fire of 1871, the Haymarket Riot, and the exposition. But I have allowed the characters to create a new—and, I hope, more compelling—story than is found in the factual accounts of the exposition and one lone biography of Cissy Palmer.

For historical background, I am indebted to several sources. *The Fair Women: The Story of the Woman's Building at the World's Columbian Exposition of 1893,* by Jeanne Madeline Weimann and Anita Miller (Chicago: Academy Chicago, 1981), a lengthy, detailed, and superbly researched account of women's role in the exposition, provided much of the meat of this story. Also helpful for information about the exposition was R. Reid Badger's *The Great American Fair: The World's Columbian Exposition and American Culture* (Chicago: Nelson Hall, 1979) and Robert Muccigrosso's *Celebrating the New World: Chicago's Columbian Exposition of 1893* (Chicago: Ivan R. Dee, 1993). For general history of Chicago I consulted *City of the Century: The Epic of Chicago and the Making of America,* by Donald L. Miller (Simon & Schuster, 1996), *City of Big Shoulders: A History of Chicago,* by Robert G. Spinney (Northern Illinois University Press, 2000), *Chicago, Crossroads of American Enterprise,* by Dorsha B. Hayes (New York: Julian Messner, Inc., 1944), and *Chicago: A Pictorial History* by Herman Kogan and Lloyd Wendt (New York: E. P. Dutton and Company, Inc., 1958). Most recently, I read *The Devil in the White City: Murder, Magic, and Madness at the Fair that Changed America,* by Erik Larson (New York: Crown, 2003).

My primary source for details about Cissy Palmer's life was Ishbel Ross' *Silhouette in Diamonds: The Life of Mrs. Potter Palmer* (Harper & Brothers, 1960), but I repeat that Ross, a well-known biographer, must not be blamed for the direction Mrs. Palmer's life takes in these pages.

And, finally, some points of the story come with my own love for and familiarity with the South Side of Chicago. Though it is now more than fifty years since I lived there, I still carry Chicago in my heart.

42540189R10191

Made in the USA
Middletown, DE
15 April 2019